WITHDRAWN
W9-BPK-890

# NEON PREY

Also by John Sandford
Available from Random House Large Print

**Holy Ghost**

**Twisted Prey**

**Deep Freeze**

**Golden Prey**

**Escape Clause**

# NEON PREY

JOHN SANDFORD

RANDOM HOUSE LARGE PRINT

This is a work of fiction. Names, characters, places, and incidents either are the product of the author's imagination or are used fictitiously, and any resemblance to actual persons, living or dead, businesses, companies, events, or locales is entirely coincidental.

Copyright © 2019 by John Sandford

Penguin supports copyright. Copyright fuels creativity, encourages diverse voices, promotes free speech, and creates a vibrant culture. Thank you for buying an authorized edition of this book and for complying with copyright laws by not reproducing, scanning, or distributing any part of it in any form without permission. You are supporting writers and allowing Penguin to continue to publish books for every reader.

All rights reserved.
Published in the United States of America by Random House Large Print in association with G.P. Putnam's Sons, an imprint of Penguin Random House LLC, New York.

Cover design by Tal Goretsky
Photograph of the author © Beowulf Sheehan

The Library of Congress has established a Cataloging-in-Publication record for this title.

ISBN: 978-1-9848-8283-7

www.penguinrandomhouse.com/large-print-format-books

FIRST LARGE PRINT EDITION

Printed in the United States of America

10 9 8 7 6 5 4 3 2 1

This Large Print edition published in accord with the standards of the N.A.V.H.

For Becca Partridge

# NEON PREY

# CHAPTER ONE

Deese was a thin man. He was fast, with ropy muscles, and mean, like an aggressive orangutan. His face was a skull, tight, sly, except where a half dozen wrinkles crossed his sunburnt forehead. He had black eyes and a nose that had been broken into angles like a lump of shattered pottery. He had a red-and-blue tattoo, on one shoulder, of a wolf with a biker's head in its jaws, and, on the other, a witchy Medusa in black ink, with spitting cobras for hair.

Smart? Smart enough for the job anyway.

People who got close to him usually stepped back: Deese smelled bad. He didn't know it, and people didn't tell him because . . . well, because he was Deese. His boss told one of his associates that Deese smelled like ferret shit; and the boss would know, because he kept a pair of ferrets as pets.

---

LIKE A LOT of Southerners, Deese was big on barbecue and wanted it done right. He brushed the meat lightly on both sides with extra virgin olive oil, seasoned with kosher salt, from the Louisiana salt mines, and coarse black pepper. He added a sprinkling of filé, a powder made of ground sassafras leaves and mostly used with gumbo; but it worked on barbecue, too. He cooked the steaks over peach charcoal, brought by a Georgia peckerwood to the Red Stick Farmers Market in Baton Rouge.

He'd take the tenderloins out of the refrigerator, slice them vertically to get two long, thin steaks. He'd cover the steaks with a pie tin and leave them on the kitchen counter, protected from the flies, while the grill got right. He wanted high heat, and then he'd lay the meat down close to the charcoal and let it go for about four minutes, which would get it done medium rare.

His old man probably would have slapped him on the face if he'd seen him putting Heinz 57 Sauce on his dinner plate, and while it was true that too much sauce could flat ruin a steak, all Deese wanted was a tiny dab per bite. Every once in a while, he'd get a fresh liver, slice it and cook it with onions in his oven, crispy, then pile on the ketchup.

---

COOKING WAS a form of meditation for Deese, though he'd never think of it that way; meditation was for hippies and nerds and people you pushed off the sidewalk. On this night, as he went through his routine, he thought about the man he'd been hired to hurt. Not kill, but hurt. Hurting was harder than killing.

When he was hired to kill somebody, he'd walk up and do it with a street gun, which he threw in the nearest sewer. Most of the time, he left the body where it landed. In some cases, where the target had to disappear, there was more planning involved, but usually not a struggle. He'd hit the guy, boost his ass into the back of his pickup, and bury the body in the swampland behind his house.

When you were hired to hurt someone, as opposed to killing him, or her, there was always one big problem: a surviving witness. The solution to that was to make it known that being a loud-mouthed witness would lead directly to something worse than pain.

In this case, the conversation with the boss had gone like this:

"Legs?"

"No, not legs. That'd just lay him up," the boss said, tapping his clean-shaven chin with an index finger. A ferret scuttled under the couch, between the boss's ankles. "I need something that people can see. I'm thinking hands. I'm thinking he's walking around for a year with hands that look like they went through a woodchipper."

"Hands are hard to get at," Deese had said. "I'd have to put him down first. You put somebody down, hard, and sometimes they don't get back up."

"Be careful, then. I want my money back. Even more than that, I want my money back from **everyone**, and an object lesson is always helpful. I'm still thinking hands."

"All right," Deese said. "You want hands? Hands is what you'll get."

HANDS WERE HARD. In a fight, they were flying fast and unpredictably, and he might not have a lot of time to get the job done. So, no fight. Surprise him, hit him in the face, knock him down, stand on one arm and bust up the hand, and maybe the arm, too. Then do the other side and get out.

Deese had already done the scouting. The guy lived alone in an apartment with outdoor hallways, so he answered his own door. If Deese did it just right, that'd be the spot . . . Watch him go in, and if there was nobody else around do the old shave-and-a-haircut door knock: **BOP-BODDA-BOP-BOP! BOP-BOP!**

When people heard that knock, it tended to disarm them. If you did it lightly enough, they usually thought it was a woman. And the target, Howell Paine, **did** like his women.

---

DEESE CARRIED the meat to the grill, arranged it perfectly over the oval mound of glowing hickory charcoal. When that was done, he went back into the house, dug his walking stick out of a hall closet.

He'd bought it at a cane store in London, England, where he'd once taken a vacation because a man named Lugnuts was looking for him. Lugnuts got his name because a karate guy once kicked him in the balls and he hadn't flinched. He only did one thing, which was kill people, and he was good at it.

Luckily for Deese, Lugnuts fell to his death in a hotel atrium in downtown New Orleans before he could get to Deese, although luck hadn't had much to do with it. The man who'd hired Lugnuts to kill Deese had subsequently been kicked to death by his underpaid bodyguards, who'd also been witnesses to Lugnut's crash landing. An object lessons for all assholes who needed bodyguards: pay them well or somebody else will pay them better.

DEESE SWISHED the stick back and forth, renewing his feel for it. Walking sticks had been adopted by the European aristocracy as replacements for swords. While the best of them were undeniably elegant, they were also effective weapons, especially in the administration of a beating.

In 1856, a Southern congressman named Preston Brooks had administered a vicious beating to an abolitionist U.S. senator named Charles Sumner after Sumner had made a speech attacking another Southern senator for his pro-slavery views: “The Senator from South Carolina has read many books of chivalry, and believes himself a chivalrous knight with sentiments of honor and courage. Of course he has chosen a mistress to whom he has made his vows, and who, though ugly to others, is always lovely to him; though polluted in the sight of the world, is chaste in his sight—I mean the harlot, Slavery.”

Sumner hadn’t recovered for years. Deese didn’t know that, not being a historian, or even a reader of comic books, but he knew about the uses of walking sticks.

Deese’s stick was made of coffee-brown blackthorn, with a rounded knob head, weighted with lead, and a steel rod inserted down the length of the shaft. Getting hit with the knob was like getting hit with a hammer, but a hammer with a thirty-seven-inch handle.

He closed his eyes, visualizing the approach, the attack, the departure. He stood like that for a minute or more, thinking about Howell Paine, until the smell of the sizzling steaks called out to him from the grill.

He was tired, Deese was. He’d murdered a young woman that day and had buried her body an hour ago. Now he had Howell Paine. Busy, busy, busy.

HOWELL PAINE

Howell Paine had bumped into a forties-something MILF at a downtown dance-and-cocaine club. She had a nice post-divorce seventy-footer parked at the Orleans Marina, which is why Deese wouldn't be able to find him the first four times he went by Paine's apartment.

As it happened, the MILF could dish out more than Paine could take, though he struggled manfully to stay with her. In the end, though, he left her snoring in the fo'c'sle double bunk and snuck out barefoot, until he was on the dock, only pausing to steal two bottles of eighteen-year-old Macallan scotch and the ex-husband's 18-karat solid gold bracelet as he passed through the saloon.

Dressed in a rumpled blue seersucker suit, a white shirt, and dark blue Tom's sneaks, he hurried along the dock to his Volkwagen, climbed in, and sped away.

He stopped at Hyman's Rougarou for a ham-and-cheddar quiche with waffles and a quick read of the **Times-Picayune**, before continuing on to his apartment. Paine's apartment was one of those places that might be considered a middle-income structure on its way to the slums. That is, green-painted concrete block, two floors, outside walkways to the multicolored doors. The place looked fine, at a glance, but the apartments would smother you if the window air conditioners stopped working, and there were rust stains coming through the paint on the stairways.

Paine found a free on-street parking place under a sweet gum tree and was walking down the street toward the apartment, admiring the new gold bracelet on his wrist, when Deese, who was just leaving, spotted him. Deese pulled over and watched as Paine climbed the outer stairs to the second floor and walked along to his apartment, carrying a brown paper bag and whistling.

Deese hated whistlers.

No time like the present, he thought, as Paine opened the door to his apartment. Night would be better, but Paine had been hard to find and by nightfall could be gone again. Besides, if everything went as planned, most of the beating would be administered inside the apartment, out of sight of the street.

Deese found a parking place, got his walking stick, crossed the street to the apartment building, climbed the stairs, and ambled casually down to Paine's apartment.

Instead of knocking when he got to the door, he turned and leaned on the railing, looking out over the street. He looked for a full minute, watching for eyes. He saw nothing alive except a red tiger-striped cat that padded across the street and disappeared into a hedge. There was somebody close by in the apartment building because he could smell frying bacon, but somebody who was frying bacon wouldn't be running outside anytime soon.

He slipped the tan ski mask out of his pocket, pulled it over his head, turned toward the door and knocked, raising the cane, ready to kick it open. Like many perfect plans, his didn't go quite right.

HE DID THE KNOCK, shave-and-a-haircut: **BOP-BODDA-BOP-BOP! BOP-BOP!** Inside, Paine had taken the two bottles of Macallan out of the paper bag and still had one of the bottles in his hand when he heard the knock. He assumed it was the woman from next door, with whom he sometimes shared a bed when nobody richer was available. He knew she did the same, but, still, a civilized relationship.

He was farther away from the door than he normally would have been as he reached out and twisted the doorknob as Deese kicked it and the door exploded inward and Deese was swinging his walking stick at Paine's face.

Paine blocked the blow with the whisky bottle, which shattered, spraying glass across his face and into the room. Paine screamed in pain and rage, and found, in his hand, the jagged remnants of the broken bottle. Deese was off balance, having swung at a man farther away than expected, and it took him a split second to recover. In that split second, Paine jabbed at Deese's eyes with the broken bottle.

Deese ducked, and the bottle slashed through his mask and into his scalp, and blood spattered on the wall, the door, and began running down into his eyes. The sight of the blood made Paine hesitate for a fraction of a second, which was time enough for the stick to come around again, and Deese used it to break Paine's arm, the one with the bottle.

Paine screamed as the bottle flew off somewhere and smashed into even more pieces. Paine grabbed Deese by the shirt, with his working arm, and swung him toward the couch. Deese involuntarily sat down as the couch hit him behind the knees, but he had the stick free again and this time hit Paine on the side of the head and Paine went down. Deese clambered to his feet and whipped the other man hard across the top of his back—once, twice, three times—and then pinned the broken arm, and Paine screamed again. And Deese screamed back, "Motherfucker!"

He smashed the knob of the cane into the hand of the broken arm—once, then again, and again and again—then kicked Paine over. Paine raised the other, unbroken arm just in time to catch the next blow on the forearm, which broke, and Deese pinned that arm with his foot and began beating the hand, shattering the bones.

Deese was hurting and bleeding, which he hadn't expected, and was screaming "Motherfucker! Motherfucker! Motherfucker!" in time to the beating. Paine rolled up on his side, not screaming but choking and in pain, and with Deese's pant leg now pulled up, Paine, with no other weapon, bit him on the calf, like a feral tomcat, wrenching his head from side to side as his teeth sank in.

Deese screeched again and dealt Paine a glancing blow on the head as Paine came away from Deese's leg with a half-dollar-sized chunk of meat in his mouth. He tried to roll away, but now Deese, still howling "Motherfucker!" over and over, began beating Paine on the upper arm and back with the walking stick and was so angry, with blood in his eyes and mouth now—his own blood—that it took him a few seconds to realize a young woman was standing in the doorway, gawking at them.

He straightened and looked at her. When she ran off, he staggered toward the door but tripped over one of the couch cushions and went down, cracking his head on the arm of the couch. Dazed, he floundered for a moment, then crawled to the door, his stick in his hand, and looked down the walkway . . . but nobody was there.

Wherever she'd gone, he thought, she was calling the cops. This was not one of those live-and-let-live places; she'd definitely be on the phone. He looked back at Paine, who was lying motionless on the carpet. Blood everywhere. Maybe he'd hit him too hard? He'd sort of let it out there.

Had to get out of there . . .

He half jogged, half limped out to his car, wiping blood from his eyes. Didn't see the woman come back out on the walkway with her cell phone, taking the video that would help hang him.

The cops came for him later that day.

He'd gotten all cleaned up . . . But then they pulled up his pant leg, ripped off the newly applied bandage, and looked at the half-dollar-sized hole.

Nothing to say about that, except, "I want a lawyer."

OKAY.

Seven months later.

Two dusty dark blue Chevy Tahoes turned off Louisiana 405, away from the Mississippi River and the levee, into the patchwork of black-earth cotton fields and woodlots. A quarter mile in, they slowed as they approached a dirt side road. Rae Givens, who was driving the lead vehicle, peered down the road and asked, "You sure this is right? Looks like a jungle back there."

Her partner, Bob Matees, said, "Checks on mileage . . ." He looked at his cell phone. "And on the GPS. It seems right, as far as I could tell from the satellite pictures."

"Wouldn't want to come out here at night," Rae

said, as she rolled off the highway and onto the dirt track. "The mosquitoes gotta be the size of crows."

"Or at noon. It's already hot as a bitch out there," Bob said. Though it was only ten o'clock, and not yet summer, they could see waves of heat coming off the blacktop.

"Dependin' on which bitch you be talking about," Rae said, falling into her phony hip-hop accent. Rae was a six-foot-tall black woman with a degree in art history from UConn, where she'd been a starting guard on an NCAA championship basketball team.

"Have I mentioned snakes?" Bob asked. Bob was a short, wide white man with a soft Southern accent, a onetime wrestler at the University of Oklahoma.

"No, and you don't have to," Rae said. She took the turn onto the dirt road, a two-track with weeds growing up between the tracks. "Where's that turnoff?"

"Maybe . . . another hundred yards."

There was no particular reason that they could see for there being a turnoff when they got to it: a crescent of hard-packed dirt sliced back into the jungle, partially occupied by an aging Ford F-150 with a camper back.

A man had opened the back of the camper, and they could see a cot, and, on the wall opposite the cot, a small television set with rabbit ears. He turned toward them when they pulled in, looking doubtfully at the two oversized vehicles. He was slender, middle height, with close-cropped hair the color of wheat, wearing a short-sleeved blue shirt with sweat stains at the armpits, wear-creased jeans, and boots.

Bob and Rae climbed out of the truck. They were both wearing blue T-shirts with "U.S. MARSHAL" emblazoned across both the chest and back, khaki fatigue pants, and combat boots. Both had marshal badges and guns clipped to their belts. Bob nodded to the man and asked, "How you doin'?"

"Doin' fine, sir."

"You live roundabouts?"

"Well, sir, I live right here," the man said. He patted the side of his truck. "Come down looking for work in the oil," he said, though he actually said "oll," the way Texans do. The far side of the Mississippi was lined with chemical plants. "Sorta using this as my scoutin' headquarters."

"Best of luck with that, then," Rae said. "You know the gentleman that lives down at the end of this road?"

"No, no, I don't, ma'am. I been here three days, off and on, and never seen nobody comin' or goin', except one colored lady who goes down there every morning. She down there now."

Another marshal got out of the trailing truck. He was wearing a tan marshal's T-shirt and green tactical pants, razor-type sunglasses, a baseball hat with a black-and-white American flag on the front, and boots. A second man got out of the passenger side, tall, dark-haired and blue-eyed, with an olive complexion, who would have fit neatly into the local Cajun population. He was wearing pressed khaki slacks and a blue long-sleeved dress shirt, a "New Orleans Saints" ball cap, and high-polished cordovan loafers. He had a pair of tortoiseshell sunglasses in his hand, which he put on as he climbed out onto the dirt track. They came up and the man in the dress shirt asked, "What are we doing?"

"This gentleman has been here for three days, off and on, and hasn't seen anybody coming or going except one black woman," Rae said. "So . . . let's get it on."

The third marshal said, "Oorah!" like they might have once done in the Big Army, and maybe still did, but he was a former Ranger and said it with a sarcastic overtone and trekked back to his truck and popped the back lid.

Rae did the same, and she and Bob and the other marshal pulled on heavy bulletproof vests and helmets with chinstraps. The man in the dress shirt got back in the trailing truck and closed the door, where he had some air-conditioning. Two of the marshals armed themselves with semiauto M15-style rifles, while Rae had a fully automatic M4. They went through a nearly unconscious series of checks—

everybody loaded up and ready to go—and the man in the F-150 asked, tentatively, "You got a bad guy down there?"

"Pretty bad," Rae said. "You stay here, you'll be okay. Or you might want to drive out a ways."

"Maybe I'll do that," the man said.

As they pulled away from the turnoff, Rae saw the F-150 do a U-turn and head out to the blacktop road in a hurry. She said, "The oll man's going out."

Bob was contemplating his cell phone and muttered, "We pick up Deese's ass, right? Or maybe he's run and we don't pick up Deese's ass. Either way, we go on down to New Orleans and drop off Tremanty and then get outside some crawfish boil. Should be perfect right now. Mmm-mmm."

Tremanty was the man in the blue dress shirt, an FBI agent who'd originally arrested Clayton Deese on charges of assault with a deadly weapon in aid of racketeering activities. The "in aid of racketeering activities" made it a federal crime. That is, Clayton Deese had beaten the living shit out of Howell Paine. When Deese had finished with him, Paine had been howling with pain indeed, the bones of his hands broken into pieces that, on an X-ray, looked like a sock full of golf tees.

Paine had owed a few thousand dollars to a loan shark named Roger ("Rog") Smith and had been unwilling to pay it back, even when he could. He'd been known to say in public that Smith could suck on it. A lesson had to be taught, and was, and now Paine, seriously worse for the wear, was in the Marshals Service Witness Protection Program until Deese's trial. Tremanty didn't want Deese all that bad; the one he really wanted was Smith, and Deese could give him up. Nothing like looking at fifteen years in the federal prison system to loosen a man's tongue.

Unfortunately, Deese, who was out on a bond, had failed to show for trial, and his ankle monitor had gone dead three days earlier. They would have gotten to him sooner, except . . . bureaucracy.

On the way down to Deese's house, with Bob driving now because Rae was holding the machine gun, Rae said, "Three days. Deese could be in Australia by now. Up in the mountains."

"They got mountains in Australia?" Bob asked.

"Must have. They got skiers in the Olympics."

"Could be dead," Bob said. "Deese—not the skiers."

"Could be," Rae said. "But Tremanty says he's the baddest guy that Roger Smith has available. He thinks Smith would want to keep him available if he can. Smith thinks Deese might beat the rap—the judge isn't known as 'Cash' McConnell for nothing."

"Tremanty says? You been going out for cups of coffee with the FBI? Meetin' Agent Tremanty for a little tit-à-tit?"

"It's pronounced tête-à-tête, not tit-à-tit, you

ignorant Oakie," Rae said. She always got tight on a job like this. Her M4 had a sling, and she was clinking the sling's swivel against the handguard and it went **dink-dink-dink** as they talked.

"It's pronounced tête-à-tête if you mean a face-to-face meeting," Bob said. "It's pronounced tit-à-tit if you mean . . ."

"Off my back, dumbass," Rae interrupted. "Here we go."

DEESE'S HOME was a low, rambling building clad with wide, unpainted pine weatherboards gone dark with the sun and wind. The house looked old, nineteenth-century, but wasn't; it had been built in 1999 on a concrete slab, according to the parish assessor's office.

A narrow porch stretched down the length of the structure, a foot above ground level, with a door opening off the middle of the porch. Two green metal patio chairs on the porch, their paint faded by sunlight and rain. The third marshal popped out of his truck and ran toward the back of the house, while Bob and Rae went straight in from the front, watching the windows for movement, their rifles already up, safeties off, fingers hovering over the triggers.

Rae crossed the porch and stood to one side of the door and pounded on it with her fist and shouted, "Mr. Deese! Mr. Deese!"

Bob was to one side, in the yard, watching windows, but with his rifle now pointed in the direction of the door. Rae pounded on the door again. "Deese! Deese!"

No reaction. Bob stepped back to the center, at the bottom of the porch steps. "Ready?"

"Anytime," Rae said.

Bob cocked himself to kick the door, but then the door moved—and he went sideways and shouted, "Door!"

The door opened farther and a frightened, round-faced black woman stuck her head out. She said to Rae, who was pointing a gun at her, "Mr. Deese ain't here."

"Where is he?"

"Don't know. He been gone."

Bob said, "Please step back, ma'am."

They followed the muzzles of their rifles into the house, which was dark and well cooled. They walked through to the back, shouted out at the other marshal, then opened the back door to let him in. Together, they cleared the place.

The black woman was named Carolanne Pouter and she worked three days a week cleaning house, doing Deese's laundry and occasional grocery shopping, mowing the yard, and keeping a daily eye on the place when he was traveling.

"Did he tell you where he was going?" Bob asked.

"No, sir. He never does. But this time . . ." She

eyed their marshal shirts. "This time, it ain't like the other times. He was two days burning paper out back. He was coming and going and coming and going for three weeks, and then he loaded all his baggage into his pickup and he went on down the road. Took all his cowboy boots, too. Told me to lock up and gave me five hundred dollars to watch the house for six months. Which I been doin', faithful."

Tremanty had come inside, and now he asked, "Did Mr. Deese have an office in the house or a place where he did his paperwork?"

"Yes, sir, upstairs, next to the bedroom."

Tremanty said to Bob, "Why don't you get Miz Pouter to show you where he was burning paper. See what the situation is. I'll check out the office."

Rae followed Tremanty up the wooden staircase, and Tremanty said, "The whole place is pine. If he's running, I'm surprised he didn't torch it. It'd burn like a barn full of hay."

Deese's office space was small, only about ten by ten feet, with one window looking out toward the jungle in back. An inexpensive office desk, the kind you might buy from a big-box office supply store, sat next to two empty filing cabinets. There were no closets, no place to hide, so when the marshals had cleared the house, they'd spent no more than five seconds in the room.

Tremanty said, "He's gone and we won't find him in a hurry."

"That's some fine detectin'," Rae said. "Since we only been here one minute."

"I found a clue you missed," Tremanty said. He was really handsome, and when Rae had first seen him she'd had to bite her lip. "On the desk."

Rae stepped over to look. Sitting on the desk, on a sheet of white computer paper, was Deese's ankle monitor, which had been severed with a pair of wire cutters. The paper had a straightforward note, apparently to Tremanty: "Fuck you."

"That's so rude," Rae said.

OUTSIDE, Bob and the third marshal, with Pouter, were looking at a fifty-five-gallon drum that had been used as a burn barrel and was half full of powdered ash. A six-foot dowel rod, heavily singed, was lying on the ground next to the barrel. Bob used it to stir around in the ash and found nothing but more ash. Deese had not only burned a lot of paper, he'd carefully broken it up so there'd be no chance of reconstituting it; and there were no partially burnt pages. It was all gone.

They had turned back toward the house when Rae came out, followed by Tremanty. "Lot of ash," Bob said. "Nothing we can save."

"He's cleaned the place out," Rae said. She turned to Pouter. "Did Mr. Deese have a computer?"

"Yes, ma'am, and a printer, too. They were old, but they worked okay. They gone now."

"We noticed," Tremanty said.

He walked down to one back corner of the house, looking this way and that, and then down to the other corner, and when he rejoined the group he said to Bob, "There's a walked-in trail goes back into the trees, right over there. Go back and take a look, see if there's anything we need to see."

"Ah, man, it's a swamp . . ."

"So stay on the path."

"Shouldn't do that. There're poison snakes back there," Pouter said. "Mr. Clay said he seen moccasins bigger 'round than his leg. He told me, if I ever go back there, he'd fire me because he didn't want to go hauling some dead black ass out of the woods. That was what he said. Except he didn't say 'black.' You know what I mean."

"I do," Rae said.

"But he paid regular," Pouter said.

"You hear that?" Bob asked Tremanty. "Snakes. Water moccasins the size of tree trunks."

"Life sucks and then you die," Tremanty said. "Besides, I'm wearing loafers, and if there are snakes back there I got nothing between my ankle and the snakes except a pair of Ralph Lauren dress socks."

"I'll go with you," Rae said to Bob. "Bring that pole."

"Ah, jeez."

But Bob went, and even led the way. The trail looked like something that might have been used by deer, or even pigs. It was only a foot wide and, here and there, overgrown with sedges, which Bob carefully probed with the dowel before crossing. The place had a wet dirt odor, but when Bob broke through some round green plant stems the air was immediately suffused with the smell of green onions, or garlic. A tiger swallowtail flittered in and out of shafts of sunlight—now here, now gone, now here again.

They saw no snakes, but the trail went on, and so did they, cutting through downed trees and live ones, stepping around low spots filled with stagnant water, until Rae said, "Bob? Look."

She pointed at an oval depression, six feet off the trail, in which the weeds were half the height of the surrounding foliage; they were younger, and a lighter shade of green. "What does that look like?"

"Looks like this one, over here," Bob said, pointing to a similar-sized depression on the other side, well off the trail. Ten feet farther along the track, they saw another, but with taller brush growing over it.

"Let's go have a tit-à-tit," Bob said.

They went back out, told Tremanty that they hadn't seen any snakes, but that they needed an opinion. Tremanty followed them back, stepping high, keeping a sharp eye out for slithers. When they showed him the low spots, he looked at them and said, "Could be natural."

“Nature often fools the eye,” Bob said. “Since that’s decided, let’s get out of here and down to New Orleans and get some crawfish. I’ll buy.”

“Goddamnit. Every time I go out with marshals, weird shit happens,” Tremanty said. He took a cell phone out of his pocket.

“So, in your opinion . . .”

“My opinion is, those are natural depressions, or maybe Deese was burying something back here.”

“Let me say it again,” Bob said. “Crawfish.”

Tremanty shook his head. “I gotta make some calls.”

“If those are graves, there could be a hundred of them back here,” Rae said, looking into the twisted, fetid brush around them.

“Pray that they’re not,” Tremanty said, as he punched a number into his phone. “I’m serious. Pray.”

# CHAPTER TWO

Five guys sat in the bar's back room, playing dealer's choice poker, five-card draw on this particular hand, and they were cheap. The most valuable chips, the white ones, were worth a buck.

Lucas Davenport was in the awkward position of holding a pair of fives after the draw, with three people still in the pot, and, at the same time, defending the FBI.

"They're not **all** assholes," he said. He was the only one wearing a suit, a silvery-gray ensemble too relaxed to be currently fashionable except maybe in certain parts of Milan, where he'd never been but would like to go for the shopping. He was tieless in a checked shirt open at the collar. He looked again at his hand, threw the cards facedown in the center of the table, and said, "I'm out."

"Name one who isn't an asshole. Just one," Shrake said, referring to the agents at the FBI. The back room smelled of beer, deli sandwiches, and a hint of cigar, though none of them smoked.

Lucas: "There's this chick I met in Washington . . ."

"I mean one that I **know**," Shrake said, pointing the top of a beer bottle at Lucas. "Maybe there's one, somewhere, but here . . ."

"I gotta think about it," Lucas said. He had a corned beef sandwich sitting on a paper plate on the table, picked it up, and took another bite. The genuine French mustard—**moutarde**—bit right back.

Shrake: "See?"

Shrake and his partner, Jenkins, both large men with battered faces, wore gray sport coats over short-sleeved open-necked golf shirts—pastel green and baby blue, respectively.

"Lotta assholes in the BCA and St. Paul and Minneapolis cops . . ." Lucas said, around a mouthful of corned beef.

"Yeah, but we're not **all** assholes, like in the FBI," Jenkins said. He threw a white chip into the pile in the middle of the table. "I'm in for a buck."

"I'm telling you . . ."

Virgil Flowers, a Bureau of Criminal Apprehension agent visiting from southern Minnesota, said, "How about Terry McCullough? He never seemed that bad."

They talked about Special Agent Terry

McCullough for a couple of minutes and, by a vote of three to two, found him to be an asshole.

"Then I got nothing," Flowers said. He was wearing a canvas shirt and jeans. He'd found out earlier that week that in six or seven months he would become the father of twins, God willing and the creek don't rise. He threw a white chip and a red one into the pot and said, "See your buck and raise you a half."

Jenkins said, "Fuck you and your raise, you sandbagging piece of shit."

Lucas: "Just because all the feds got college degrees . . ."

"We **all** got college degrees," Shrake said.

"A real college, not a four-day putting school," Lucas said.

Jenkins said, "Oh."

"Feds are like classical musicians," said Sloan, a former Minneapolis homicide cop who owned the bar where they were playing cards, and who sometimes played guitar in a J. J. Cale tribute band. He was a narrow man who dressed mostly in shades of brown and wore hats with brims. "They can read music like crazy, but you want them to play a C major seventh chord, they got no idea what the fuck you're talking about."

"I got no idea what the fuck you're talking about," Lucas said.

"Take my word for it, it's exactly the same

thing," Sloan said. And, "Buck and a half to me? I'm gone."

LUCAS'S PHONE buzzed in his pant pocket and he slid his chair back and looked at the screen: Rae Givens.

"I gotta take it," he told the others.

He stepped away from the table, put a finger in his off ear, and said, "Rae. What's up, sweetheart?"

"You been reading about the bodies coming out of the woods in Louisiana?"

"Yeah, in the newspapers," he said. "Four dead, right?"

"Five, as of an hour ago, could be more. Probably more."

"Are you and Bob involved?"

"Yeah. We spotted the graves, but we're on the fringe of it for the moment," she said. "We got FBI like a rat's got fleas. We need you to use some of your political shine to get involved and take us along for the ride. Me and Bob."

"Any reason why I should?" Lucas asked.

"He's major, Lucas. A bad dude, the kind you like. I don't think the FBI is gonna find him," Rae said. "They're way too zone defense and we need a man-to-man. We need somebody chasing him down, not circulating bulletins around the places he might be."

"Five dead makes it more interesting . . ."

"How about this? He ate them," Rae said. "We think he barbecued them on his home grill. We found a woman's body—a girl, really—with the muscle taken out of her lower back. And we found some unburnt fat in the grill with human DNA."

"What?"

"He's a fuckin' cannibal, man," Rae said. "Don't go telling anybody, it hasn't leaked out yet."

"Huh. Any idea where he's gone?"

"No. But get your slow white ass down here before the musical chairs stop. We need a chair if we're gonna do this," Rae said.

"Bob's in?"

"He's standing right here next to me and he's already been emailing back and forth with Washington. He wanted me to call because, you know, I'm better-looking, and he knows that's important to you."

"Let me make some calls tomorrow morning," Lucas said. "Who's the agent in charge at the scene?"

"A guy named Tremanty. I gotta tell you, he's cute."

"Spell it."

"C-U-T-E." She laughed, said, "I slay myself," and then spelled out the name: "T-r-e-m-a-n-t-y."

Lucas told her he'd get back before noon the next day. When she'd rung off, Lucas went back to the table, and Flowers asked, "What was all that about?"

"That killer guy down in Louisiana? You know,

where they're digging up the bodies? Turns out he ate some of the victims," Lucas said, ignoring Rae's warning about leaks.

Shrake: "Say what?"

"Barbecued them."

Jenkins: "Do they know what kind of rub he used?"

"Not yet, apparently," Lucas said.

Flowers: "They want you to buy in?"

"That's what they say."

Flowers: "From what I read, he sounds like he's on the dark side of deranged. Don't get shot."

Sloan asked, "Are we gonna sit here and bullshit or are we gonna play cards?"

Jenkins: "Asked the man who's losing his shirt."

"We all lose our shirts when that fuckin' Flowers is in the game," Shrake said.

Flowers: "I have been lucky, I guess. I can't apologize."

The other four all said "Right . . ." at the same time, and Jenkins added, "Deal, dickweed."

LUCAS DAVENPORT was a tall man, broad-shouldered, with dark hair speckled with gray, blue eyes, and a smile that could turn mean. He was fifty-two and a dedicated clothes horse, which was why he was wearing a suit to play poker in the back of a bar.

When the game broke up at midnight, he and

Flowers chatted for a while in the parking lot about Flowers's upcoming fatherhood. "I gotta tell you, I'm about as excited as I ever get, but my mother is totally out of control," Flowers said. "I think my folks had given up on having grandchildren. Now I think my mom wants to move in with us."

"No, no, no, no . . ."

"Nah, that ain't gonna happen," Flowers said.

"There was some talk that you might leave the BCA and run for sheriff down there," Lucas said, leaning his butt against the back corner panel of his Porsche 911.

"That's not something I have to decide right away—the current guy's got almost four more years, but he's sorta recruiting me to run when he retires," Virgil said. "There'd be some advantages—I'd be home all the time . . ."

"I got two words for you," Lucas said. "'Health insurance.' Your state insurance is terrific, and with twins, you'll need it. When my kids were small, they were down at the clinic once a week. Elementary school is a germ farm: the kids get everything known to mankind. Look before you leap . . ."

They went on for a while, and Lucas finally patted Flowers on the back and said, "The best advice I got is, Virgie, is stop worrying and enjoy it. Kids are wonderful, even when they're not."

"Thank you."

---

WHEN HE GOT HOME, Lucas's wife, Weather, was asleep. Lucas tried tiptoeing around the bedroom, but she woke up and asked, "Talk to Virgil?"

"Yeah. He's all over the place about the kids," Lucas said. "We gotta get them up here this summer. More than once. Maybe you can calm him down. He asked me the difference between Huggies and Pampers and wanted me to recommend one, for Christ's sakes."

"How about next week?"

"Ah, Rae called. She might have a job I want to look at," Lucas said.

"Louisiana?" Weather asked.

"Yeah."

"Talk in the morning," she said.

LUCAS HAD an office in Minneapolis, but didn't work out of Minneapolis. He worked out of Washington, D.C., and reported to a bureaucrat named Russell Forte. The relationship was purely notional.

Because of the political arrangement that had brought Lucas to the U.S. Marshals Service—he was a deputy U.S. Marshal—he was free to pick his own cases. There was a caveat: if a Washington politician called for help, he was bound at least to listen. The arrangement initially created some dissension within the Minneapolis office, but that had mostly gone away. The U.S. Marshal for the Minnesota District, Hal Oder, had been warned to keep his hands off Lucas, and he did, though he didn't like it.

If that were to change, Lucas would quit; and he'd proven valuable to a number of powerful politicians of both parties, so his protection was unlikely to go away. Not that he completely trusted any of them—even the best politicians were, in his mind, sneaky, unreliable motherfuckers. While he did occasional errands for them and sometimes took cases for the Minnesota District, his main occupation was chasing down hard-core killers.

Not just any killers. Because of the way the federal law enforcement bureaucracy divided up tasks, he was mostly limited to killers who'd already had some contact with the federal court system. He didn't have the backup resources of the FBI, but that was okay. Chasing down fugitives was more a matter of street work than technical processes, and that was what he was best at.

He was happy, as much as he'd ever been inside a law enforcement unit. Being a vigilante would be even better, but, of course, that was both expensive and illegal.

He and Weather talked at dawn, before her first surgery—she was a plastic surgeon, and for reasons that seemed crazy to Lucas, most surgeries were begun when normal people were still asleep. A bit later, when he woke up the second time, he called Russell Forte in Washington.

"I've gotten some rumblings that the Davenport machine may be cranking up," Forte said. "I looked into it, and while the FBI might not necessarily actively seek your help down there in New Orleans, they probably wouldn't drive you away with nunchucks."

"Bob and Rae?"

"Absolutely. Bob sent me a note yesterday saying that you might call and beg to get in on it, poor bastard," Forte said. "Listen, this guy, this Deese, this cannibal—man, it would be nice if a marshal were to nail him. The PR would be, like, galactic."

"So I can pack my bag?"

"Yes. The FBI guy in charge of the site is named Sandro Tremanty, and my friends among the FBI say that he is competent, which means he's probably on his way up. Try to treat him as an equal."

"That's not realistic, but I'll try."

"Then we're set. Sally's cutting your travel orders now. Usual terms. Did you ever get your LEO traveling armed certification?"

"Yeah, I'm all set."

"Keep me up on what happens. And try to keep better track of your expenses. Sally said that last batch of your forms looked like it was compiled by chickens."

———

THREE DAYS after Rae's late-night call, Lucas kissed his wife and two at-home kids and flew out of MSP and into MSY—Minneapolis–St. Paul International to Louis Armstrong New Orleans International—his Walther PPQ tucked away in his carry-on pack. Bob met him in baggage claim wearing a black T-shirt, tan cargo shorts, and cross-training shoes. Bob was a wide man, with a neck that extended out past his ears.

"Nice to see you, man. Bring your gun?" he asked, as they shook hands.

"Right in my pack. I'd take it out and show you, but somebody would shoot me," he said, looking around the crowded baggage claim area.

They got Lucas's bag and went out the door, which was like stepping into a bowl of Slap Ya Mama hot sauce: fiery and wet. Bob was driving a Tahoe and was parked in a police-only zone: "I showed them my badge and told them I was undercover, investigating aggravated interstate mopery, and they said okay," Bob explained. "We gotta get out of here before they look up 'mopery' in the dictionary."

"Like a cop would have a dictionary," Lucas said. "Where's Rae?"

"She's still up at the site," Bob said. "I'll tell you, Lucas, I've seen some disgusting shit in this job, but this one takes the cake. These bodies are straight out of a horror show. And that fuckin' Deese was eating these people. Most people, he eats what

Tremanty says is the tenderloin, or would be the tenderloin on a deer, but this one guy, it looks like he ate his liver."

"Jesus."

"And then he buries them in this boggy ground. When they bring them up . . . ah, you'll see. The FBI brought in cadaver hounds, and we're going over his property inch by inch, but it's six acres of jungle and it's nasty out there. We think we've got another grave spotted and we're not even halfway through yet."

"News media?"

"Parked all over, all day. WVUE outta New Orleans is running a promo saying they've got big breaking news on it, and I suspect they've heard about the barbecue thing. They're holding it close, they wanted to interview Tremanty at 6:05 this evening, but he told them to suck on it . . . So . . . you bring anything but suits?"

"Oh, yeah. Talked to Rae. I got my backwoods gear. Even brought a pair of gum boots."

"You'll need them. We've killed three canebrake rattlers and a cottonmouth. We had a Fish and Game guy there who didn't like it, he wanted to catch and release over by the river, but most of the guys shoot first and talk to Fish and Game later. Somebody bought a box of CCI snake shot, and we're all loading it at the top of the stack."

"I basically don't do snakes," Lucas said.

"I noticed that about you when we were down in Texas," Bob said.

ON THE WAY NORTH, they talked about their previous work together in Washington, D.C., and Texas, and about the Minnesota senator who was shot to death, after their Washington investigation had ended, and exactly who might have done it.

Bob gave Lucas an inch-thick stack of paper on Deese and the man believed to be his main employer, Roger ("Rog") Smith. Smith was a graduate of the University of Alabama's law school in Tuscaloosa who'd turned to loan-sharking as a natural outgrowth of his law practice, along with his principal ownership of a major bail bond business. Lucas tucked the paper away in his pack. "I can't read in a car, I'd puke on your front seat. Just talk to me."

"Smith loans some chump twelve hundred dollars at twenty percent so the chump can call up Smith's bail bond business and give the money back on a ten-thousand-dollar bond, which requires him to hire Smith's firm to defend him."

"Got the whole thing sewn up," Lucas said. "What happens if the client is convicted?"

"Well, for one thing, the judge would probably have to give back his share of the twelve hundred dollars in bond money."

"You're a hopeless cynic," Lucas said.

"I'm a hapless Louisianan," Bob said.

THEY ARRIVED at Deese's place at two o'clock in the afternoon. A line of TV vans was parked out on the highway, but the track to Deese's house had been closed, with a Louisiana state police car parked across it. The cop recognized Bob and waved them through.

"I understand this Tremanty is cute," Lucas said.

"Rae is mooning over him." He glanced sideways at Lucas. "She told him that he looks like your son. And you know? He does."

"I'm not old enough to be an FBI agent's father," Lucas said.

"Sure you are, if you started early, maybe on one of those out-of-town college hockey trips." They had to pull to the roadside fifty yards short of the house because of the accumulation of parked cars. "Come on, I'll introduce you to Sandro."

"Not Sandy?"

"No. It's Sandro. Or Tremanty. Rae calls him Ess-Tee," Bob said.

"He's not a total asshole?"

"I hesitate to say it, but he's okay."

"That helps. Let me get my boots."

They got out of the truck, and Lucas popped the back door, unzipped his Tumi suitcase, folded his suit coat into it, got the gum boots out, traded his shoes for the seventeen-inchers, and tucked his pant legs neatly inside. They walked down to the house, past another cop checking IDs, and went in. Several tables with folding legs had been set up in the living room, stacked with computers and paper. The house was cool, an air conditioner rumbling on the second floor, but humid enough to make the air feel liquid.

Tremanty was standing behind a computer operator. The FBI agent was as tall as Lucas, with the same dark hair and blue eyes, but slender. Looking over his shoulder, he saw Lucas and Bob, came around the table, and said, "How ya doing, Dad?"

"I'm okay," Lucas said, as they shook hands. "As your father, I'd like to tell you how to run this investigation."

"Fuck that," Tremanty said.

Lucas turned to Bob. "A fed said 'fuck.'"

"Not for the first time. It's shocking, I know."

Rae came in from the back. "Lucas Davenport, suites hotels and business-class travel. You sweetie."

She gave him a hug and said to Tremanty, "See? I told you. He must have visited Virginia thirty-one years ago."

Tremanty said, "I'll check with Mom." To Lucas: "Listen. I'm glad to have you. I've heard about you from a couple people in Washington. You're welcome to everything we've got, but you ought to start by following Bob and Rae around the scene in the back."

"I'll do that," Lucas said. "And thanks. I'll try to help without getting in your way."

They nodded at each other, and Rae said, "This way . . . Hey! Like your shoes."

RAE CALLED the back lot a jungle, and it was, but now roped with crime scene tape and new-cut trails. The undergrowth was so heavy that Lucas worried about getting bit above the knee by a snake wrapped around a vine. He'd seen pictures like that—Garden of Eden pictures, with a snake encircling the Tree of Knowledge of Good and Evil.

He said that, and Rae said, "Garden of Evil. No good in here."

Fifty yards back into the jungle, all of them yet un-snakebitten, they found a tall, skinny, weathered man wearing mud-caked white Tyvek coveralls, a baseball hat, and gum boots identical to Lucas's. He wore a belt over the coveralls, with three holsters, one carrying a .40 caliber Glock, the second a plastic canteen, and the third a Marshalltown trowel.

Bob asked him, "What about six?"

"Doc's down there taking DNA samples. It's old, it's all falling apart, we're gonna box the skull, we can see some dental work. He says it's male, for sure. We got one hand, but the flesh is gone, so there won't be any prints. Barb thinks she's got seven, by the back lot line, and Dave thinks he has eight. The dogs aren't indicating, so they may be really old, and there's so much organic matter on top that they get confused. Whatever, we'll have to dig them out."

Rae said to Lucas, "This is Cory Laird, FBI, he does old bodies. Cory, this is the marshal I was telling you about, Lucas Davenport." They shook, Laird smiling and saying, "Clean hands. We all work with gloves, in case you're worried. You need the tour?"

"Like to take a look," Lucas said. "You got IDs on any of the bodies?"

"On two of them. We're shipping the DNA scans everywhere, seeing if we can pick up the others. We think that most of them come from New Orleans, or the parishes right around New Orleans. We're looking for relatives of missing people that we think might have been Deese's targets, so we can cross-check the DNA with them. Deese worked for several different mob guys over the years, some of them are dead, so figuring that out has been complicated. My best bet is, we'll get all but one. It seems like in these situations, there's always one you can't identify."

Laird led them along the narrow but now well-worn path, and, behind Lucas, Bob said, "Newest body is only about seven or eight months old, a woman named Bailee Wheelwright, nicknamed Bill, who kept company with Rog Smith, who I told you about."

"The lawyer, bail bondsman, loan shark."

"Right. She was his best girl for two years, and Tremanty said they were having problems and she supposedly moved to Chicago and disappeared. He'd been looking for her, hoping she'd talk about Smith, but never made contact. Tremanty thinks that when they had their falling-out—she might have known too much about his operation—so . . . Deese. The body's missing a strip of muscle from the back."

They'd been stringing along the narrow track behind Laird, walking through shallow mud puddles along the way, around the larger trees, past deep excavated pits. Somebody had used a chain saw to open up pieces of the swamp, with the cut limbs stacked back in the heavier brush.

They took a new-cut side track to an isolated pit, where two people were working side by side in the hole, both dressed in Tyvek. A lunch-box-like container sat outside the hole, filled with cylindrical bottles with screw-on tops. The excavations had been cut wide enough to allow the men to stand on clean earth separate from the grave's hole.

"All the digging is done with trowels, an inch at a time," Laird said. "It takes a while."

Peering into the hole, Lucas could make out a dirt-colored skeleton with some rags of clothing and skin and hair. The visible bones had collapsed on top of one another, the vertebrae, arm bones, and ribs crushed down over the folded leg bones, the skull on top. The only odor was that of swamp mud.

The men looked up, and one of them said, "Where's Larry? We need the box."

"He's coming," Laird said. "You see anything?"

"Shot in the back of the head, bullet passing through the brain and out through the left eye socket. Looks like the subject was kneeling, to get that angle. Or, the shooter could have been standing on a chair, but . . ."

Laird said, "Yeah?"

The other man in the hole said, "This goddamn mud gets on everything. Drives me crazy. You scrape it off and one minute later it's back on."

Lucas took the rest of the tour: two unexcavated suspicious depressions were pointed out, with Laird saying one was a sure thing, in his opinion, the other was fifty-fifty. "We're more than halfway through and there are spots in the other half that we think would have been obvious choices for burials. So . . . it's a big deal and getting bigger."

Rae asked Laird, "You remember that case up in Minnesota a few years ago? The Black Hole?"

"Sure. Seventeen murders and a few old skulls stolen from cemeteries, if I remember correctly. Crazy guy living with a dead man. It's a classic."

"Lucas is the guy who broke that down," she said.

"No kiddin'." He looked at Lucas with raised eyebrows. "Glad to have you, then. I hope to hell we don't have seventeen, though. That's not a record I'd want to mess with."

Of the six recoveries, including the one in the grave still being excavated, the means of death had been determined in five—all gunshot wounds to the head. "It looks to us, from what Tremanty's uncovered, that Deese used a club to punish and guns to kill. Never straight-up fights. He favored ambushes."

In the last one, the one that had got him arrested, the victim, Howell Paine, said he had answered the door and had been hit in the face and was on the floor before he even understood what was happening.

By then, he'd been unable to resist. He never would have known who his attacker was—the man had been wearing a ski mask—if his next-door neighbor hadn't taken a picture of the attacker's car, including the license plate. He'd also taken a bite out of the man's leg, and the meat he'd spit out had matched the DNA of the meat still intact on Deese's body. Tremanty had had a watch on anything Deese-related. Howell had been put under guard, in the hospital, and when he got out he was hustled into the Marshals Service Witness Protection Program.

"Never would have found this place if he'd gone to trial," Bob said, tipping his head back to look up through the jungle to the skies. "If he'd been convicted, he might've gotten ten years, or fifteen, with the wrong judge. With Roger Smith's influence, he might have gotten two, maybe none. But he would've gotten out. Now, since he ran . . . and we found this place . . . he's looking at life, at a minimum. And the needle is a real possibility."

Lucas looked around. "I've seen what I need. I want to look at Tremanty's paper and maybe get a beer with him, if he's the beer-drinking type."

"He can be," Rae said. "You've got to be careful, though. He's pretty straight. He won't want to hear about . . . unorthodox investigative techniques."

On the way out, Bob suddenly blurted, "Snake!" and pointed at Lucas's foot. Lucas levitated, and Rae and Bob fell out laughing.

Lucas said, "I won't kick your asses right now. Revenge is best when it's cold, and I've had time to think about it. Can you say 'economy class'? Can you say 'seventeen-inch seats'? 'Motel 6'?"

"You wouldn't fuckin' do that," Bob said. He looked at Rae. "Would he?"

Rae: "Who are you again?" And to Lucas: "Do I know him?"

"Best for you if you don't," Lucas said. He looked around his foot and back into the weeds and muttered, "Snakes . . ."

# CHAPTER THREE

Back in the house, Tremanty asked Lucas if he'd had a chance to look through the printouts that Bob had given him. "I can't read in cars," Lucas said. "I need to do that now."

"There's a spot upstairs," Tremanty said. "Deese's office. It's cool, and there's a decent chair in there."

"Any guesses on how many bodies you'll find?"

"I'm thinking ten, twelve. That's only a guess," Tremanty said. "What worries me is all the publicity we've been getting. By now, Deese knows for sure that we've found the bodies, so he's gotta be digging himself in deep. He hasn't had a lot of time to do that yet, but the longer it goes . . ."

"Does he have the resources to do that?" Lucas asked.

"I dunno. When we busted him, we went after his bank accounts and got eight thousand dollars. This is a guy who was probably spending that much every month on hookers and blow. So, he wasn't keeping his income in his aboveground bank account."

"If it was hookers and cocaine, over any long period of time . . . those guys tend to spend everything they have. They're both addictions."

"Yeah. Even if he had a stash, it might not have been too much. His housekeeper never saw any money around the house and she was all over it. It's possible that he's broke."

"Okay. Let me read," Lucas said. "Preferably in a place that's snake-free."

"Hey. Snakes are more afraid of you than you are of them. Not many rattlers survive an encounter with a human being, but it's a rare thing when a rattlesnake kills a human," Tremanty said.

"Right. I needed a pro-snake lecture. I'm gonna go read," Lucas said.

HE SPENT the rest of the afternoon working through the paper with a highlighter pen, taking breaks for Diet Cokes supplied by Rae, to walk in the jungle and look into the pits while avoiding snakes, and once, as the day faded into evening, to chat again with Tremanty.

"We need to go somewhere quiet and talk," Lucas said. "Maybe when you quit for the day?"

"There's a bar a few miles out where people go when we finish," Tremanty said. "It's got booths that give you a little privacy."

"Then let's get Bob and Rae down there and talk."

At six o'clock, everyone in the house gathered around Deese's wide-screen television to watch the news. The talking head immediately passed the camera off to a dark-haired woman who began by saying, in her best hard-news voice, "We have learned exclusively that the bodies being dug up at the home of Clayton Deese are showing signs of cannibalism . . ."

Everyone in the room groaned, and a neatly dressed woman in a blue dress said to Tremanty, "There goes my night."

Rae leaned toward Lucas and muttered, "FBI spokeswoman."

"I'm two-thirds of the way through the paper," Lucas said. "I'm going back upstairs."

SUNSET WAS about eight o'clock, but the jungle started getting dim at seven, even dimmer in the muddy pits, and the recovery crews began pulling out. Six men and a woman who were doing the excavations took turns in Deese's shower and were gone by eight. A dozen overnight guards began patrolling the site, under perimeter lights supplemented by laser trip wires.

Lucas, Bob, and Rae followed Tremanty out at eight o'clock, seven miles to a low, rambling concrete-block bar called Remy's. The bar was decorated with beer signs, and, on the door, a black-and-white poster that showed a man's fist holding a revolver, with the words "We Don't Call 911."

A twenty-foot-square dance floor sat at one end of the building, with an elevated platform against the wall that might have accommodated a five-piece band. Everything inside was old wood, fake wood, or concrete blocks, including a digital jukebox that was a bit of all three; a Brooks & Dunn song, "Neon Moon," was burbling out into the dim interior.

The bar was populated by wary locals, most in working clothes—jeans and T-shirts—who were gathered at the dance floor end; by a few reporters, who were jammed into the middle; and by cops and technicians from the Deese crime scene, who dominated the other end. Everybody seemed to be eating deep-fried shrimp or deep-fried catfish or deep-fried potatoes, string beans, or cauliflower buds.

As they walked past the reporters, a photographer lifted a hand-sized camera and took a picture of Lucas. Annoying, but perfectly legal, and the photographer nodded at him. Tremanty led the way to the last booth, the only one that was empty. Lucas got the impression that it was reserved for him, and a waitress hustled over as soon as the four of them slid into it.

———

THEY ORDERED DRINKS, and when the waitress had gone Tremanty looked at Lucas and asked, "What do you think?"

"I won't be any help for you at the crime scene. Neither will Bob or Rae, except maybe as tour guides. We need to go after Deese," Lucas said. "Starting now."

"How would you do that?" Tremanty asked.

"I've had some complicated dealings with the FBI," Lucas said. "In my experience, the FBI doesn't always want to know how the sausage gets made."

"I don't want to hear about anything overtly criminal, but if it's arguable I do want to hear about it," Tremanty said.

The waitress arrived with the drinks—beers for Bob and Rae, a lemonade for Tremanty, and a Diet Coke for Lucas—and they shut up for the minute she was there, and, when she was gone, Lucas said, "I want to interview Roger Smith. I want to ask him where he thinks Deese went."

"Good luck with that," Tremanty said. "There's no way he'll tell you a thing. If Deese flipped on him, he could be looking at the needle himself."

"This would not be a formal recorded interview," Lucas said. "I'll ask him to take a walk. I might lie to him a little."

Tremanty gazed at him for a moment, then said, "Huh." And, a moment later, "Now that the cannibalism thing is out, the pressure is going to get intense."

"That's exactly what I'm thinking," Lucas said.

Rae was sitting next to Tremanty and pushed an elbow into his arm. "We wouldn't want to use the word 'blackmail' about a Smith interview. That would be wrong."

"Why would the word even come up?" Tremanty asked.

"We've worked with Lucas before," Rae said.

"Ah. If you did use the word, what would scare him enough that he might cooperate?" Tremanty asked. "He's got a lot of reasons not to."

"That might be something that you don't want to discuss," Lucas said.

"Let's try not to wreck my career," Tremanty said. "But if you were to do this, when would you do it?"

"Tomorrow morning, early. If you have an address for Smith? And a phone number?"

"Oh, yeah. We've got all of that. He's out late every night and sleeps in. Usually starts stirring around about ten o'clock," Tremanty said. "He has live-in help. A housekeeper, plus a driver who carries a legal gun."

"You've done surveillance on him," Lucas said.

"Sure. He's got links to every organized crime outfit in the city. Actually, more disorganized crime than anything else, but you know what I mean. Ratshit gangs trying to peel money off anything they can. A lot of dope goes through here; that's where the money is. There's some gambling and so on, but not like it used to be. Smith knows the players, and his law firm does a lot of work for them."

"Was he a competent lawyer?"

"He was okay, when he was practicing," Tremanty said. "He doesn't practice anymore. He has a dozen or so associates to do the trial work. He's the CEO; he mostly coordinates. He's the biggest loan shark in town. We've heard . . . no, we **know** that he's got a million or more on the street at any one time. He charges ten percent per week, that's around five hundred percent per year. It comes back all cash."

"Ten percent isn't bad, for a shark," Lucas said. "New York, Chicago, they get fifteen or twenty percent."

"That's why he's the biggest in town. He's driven most of the others out of business," Tremanty said. "He's smart. Takes a smaller bite that still brings in five mil a year, donates money to widows and orphans at Christmas, only gets mean when he really has to. Like with our boy Howell Paine."

They talked through a second round of drinks, and when they were done Lucas said, "I'll roll this out tomorrow. Right now, I need to know where there's a Walmart."

BOB AND RAE were staying at a Best Western in Plaquemine, but Lucas suggested that they check out and go with him to New Orleans. "I've already got rooms reserved for the three of us. I'll need you down there. Depending on what we find out tomorrow, we might be flying."

"We thought we might," Rae said. "We're basically packed; we've got our gear bag."

Lucas nodded. Their gear bag contained enough weaponry to start a revolution.

After leaving the Best Western, and a brief stop at a Walmart, they went on to downtown New Orleans and checked into a Hampton Inn. The trip down took an hour and a half, and they agreed to meet in the restaurant for breakfast at eight o'clock. "We should be at Smith's place by nine o'clock at the latest. I don't want to miss him," Lucas said.

Alone in his room, Lucas opened up his new burner phone, the one he'd bought at Walmart, and called WVUE. "I need to talk to the producer on the Clayton Deese cannibal story. I just got back from there and I have a tip for you."

They put him on hold for two minutes, then a producer came up and asked, "You're calling about the Clayton Deese story?"

Lucas gave his voice a querulous tone. "Yes. I've been working up there, and I don't agree with the way the FBI is handling the information. Your story about the cannibal aspects is correct, but what they're not telling you is that some of the victims are children. He was kidnapping and eating children. Check with the FBI and they'll be forced to tell you the truth about this."

"Could we get your name . . . ?"

Lucas clicked off, yawned, went online, emailed Weather about his day, read her email about her day, turned on the TV and watched a ballgame. He was asleep by midnight and up by 7:30.

He turned on the television before he went into the bathroom, hoping to get the news, and was shaving when an alert came up, and a woman said, "After our exclusive report last night, that cannibalism was involved in the Clayton Deese serial killer investigation, a tipster called a producer at this station and alleged that some of the victims now being uncovered were children. The FBI refuses to comment . . ."

Lucas took the razor away from his chin, smiled at himself, and muttered through the shaving cream, "You're so great, Davenport. You're a fuckin' PR genius, you know that?"

Lucas wrote a note to Roger Smith before he went downstairs. Bob and Rae were waiting in the restaurant. They all had pancakes and sausage, and Rae said, "Smith is going to tell you to stick your note where the sun don't shine."

"Maybe," Lucas said. "Or maybe not."

Bob said he was intimately familiar with New Orleans, so he drove, promptly got lost, and resorted to the navigation system. They went past Audubon Park, and Lucas said, "I've heard of that place . . . never seen it."

"You should go someday," Bob said. "Great place to bird-watch."

"You bird-watch?"

"Not unless it's buffalo wings on a platter," Rae said.

"But I **see** people bird-watching," Bob said. "It's a nice place. This whole area is nice."

"As long as you got a Porsche," Rae said.

Smith lived in a pale green two-story house behind a wrought-iron fence on St. Charles Avenue, a few blocks from the park, with a lush yard spotted with flower gardens and manicured trees. The street was actually a boulevard, with a grassy strip between lanes and trolley tracks down the middle of the strip. There were narrow on-street parking lanes, and Bob pulled into one, behind a Porsche Panamera, a half block down from Smith's house. "You sure you don't want us to come with you?"

"Nah, I'm fine. I want to be as unintimidating as I can be, at least until I get inside," Lucas said.

Entry to Smith's yard was either through the driveway gate, which had an elaborate lock, or through an old-looking wrought-iron gate that led up a stone sidewalk to the front door. The gate was closed with a simple latch, but when Lucas pushed it open he noticed a copper stud on the side latch: an electronic switch. He'd triggered an alarm inside the house.

The front door was set up three limestone steps

and into a deep recess; there were both a lighted doorbell and a bronze knocker on the door, and he leaned on the doorbell for an extra beat and then banged the knocker a few times. A moment later, a slender, dark-complected man with close-cropped curly black hair opened the door, looked at Lucas, and asked, "Jehovah's Witness?"

He made Lucas smile, and Lucas said, "No, I'm a U.S. Marshal. I want to visit with Mr. Smith for a moment. No warrant, no recording, just a friendly conversation. I have a note for him."

"He may not be up, but after you nearly knocked down the door he may be. Can I have the note?"

Lucas passed it to him and asked, "If you can't knock down a door with a knocker, what can you knock it down with?"

The dark eyes flicked up at him and then back down to the note, which he read aloud: "'Your employee ate children? Really?'"

"I thought I should ask," Lucas said.

"Wait here," the man said.

HE WAS BACK in five minutes. "Roger will be down in a minute. He was awake, but he wanted to brush his teeth and splash some water on his face."

Lucas stepped inside, and the man said, "Stand there for a moment." Lucas noticed that he had an electronic device in his hand that looked something like a television remote control. He passed it over Lucas's suit and up and down his legs, and Lucas said, "No wire. Or gun."

"I see that," the man said. He pushed a button on the device, which made a high-pitched beeping sound, and added, "And your phone isn't recording. Come this way."

As Lucas followed him through the professionally decorated living room, down a hallway with a thirty-foot Persian runner underfoot, into a sprawling kitchen, he asked, "What's your name?"

The man thought about it for a while, then said, "Dick."

He put Lucas at a long breakfast table that appeared to be hewn from a single log and went to the coffee machine. "Cappuccino?"

"A cappuccino would be great," Lucas said. The table had a centerpiece: three ceramic chickens, molded as one piece and unglazed. They weren't simply chickens, Lucas realized, but Art with a capital A.

Dick brought Lucas a cappuccino in a china cup with a matching saucer and went back to the coffee machine. A moment later, Smith came through the kitchen door. He was middle height with blond hair, cut like a banker's, over pale blue eyes and a short nose. He was stocky, not fat, with a clear pink complexion. He was wearing blue-and-white vertically striped pajamas and blue slippers. He looked, Lucas thought, as though he spent a lot of time swimming.

"Could I see some ID?" he asked, as he took a chair across from Lucas.

Lucas passed his ID case, with its badge, across the table, and Smith studied it, then passed it back and said, "No recording, no warrant, a friendly conversation."

"I can explain about that," Lucas said. "I've spent most of my life as a homicide cop in Minneapolis and with the Minnesota state police. I got the marshal's appointment through political pull. I chase guys down and put them in prison. Or kill them, if they need killing. I'm looking for Clayton Deese. I understand he worked for you from time to time and I thought you might know where he is."

"I do not," Smith said. He turned to Dick. "Do you know where Deese is?"

"I have no idea," Dick said. He gave Smith a cappuccino in another china cup and saucer. "Haven't seen him for what? A year or two? That was down at a club somewhere."

Smith turned back to Lucas. "So, are we done here?"

"In a minute," Lucas said. He and Smith both took a sip of their cappuccinos. "Here's where the street cop thing comes in. I don't really operate like a fed. I spend most of my time talking to dirtbags. Like you two."

Neither man flinched, or commented.

Lucas continued: "My spider sense is telling me

that you might have some idea of where he might have gone, and that's all I'm looking for. I need something specific to work with. I won't tell anyone where the information came from. If I can confirm it from federal files, I'll tell anyone who asks that the files were my source, not you guys."

The two glanced at each other, then Smith asked, "Or what? There's something else in here, isn't there? The iron fist in the velvet glove."

"The children Deese ate," Lucas said.

"I seriously doubt . . ."

"Yeah, but the media doesn't."

"The media are a crowd of morons," Dick said.

"Who can be seriously annoying. If all the television stations were to find out that you were Deese's boss and that he ate children, I doubt you could find a parking spot out on your street. It would be filled with TV vans with those twenty-foot Christmas tree antennas sticking out of their roofs. Your neighbors would love that. 'The cannibal's employer, right here on St. Charles.' And every time a car came down the driveway . . ."

"I get the picture," Smith said. "You can guarantee that wouldn't happen anyway?"

"I can't guarantee anything," Lucas said. "I **can** tell you two things for sure. Nobody would hear anything from me. And you know what the FBI is like, with evidence: they won't be talking. You also have to consider the fact that not only did Deese butcher and eat his victims, but, on at least one occasion, he ate a guy's liver. With onions, I'm guessing."

Again, neither man flinched, but they did exchange another glance.

Lucas added, "By the way, Rog, one of the victims was your ex-girlfriend, Miz Wheelwright. She was one of the first bodies they pulled out of the muck. And, yeah, she was eaten."

For the first time, Smith seemed perturbed, his face going a shade paler. "Don't tell me that."

"I'm telling you that," Lucas said. "More grist for the media mills, since your relationship was well known around town. I can't promise that won't get out, either, but it won't come from me."

"He really ate kids?"

"That's what WVUE is saying, on its morning newscasts."

Dick closed his eyes, tipped his head back, and said, "Oh, shit."

Smith said, "Give me a minute."

He turned away from Lucas and stared at a pastel blue wall for at least a minute: thinking.

Then he turned back and said, "Sit right here. I've got to run upstairs."

He left the kitchen, and Lucas asked Dick, "Where's he going?"

Dick shrugged. "Maybe he didn't take his morning pee."

Smith was back in two minutes, "I don't know where Deese went. You think he worked for me, but that's incorrect, in a sense. Deese was a freelancer and he worked for anyone who could pay him, as long as he didn't cross . . . certain lines."

"As long as he didn't work for your rivals," Lucas suggested.

"You said that, not I. As I said, I don't know where he is, but I could speculate. He has a half brother out in Los Angeles. They are close. Very close. His brother is some kind of hard-core stickup man," Smith said. "That's what I've heard, but I've never met him or spoken to him. He would have some resources that Deese needs, if he's running. I know that Deese would meet him in both in LA and in Vegas, when he went to visit. That would happen every few months. The brothers like to gamble, and I think they may have an uncle out there, too. Out in the desert, near Vegas. Deese was joking about him one time. Called him a desert rat, said he mined for turquoise."

"His brother's name is Deese? Deese what? What's his first name?"

"No, it's Martin Keller or Martin Lawrence. Those are the two names I've heard. If either of those are his real name, you should be able to find substantial files on him. I know he's been in prison. A couple of years ago, Deese told me that if I ever had to get in touch with him in a hurry, in an emergency, when he was traveling, I could call a number. It's a . . . switchboard, so to speak."

He handed Lucas a piece of notepad paper with a phone number scrawled on it in blue ink.

"That's an LA area code. I've never called it because I've never had to, and, to tell the truth, if I ever did call it I'd do it from a pay phone, or something. He said to call only after nine o'clock at night, LA time, and ask for Martin Lawrence. That's all the help I can give you, because that's all I know. From one dirtbag to another, I can tell you I'd like to find that sonofabitch Deese myself. I won't explain that, other than to say, he never should have run."

"Why didn't he have a cell phone you could call him on?" Lucas asked.

"Think about that," Smith said.

"Okay. The FBI is probably wired into your testicles. And if Deese hadn't run, you wouldn't have this problem."

"No comment, though I'd appreciate it if you'd kill him," Smith said. And: "I'd offer you another cup of coffee, but I have a business meeting downtown in an hour and I need to get dressed."

"One more question: do you think, or have any reason at all to believe, that Deese had a lot of money stashed?"

Smith said, "I don't know. I'm sure he had some, but I don't believe he had much. The guy put more cocaine up his nose than the average country singer. That kind of habit really eats up your cash."

Lucas stood up, nodded, and said, "I hope I don't have to talk to you again."

"I share that hope," Smith said. He turned to Dick and said, "Show the marshal the way to the door."

On the way out, Dick said, "I believe Roger misspoke. Clayton once told me his brother hung out in Marina del Rey, not in the city of Los Angeles itself. Deese said the Marina is a pussy-rich environment, which is why he'd go out there, in addition to seeing his brother."

Lucas said, "I'll check that."

Dick said, "Don't fall down the steps," which made Lucas smile again.

Dick was sort of a card.

WHEN DAVENPORT was gone, Santos made sure the door was shut, then watched him walk out to the street. A moment later, he was out of sight, and Santos climbed the stairs to Smith's bedroom, where Smith was buckling up a pair of dress pants.

"He's gone," Santos said.

"Luke Davenport. Do some of your computer shit, look him up, see if we need to worry. I have a feeling that he's not your average flatfoot. See if he might have money problems or any other levers we could use."

"I can do that."

"I'm talking to Dixon in"—Smith glanced at his Patek Philippe—"fifteen minutes. Larry's coming with me; we're meeting outside the bank. Dixon's going to want to do something about Phil, and we might have to. Shouldn't take long to figure it out. I'll see you back at the office in an hour or so."

Santos nodded. "What about Deese?"

"Call him. Carefully. One of two things has to happen: Deese has to have enough money and ID that he can get out of the country and stay there; or, he's got to be killed. I'll take either. Getting the marshals to kill him would be a huge bonus. But, just in case, call him and see how much cash he needs."

"Remember how he said that if the cops caught up with him, he'd shoot his way out or die?"

"A lot of guys say that, but when it comes time to take a bullet they pussy out," Smith said. "Make the call."

"I can do that. I'll go to the office first, then call from a pay phone over in Slidell later in the afternoon. Different area code. And I think the marshal's name was Lucas, not Luke."

"Whatever."

SANTOS DROVE to Smith's law offices, where he had a corner cubicle at the back, overlooking a neighbor's garden. He liked to open the windows in the spring, when he could smell the lilacs and see the new flowers pushing up and opening. A neighbor two houses down the street had a chicken coop, and he could sometimes hear the chickens complaining to one another. He'd never heard a rooster crow, and one of the women in the office said that roosters were illegal in New Orleans, but not hens.

Way of the world.

Santos sat behind his desk, turned on his laptop computer, with software that would ricochet across a couple of different continents before opening targeted websites. The NSA might possibly be able to track him, he thought, but Smith was too small-time to draw that kind of attention.

When he put Davenport's name into the machine, he got several hundred hits. He took notes on a legal pad because, unlike with a computer, the paper could be fed to a shredder.

There was always a lot of hustle around the office—people coming and going, office doors opening and closing, talk in the hallways, phones ringing. He ignored it all until Smith stuck his head in the doorway and asked, "Well?"

Santos leaned back.

"Davenport's smart and violent. Years ago, when he was a Minneapolis cop, he made some money designing role-playing games. Like **Dungeons and Dragons**, that kind of thing. Not a lot of money, but some, and he became known for it. Later, he apparently got run out of the police department because of charges of brutality that were covered up. So he started a computer company that focused on software for cops and based on the kind of games he used to invent. He wrote out the concepts and hired some college kids to do the coding, and he made a fortune. He's got more money than you do, Rog. We won't get at him that way. Then he joined the state cops, quit there after a few years, and became a marshal. He's politically connected all the way up to Washington, and with both parties."

"All reasons not to mess with him, then," Smith said.

"Here's another reason. It's hard to tell exactly what happened—gotta give me a little rope here—but he was apparently investigating freelance military guys in Washington who were hired to kill a U.S. senator. They tried to get Davenport off their backs by going after his wife. They faked an auto accident, almost killed her."

"If it'd been us, we wouldn't have missed . . ."

"But here's the point," Santos said. "The military guys? They're dead. Well, one's missing and one's in prison, but the others are all dead."

"Huh. All right. If we have to get any further involved in this, we stay away from him."

"A good idea, I think," Santos said. "I'm worried about him getting to Deese. Deese knows—"

"Way too much."

Later that afternoon, Santos drove over to Slidell and called Deese to tell him about the marshal. Deese asked, "What's it to you? Don't tell me that Rog is worried about my personal safety."

"No, he's worried about **his** personal safety. If these marshals grab you, you'll be looking at the death penalty and you might be tempted to make a deal. Rog wants you gone and he's willing to pay. He thinks you probably need the money."

"How much?"

"Quarter million."

Deese laughed. "Man, I had a quarter million six months ago and I spent it. That ain't gonna do it. Tell him to call me when he gets real."

# CHAPTER FOUR

When Lucas got back to the Tahoe after talking with Smith and Santos, Bob asked, "Well?"

"We're looking for a guy named Martin Keller, or Martin Lawrence, who may live in Marina del Rey, or maybe Los Angeles or Las Vegas, and who has done time."

"Who's he?" Rae asked.

Lucas replayed the conversation he'd had with Roger Smith, and Rae said, "If Keller or Lawrence has been in the system, Tremanty can find him for us. We've got to tell him about this."

Lucas called Tremanty, put the phone on speaker so the others could hear, repeated the conversation with Smith a second time, with some editing, and included the phone number Smith had given him. Tremanty asked, "You're going to Los Angeles?"

"Depending on what you find out," Lucas said.

"I'll put a priority on this and bounce everything we've got to your federal email. If either of those names are real or known aliases and he's in the system, you'll have it before you get back to your hotel."

"All right. There was another guy there, with Smith. He said his name was Dick."

"What'd he look like?"

Lucas described him, and Tremanty said, "His name is Richard, or Ricardo, Santos. He's a second-generation Cuban American; his grandparents left the country when Castro came in. He seems to be Smith's assistant, but there are rumors that he's Smith's connection to the other bad boys in New Orleans. He has a degree in chemistry from the University of Miami."

"Chemistry? Really?"

"Apparently legit. Of course, a chemistry degree can be used for a lot of things that aren't legit."

"I can tell you he makes a nicely foamed cappuccino," Lucas said.

"There you go," Tremanty said. "I've started a file on him; not much in it—yet. I'll send it to you, with the files on Martin Keller or Martin Lawrence."

Bob: "Back to the suites?"

THEY GATHERED in Lucas's room and looked over his shoulder as he paged through the incoming FBI files.

Martin Keller/Lawrence's real name was Marion Beauchamps. He was first arrested for armed robbery in New Orleans in the early 2000s. He spent two years in the C. Paul Phelps Correctional Center, released a year early for good behavior. He never showed with his parole officer, and a brief investigation indicated that he'd gone to Los Angeles. Louisiana put a hold on him with the Los Angeles police, but he was never picked up.

He was arrested in Los Angeles in 2010 on a robbery charge under the name Raymond Carter, but was released on bail before his true identity was determined, and he never showed for trial.

He was arrested again in 2014 under the name of Martin Keller after he was badly beaten in a fight at a nightclub, which he'd apparently started, a serious miscalculation on his part. When he was transported in an ambulance, he was found to be holding an ounce of cocaine. Through a processing error at Los Angeles County–USC Medical Center, he was not confined to a secure ward and walked out of the hospital on his own, again before his real identity had been established.

A note in his file said "Contact LuAnne Rocha, Los Angeles Police Department, Robbery Special Section."

"Nobody's heard from him in years," Rae said. "He could be anywhere. He could be dead."

"Maybe LuAnne Rocha knows," Bob said.

---

THE PHONE NUMBER that Smith had provided went to a bar in Venice, California, called Flower Child's. Lucas had been both in Marina del Rey and Venice. "They're on the coast, right next to each other, and right there in LA," he told Bob and Rae. "Smith might even have been telling the truth about some of this."

LUCAS CALLED LuAnne Rocha, identified himself. "We're looking for a guy named Marion Beauchamps, who you guys have arrested under the names Raymond Carter and Martin Keller, but you might also know him as Martin Lawrence . . ."

"I mostly believe you, but how do I know for sure you're not actually Beauchamps calling to find out what I know?" Rocha asked.

Lucas routed Rocha through the U.S. Marshals Service to Russell Forte, who confirmed Lucas's identity, and Rocha called back. She had a sweet soprano voice that might have belonged to a young kindergarten teacher. "If you find him, let me know. That asshole has caused me more trouble than any other ten guys I can think of," she said sweetly.

"He's still in LA?"

"Almost for sure. I hadn't heard that Lawrence name, though. Where did you get that?" she asked.

"We've been asking around here in New Orleans. We're actually looking for his brother, a man named Clayton Deese," Lucas said. "He's the guy who killed and buried all those people we're digging up in Louisiana. We think he might have run out there, looking for help from Beauchamps."

"Jesus, must have had great family gatherings, huh?" Rocha said. "Sit around and bullshit about mugging techniques."

"Why's Beauchamps so high on your list?" Lucas asked.

"Because he's involved in home invasions in Beverly Hills, Brentwood . . . uh, one in Pacific Palisades, two in Malibu, a couple in the Hollywood Hills . . . Like that," Rocha said. "We picked up his prints on a pen we found in a driveway of one of the homes his gang hit, probably fell out of the door of their van. They've got a regular pattern: four guys, masked, driving a fake service vehicle—a plumber's or an electrician's, or maybe cable TV."

"Same van, not stolen?"

"No, probably not stolen, as far as we know, but really common: a white Ford Transit. We think they've got magnetic license plates, or some other way, to get them on and off in a hurry. When they get to the house, we can see the Transit, but they've pulled the plates, so they're not recorded on security cameras. There are a billion vans exactly like it in LA."

"Interesting," Lucas said.

"Yeah. They've thought about it, how to do it. They do their research, they know how many people are in the house, never hit anybody with a huge profile—no movie stars, nothing like that. The victims are always way rich, always have at least a few hundred million, and a couple were legitimate billionaires. Houses are always secluded, behind electronic gates. We think they use a code reader to pick up the signals between a victim's car and the gates. They go in immediately after the owners come back from a night out. They pull in, close the gates, drive up to the front door, hit the door with a battering ram cut from a telephone pole—the victims have seen it; it's one of their signature techniques—and they are all over the victims in a matter of a minute or so."

"Anybody get killed?"

"Not yet, but they go in with guns, and they've beaten a few people pretty badly. They'll kill somebody, sooner or later. They threaten to rape the wives or daughters, if they're around. They loot the house. They don't just take cash, they take watches, jewelry, coin collections, anything valuable that can be broken down and sold. No easily identifiable artworks, like paintings," Rocha said. "Their net, believe it or not, is close to a million bucks a hit. They probably only clear two hundred thousand or so, but still. And no taxes. The people they hit are always very rich couples, and the wives usually have a pound of diamonds stuck in a bedroom safe," Rocha said.

"And Beauchamps is involved in all of them?"

"Yes, we think so. We think he's the leader. One victim had a solid gold paperweight commissioned by his wife. It was a lump of gold the size of my fist, made by melting down a pile of pure gold coins and having an artist sculpt it to look like the victim's wife's breasts. The raw gold was worth something like forty thousand dollars. Anyway, we put out a bulletin, and the Vegas cops happened to raid a fence a couple weeks after the home invasion and found the gold tits before the fence could melt them. One of the cops remembered our bulletin and called. The fence identified Keller—Beauchamps—from his mug shots."

"Okay. He's around."

"Yeah. We've got one other suspect—and when I say 'suspect,' I mean 'for sure'—named Jayden Nast. He's a very large, violent black guy. He goes straight for the wives, tells them what he'll do to them if they don't pop that safe, how he's going to pop her balloon knot. These are well-tended women who can't deal with, uh, you know, the situation, the threats. It's all very calculated: he's a frightener and knows how to do it."

"I don't know . . . What's a 'balloon knot'?"

"You know, you look inside a balloon knot, it

sort of looks like a sphincter muscle," Rocha said. "Like an anus."

"Got it," Lucas said. "How'd you ID him?"

"One of the women gave him some lip and he smacked her in the face, broke her nose, knocked her down, and she grabbed his ankle and scratched him. He pulled her back up—by the hair—and she gave up the combination to the safe, but she kept her hand curled up and got us some solid DNA. He went in the database in 2011 on a felony assault charge, pled down, got out, but stayed in the base. So we're sure."

"Then we're looking for Beauchamps or this Jayden Nast, who could take us to Beauchamps, who then could take us to Deese."

"If you get even a whiff of Beauchamps or Nast, I want to hear about it," Rocha said. "Do you have any idea what it's like to have a dozen billionaires on your back, and on the chief's back, and on the mayor's back, some of them major political donors, all of them demanding that the guy get caught and hanged?"

"You think that's worse than chasing a cannibal?"

After a few seconds, Rocha said, "I gotta hand it to you, a cannibal serial killer would be right up there. But he's not my cannibal, he's yours. You coming out here?"

"Very soon," Lucas said.

"Call me. Pay attention when I say that Nast is violent. We've backtracked him all the way to his gangbanger days down in South-Central. This is a guy who likes to hurt people. He supposedly once worked over an ex-girlfriend with brass knuckles, ruined her face. Everybody says one other thing: he hates cops. There are rumors that he's killed cops. We don't know if that's true or where it might have happened. Probably not here, but the rumors are persistent. Pay attention, okay? A guy, with guns, who hates cops."

"Gotcha."

LUCAS HAD HAD the phone on speaker, and when he hung up Bob asked, "We going?"

"We're going."

"Hot dog. We going," Bob said to Rae.

Rae said, "Be still my beating heart."

Bob said, "You didn't tell Rocha about the phone number."

"I want to take a look at this bar, see who we can find," Lucas said. "Rocha would take down Deese if she had the chance, but she really wants Beauchamps and Nast. That's her priority, not ours. If she grabs Beauchamps, we might lose our connection to Deese."

"I'll buy that," Rae said. "If we get Deese, we'll probably get Beauchamps anyway. Might not work the other way around. When are we leaving?"

"I'll call Russ Forte's assistant," Lucas said. "We've

got reading to do . . . I'm thinking tomorrow morning—early."

GETTING FROM New Orleans to Los Angeles wasn't as simple as it should have been, and they didn't get out early. Check-in always took time, with the bag full of guns and armor that Bob and Rae traveled with, and they finally made it into LAX on a Delta flight at one o'clock in the afternoon.

Because feds were so identified with SUVs, and local cops with beaters, they rented two Chevy Malibus from Avis. Lucas had been in Los Angeles any number of times and usually stayed in Santa Monica, at Shutters on the Beach. He didn't think it was likely that the Marshals Service would go for rooms at Shutters, so they checked into the Marina del Rey Marriott. They didn't get suites, which disappointed Bob and Rae, but they did get views of the marina and, Bob noticed, a Cheesecake Factory. They were a ten-minute walk from Flower Child's Bar and Grill on Washington Boulevard.

They were out of the hotel by four o'clock; the day was clear and warm, the temperature in the upper 70s, with only a fitful breeze coming off the ocean and into their faces as they walked down to the bar: all reasons to live in LA, including the smell of the ocean.

Flower Child's was in a low, two-story stucco building a few blocks from the Pacific, with a pink-striped awning over the sidewalk. The awning was also decorated with painted flowers, marijuana leaves, and ukuleles.

Inside, a central bar divided a front room from a room in back. The bar was wrapped with thin lighted tubes in pastel pink, green, and yellow that made it look like a vintage jukebox. The front room had open tables of various sizes and was brightly lit, with customers reading newspapers as they ate. The back room was darker and lined with booths, about a third of them occupied.

They took a booth in the very back, Bob on one side of the table, Lucas and Rae on the other. A waitress came over and said, "The burgers are great . . . What do you want to drink?" She was wearing turquoise eye shadow, a tube top, and short shorts, and had a collection of rings piercing the lip of her navel. A tattoo of a boa constrictor started at the nape of her neck, ran down her back beneath the tube top, reappeared below it, and followed her spine down into her shorts. She was chewing gum.

"Nice ink," Bob said.

"Thanks. An old boyfriend did it for me. It goes all the way down between my cheeks."

"That's a lotta fine information," Rae said.

"Well, you know . . ." she said, rolling her eyes. "Whatever . . ."

They all got burgers and fries, and Lucas got a Diet Coke and Bob and Rae ordered Dos Equis. A song that sounded vaguely familiar to Lucas was playing through the sound system but he couldn't quite place it. Bob identified it as "Plastic Fantastic Lover" by Jefferson Airplane, "which is about right for this place."

When the waitress came back with the Coke and beers, she told them that a flower child tribute band played in the back room in the evenings: "Mamas and Papas, Lovin' Spoonful—that kinda shit. I get outta here before it comes on, to tell the truth. I'm afraid it'll suck the brain right outta my ear."

"Is the owner a flower child?" Lucas asked.

She snorted. "No. He's whatever he thinks the bar should be. It used to be called Hang Eleven, because he thought he might get the wannabe surfers. Before that, it was called Duder's, because of that movie. And, before that, it was called Shredder's. The name changes, nothing else does. We even use the same 'Under New Management' sign. Tourists and locals during the day, middle-aged meat rack at night. Guys with gold chains."

"Guys still do that?" Rae asked.

"They do here." She checked out Lucas, then Bob. "If you two're looking for love, you'd do okay." And to Rae: "You're more upscale."

Made them laugh, and when she went to get the burgers Bob said, "She's workin' us for tips."

"Probably gonna get 'em, too," Rae said.

---

THE BURGERS were great, like the waitress said, the fries hot, salty, greasy, like they should be. They were halfway through the meal when a couple of uniformed LA cops came in, pulled off their sunglasses, and looked around. They picked a booth in the back, and both of them looked long and hard at the three marshals as they went by. The waitress knew the two, called them by their first names.

After they ordered, they were still looking at Lucas and Rae—they couldn't see Bob from where they were sitting—and Rae muttered, "The cops made us."

"Yeah, I think." He fished his ID out of his pocket and said, "Be right back."

With the waitress nowhere in sight, he slid out of the booth, walked over to the cops, and laid the ID on the table. "Appreciate it if you could keep quiet about this," Lucas said.

"Something happening here?" one of the cops asked.

"We're looking for a guy who might come in here sometimes," Lucas said. "You know the owner?"

"Tommy? Yeah. He's okay," one of the cops said, "mostly."

"Mostly?"

"He used to sell a little cocaine and weed, to make ends meet. Not so much the last couple of years, though. Too much competition."

"You think he'd talk to us?"

"Oh, sure. He's friendly enough. He likes to have cops come by—keeps the riffraff down. He's got an office upstairs, the stairway's back by the restrooms. Name's Tommy Saito. He's usually up there afternoons and evenings, if he's not down here."

Lucas rapped his knuckles on the table. "Thanks."

WHEN THEY'D finished the meal and paid and over-tipped, they wandered down the hallway in back, past the restrooms, then up a flight of wide wooden stairs to the office suite. A door with a tall glass window had a sign that said "Come In," so they went in, where they found a heavyset woman sitting behind a wooden desk, going through what looked like charge slips and pounding on a dictionary-sized calculator.

She looked up and said, "Not guilty!"

"Tommy around?" Lucas asked.

She turned to a door recessed into a short hallway and shouted, "Hey, Tommy. There are some cops looking for you. Might be federal."

Tommy Saito poked his head out of his office, looked at the three of them, and said, "Federal? Well, come in, I guess. What can I do for you? I pay all my taxes on time."

"Ahead of time," the woman corrected.

Saito held his office door open. Lucas led Bob

and Rae in, where they found another wooden desk, sitting on a burnt-orange shag rug, with three visitors' chairs facing the desk. Saito, a short, balding Asian American, maybe sixty years old, dropped into the chair behind the desk. The wall behind him was covered with framed photos, snapshots of the same woman and three children at a variety of ages, and some shots of other kids, even younger, who might be grandchildren.

Lucas showed Saito his ID, then took copies of Deese's, Beauchamps's, and Nast's mug shots out of his jacket pocket, unfolded them, and pushed them across the desk.

"Have you seen any of these guys in here?"

Saito looked at all three, pushed Nast's back across the desk, and said, "We don't get many black dudes in here. Of those we do, he ain't one of them."

He lingered over Deese's photo for a moment, then pushed it back across the desk as well. "This guy looks sorta familiar, but if he's been in it was a long time ago. I'm saying, like, more than a year, and maybe a few. He's got a face you remember."

He looked at Beauchamps's photo the longest, then said, "This guy comes in every once in a while, checking out the divorced chicks. Usually takes one home with him—wherever home is. I don't know why I think this, but I don't believe he's from right around here. Maybe he told me once that he comes over here for business reasons and likes to stop in for a burger, fries, and a divorcee."

"You know any divorcees he's taken home?"

Saito looked at the photo for another moment, then yelled, "Heather! Come here a minute, will you?"

The woman came in, said, "I heard the question," looked at the photo, then turned and peered at a window covered by drawn blinds, pointed a finger at Saito, and said, "Suzie-Q."

Rae: "Really? Suzie-Q?"

Saito said, "That's not really her name. We call her that because she used to play an old Creedence song on our jukebox every time she came in. She lives at one of the condos in Marina, I know that for sure. She walks over here couple times a week. What the hell is her name? I know it . . ."

Heather had gone back to staring at the blinds, then said, "Jackman."

Saito said, "Barbara . . . ?"

Heather said, "That's it. Barbara Jackman."

LUCAS WROTE the name in his notebook. Then he said, "A friend of Mr. Beauchamps said he could be contacted by calling here. Do you know why that would be?"

Both Saito and Heather looked genuinely surprised; either innocence or excellent acting. Saito shook his head. "Not here. Are you sure it's ours?"

Lucas looked in his notebook and recited the number. Saito said, "That's not our number," but Heather said, "That's a pay phone."

Saito said, "Really?" like he wished Heather had kept her mouth shut. Then to Lucas: "We have a pay phone back by the restrooms. Some of our customers don't want to use their own sometimes . . ."

"I know how **that** goes," Rae said. "Don't want your dealer calling you up or even having your cell number on his phone."

"Not just dealers . . . Okay, maybe sometimes," Saito said. "But what are you gonna do? The phone kicks out two hundred dollars a week, so . . . we need the cash."

"If you want to get in touch with Beauchamps, you couldn't call the phone and hope that he's walking by. Not if he comes in only every few weeks," Bob said.

Lucas: "We were told you had to call after nine o'clock Los Angeles time."

Saito said, "After nine o'clock?" and looked again at Heather, who said, "It's that goddamn Englishman. I kept telling you he was gonna be trouble."

Saito said to Lucas, "Ah, jeez. It's gotta be Oliver. God, I hate that. He's been with us for, what, eight years?"

Lucas: "Oliver?"

Saito sighed. "Oliver Haar. He's this English

guy that works the door at night. Got a hard nose, when he needs it, keeps the peace when required. The phone's right down the hall from his spot at the door. He come on at six, works until we throw everybody out at two."

Bob: "Has he had any trouble with the law?"

Heather: "There was a rumor—"

Saito: "Just a rumor."

Heather: "That he needed to make himself scarce in London and wound up here. He's at the door, the women like him—the accent, and all that."

Saito: "And he looks good."

"All right," Lucas said. "We may want to talk to him later. Don't say a word to him about this. And don't give him a hard time, no hints there might be a problem. Just let him work. Okay?"

"Are you going to watch him?" Saito asked.

Lucas shook his head. "No. If Oliver is only passing messages, he might not have any idea of who he's talking to—or even that he's talking to bad guys. It could be he's calling burner phones, which wouldn't get us anywhere."

"I gotta say, I'd hate to lose him," Saito said.

"I wouldn't," Heather said. "He's a jerk."

"You need a jerk on the door," Saito said. "Especially one with refined British manners."

"I'll give you that," Heather said, grudgingly.

"I leave all that up to you," Lucas said. "Again,

don't tip him off. This is a serious matter and you don't want to be touched by it. But it's also possible Oliver's completely innocent."

Heather shook her head, not buying it.

RAE CALLED TREMANTY, who opened by telling her they'd found a seventh grave and were pretty sure they had eight. "The pressure is building."

"We're working," Rae said. "We need to find a woman named Barbara Jackman who lives in Marina del Rey. Could you have somebody look?"

"You got an actual lead?"

"Maybe."

"Call you back soon as I can," Tremanty said.

Lucas, Bob, and Rae went back to the Marriott. Tremanty called as they were walking in the door. "I've got an address and some details. She's had three traffic tickets over the past five years—speeding—and a small amount of marijuana picked up on one of them, before it was legal out there. She had the baggie sitting on the passenger seat. She got a fine, nothing else. Her driver's license has a current photo. She works part-time as a real estate agent. There's a better photo on her website, but she looks a lot younger than her license, so it may not be up-to-date. I asked for a credit report. It'll all be in the email."

In Lucas's room, they pulled up the email from Tremanty. Jackman's driver's license had a Marina del Rcy address, a condo on Marina City Drive. They spotted it on Google Maps, a half mile away, and decided to drive over.

"I'm feeling **too** lucky," Bob said. "It's making me nervous. We're not working hard enough for this."

JACKMAN'S CONDO, a tall, circular, cake-shaped building, had a gatehouse with nobody in it. They parked in a "No Parking" area, along a curb, Rae unrolling a "Marshal's Service" dashboard sign, but then an employee of the condominium jogged over to run them off and wound up guiding them into a legitimate spot and showing them to the elevators.

"Five dollars says she isn't home," Bob said, as they went up. "It's too easy, I'm telling you."

They found her door, knocked, and ten seconds later Jackman cracked the door, peered over the chain, and asked, "Yes?"

"I WANT TO KNOW who told you I went home with him," Jackman said, when Lucas asked. They were inside her apartment, looking over the marina and out toward the ocean. She was angry. "It's Oliver, isn't it?"

Jackman was a tall, attractive forty-three-year-old—they got her age from her license—with bouncy honey-blond hair and darker eyebrows and real two-carat diamonds in her ears. If she worked only part-time at the real estate office, she had money of her own, Lucas thought.

"We haven't met an Oliver," Lucas said. "Even if we had, we couldn't tell you who our source was. Listen. We don't think you did anything wrong. Your social life is your social life and we're not interested. We want to know where you went, that's all."

"I don't know where, exactly," Jackman said. "It's over by Pasadena, north of the 210. It was a half hour from here, at eleven o'clock at night, in a Cadillac, and forty-five minutes coming home at three o'clock in the morning by Uber."

"That's raw," Rae said. "He didn't drive you home?"

"Called an Uber, put me out on the street," she said. "I haven't seen him since. If I had, I'd have given him another piece of my mind, on top of the piece he'd already got."

"You think you could find—"

"No, I couldn't. It was almost midnight when we got there, and I'd had a few drinks and wasn't paying much attention. It's a standard suburban, upper-middle California neighborhood that looks like a million other places. Saw a nice Spanish Revival house on the way—I'd put it at a million-five, maybe two, depending on condition. Now that I'm thinking about it, it was probably not in Pasadena but maybe Altadena. But you know what? Since you're the FBI—"

Bob: "Marshals Service."

"Whatever . . . I know how you could find him. He had a regular phone in the bedroom. When he went off to the bathroom, I called myself on it."

Rae: "You called?"

"Yeah. So I'd have a record of his phone number, if I wanted to call him up. I never wanted to, it turns out. I didn't tell him about calling myself, though."

Lucas: "You still have . . . ?"

She got her purse, got her phone, thumbed through it, and said, "Ready?"

WHEN THEY LEFT, going down in the elevators, Bob said, "I'm telling you, it's too easy."

"Gift horse," Lucas said. "Don't look in the mouth."

"I'm with Bob," Rae said. "You haven't been on many fugitive things like this, Lucas. Maybe one, down in Texas, right?"

"A couple more up in Minnesota," Lucas said.

"Yeah, but those were amateurs. You've only done one hard-core guy," Rae said. "What you find out is, you always have trouble. It might be spread out, so you have trouble all the way through the operation, or everything can be sweet, but then, right at the end, a pile of trouble jumps up and bites you on the butt. Always."

"I'll keep that in mind, but it sounds like superstition," Lucas said. They walked out through the lobby, and Lucas put his sunglasses on. "You two haven't worked with a sophisticated, well-dressed investigator like myself, so you don't appreciate how smoothly things can go. With you guys, it's always combat fatigues, guns, kicking down doors."

"Nothing wrong with that," Bob said. "And you can take your well-dressed sophistication with about two pounds of beach sand and pack it up your ass."

"That's the Marine Corps talking," Rae said to Lucas. "The whole packing sand thing."

"Ask Tremanty to check that phone number. We need to get over there—Pasadena, or wherever it is," Lucas said. "She said forty-five minutes at three in the morning. At this time of day, it could be two hours. The fuckin' traffic here is unbelievable."

Rae called Tremanty, who was back to them in five minutes with an address for the hardwired phone. "You guys are like some kind of geniuses," he said.

"We already knew that," Lucas said, "but we try to keep it quiet." He wrote the address in his notebook and said to Bob and Rae, "Altadena Drive. Suzie-Q knew where she was."

# CHAPTER FIVE

They took both the Malibus, one silver, one black, Lucas driving on his own, Bob and Rae together, following their iPhone navigation apps up a number of freeways that began to sound like a bad California surfer song: the 405 to the 10 to the 110 to the 210—the thighbone connected to the hipbone, the hipbone connected to the iPhone—and then off into a welter of streets that began climbing the first low foothills of the San Gabriel Mountains.

The landscape was lush: towering royal palms mixing it up with darker, heavyset pines, and flowering bushes in scarlet and brilliant yellow, and everywhere two thousand shades of green, all behind wrought-iron fences with long, wide driveways.

They cruised, a hundred yards apart, past the target. The house was a sprawling, single-story ranch, with a curving driveway that led to a two-car garage partly obscured by foliage. A six-foot hedge ran along the front and sides of the property, separating it from its neighbors. They couldn't see the backyard, but it looked as overgrown as the front.

After cruising the place, they drove out to a coffee shop on Lake Avenue and got coffee, and Bob also got donuts. Lucas brought up an Altadena map on his iPad and then a satellite view of the house, which told them almost nothing because of the heavy foliage across the whole block. They could see the bright blue corner of a swimming pool at the back.

"Did you see the house for sale across the street, a couple houses down the block?" Bob asked. "Bart Carver Realty?"

"I saw it, didn't think about it," Lucas said. "Why?"

"Because it looked empty, unswept, like maybe there's nobody living there right now, or only part-time. You can see Suzie-Q's house from there; you're looking right up the driveway. If the for sale house is empty and we could get in there . . ."

"We've done it before," Rae said to Lucas. "We can get comfortable, and it gets the cars off the street."

"I've done it myself, but I knew the real estate guy," Lucas said. He thought about it, then said, "I'd rather not ask Rocha for help, not until we know what we've got. She'd want in."

"Why don't we go lay some heavy-duty marshal

shit on this Bart Carver?" Bob suggested. "Can't hurt."

Lucas nodded. "Okay. That's better than anything I've got."

AS A REAL ESTATE BROKER, selling million-dollar houses, Bart Carver should have been easy to find, but wasn't—there was nobody at his office at eight o'clock, and the first of his associates that they managed to reach didn't believe they were marshals and thought Lucas was trying to lure her out of her town house to sell her into sex slavery. The second associate had a similar attitude, without the paranoia, but agreed to call Carver and ask him to call Lucas.

Carver, who didn't call back until ten o'clock, happened to be at a chamber orchestra performance that his wife made him go to—or so he claimed when they spoke with him. The house, he said, was indeed empty, but he couldn't possibly let anyone in the place without checking with the owners, who'd certainly be asleep at ten o'clock. When Lucas doubted that and got loud, if not actually threatening, Carver agreed to try to call.

"Have them call me," Lucas said.

The owners called Lucas ten minutes later. "We're happy to cooperate with law enforcement officers, but that's an expensive house and we don't want it damaged in any way."

"We will be sitting in a window with a pair of binoculars. Your neighbors will never know that we are even there," Lucas promised.

"Could we talk about it tomorrow? We're down in San Diego, but we've got to come up there in the morning."

"Let me check with my guys," Lucas said. "Hang on."

"It's already late," said Rae, who'd been listening. "What are we gonna do in the middle of the night? Let's bag out at the hotel, do some planning, meet the owners up here."

Lucas agreed and told the owners that they'd meet in the morning. The guy they were talking to said, "Listen, wear jeans. And T-shirts . . . Maybe bring some gloves."

"Why?"

"To scratch our backs if we scratch yours."

THEY MET with the owners at a Jack in the Box. They turned out to be two burly, middle-aged gay men, Stephen Barnett and Luis Jimenez, who'd decided to get out of LA. "We expect that next summer will get days that are 120 degrees, if not hotter. It'll be Saudi Arabia, only with margaritas and the dumber movie stars."

They were transferring their construction business to San Diego, they said, which they expected to stay cooler.

"We're moving down there piece by piece," Barnett said. "There's still some furniture in the house. I imagine you're looking for Craig, right? Big black guy?"

"We're uncertain of the names they're using," Lucas said. Rae pushed the mug shots across the table, and they instantly picked out Nast.

"He's an asshole," Barnett said. "When I say that, I'm insulting other assholes. He'd see us driving by and stick his thumb in his mouth and suck on it. I've been tempted to go after him with a baseball bat."

"You'd need a baseball bat," Jimenez said. "The guy is huge. And he's no debutante. He looks like he's done hard time. He's got the attitude."

"He's never done anything physical?" Bob asked. "Nothing we could go over and talk to him about?"

"Not other than the thumb sucking. I don't know how that would look on a search warrant," Barnett said.

Rae smiled. "Not all that convincing."

Jimenez said a couple of other men either lived at the house or were frequent visitors. "There are at least two people in there, maybe three. One of them told a neighbor lady that they were traveling sales guys and weren't here most nights, so they decided to share a place so they could have a nice house with a pool and only have to pay part of the rent."

They talked for a bit longer, and then Lucas asked, "What do you think? Can we have a key?"

The two men looked at each other, then Jimenez nodded and said, "We're going over to the house right now. We brought our truck, we're gonna take some things out. You could come over, put your cars in the garage, help us move some furniture . . . Nobody will think anything of it. Besides, most people on the street are working during the day, there's almost nobody to see you."

That's what they did. As requested, all three marshals wore T-shirts and jeans. And one very clear reason for all the cooperation emerged as Lucas and Bob, along with Barnett and Jimenez, struggled to get two huge custom-made couches out the door and into the truck. "We got some guys at the other end to help get them into the new place, but we didn't have anybody to help up here," Jimenez said.

For the next hour, the marshals helped carry coffee tables, lamps, rugs, paintings, boxes of books, and an electric piano out to the box truck. The only neighbor they saw was an elderly man walking a blue heeler, who both ignored them.

Before the two men left, Rae went out to a Super King Market and bought three days' worth of food and drink and then dropped down to Vroman's Bookstore in Pasadena and bought a supply of books and magazines. The power in the house was still on, so they had a refrigerator, stove, microwave, and air-conditioning. The WiFi had been turned off, but Rae had a hotspot they could hook their laptops into.

"Please don't shoot anyone and get blood all over. It's impossible to get it out of the drywall," Barnett joked as they were closing up the truck.

"We'll try not to," Lucas said. "And thank you,"

BARNETT AND Jimenez left behind two small couches and an oversized easy chair in the living room and two single beds in a guest room. They were hoping to sell the beds with the house. The windows were still covered with curtains.

The best view of the target house was from a corner of the living room. They put an easy chair and ottoman next to the window, opening the drapes just enough that they could use binoculars and Bob's night vision goggles without moving the fabric. Lucas and Bob carried the couches to a family room in the back, where they could turn on lights that wouldn't be visible from across the street.

After Barnett and Jimenez left, Bob, Rae, and Lucas did an odd-man coin flip. Bob lost and took the first two-hour watch at the bedroom window. Lucas took the second watch and Rae the third. Bob came back on at eight o'clock, and, at ten after, he shouted, "Right now!"

Lucas was lying on one of the couches, reading

a Mick Herron thriller, and Rae was sitting at the breakfast bar, looking through a book about architecture left behind by the owners and eating baby carrots. They both ran for the living room, and Bob, who was looking between the curtains with the binoculars, said, "Car pulled in, a Lincoln SUV, on this side of the street, so I couldn't see the driver at all. Used a garage door opener, went straight in, dropped the door."

"So we know it's live anyway," Lucas said, peering out the window. There was nothing to see.

"It's live," Bob agreed.

He shouted "Right now!" again forty-five minutes later, and Lucas and Rae bolted for the living room. This time, they saw the SUV, a steel-gray Lincoln Navigator, backing out of the driveway. This time, it drove past the house and there was enough light that they could see the driver was a black man.

"Bob, stay here," Lucas snapped. "Rae, let's go. Run, goddamnit."

They ran out through the kitchen to the garage. Rae had left her Glock in its holster sitting on the kitchen counter and grabbed it as they went by. Lucas punched the button in the garage and the door rolled up. He backed out and nearly hit a passing car, but jammed on the brakes at the last second, then continued into the street.

The Prius ahead of them was dawdling, as

Priuses will, and as Lucas burned past it Rae said, "She gave us the finger."

"We deserve it," Lucas said.

Altadena Drive was a through street, and the Lincoln was well ahead of them as they went after it, but it was moving as slowly as the Prius.

"He doesn't want to be stopped for speeding," Rae said. The limit was twenty-five, and Lucas kept the Malibu at forty until they'd closed within a hundred yards, with another car between them.

They followed the Lincoln along a couple of freeways and off at an exit, now with a half dozen cars between them, and watched as the driver threaded down a few more streets and then parked in the lot at, and walked into, a grubby-looking club called Eagle Rocks. Lucas parked on the opposite side of the lot, from where he could still see the front door.

"I'll take it from here," Rae said. "I'm looking for my boyfriend. Watch my gun."

"Call me on your phone right now and leave it open," Lucas said. "Carry it in your hand. If you need help inside, yell and I'll be there."

RAE LEFT HER GLOCK on the passenger seat, got out, tucked her shirt into her skinny jeans, and disappeared through the doors of the club. She was back out a minute later, slid into the passenger seat.

"He was right inside the door, talking to a waitress," Rae said. "I went by and asked the bartender if he'd seen Bobby and he said he didn't know any Bobby, so I came back out. I looked right at Nast from a foot away. I think he kinda liked my looks, but I'm holding out for Tremanty."

"It's Nast for sure?"

"One hundred percent," Rae said. "I'll tell you what: Jimenez was right. The guy is a hulk. He lifts serious weight, he's got a neck like a pyramid, way bigger than Bob's. He's got prison ink on his arms and a nasty keloid down one cheek."

"So we're careful with him. And we've got him—we know where he lives. Let's get back there in case somebody else shows up," Lucas said.

On the way, Bob called. "We've got another guy at the house, couldn't see this one, either. Driving a BMW sedan. I'll tell you what: when I saw him slowing down to pull in, I ran out back and pushed through the hedge far enough that I could see into the garage. Still didn't see the guy's face, he was already going inside. But what looks like a two-car garage over there isn't. It's two cars deep, making it a four-car, and I saw a white panel van in there, pulled all the way up against the back wall. So . . . it's them."

"We know the guy we're following is definitely Nast," Rae said. "Maybe they're all in there."

"I doubt it," Lucas said. "Four guys, probably bringing women home from time to time . . .

That'd be too much like a college dorm. I could buy two of them living there, but not all four."

"What do you want to do?" Bob asked.

"We need to trim a couple of hedges. In the middle of the night," Lucas said. "You got a hedge trimmer in your kit?"

"Got a big, sharp knife," Bob said.

"That'll work."

BARNETT AND JIMENEZ had left lamps near the windows in the living room, kitchen, and one upstairs bedroom with timers that turned them on and off randomly, to discourage burglars. They all went off by midnight, except the bedroom, which came back on hourly, for five minutes at a time, between one and six in the morning, as though somebody were getting up to pee.

When the lights went off at midnight, Lucas and Bob slipped out to the back door and then down the side hedge to the front of the yard and in the dim ambient light cropped a few branches out of the hedge to create holes that would allow them to better see the target house.

The house showed lights until after one o'clock, when all but one of them went off.

Lucas took the four-hour watch from one o'clock until five while the others slept. The Lincoln Navigator returned at two-fifteen, and when it pulled into the right-hand slot in the garage he could see a black BMW sedan in the left. Then the remote-controlled door rolled down, the light at the front of the house went out.

Rae, who had gone to sleep at ten o'clock, took over from Lucas at five. When Lucas woke at eleven, she said, "The Lincoln is still there, but the Beemer left at nine. Bob's gone after him, they're over in the Hollywood area right now. He says there were two white guys in the car, so it's not Nast. That makes at least three different guys in there."

Lucas got cleaned up and went back downstairs to eat some Cheerios. Bob called ten minutes later and said, "I tracked these guys into a café on Sunset Boulevard. My phone map says I'm either in Hollywood or the Hollywood Hills, I don't know which, but one of the guy is Beauchamps. He's got a beard now. And he's going bald, tries to hide it with a tennis hat. But he's our guy. Another guy came in and met our guys, sat with them for a minute. I'm no narc, but if Beauchamps didn't pick up some dope you can butter my buns and call me a biscuit."

"Beauchamps and Nast are living together," Lucas said. "It might be time to call Rocha."

"Give it a few more hours," Rae suggested. "See if anyone else turns up. Like Deese."

Lucas agreed to wait. He called Bob off tracking Beauchamps. "There's a chance he'll spot you. We know he lives here, so let's not take that chance."

---

BOB WAS BACK, and at the window, when another car pulled into the target house's garage, this one a red Jaguar convertible. The top was down, and the driver was a white man, neither Deese nor Beauchamps.

"Rocha told us there were four of them and that guy makes four," Lucas said.

"They **are** living in a dormitory," Rae said. "I wonder why? That seems wrong to me."

"Gift horse?" Bob said.

"I worry about shit I don't understand," Rae, kneeling at the window with the binoculars, watching, said.

LUCAS CALLED ROCHA. "We'd like to get together to strategize," Lucas said. "We're up in Altadena."

"Why are you in Altadena? You got something?"

"We found Nast, Beauchamps, and at least two other guys we haven't yet identified," Lucas said.

"What! You've been here two days?"

"We got lucky," Lucas said. "And we **are** the Marshals Service."

"Bullshit. You don't get lucky in a city this size. And the Marshals Service can kiss my ass," Rocha said. "You didn't tell me something."

"Maybe. Anyway, you want to hook up?"

She suggested they meet at the Pasadena Police

Department, but Lucas wanted both Bob and Rae to be at the meeting and didn't want to leave the target house unwatched, so Rocha agreed to come to the house.

"Don't come in one of those goddamn beaters you guys use. Come in a personal car, or something, pull right into the garage. We'll have the door open. We're right across the street from Nast and Beauchamps," Lucas said, as he gave her the address.

"I'll be in my own vehicle. I'm bringing a couple of guys," Rocha said.

NAST LEFT shortly after Lucas made the call to Rocha, driving the Lincoln. The Jaguar and its driver were still at the target house. When Nast was out of sight, Bob backed one of their Malibus into the driveway to make room in the garage for Rocha.

LuAnne Rocha and two male detectives, Lewis Lake and Darrell MacIntosh, arrived an hour later in Rocha's Dodge minivan, the most un-cop-like of vehicles. Rocha called when they were two blocks away and Lucas went out to the garage and pushed the button that lifted the door and dropped it when they were inside.

They trooped into the kitchen, made introductions and shook hands, and Rocha said, "Tell me how you did this."

"We had a phone number for a bar," Lucas began. He told them the story, didn't mention Oliver Haar but did tell them about Suzie-Q and pointed out the house across the street.

"You're sure it's Nast and Beauchamps?" Rocha asked. "That seems almost too good to be true." She was an athletic-looking woman, with short brown hair and brown eyes. She wore a dark green cotton jacket over a light green blouse, black slacks, and low heels. The jacket proved not very subtle camouflage for her handgun.

"I brushed past Nast, a foot away, in a nightclub last night. Looked him right in the face," Rae said. "Bob sat a couple of tables away from Beauchamps and his friend while they were eating breakfast this morning."

MacIntosh asked, "You guys basically are a tracking and SWAT squad, right?" MacIntosh looked like an LA weatherman, too-white teeth, a touch of coloring in his hair, the Beverly Hills sport coat. Lake tried to dress sort of like Steve Jobs—black pants, black T-shirt, black cotton jacket.

Lucas said, "I'm not so much SWAT. I was homicide back in Minneapolis and with the Minnesota state cops. Bob and Rae are more tactical. If there are four guys over there and they're hard-core fighters like LuAnne says, then we're probably going to need one of your SWAT teams to back up Bob and Rae."

"For sure," Rocha said. "I'll get that organized,

but it'll take a while. I'm thinking we'll do it tomorrow at dawn. That gives us plenty of time to pull things together. And if they stay out late, like you say, they ought to be pretty out of it if we hit the door at six o'clock."

"The option would be to watch them come and go, track them individually, and take them when they get out of their cars," Lucas said.

"Could do that," Rocha said. "But that'd be asking for a shoot-out in a parking lot with people around. I think I'd be happier with a SWAT team doing their thing at dawn."

They talked about that for a bit, but it was LA territory. Rocha said, "For now, we basically want to sit here with you, do some watching of our own."

Bob had noted the license plate on the BMW and Rocha ran it. "Goes to a Douglas Moyers, at that address," she said, nodding at the house across the street. "We have nothing on him at all. Not so much as a traffic ticket."

"Fake name," Rae said.

Rocha nodded. "Yup."

They were watching for half an hour when the garage door went up at the target house and the Jaguar backed into the street. MacIntosh got the tag number, Rocha ran it. "Goes out to a Jacob Barber, again at that address, again not a single violation of any kind."

MacIntosh: "Fake. That pretty much clinches it."

Rocha looked up from her tablet screen and said to Lake and MacIntosh, "Let's get it going. We need to talk to the sheriff's office. If they're still at home, we'll hit them tomorrow at first light."

# CHAPTER SIX

Genesis Cox was sleeping as deeply, and as naked, as a newborn baby, so accustomed was she to the stentorian snoring of her partner that even the rapid-fire wheezes, snorts, and grunts of his dream episodes failed to disturb her.

Cox was a standard big-boobed, bottle-blond, bar menu Long Beach babe, with curly hair like Meg Ryan's in that movie **When Harry Met Sally**, which was, like, her way favorite forever. Several other Ryan vehicles were in her top ten, mostly because of the star's way-amazing hair. Even when Meg was, like, flying a fuckin' Black Hawk helicopter in some kind of fuckin' war, or something, her hair was way fuckin' epic.

Cox knew the guys she was living with were criminals, but really it was more like the redistribution of wealth from Beverly Hills to Long Beach, almost like being a Democrat, so it was hard to see too much wrong with it. And nobody ever died.

She was currently working her way through a self-help book called **You Are a Badass—How to Stop Doubting Your Greatness and Start Living an Awesome Life**. It was wedged between the pillow and the top of her head, where she'd left it when she turned off the lamp. Cox's life had not yet reached the awesome peak she was sure was on its way, but it was nothing less than what she deserved. She hadn't yet made out its substance. Probably something in Hollywood, she hoped. Like fuckin' a producer. That would be awesome, all right. Though she'd have to be careful: sometimes you thought you were fuckin' a producer and he turned out to be a writer or something.

Cox slept well, especially after a round of athletic sex, and was proud of her ability to take a lickin' and keep on tickin'.

MARION BEAUCHAMPS, who Cox called Marty, even though when she snuck a look at his real driver's license one time, which he kept in a chest of drawers, it said Marion. Beauchamps slept in a T-shirt and also workout pants, because his legs got cold when he threw the covers off, which he did every night.

Beauchamps was a criminal, but of the relatively

intelligent and thoughtful sort, who believed he could do home invasions in Beverly Hills, Hollywood Hills, Holmby Hills, Cheviot Hills, and any other hills you might have, for as long as he wished, with minimal chance of getting caught as long as nobody got hurt and it didn't make the front page of the **Times.**

His ideal target was the early-retirement Silicon Valley exec who'd gotten his monster stock payout and thought that Hollywood was way more glamorous than Nerdville because you get to hang out with movie stars and maybe get a piece of movie star ass from time to time. What was a billion dollars for anyway, if you couldn't do that?

Beauchamps would never touch a media light of any kind—movie, video, singer, not even one of the talking heads on **E!**—because the publicity would go on forever. Publicity, he thought, was his biggest enemy and he was careful not to attract any.

IN A SECOND BEDROOM, John Rogers Cole was working his way through **Infinite Jest** by David Foster Wallace. A morning insomniac, he found **Jest** usually helped him grab a couple more hours of sleep before he had to start the day.

Cole was a nondescript sort, which was the way he liked it. If you were nondescript, you didn't have a cop looking in the driver's-side window at a traffic stop and asking himself, "Say, don't I know that face?"

Of middle height, he had fine brown hair, worn short, brown eyes, an ordinary nose and chin, and narrow shoulders. He usually wore a dress shirt with the sleeves rolled above the elbows. The shirt concealed a gym rat's body: he had biceps like a drywaller and could run three miles in eighteen minutes. His current driver's license and Visa card said his name was Douglas Moyers, but the gang all called him Cole.

His lack of facial drama didn't help him with women, who always went for the square-jawed, blunt-nosed, big-shouldered guys like Beauchamps, but he did all right. In Cole's experience, if you sat around in Starbucks long enough, drinking lattes and reading **Jest**, something would come along. He dug librarian types, black-rimmed glasses and an overbite.

ALSO SLEEPING ALONE, on a mattress on the floor of the home office, was Beauchamps's half brother Clayton Deese, the cannibal. He'd been all over the internet since the FBI said he'd eaten some lady, and maybe a couple of guys, which Cox and Cole and even, to some extent, Beauchamps found disturbing.

Not only the eating part but the fact that cannibals tend to attract the eye, and Deese had a distinctive face and those tattoos. He'd always been clean-shaven, right up to the time he left New Orleans. He now wore a reddish beard that qualified him to hunt alligators down in the bayous, but there was something about his eyes that still attracted attention.

He looked like a mean motherfucker, and there was no way to cover it up. When a normal law-abiding citizen looked at Clayton Deese, his first thought was that Deese belonged in jail. Not that Deese ran into many normal citizens.

Deese dreamed in full-color porn; in between erotic dreams, he'd wake and his mind would snap to his problem, which was the same it had been in New Orleans. He had to get away. He was gone, but he hadn't yet gotten away. He needed a bunch of money for that and he didn't have it.

THEY WERE all sleeping soundly when, at sunrise, there was a sudden burst of dings from the living room. And then another burst, at a slightly different pitch. Beauchamps quit snoring and launched himself from the bed and went running out of the room, his REM sleep hard-on leading the way like a wobbly flashlight.

And then the shit hit the fan.

Like a fuckin' machine gun, which is what Cox screamed it was.

When it had ripped open the dawn, she'd sat

up in bed, her mouth dropped open, she'd shrieked, "Fuckin' machine gun," she'd grabbed a terry-cloth robe, and run after Beauchamps, pulling the robe on as she ran.

Deese bolted out of the home office, and Deese and Cox followed Beauchamps to a tinted-glass window in the family room that looked across the backyard to the house behind them. Men in dark uniforms were running through their yard and setting up behind palm trees, the deeply shaded lawns sparkling with muzzle flashes of dozens, and maybe hundreds, of fired cartridges, going both in and out of the house.

Beauchamps said, "Cops," and then Cole ran in, fully dressed and carrying a book, and Beauchamps said, "They're all over Nast's place. They'll get here, sooner or later. We gotta get outta here. Grab what you can, meet in the garage. One fuckin' minute." And they all ran back to their respective rooms.

The battle continued outside, the volume of gunfire like something from a war video. In what was a little more than one fuckin' minute, they were all more or less dressed. Cox, still naked under the robe, had jammed an armful of pants, blouses, underwear, and seven pairs of shoes into two fake Louis Vuitton tote bags and had run toward the garage, where she bumped into Cole, who'd just thrown a bag in the back of Deese's pickup. Her robe had parted as she ran, and Cole said, "Whoa!" as he took a look, and Cox said, "Hey, there," but not as a firm objection, and she didn't bother to close it as she threw her clothes in the Cadillac and headed back into the house, her long pale legs flashing in and out of the flapping robe.

Beauchamps ran into the garage with an armload of stuff, threw it in his Cadillac, and Cole said, "Don't touch the lights, don't open the doors, and when we do open them don't talk loud." As Beauchamps ran back out, Cole picked up a broom and used the handle to smash the overhead door's lights.

Deese ran in carrying a dog shit brown Filson duffel bag, which he threw in the back of his pickup. He was wearing jeans and a T-shirt but was barefoot. Cole said, quietly, "I broke the lights, watch the glass." And there was more shooting from the back and also men shouting. Beauchamps ran in and said, "I don't see anybody out front," and, "Everybody got their money?"

And Cox cried, "Oh, shit," and dashed back into the house and was back fifteen seconds later with a Christmas cookie tin. "We almost forgot the coke," she said. And Beauchamps said, "Clay, you take Cole and I'll take Geenie. Let's go! Push the button."

Cole pushed the button and ran around the front of Deese's truck and got in and pulled the door closed with a quiet click and five minutes after the shooting started they followed Beauchamps's two-year-old Cadillac SUV out of the dark garage and down the driveway. There were lighted windows everywhere, and a few people already out on lawns. The shooting behind the house continued.

Eight blocks out, Beauchamps pulled over to the curb. Deese rolled up behind him. Beauchamps stepped back to his half brother's truck and said through the lowered driver's-side window, "We're busted. They'll figure out the house, they'll print the place, and we're all over it. That'll take a while. I'm thinking Vegas. At least until things calm down."

"Maybe they got Vegas, too," Cole said, leaning forward to talk past Deese.

"I don't think so," Beauchamps said. "Somebody spotted us. I'm thinking they spotted Nast because he's so damn visible and he's been hitting the clubs. They didn't even know about the back house."

"If they got Nast and Randy and they talk . . ."

"Nast and Randy are dead," Beauchamps said. "You heard what was happening. Nast hated cops, he was hosing them down with that fuckin' M16. No way they let him walk away from that. They're deader'n shit, both of them."

Deese said, "Vegas is okay. But we gotta go. We're still too close."

"Right out the 210 to the 15, stay in touch on the phones and not too far apart in case there's a problem."

"Go!" Deese said.

———

COX STARTED ragging on Beauchamps before they got past the racetrack at Santa Anita.

"I knew this was gonna happen," she said. "I told you we were pushing our luck. We shoulda been outta there a year ago. And now Nast and Randy are dead, not that it's a huge loss. Especially Nast. What an asshole he was. Or maybe still is—"

"Was," Beauchamps said. And, "Be quiet, for Christ's sakes, I'm trying to think."

"Maybe you shoulda tried thinking before you threw me in a car half naked and we . . . What are we gonna do? I'm not gonna live in that fuckin' trailer, not in May in Vegas . . . I've never been arrested for anything and my fingerprints are all over that house. And now the cops will be looking for me. And if Nast killed some cops, then it might be murder . . . Oh, Jesus Christ. I didn't even think of that until now. Murder!"

"I'll tell them you were a hooker we brought in, you didn't know anything about it. Now, shut up."

"Like that's gonna work. You know any hooker's never been arrested? Me, neither," she said. "We gotta go a lot farther away than Vegas. And I'm not staying in that fuckin' trailer, I did that once and once was enough. You got fake IDs. We oughta check into the Mandalay, or something. Or the Wynn . . ."

She really never stopped until they were up the hill at Victorville, an hour out of the house, not even when she'd bent herself over the seat to get a different set of clothes out of her bag and her naked and, honestly, totally excellent ass was rubbing Beauchamps's right cheek, which made it even harder to maintain his lane. In Victorville, they pulled into a Mobil station for gas and food and cold drinks.

As they were gassing up the vehicles, Cole told Beauchamps and Deese, "I got my laptop, if we can find some WiFi, and we can get the news."

"Wait until we get to Vegas. There won't be anything yet anyway," Beauchamps said. "We need a better place than the trailer park, we can't all four stay there. Geenie's already driving me crazy with her whining."

"You think Vegas is far enough?" Deese asked.

"Orange County would have been far enough, except for that fuckin' LA television. Vegas is quick, and we got the trailer and can lay low for a while until we can find a house to rent," Beauchamps said. He looked at Cole. "We'll get to Vegas, buy some wedding rings for you and Geenie, and you can rent a couple of houses. Nobody knows your face. And it's easy renting houses there."

"We can do that," Cole said. He lit a cigarette. "If Geenie's getting on your case, she could ride with me."

"There's an idea." Cox had gone to the restroom to change clothes. When she came back, they'd transferred Cole's stuff to Beauchamps's car and Beauchamps's stuff to Deese's truck.

Beauchamps told her about the wedding rings and renting houses, and she said, "Hey, my friend rented an apartment for two months with that Airdnc thing. She said there was this girl in Vegas who'll get you into one of them, no questions asked, and you can stay as long as you want, if you pay up front. All furnished with WiFi and TV and everything."

"That's a possibility," Beauchamps said. "We'll check it out when we get there."

"How come I'm riding with Cole?" Cox asked, looking among the three men.

"'Cause Deese and I got things to talk about. And because you're driving me fuckin' nuts," Beauchamps said. "Besides, you and Cole can work on your husband-wife act."

THEY WERE out of Victorville before it got hot, and Cox, who'd changed into shorts and a T-shirt in the Mobil station restroom, started talking again, about leaving California, about life in general, and though Cole didn't have much to say, he'd chip in with a word every now and then, encouraging her to go on, which she appreciated, because sometimes she had the feeling she talked too much.

Once past Barstow, with the sun now getting up in the sky, she said, "This is the part I hate. There's nothing from Barstow to the Nevada line.

Two hours of nothing. Down in Tucson, they got great-looking cactuses. Up here, we got shit."

"Time passes," Cole said. "Mind if I smoke?"

"I don't mind, but crack the window and blow the smoke out," she said. She looked out the window at the Mojave as he lit up. "Absolutely nothing out here. It's like looking at a TV with the power off. We'd usually get about halfway up there and Marty would make me go down on him."

"Yeah?"

"Yeah. Something we did. He'd be swerving all over the highway when he got close. Couple of times, we got passed by a semi and the driver saw what we were doing and he'd honk his horn at us. You know, real long . . . **Hoooooonk.**"

Cole grinned and took a long drag off the cigarette.

Deese's truck was a quarter mile ahead of them, both vehicles rolling along at a steady 80 miles an hour. "So fuckin' boring," Cox said. Then, "You know, the brothers are going to take care of themselves. They're not going to take care of us. I don't even know why they're taking me along. I could go back to LA and who'd guess I even knew you guys?"

"Remember about the fingerprints," Cole said. "If you've ever been printed—"

"I haven't been. I never been arrested for anything," Cox said.

"Really?"

"Really. What'd you think, that I was on the corner?"

"Well, I never figured out you and Marty," Cole said. "You didn't exactly seem like a girlfriend. Like when he was banging that actress chick, he was right out front about it. You didn't seem to care."

"I didn't. Less wear and tear on me," Cox said.

"So . . . I thought maybe he was paying you to hang around."

"He was, sorta. Not like a hundred bucks a time, or whatever," Cox said. "But, well, two words: 'money' and 'cocaine.' I wasn't on the corner, but I do like money and cocaine. I like rich guys, especially the ones who like to spend the money and who like to go out clubbing. Dancing. Who'll loan out their Amex cards. I dated a lot of Arab boys from USC."

"Huh." Cole thought about that, then said, "I only had one legitimate credit card in my life. From Sears, and I think they went broke. I got it when I was a kid so I could buy tires and tools and shit."

Cox reached across the seat and patted him on the leg. "You always seemed like a nice guy to me, a lot nicer than the others," she said. A minute later: "If Marty and I develop a problem, would you take care of me?"

"If I could," Cole said, "I guess. I don't know what I could do. I lost a lot of money in this deal. I kept it in my car, down below. Cops got it now."

"Oh my God."

"No kiddin'."

"Something bad is going to happen," Cox said. "Marty's not a guy to keep his head down. You seem more responsible that way. I know he and Deese are going to start gambling up in Vegas because . . . because that's what they do."

"That'll get them caught. They got cameras, tight security, and smart cops up there," Cole said. "We need to lay low until we can get a little cash together."

"If we worked on this husband-and-wife stuff, like Marty said, we'd have a better chance to get away. Couples up in Vegas are invisible. People look at single guys and single girls, but not couples, because they aren't . . . available. There are millions of them, all over. Nobody even looks."

"But what's to work on? Being a couple? You just go around together, right?"

"People who are couples act different than other people," she said. "You can tell."

"Tell what?"

"That they're together," she said. "You know, that they're intimate with each other."

"You mean, sleeping together?"

She shrugged. "Or whatever. Intimate." Long silence, the two of them looking out at the overheated desert, which definitely wasn't as picturesque as the one in Tucson. "Listen . . . you wanna blow job?"

Cole scratched his head, looked at her, checking

to see if she was serious. She seemed to be, her eyes flat and not wise. Finally: "Sure, if you think Marty won't mind."

"I don't plan on telling him," she said. And, "You know his real name is Marion?"

"Yeah, but he wanted everybody to call him Marty because he's had legal problems with the Marion name."

Neither said anything for another minute, then Cox said, "You probably ought to slide the seat all the way back."

"Oh. Sure. Let me get rid of the smoke first. It is pretty boring out here."

# CHAPTER SEVEN

They had driven Bob's Malibu around the block and parked it, leaving the driveway empty. Rocha left in the minivan and came back an hour later with two sheriff's deputies to help with the surveillance. They brought more groceries.

The Jaguar came back late in the afternoon, followed a few minutes later by the BMW. One of the deputies took photos with a telephoto lens.

As they waited through the afternoon for Rocha to coordinate the raid with the three different departments involved, Lake hooked a laptop into an industrial-strength hotspot and brought up all kinds of official documents regarding the target house—building permits, tax assessor's reports, plat maps, aerial views. The original permits, thirty-five years old, showed the house as having three modestly sized bedrooms, but a later permit hinted at extensive internal remodeling but didn't include detailed plans.

"We don't really know what it's like in there," Rocha said. "The building permits are mostly about new HVAC, but those are old-style family bedrooms, and I wouldn't be surprised if they'd combined some of them into one- or two-bedroom suites. We can't count on the doors and bedroom access being where the plans say they are."

"But there are at least four people using the place," Rae said.

"First-floor family room could have been converted into another bedroom suite," Lake said. "Maybe even two."

"We don't know, though," Rae said. "I'm thinking we go in really hard, flashbangs through exposed windows, hit the door with a ram. There's CBS construction up to waist height; that'll be a problem for lighter weapons if there's a fight."

All the overhead views of the house were obscured by the heavy year-round foliage. "There'll either be a fence or a hedge to separate it from the house behind it," Rocha said. "We'll have SWAT guys coming in from the backyard and they'll have to cross that before we hit the front of the house."

"We need all the tactical people copied in on this and that includes Bob and Rae," Rocha said to Lucas. "You're not tactical, so you stay behind. Mac isn't tactical, either, so he stays. Lake is technical, and I'm the boss, so we gotta be there for the meeting. You guys get to sleep in."

"I'd like to be involved."

"Well, you'll be here. But not running around in the street—we'll have ten or twelve guys with rifles and vests and helmets and we don't need some guy in a suit confusing things. I won't be out there, I'll be in a truck with Lake."

Lucas gave in. "But I'll be there as soon as it's over."

"That's fine. You're invited." She patted him on the back and he didn't like it.

BOB AND RAE went to bed early because they'd be meeting with the SWAT team at the Altadena Sheriff's Station, which was only a few blocks from the target house, before dawn the next morning. They took the two beds, while Lucas read into the night and sheriff's deputies watched the target.

The BMW, and, presumably, Beauchamps, returned to the house at eight, although they didn't see him, and the Jaguar showed up at ten. The Navigator didn't return until almost midnight. It was then that Lucas and MacIntosh laid eyes on Nast for the first time. He stood under the garage light, arms akimbo, shaking his head, and, a moment later, rolled the garbage can out to the curb. He went back inside and dropped the door.

Rocha had gone home to get some sleep but said she'd be up late, and MacIntosh called her: "We got him, Lu. Rae was right on. I got a close-up of his face in the garage light and it's Nast. We got all three of them in the house. And maybe four, if that BMW was two guys in it like when Bob was trailing it . . ."

A half hour later, with no more movement at the target, Lucas pulled the cushions off the couches in the family room, threw them on the floor, and stretched out.

The raid was complicated, he thought as he slipped into sleep. Three different agencies were involved—LA city cops, LA County sheriff's deputies, and the Marshals Service.

He, Bob, and Rae had tracked down the LA suspects, who were wanted by the City of Los Angeles and a couple of other jurisdictions, but not by any of the cities covered by the sheriff's department or by the Marshals Service. The one suspect wanted by the marshals, Clayton Deese, wasn't wanted by any of the local agencies and might or might not be in the house.

Whatever the outcome of the raid, the legal entanglements would be intense. Which was why there were about a billion lawyers out there, he supposed . . . It was almost like they deliberately tangled the laws to keep themselves in fees. But, nah. Too cynical. He smiled into the darkness and went to sleep.

---

LUCAS WAS sleeping soundly when one of the sheriff's deputies shook him awake. "It's quarter 'til six, if you want to brush your teeth. They're saying they're gonna hit the place about quarter after. It's already getting light outside."

Lucas rolled off the cushions, feeling stiff. Bob and Rae had gone an hour earlier to rodeo with the other agencies at the sheriff's station. He brushed his teeth, looked at his phone to check the time, decided to shower and shave, and got down to the living room in time to hear Rocha say, on the radio, "Saddle up. You all know what you're doing. Let's do it."

THE SWAT TEAM, including Bob and Rae, would be traveling in several different vehicles and would come at the house both from the front and from the back through the yard of the house behind the target. The team coming in from the front would freeze fifty yards out, where they couldn't be seen from the target, while the team in the back would cross whatever barriers were between them and the target—most likely, a low fence or a hedge.

When they were in the backyard, they'd alert the team in front, and designated members would heave flashbangs through the windows believed to be bedrooms at the same instant a battering ram took down the front door.

Everything would be done silently until the flashbangs went off: no screeching tires, no cops running in the street.

"These guys do it all the time," MacIntosh said. "When they hit it, I'm not going to sit here and watch. I'm going over there."

"I think you ought to stay," Lucas said. "You're not tactical."

"Fuck that," MacIntosh said. "What are you gonna do?"

"I'm going," Lucas said.

"Attaboy!"

LUCAS HAD HAD an interest in poetry since taking a class at the University of Minnesota. The class was taught by an aging professor who was also an avid hockey fan. Lucas, a first-line defenseman, had been plugged into her class to make sure his grade point average stayed high enough to keep him on the ice. As it happened, he got an A. Poetry, he thought, was a hell of a lot more interesting than Minnesota history, which was also taught by a hockey fan and had been the other option.

In any case, when the SWAT team came creeping in, he thought momentarily of Carl Sandburg's "The fog comes on little cat feet . . ."

The SWAT vehicles had stopped well down the street, and the armored cops, in their green tactical uniforms and helmets, were nearly invisible in the early-morning light against the heavy foliage as they closed in on the target house.

"I'm going out the back," MacIntosh whispered, even though they were still inside the surveillance house with the doors and windows closed.

"Don't freak anyone out," Lucas said. "Stay clear and let them work."

"Got it," MacIntosh said. "You coming?"

"Right ahead of you," Lucas said, heading for the door.

They went out the back door and down the side of the house, along the hedge Lucas and Bob had cut the holes in. Looking through one of the holes, Lucas saw the SWAT guys settling in at the neighboring houses. And then, at some command they couldn't hear, two cops suddenly ran onto the lawn of the target house.

"Flashbangs," MacIntosh muttered.

It all went to hell in an instant.

A FULLY AUTOMATIC weapon opened up from a corner window of the house, and the two approaching officers fled, one falling, and Lucas called, "Shit, he's hit," and there was immediate returned fire from other SWAT team members.

"It's a fuckin' war!" MacIntosh shouted. He'd

drawn his weapon and started down the hedge toward the street, and Lucas hooked his arm and said, "The SWATs will only see a man with a gun."

MacIntosh hesitated as the machine gun went silent. Fire continued to riddle the front of the house, and the man who'd gone down, and who Lucas thought had been hit, got to his hands and knees and scrambled off the lawn, apparently unhurt. Then shooting erupted at the back, and then there was more shooting from the front of the house, the muzzle flashes blinking from one window and then the next, a pistol pecking away at the hedges where the SWAT team was digging for cover.

"Fuck it, I'm going," MacIntosh said, and he scrambled in a deep crouch down the length of the hedge. Though Lucas knew better, he followed. At the end of the hedge, MacIntosh shouted to someone across the street and then ran there, with Lucas behind him, out of sight of the windows of the target.

A couple of SWAT team members had taken cover behind the six-foot-thick trunk of a camphor tree, and one of them shouted, "Stay the fuck down and out of the way."

A SWAT guy dashed in from the side, close enough to put a couple flashbangs through a side window, then a couple more through a back window, and when the flashbangs went off it was like standing next to a lightning bolt.

Then silence.

Then somebody called out, "They down?" and other cops were shouting from the back and sides of the house.

Then Rocha's soprano voice shouting, "Everybody sit tight . . . Everybody sit tight . . . Sit tight."

One of the SWAT team guys with Lucas and MacIntosh stood up and eased his weapon around the tree, aiming at the front windows. The second guy did the same after a couple of seconds, but around the other side of the tree trunk.

Lucas couldn't see anything with the heavily armored cops hanging over him; neither could MacIntosh, who was sitting on his ass with his gun in his hand, who said, "I can't see a fuckin' thing."

Lucas stood, tentatively, and eased out from behind the SWAT guy to get a look. Laser dots played over the side of the target, focusing on the front door and the windows.

The SWAT guy said, "They gotta be down. We put five hundred rounds in there and that ain't no bullshit."

MacIntosh said, "Hope none of our guys got hit, that was a fuckin' machine gun in there."

"Probably oughta enter from the back," Lucas

said. "I wouldn't want to be the one who runs up that driveway."

"That ain't gonna happen," the SWAT guy said. And, "Who are you anyway?"

"Marshal," Lucas said.

"Pleased to meet you. Bob and Rae seemed like nice folks."

"They are," Lucas said. "That was a hell of a thing there. Hope nobody got hurt."

He edged farther out from behind the SWAT guy, trying for a better view.

IN THE BLINK of an eye, the automatic weapon opened up from the nearest window, powdering the camphor tree where they stood. A slug hit Lucas in the chest and he went down. And he heard MacIntosh screaming and felt somebody pulling on his ankles, dragging him farther behind the tree. He was then looking up at the underside of a tree, heard more hundreds of rounds pounding the house, and then everything started going weird, not a lot of pain but somehow a lot of hurt, and he thought, "Hope I'm not dying," and then, "Maybe I am."

Somebody was screaming, "Get it down here, get it rolling, get the fuck over here," and he felt himself picked up like a rag doll and put on a gurney, which felt comfortable and soft around his head and ears, and then he was in an ambulance and he heard the ambulance tech shouting, "You gotta roll, man, you gotta hurry," and the siren was going and everything got dimmer, and farther away, and even dimmer.

Then it all went dark.

# CHAPTER EIGHT

When he thought about it later, the darkness was the worst of it, worse than the pain. Sleep isn't dark, it's not black. There's something in your brain that's always awake, so when the sabre-toothed tiger comes to the cave, your brain wakes you up and tells you to get the family spear.

The dark that Lucas fell into wasn't like that. No part of his brain was awake. Then, at some moments, he floated into the still-living gray sleep state, only to fall back into the dark. Going back down was like dying all over again, every time it happened.

HOT AUGUST NIGHT, streetlights vibrating with humidity rings along Mississippi River Boulevard. Lucas pulled his T-shirt over his head and ran shirtless and sweating for the last two blocks to his house and up the driveway. He wasn't moving as fast as he had in the spring, before he'd been shot. When he got to the garage door, he bent over, hands on knees, gasping for breath.

The bullet hole in his chest and the exit wound in his back showed as pink knots of new skin and scar tissue. A wave of nausea swept over him and he gagged, pushed it back, and finally stood up, sweat rolling down his chest.

His back ached, and maybe always would. The slug had hit him below the collarbone, punched through a corner of his pectoral muscle, knocked a hole in his shoulder blade, clipped the top of a lung, barely missed his deltoid, and exited through something called the infraspinatus.

He'd bled, Bob told him, like a stuck pig.

The docs told him it'd be a year before he'd be all the way back. He refused to accept that. And even when Weather pleaded with him to ease up, he couldn't. He couldn't because he was afraid of the darkness—the death—that had come over him over and over again.

And he was afraid of the weakness, that his body was betraying him. When he began going out, to the supermarket, to the drugstore, he sometimes had to put a hand on a shelf to steady himself. That hadn't happened before. Ever. The docs said the shakiness would go away but it would take some time.

He suspected he had more gray hair two months after being shot than he'd had before, more lines in his face. He'd always thought that stories of hair turning gray overnight was an old wives' tale, but he was no longer sure of that.

THE LAST THING he remembered, before waking up in the hospital, wearing a respirator mask and with an arm full of intravenous needles, was the ambulance attendant shouting for the driver to go faster. He'd been taken to a Level 2 trauma center at Huntington Hospital in Pasadena and had spent eleven days there. Bob and Rae arrived a few minutes after he did. His adopted daughter, Letty, a student at Stanford University, had arrived at the hospital at noon, and Weather in the late afternoon.

When Letty walked in, she put both fists on her hips and said, "You better get well. I'm not putting up with some blanket-covered invalid shit." He heard her say that, then dropped into a drug-induced hole, remembering it when he came back up.

A doc told Weather that Lucas had apparently been hit by a full metal jacket round, which left a cleaner wound than a jacketed hollow-point would have. Rae confirmed that a day later, after the shooting site had been worked over, saying, "One of the SWAT guys said some of the hard-core assholes use full metal jackets because they think they'll punch through vest plates."

And that was what Weather talked about. The technical stuff. She cried occasionally, looking at him, even when he was smiling at her, and the rest of the time she went all technical with the docs, looking at videos of the MRIs and other electronic probes and talking SWAT tactics with Rae and how it should have been done.

Lucas's back muscles now contained tiny bone splinters that would always be there; a surgeon would do more damage taking them out than if they were left alone. He also had a carbon fiber patch over the hole in his shoulder blade, held in place with screws, to stabilize the bone, which had cracks radiating from the bullet hole. The cracks would eventually heal, but the patch would remain.

Letty had said, three days after the shooting, "You've actually got a hole in your back. I mean, like a **hole**. I could stick my thumb into it."

"Don't do that," Lucas said. "It already hurts a lot."

By June, with the help of the skin grafts, the hole was gone.

---

NAST AND A MAN named Randy Vincent had been killed in the raid. Nast had been firing the full-auto .223 that had taken Lucas down. Nast had been riddled with bullets—he'd probably been hit three or four times before he fired the last burst that hit Lucas, and maybe ten times afterward. Vincent, who'd been firing a 9mm pistol, had been hit once in the eye and killed. He was the man who owned the car registered to Jacob Barber.

The fourth man, who owned the BMW and was the one seen at the breakfast place by Bob, was identified by his fingerprints as John Rogers Cole, who'd done seven years in prison in Nebraska for robbing a credit union.

He'd gotten a heavier than normal sentence because a pre-sentencing investigation by the Nebraska authorities suggested that he'd probably done at least eight other credit unions in Nebraska and in Kansas. He showed one other arrest in Omaha, when he was eighteen, for peeping. That charge had been nol-prossed and he walked. The file didn't say whether the charge had been sexual or likely the prelude to a burglary.

"We should have done more research," Rae said. She and Bob were sitting next to Lucas's bed, two days after the fight. "These guys had been living there for three years. We thought it was strange that they'd all be in there like a dormitory. They weren't."

"They weren't?" Lucas's voice sounded like a rusty gate.

Bob shook his head. "Nope. They also owned the house behind the one we were watching and they'd planted a double hedge between the two. You couldn't see it, and we didn't see it until we'd been there for an hour and had been all over the yard. The two hedges ran parallel to each other, two feet apart, at the edge of the backyard, up a slope to the house behind. You could go from one house to the other without ever being seen. They set it up that way in case there was trouble at one house, they could make it to the other."

Rae said, "They couldn't deal with a full-out raid with cops coming from both front and back, though, so they shot it out. We don't know for sure when Beauchamps left the front house, but probably the night before. He could have actually snuck back, between the two hedges, while the fight was going on, right past the SWAT guys, but there was a bed in the second house that was apparently his and it had been slept in."

"Then why did they all park at the target?" Lucas asked.

"We're not sure, but I think I can guess," Bob said. "The garage at the target house looked like a two-car, but it had been remodeled years ago to take four. We'd already seen that, which made us think that all four guys were there. We'd seen four coming and going in three different cars. The house in back had only a two-car garage. We think Beauchamps and Cole lived there and Nast and Vincent lived at the front house. Then Deese showed up. We have his prints, Deese was definitely there at some point. I think he moved into the back house with his pickup and Cole started parking that BMW at the target house."

"We took seven hundred and forty thousand dollars in cash and gold out of the BMW, by the way," Rae said. "Almost another half million out of the two houses, put together."

"The other thing was, the whole place was alarmed," Bob said. "They had yard alarms, both front and back. The guys coming in from the back woke them up. By the time the guys from the front went in with the flashbangs, they were already up and armed."

"Would have taken a lot of research to see the alarms," Lucas said.

"Even with lots of research, we might not have seen them," Rae said. "The things were the size of your finger, attached to trees, hooked up wirelessly. We might not have seen that hedge, either. I mean, you really can't see it, even in the daylight, from the next yard. It looks like one thick hedge. You can't see that it's two, with a path between."

There had been hundreds of shots fired during the fight: three empty thirty-round magazines had been found scattered around the windows from where Nast had been firing the full auto, and another magazine in the gun itself, which was mostly empty when he went down. Vincent had gone through one seventeen-round magazine and had been working through another when killed.

Lucas never found out how many rounds the cops had fired, but it was probably several times the number fired by Nast and Vincent.

Deese, Beauchamps, and Cole had driven away during the fight, and they weren't alone. Several neighbors on both streets had also fled, and a man across the street had seen the occupants of the back house driving away in a SUV and a white pickup. They'd never been seen again. One of the neighbors thought there was a woman with them, a blonde. The LA cops had found a fourth set of prints in the back house, small, like a woman's, but they'd gotten no hits from the feds.

"THERE WERE SWAT guys who were supposed to stay up on the street, by that back house, in case there were runners, but when the shooting started and people started screaming about cops going down they ran around the house and left nobody back in the street," Rae said. "There was nobody in the street for twenty minutes. We think Beauchamps and the others just got in their vehicles and drove away. The garage door was open, but the overhead door lights had been broken out."

"Seems like bad discipline by the SWATs," Bob said. "But when you got cops down, everything tends to go up in smoke. I don't blame those guys for leaving the street. They were risking their necks trying to help."

ONLY ONE SWAT team member had been injured, which was nothing short of a miracle given all the gunfire. He'd taken a single round in what the press releases called his hip, but Rae said was his butt. "I'm not saying he's a half-assed cop, but he's a half-assed cop."

The wound was actually more serious than Lucas's. The cop was hospitalized for almost six weeks, and he still hadn't returned to duty in August.

The LA cops and the LA County Sheriff's Department had launched an all-out search for Beauchamps, Cole, and Deese and had found exactly none of them. "LA has their mug shots all over California and up in Vegas and Portland and Seattle, and down in New Orleans, but we never got a hint," Rae said. "We believe that all four of them were ready to run at the drop of a hat. Both Nast and Vincent each had two fake IDs, including real California driver's licenses with paid-up auto insurance. Wherever those three guys went, nobody's found them. And nobody knows where to look, either."

"It's possible that they're still around," Lucas said. "How many people in Southern California? More than twenty million. These guys have already got California driver's licenses, and car tags, and they're familiar with the territory."

"Rocha doesn't think so," Bob said. "She says it's too hot down here—too many chances they'll run into an acquaintance who'll know who they are and who needs a favor from the cops. You could get one big favor for turning in a gang that shot a couple cops in a gunfight even if they **didn't** do the shooting. To say nothing of a cannibal."

"Could be right," Lucas said. "But could be wrong,"

During the gunfight, Nast had managed to hit a house across the street with a dozen bullets. It was made of concrete blocks and none of the bullets had penetrated all the way through. Nobody got hurt, but the owner had sued LA County for reckless endangerment, and Lucas, Bob, and Rae would probably be called to testify if it ever went to trial.

NOW LUCAS, on this hot August night, stood in his driveway, dripping sweat, fighting the nausea.

He knew he'd heal sooner or later, but what bothered him most was the persistent weakness.

He'd started playing hockey in elementary school, and back then, in the bad old days, there'd been a lot of emphasis on gutting it out and hanging tough. He'd never felt weak, even as a kid. He knew, in theory, that if he managed to survive to old age, at some point he'd probably start feeling weak.

But when you got old, you'd adapt, and you'd have time to adapt. He hadn't had any time. At the hospital, when he could walk again, the nurses had to help him get out of bed, to use the bathroom. They'd led him down the hall to the imaging department, pushing a pole with a saline bag on it, shuffling along in a robe like an old man. They'd flown home on a private jet, and he'd had to walk down a set of stairs to the tarmac and had held on to the handrail for dear life, afraid his legs wouldn't hold him upright.

Unlike any of his other injuries—he'd been shot twice before—this one had gotten to his head.

As he stood there, catching his breath, Weather walked out and put a hand on his back and asked, "Have you thrown up?"

"Not quite."

"Goddamnit, Lucas, you're pushing too hard," she said.

"Gotta push. Better to break than to rust."

"Those aren't the only two choices . . . Anyway, Rae's on the phone."

LUCAS FOLLOWED her inside, picked up his cell phone, and said, "Hey, babe. Have you nailed Tremanty yet?"

"Can't talk about that," Rae said. "Listen, you said to call you tonight. I'm calling. How're things?"

"I'm going back to LA," Lucas said.

"Are we coming with you?"

"If you want," Lucas said. "I'd like the company."

"Hell, yes." He heard her turn away from the phone and call, "We're going back."

"Bob's there?"

"Yes. We came down to watch them close the scene at Deese's cabin. They're running an eight-foot hurricane fence around the entire site. They spent the whole day putting up posts, pouring concrete around them. They're turning it into a fort. Eleven graves, twelve bodies."

"Speaking of forts, I'll call Russ Forte tomorrow," Lucas said. "I don't know exactly when . . . What's your schedule look like?"

They talked schedules, and since they were going back to California anyway, Lucas wanted to take a day to swing by Stanford to see Letty. She was going into her final year and trying to figure out what to do next: grad school or a job.

"I'd say a week or ten days," Lucas said. "I talked to Rocha a couple of days ago, and the LA cops are dead in the water. They'd love to get their hands on Beauchamps and Cole, but they believe they're gone. They're probably right."

"Where are we going to start?"

"That Englishman at the Flower Child's bar. You didn't mention him to Rocha, did you?"

"I might have forgot," Rae said.

"Good. We'll start there."

WEATHER HAD KNOWN that Lucas was getting ready to go back to Los Angeles. She didn't resist but was worried about his head as much as his body.

"When you got shot in the throat, it didn't affect you like this has," she said. Years before, Lucas had been shot by a young girl with a piece of crap .22 and might have died if Weather hadn't been there to open an airway with a jackknife.

"That's just the shit that happens if you're a cop. I didn't do anything wrong. There was no reason to think she had a gun, she was a kid," Lucas said. They were sitting in the kitchen, munching cantaloupe chunks from a plastic cup. "This was different. I did something really, really stupid. I should never have even been behind the tree and stepping out there when I knew there was an experienced, hard-core shooter in there with a machinc gun . . . That was really stupid. I thought the fight was over and I just stepped out to look at the house. I keep coming back to that. Would I have ever done that when I was younger? Have I lost the edge?"

"You haven't lost any kind of edge, for Christ's sakes," Weather said, exasperated. "You're too young to lose your edge. Everybody does stupid stuff from time to time."

"Even when being stupid can kill you?"

"I saw a story on the news that said thirty-seven thousand people died in automobile accidents last year and more than two million were injured. Most of those were caused by momentary stupidity," Weather said. "If you're driving a two-and-a-half-ton vehicle at 85 miles an hour and talking on your cell phone, you're stupid. But everybody does it. Including you. When Shrake got hurt last spring and Virgil had to drive him to that hospital in Fairmont, Shrake said the scariest part of it was when Virgil was driving and talking to the Highway Patrol at the same time, said Virgil almost got them killed a couple of times. He probably saved five seconds by being stupid, and Virgil isn't normally stupid."

"A Shrake exaggeration," Lucas said.

"Not much of one," Weather said. "Stop brooding. You did something stupid. Get over it."

He knew she was right; she'd gotten over a

couple of awful moments herself. But this was . . . different.

Lucas didn't in theory believe in revenge, but there was that long hockey life, from Mite to Squirt to Peewee to Bantam to Midget to high school to university. If somebody gave you a shot, you gave him a shot back. Harder. In this case, the guy who literally gave him a shot was beyond reach, being thoroughly dead.

Psychologically, though, it felt like unfinished business: there were still three other guys out there. He needed to give them a shot . . . And harder.

WEATHER HAD BEEN tough on him after he got home. When she arrived at the Huntington, she'd half expected to find him dying or dead, but when she'd come into the room and he'd tried to smile at her she'd turned around and run back out. Letty went after her and later told Lucas that Weather had collapsed in the hallway, unable to handle the instant departure of stress.

Then she got tough.

At home, she enforced a rigorous regimen of healing and recovery. By the middle of June, he was going on long walks; by the first of July, he was fast-walking. By the middle of July, he was running but weak. By the first of August, he was running harder. By the middle of the month, he was ready to kill, and Weather released him, to go do it.

But he still hurt, and occasionally felt weakness hiding down deep.

ON AUGUST 18, Lucas flew into San Francisco, rented a car, and drove to Palo Alto, where Letty had taken a summer lease on a condo from an economics professor who was in London, studying money.

"I got a deal on it," she told Lucas when she'd called him about it a few days before Lucas got shot. "I can get it for two thousand dollars a month. It's got a great pool, though it's stuffed with geeks. All I have to do is take care of the dog. I don't even have to fuck the professor."

"That's good, because then I won't have to come out there and kill him," Lucas said.

"I knew you'd approve. Can you send me a check?"

He could.

HE PICKED HER UP at the condo. When she opened the door, she took a step back, and he asked, "What?"

"You're a bag of bones," she said. "Are you okay?"

"I'm down a few pounds," he said.

"A few pounds? Don't lie. You're down ten or fifteen pounds, and you weren't carrying any fat to begin with. You've lost muscle. What do you weigh now?"

"I haven't looked lately, but I'm running hard. I'm fine."

She wasn't convinced but went to get her shoulder bag. Lucas checked the professor's bookshelves, which were heavy on economics. And erotic photography. He looked at a couple of the photo books, and asked, "Say, are you sure you're okay with this guy?"

"Positive. He hinted he might like to takes some pictures of me someday, but I told him my dad's first two rules for a girl's life," Letty said.

"I'm not entirely sure I remember those," Lucas said.

Letty counted them off on two fingers: "No ink; pierce anything you want, but no ink. And never take off your clothes around a camera."

"Now I remember," he said. "Excellent advice, I have to say."

"But you never told me how much it hurt to get your labia pierced . . ."

Lucas blanched. "Jesus Christ, Letty . . ."

She laughed merrily and said, "Gotcha. Let's go eat."

---

THEY ATE a late lunch at a nice California-style outdoor café, chicken sandwiches with avocado slices and fries with Indonesian pepper and some kind of healthy tea that was supposed to bring peace to your soul, or clean out your colon, or possibly do both simultaneously.

"Two different futures," Letty said. "An important guy at Yale says he can fix me up with a scholarship at least through a master's degree and probably a Ph.D. if I want to take that track. And second, Slocum Haynes—you know who he is?"

"Zillionaire. Oil and airlines and ships and . . . other stuff. Rockets."

"Yeah. He's offered me an internship where I'd be one of his assistants. Pay is barely okay. I could afford a one-bedroom apartment in Oklahoma City. I'd travel a lot. He also says that in two years with him, I wouldn't need a master's or any other kind of degree."

"Sometimes good-looking young interns—"

"Get preyed upon," Letty said. "You gotta stop worrying about me, Dad. Haynes said I wouldn't have to fuck him. Or anyone else at the company. Said he didn't allow it. Actually used the f-word."

"I wish you'd start saying 'f-word' more often."

"Dad, if you didn't say 'fuck' at least once every five minutes, your head would explode."

"I'm not a young woman," Lucas said.

"Yeah, well, neither am I, not so much." She was twenty-one, but he knew what she meant.

"I don't know enough to advise you," Lucas confessed. "It's interesting that you're balancing a Yale degree against a bad-paying job. That suggests to me that you think the job might be more valuable . . . in some ways."

"I think it would be. Haynes is a genius. And I could always go back for the degree," Letty said.

"How'd he hear about you?"

"He was invited out here for a seminar," Letty said. "I was interested, I sat in and asked a bunch of questions. He asked me out to dinner, along with a couple of faculty members. We talked, and a couple of days later he called me and made the offer."

"Did you ask your porno economics professor about it?"

"Yeah. He asked me if I didn't take the Haynes job, would I recommend him? I think he was joking, but I'm not sure. He told me that if Haynes liked me, I'd wind up rich and powerful."

Lucas rubbed his chin and said, "I don't like to talk about this shit, but . . . I could have gotten killed last May. Another inch lower, an inch to the right . . ."

"I know that. Exactly what shit are you talking about?"

"My will. Weather gets most of it, but if I got killed tomorrow you'd get ten million."

"Jeez. And I forgot to bring my gun with me."

"I'm not joking," Lucas said. "What I'm trying

to tell you is, whatever you do, you don't have to start saving for your retirement. When I croak, you get somewhat rich. When Weather croaks, you get even richer. You're basically trust fund scum. You don't need Haynes."

Letty looked down at the tabletop, then said, "You're telling me I can do what I want. I don't have to do something I might not like because I think it would be prudent."

"That's right."

"That's a pretty heavy burden. Thinking for yourself."

"Yes, it is."

THEY STOPPED talking about money and spent some time driving around, chatting about the Deese case, and Bob and Rae, and Virgil Flowers and Jenkins and Shrake. When he dropped her off at the condo, he was looking at six hours down to LA.

She kissed him on the cheek, before she got out of the car, and said, "Thanks. I needed the talk."

"Gimme a last thought."

"Slocum Haynes said I could call him at home any evening after seven o'clock his time. To chat. I'll give him a call tonight. See what more he has to say for himself and his job."

---

LUCAS SPENT some time thinking about Letty as he drove south through the Central Valley. When she said, "And I forgot to bring my gun with me," she was joking, but she did have a gun. She kept it stashed in a safe-deposit box, and a cop friend of Lucas's with the California Bureau of Investigation would take her out to a range a few times a year to burn up some 9mm. Lucas had thought she might aim for the FBI or possibly the CIA, or some other gun-toting law enforcement agency, but her interests had changed at Stanford.

He had no idea where she would wind up but didn't doubt that it would be interesting.

THE TRIP TO LA was fast: he arrived after rush hour, and the 5 and the 405 fed right into Marina del Rey. He checked back into the Marriott, called Bob and Rae, and met them at the entrance to the bar.

They both looked at him for a long five seconds, then Rae took hold of Lucas's biceps and said, "You're okay."

"I'm okay," Lucas said.

Bob: "You look like shit. You're kinda gray. You gotta start eating, man."

"Yeah, yeah, I'm fine," Lucas said, pulling away from Rae. "It'll take a while to get it all back, but I'm right there . . . What are we doing?"

"That English dude comes on at six o'clock at Flower Child's," Rae said. "We could have a fcw beers and go to bed and start tomorrow or we could walk down there right now and jack him up."

"I don't need a beer," Lucas said. "And I got the jack."

# CHAPTER NINE

Los Angeles had been working its way through a heatwave, with rolling brownouts killing power across the basin. Washington Boulevard wasn't dark, but it wasn't as brightly lit as it had been in May.

As they walked toward Flower Child's, Rae said, "All right, we're gonna jack him up and you said you got a jack. What's the jack?"

"I'd rather talk about your love life," Lucas said. "I can't believe that it's taken this long for you to nail Tremanty."

"She can't, either," Bob said. "I told her why, but she's not buying it."

"Shut up," Rae said.

"What's the reason?" Lucas asked.

Rae said, "Shut up, both of you."

"Quiet. I'm talking to Bob," Lucas said.

Bob said, "Well, being a handsome guy with a

job, a nice car, expensive threads, and a gun, and being located in downtown New Orleans, with one of the largest known concentrations of redheads, hairdressers, and cocktail waitresses outside of Dallas, I believe Tremanty is well tended to. Rae made the mistake of indicating her interest, which means she's always there if Tremanty needs a backup, or, you know, feels like going out of town for a long weekend."

"Big mistake," Lucas said. "Can't believe she made an amateurish error like that."

"I'm heavily armed," Rae said. "Shut up and tell me about your jack."

"I could have a word with Tremanty," Lucas said to Rae. "He's like a son to me."

"One more fuckin' word . . ."

Lucas said to Bob, "She's not only armed, I think she's actually suffering, at some level, from heartbreak. We'd best leave it alone."

"You could be right," Bob said. "Tell me about the jack."

They stopped to let a right-turning car nearly run over their toes. "While I was sitting on my ass in St. Paul," Lucas said, as the car drove on, "I called up an old friend who happens to be a deputy director at the FBI."

Rae said, "Louis Mallard."

"That's correct. Not only a deputy director but a major law enforcement politician. He called up a pal with Scotland Yard—"

"You gotta be shittin' me," Bob said. "There really **is** a Scotland Yard?"

"And asked, politely, for any information about Oliver Haar. They had a file. Haar was the youngest member of a smash-and-grab gang in London. He ran his mouth too much and the London cops busted him. They gave him the old 'Don't drop the soap in the showers' talk, being a nice-looking young kid looking at five years or so. He cut a deal to serve no time and ratted out the rest of the gang."

"Should have taken his chances with the soap," Rae said.

"Maybe. The guys he ratted out are a rough bunch. It gets better. The leader of the gang, whose name was George Wilks, and who had a lot of experience, was responsible for fencing the stuff they stole, and he parceled out the money to the gang in weekly payments. He told them he didn't want them buying Series 7s or anything else that would catch the eyes of the cops. They had enough to live well, buy decent cars and dope, go to Italy or Portugal in the winter, and so on. Anyway, Wilks and the others all went to prison. Not long after they went away, somebody kicked in the door of Wilks's house while his wife was out, pulled a dummy wall out from behind a toilet, and took out the two hundred thousand pounds that Wilks had stashed there. Haar knew about the stash. That's just a rumor, but the London cops think it's probably true. In the meantime, the Brits let Haar keep his passport—wink wink, nudge nudge—and he hasn't been seen in England since Wilks's bathroom got robbed."

"What a bad boy Oliver is," Bob said.

"That's what everybody thinks," Lucas said. "That was twelve years ago. All the gang members got out of prison since then, although two are back in again. The others are still involved in various kinds of crime, according to the London cops. If Oliver were discovered by U.S. Immigration to have come here with an undisclosed criminal record, and to be involved in criminal activity here, he'd be deported. Back to England. Where he probably doesn't want to go."

Rae: "Oh-oh."

"Yup."

"That's an excellent jack you got there," Bob said.

"I thought so," Lucas said.

A young couple walked past. The guy was wearing a T-shirt, shorts, and flip-flops, and the woman was wearing a brief strapless top, tiny shorts, and sandals. Rae said, after they passed, "Here we are, walking down the street wearing long pants and jackets. You think anybody in LA hasn't made us as cops? We need to revise our dress code if we have to work here."

"What are you thinking?" Bob asked.

"What that guy was wearing: shorts, T-shirts, but maybe running shoes. We carry some weight, so maybe cargo shorts. We need to go shopping."

"Tomorrow," Lucas said. "Though I'm feeling a little moist right now. And I can tell you up front, the Davenport doesn't wear cargo shorts."

FLOWER CHILD'S was nowhere near crowded. As Lucas remembered the waitress saying during their first visit, it was pretty much a middle-aged meat market, gold chains and all, though no leisure suits were in sight. Or any suits at all, for that matter—too hot.

Oliver Haar was standing at a podium-style reception desk, talking to a woman who looked like a customer, a friendly chat. Lucas recognized him from mug shots sent by the London cops. Haar was a decade older, but he'd aged well, with wavy blond hair over a high forehead, blue eyes, a long nose over perfect teeth, and a mild tan. He also looked like he'd been hit by a Tommy Bahama truck, wearing an open-necked Hawaiian shirt, pale cotton slacks, and canvas shoes without socks.

Even as he was talking to the customer, his eyes clicked to Lucas, Bob, and Rae, and Lucas picked up the crook's involuntary flinch, the impulse to run, though it was quickly smothered.

Lucas stepped up to the desk and said, "Oliver. Would you have a minute to run upstairs to the office and chat?"

He nodded. "I suppose so." To the woman he'd been talking to, he said, "Back in a minute, darling."

As they followed him through the back, he turned to Lucas and asked, "Who are you?"

"U.S. Marshals," Lucas said.

"I haven't done anything at all, except work hard," Haar said. "I do have a green card."

"We're not interested in your immigration status, though we could be," Lucas said. "Why don't we talk upstairs."

THE OUTER OFFICE occupied by Heather, Tommy Saito's assistant, was empty, and there were enough chairs to accommodate all four of them. Haar laid back in one of them and asked, "So . . . what's going on?"

"We need your cooperation on something. And if we get it, we walk away. If we don't get it, we talk to Immigration about some things you may have left off your green card application," Lucas said. "I'm not trying to be unfriendly, I'm trying to outline the . . . realities."

Haar nodded and asked, "What do you want? Specifically?"

"You use the pay phone downstairs as a kind of switchboard or answering service," Lucas said. "No cops know that except the three of us, and nobody needs to know that we ever talked to you. We're looking for a man named Marion Beauchamps, who you might know as Martin Keller or Martin Lawrence, if somebody called for him."

Haar stared at Lucas for a moment, showing some teeth in what wasn't a smile, then bobbed his head. "He's a hard one. If he knew I'd talked to you, I could get hurt."

"We will try to prevent that. If we can find them, they'll be going to prison forever," Rae said.

Haar thought about that for a second, looked carefully at Bob and Rae, and then back to Lucas. "It was Martin Keller and Martin Lawrence until a few months ago. Now it's Raymond Sherman. I don't know where he is, but if somebody calls for him I have a number to pass along."

"A current one?" Bob asked.

"Like I said, everything changed a few months ago, including the number. If anyone calls for Keller or Lawrence, I don't know who they're talking about. If somebody calls for Sherman, I pass along the new number. I've only had one call for Sherman."

"Have you called the number yourself?"

Haar shook his head. "No. I don't need that kind of trouble."

"How many clients do you have?" Bob asked. "For your forwarding services?"

"A few . . . twelve or fifteen. Most of them completely legitimate. I hook up people who need lawyers or real estate agents . . . I have a dog groomer, even."

"Dope dealers?"

"I don't do dope," Haar said. "I've been asked,

but dealers get caught. Always. Then they cough up everything they know. So I don't do that."

"How did you connect with Sherman? I mean, originally?" Lucas asked. "Whatever his real name is. Or was."

"There's a guy who used to hang out here a lot. He said he was on the run from his wife, he said he owed a couple hundred grand in alimony and child support and he told me he'd give me fifty bucks a call if I'd be his switchboard," Haar said. He shrugged. "All I had to do is take two steps down the hall to answer the phone, so I said yes. Then another guy came along. My name was passed along by these chaps. I don't know who any of them were or what they did. I just passed numbers. After a bit, I began to realize that some of them were . . . bad people. Two of them, maybe three, made the **Los Angeles Times**, and the **Times** doesn't write about anyone unless they've done something noticeable."

"What was your relationship with Sherman?"

"I passed numbers to him. Most of these people I never met. Sherman—I actually knew him as Keller—came in to see what was what. I knew right away that he was the wrong type. But he liked this place, he liked the women. He'd come in, like anyone else. Rougher but not crazy. A certain kind of woman definitely had a taste for what he was selling."

"Give me the phone number you're calling," Lucas said.

Haar dug in his pant pocket, took out a black address book the size of a credit card and an eighth of an inch thick. He read out the number and said, "I hope you'll use it with care. It's possible that nobody calls that number except me, so if you call it, they'd know who gave it to you."

"We'll be careful," Lucas said.

"I'm surprised you don't use a smartphone for the numbers, maybe with some encryption," Rae said.

Haar smiled for the first time, a brief flash of white teeth, and said, "You know the best encryption? Two pieces of paper wadded up and swallowed."

"All right," Lucas said. He took a card out of his wallet, wrote his phone number on the back, and said, "If Sherman calls, give me a ring. Don't forget. When we get him—and we will—we'll look at his phone to see who he's been calling . . . And who's been calling him."

Haar looked at the card, then at the reverse side, and said, "I need to get some cards like this."

Rae asked, "Like what?"

Haar showed it to her: the card was blank on both sides, except for the handwritten phone number. Rae looked at Lucas and said, "Explain."

Lucas said, "Sometimes assholes don't want to carry a cop's card around with them." And to Haar: "Not saying you're an asshole, or anything."

"I'm actually a pretty decent bloke," Haar said. "With some quirks."

After some more talk, and more warnings about the consequences if he spoke to anyone about their visit, they let Haar go back to his reception desk.

RAE CALLED TREMANTY from the sidewalk outside the bar. "I'm with Lucas and Bob. We have a phone number, but we need to be careful."

Tremanty called her back as they were walking into the hotel. He'd talked to the FBI's overnight phone guy, who was named Earl.

"Earl didn't do anything that might trip any wires. He looked at records and nothing else," Tremanty said. "The phone's a burner, and there have been four calls to and from. It's in Vegas. I told them to email you a map of where the phone was when the calls were made. That could take a few hours."

"You know what we're talking about here," Lucas said. "We want to get on them before they take off again."

"I'm pushing Earl."

LUCAS, BOB, AND RAE were all on the same floor at the hotel. They went up in the elevator and walked down the hall to Lucas's room to figure out what to do next.

"I'd rather stay here. This is hot, Vegas is gonna be a goddamn furnace," Bob said. He was looking at the weather app on his phone. "It's 108, 110, 111, respectively, for the next three days. If we have to work outside . . ."

"Rae's right," Lucas said. "We'll need new wardrobes. Maybe pick up some stuff tomorrow. I'll call Forte tomorrow morning and get plane tickets . . . Or we could drive."

Bob went to his mapping app. "We gotta get to the airport three hours ahead of the flight because of our gear, the guns, and it's a half hour to the airport. Plus, LAX is a world-class shithole. Flight time is an hour, then we'd have to collect the gear and rent cars at the other end. Total, probably five and a half hours. Or, we could drive, get there in five hours or less, and we wouldn't have to mess with checking in the guns and renting cars. And we could leave here anytime we want."

"Drive," Rae said.

"Shop, then drive," Lucas agreed. "We ought to have the phone maps later tonight or tomorrow morning for sure."

"Meet at breakfast," Bob said.

"Nine o'clock," Lucas said.

LUCAS WAS UP at eight, cleaned up, and checked for the overnight email from the FBI. The phone number they'd gotten from Haar showed four calls, three going out, one coming in. All three outgoing calls had been made from the Forum

Shops at Caesars, a mall attached to the hotel and casino.

"Probably because it's all crowded and confused with a lot of traffic and you could never find a guy in there," Rae said.

More interesting was the single incoming call, which had been taken at a trailer park west of Caesars.

"We'll have to take a close look at that place," Lucas said. "That's about a ten-minute drive from Caesars, so they might have been making calls from Caesars because it's also convenient. Maybe they hang out there."

"Sounds reasonable," Bob said.

Lucas spent five minutes looking at a map of the Vegas Strip, then called Forte's secretary and told her to book them into the Bellagio Hotel. She called back five minutes later and reported that there was a Best Western within walking distance of the Bellagio and it was more economical. "I don't care how short the walk is, or how economical it would be, it's going to be 108 in Las Vegas today and we know the guys we're tracking hang out at Caesars, which is next door to the Bellagio. Book us into the Bellagio and fuck economical," Lucas said.

She called back in another five minutes to say they had three rooms in Lucas's name.

"We're all going to jail," Rae told Bob, when Lucas had rung off. "Sooner or later, somebody's going to add up the business-class travel and the four-star hotels and they'll put us in jail."

"Not us," Bob said. "It's Forte who's doing the bookings. Besides, after what happened last year in D.C., I don't think anybody anywhere would want to take us to a trial."

"So they'll have the CIA kill us," Rae said. "That'd be more economical, too."

THEY HAD BREAKFAST, drove over to Santa Monica—Lucas was driving a rental Volvo S90 and Bob and Rae had a three-year-old government motor pool Tahoe arranged by Forte—and walked into a Nordstrom's at the end of the Third Street Promenade as soon as the doors opened. At eleven o'clock, carrying shorts, short-sleeved shirts, and golf socks in their shopping bags, they were back in their cars and headed for Las Vegas.

Bob's mapping app reported a traffic disaster on the 405 North across the Valley, that suggested they wouldn't get to Las Vegas until September, so they went east across town, eventually catching the 210 into San Bernardino and then the 15 through Victorville, home of an ongoing federal prison humanitarian disaster, and then Barstow, across the hard desert and into Vegas.

The 15 at San Bernardino ran parallel to, and very close to—eventually crossing—the San Andreas Fault. Lucas had read in a magazine article that if the Fault slipped a disk, the 15 would wind up in the bottom of a canyon. Two months later, the story said, there'd be tumbleweeds blowing down a Las Vegas Strip that was cut off from the Los Angeles high rollers.

He didn't necessarily believe that, because there was always the 405, but the 405 also crossed the Fault, so it might also be discombobulated by the Big One.

As a dedicated resident of Minnesota, he didn't much care about all of that as long as the Big One didn't pop open the earth as he was driving over the Fault.

Rae had ridden with Bob for the first part of the trip, but switched over to ride with Lucas at Victorville because Lucas wanted to talk through some ideas and to make some phone calls, which he didn't want to do while he was driving.

THE FIRST CALL went to Investigative Services Division on the Las Vegas Metro Police. Rae got through to the relevant lieutenant, identified herself, and asked for help on recent home invasions in the Vegas area and for DMV auto transfers for any Cadillac Escalade or Ford F-150 around the first of June. The cop said he'd get the information and an investigator named Bart Mallow would meet them at the snack bar at the Bellagio. "Call when you get close. I'll give you his direct line."

They made it into Vegas, with a couple of stops, before four o'clock on an afternoon so hot that the waves of heat coming off the concrete made the Louisiana waves look like amateurs. They turned into the Bellagio, past a shirtless man wearing a red Speedo, red-striped toe socks, and lipstick, with glitter sprinkled on his cheeks and a plastic olive wreath atop his purple hair; he was rocking out to the street music. Three seminude fat women with glittery stars pasted on their nipples were digging his act.

As they checked into the hotel, Bob said, "Guess what they got over in the Caesars shopping mall?"

"Does it have something to do with food?" Rae asked.

"A Cheesecake Factory. We never got to go to the one in Marina del Rey."

"Tomorrow maybe," Lucas said, "though I can already hear my arteries seizing up. Let's find this snack bar place and see what Mallow has to say for himself."

MALLOW WAS a fortyish fireplug, something like Bob, but with more bounce and less muscle. He wore his hair in a neatly oiled blond flattop and had a nose that had been broken a few times. He had a white bandage on one side of it, sticking out like a chicken's beak. "Mohs surgery for one of those cancer dealies. My looks are gone," he said, as they introduced themselves.

"This's gotta be ground zero for skin cancer," Bob said. "I think I caught some on the drive up here."

"You're right, it is," Mallow said. "On the other hand, I don't get frostbite anymore. I was raised up in Rochester, New York."

"Fair trade," Rae said. And, "You got anything for us?"

Mallow nodded. "I do. If you want to get something to eat . . ."

They went through the line, for burgers and fries and pizza and Cokes, and settled back down to look at Mallow's paper.

"I looked you up on the internet and saw that stuff about the fight back in May." He looked at Lucas. "You seem to be doing okay."

"I am now. Felt bad at the time."

"Lucky you're not completely dead," Mallow said. "I got shot once, but it was a .22. Got hit in the foot. Not life-threatening, or anything, but it hurt like hell for a year. And still hurts sometimes . . . Anyway, I looked you up, I read all that stuff about the home invasion guys, this Beauchamps and Cole, and the cannibal guy, and I guess there's some woman running with them, maybe. A month ago, early July, here in Vegas, up at the Kensington Gardens, three guys in masks went into a house at eleven o'clock at night, scared the living shit out of this casino exec and his wife, and got out with a half million in cash and valuables. That doesn't happen here. We didn't make the connection with the LA gang until you called this afternoon. They sound like the guys you're looking for. The descriptions we have fit Beauchamps, Cole, and Deese well enough. The MO is the same as the LA robberies, the battering ram, going after the wife, threatening rape—all that. I talked to your robbery sergeant down in LA, Rocha, about an hour ago, and she agrees. She's interested. And she says hello, says you're not as bad a bunch as you might be."

"Thank her for that," Lucas said. "What about the cars?"

"Yeah. A lot of cars go through here, and there were a couple of dozen used F-150s re-registered around the first of June. Most popular single vehicle in America. Three Escalades, which wasn't so much of a problem, so I checked those and none of them sounds likely. I talked to all the sellers and they were all legitimately registered here in Nevada."

"This is good stuff, Bart," Lucas said. "Confirms what we thought: they're here."

"We'd love to catch them—we don't like people messing with casino execs," Mallow said. "I'll give you any help I can."

———

THEY TALKED for a while longer, and Mallow left them with the paper on the home invasion. Lucas told Mallow that he might want to talk to the victims and Mallow said he would fix it. "It's clear that they had been researched and watched, but they never felt a thing, never had a clue that somebody was watching them," Mallow said.

When Mallow was gone, Lucas, Bob, and Rae went up to their rooms, changed into cargo shorts and loose short-sleeved shirts, to cover their pistols. Lucas hadn't been able to avoid the shorts because of all the crap cops carry around in them, like badge cases and extra magazines. He checked himself in the full-length mirror before he left the room and shook his head. He didn't often see his knees in the sunshine. Not his look.

They met in the lobby, walked through a mass of slot machines and up and down some escalators and stairs and out into the incredible heat and into the front of Caesars. The Forum shopping mall was on the far side of what looked like two hundred yards of slot machines, most of them unoccupied, and Bob said, "I could drop ten bucks while we're here. Maybe twelve."

"Don't burn out your bank account all at once," Rae said. To Lucas: "Your legs are so white, they're transparent. Look at that, Bob. You can see right through them."

"Gimme a break," Lucas said. "I hate shorts. I feel like a fuckin' golfer."

They were coming up to the entrance to the Forum when a man in a black suit wearing a brass name tag caught up to them and touched Lucas's shoulder and said, "Excuse me . . ."

There were two other men with black suits with him, and the lead man asked, "Law enforcement?"

Lucas said, "Federal marshals." And, "I know, we're wearing shorts, but it's hot outside."

The three men looked like ex–heavy-duty cops of some kind, maybe FBI or ATF, all in shape, with carefully greased-back black hair and bright neckties. They'd spotted the weapons that the marshals were carrying. Lucas, Bob, and Rae took their IDs out of their pockets and the three men checked them. And the leader asked, "Do you have something going on here?"

"We're not sure," Lucas said. "We're tracking some people who made phone calls from the Forum. We're checking out the territory."

"All right. Be aware of how crowded it is."

Lucas smiled and said, "We won't shoot anyone. Promise."

The man didn't smile back, but said, "Okay . . . Try real hard."

Lucas said, "If you give me an email, I'll send you some mug shots of the people we're looking for. Maybe you've seen them."

"What'd they do?"

"Hard-core stickup guys," Bob said. "Part of a gang that shot a couple cops in LA last May. Home invasion. They probably took down a casino exec from Cyril's, and the guy's wife, here in Vegas a few weeks ago."

"Toni and Cal? The night robbery?"

"That's the one," Lucas said.

"That was ugly," the lead man said. "I heard Toni is still messed up about it. Hope you get them . . . though it took you a while to get here."

"Yeah, well, I was one of the guys they shot," Lucas said.

The security men glanced at one another, and the leader said, "Ouch," and another one said, "Bet that smarted," and the leader took a card from his pocket and wrote an email address on the back.

"Send me those mug shots. I'll have all our security personnel look around."

Lucas nodded and handed a card of his own to him. "Call me about anything."

"GOOD SECURITY," Rae said, as they moved on.

"You know how you can tell they're not ex-marshals?" Bob asked. "They're too skinny."

"Keen observation," Lucas said.

"Bunch of sissies," Bob muttered.

They walked into the Forum, an indoor shopping center with domed ceilings painted blue, orange, and white to look like a partly cloudy evening sky in the desert. The various hallways were punctuated by intersections that featured oversized tableaus of fake Roman sculpture—gods, goddesses, emperors, gladiators.

"Man, Roman women had really great tits," Bob said, taking them in. "I mean 'breasts.'"

Rae: "You know why? They all died when they were twenty-six."

"I'm not saying this place is cheesy . . ." Lucas said.

"I'll say it," Rae said. "It's cheesy. But not uninteresting. It's like its own art form. Vegas cheddar. I kinda like it. Remind me to write something about it and use the phrase 'Vegas cheddar.' It's both accurate and snarky."

A security guard went rolling by on a Segway; another wandered past, wearing an old-fashioned brimmed hat, like the Stetson Open Road hats once worn by the Texas Highway Patrol. He eye-checked the three of them, nodded, and moved on. A few minutes later, another one went past. And then another.

Rae said, "They must not like shoplifters."

"I get that impression," Lucas said.

From where they were standing, Lucas could see the shops: Dior, Zegna, Armani, Tiffany, Louis Vuitton, Ferragamo, Versace, Cartier. Dozens of people were gawking at a fountain like they'd never seen water before, some of them stopping to take selfies with it as the backdrop.

"Fountain makes me want to pee," Bob said.

"I'm not sure you're the demographic the designers were looking for," Rae said.

Lucas said, "You know what? Walking around here won't get us anywhere. Too many people. Even if they were here, we wouldn't see them."

"We could break up, make a sweep," Rae said.

"We could try that," Lucas said. "Give it a half hour."

AS THEY WERE doing that, one of the security guards took a slip of paper out of his wallet, called the number written on it, and said, "You asked me to look for a face. He walked past me just now."

"Is he staying there?" A woman's voice, which he hadn't expected.

"I don't know," the guard said. "I'm just standing here like I'm looking for shoplifters. He was shopping, I think, so he could be staying anywhere."

After a moment of silence, the woman on the other end said, "Probably there, I bet. It's too hot to be walking outside to get to a shopping center. Not at five o'clock in the afternoon. Maybe at nine or ten."

"Dunno. Anyway, I was told there'd be a hundred bucks in it for me, if I remember correctly."

"Yes. We'll catch you the next time we come through."

**Click.**

The guard had the sudden feeling that the hundred bucks might not be coming through anytime soon. Fuckin' hoodlums.

LUCAS WAS IN a Canali store, eying the ties, when his phone burped. A call from Russell Forte in Washington.

"You're interrupting my shopping trip," Lucas said. And, "What time is it? Are you calling from home?"

"Yeah. I'm watching HBO and eating popcorn. It's after eight here. You wouldn't be in the Forum Shops at Caesars, would you?" Forte asked.

Lucas frowned at his phone. "How'd you know that? You put a tracker on my phone?"

"No, I got a call from Earl the phone guy. An alert popped up on his screen. Somebody called the phone you're watching. The call came from the Forum Shops. About six minutes ago."

"You mean, like, somebody spotted me?"

"Or Bob or Rae. But probably you," Forte said. "After you got shot, your name was in the papers in LA, so they may know who's looking for them. There are about a million photos of you online, going back twenty years, in Minnesota."

"Goddamnit. Where was the phone when it got answered?"

"Same place it got answered before, near that trailer park. I'll bet they burn the phone after this call. They could already be moving."

LUCAS CALLED Bob and Rae. "Back to the cars. Hurry."

He hadn't seen them because of the crowds in the casinos until they were headed back to the Bellagio. They all got in the Volvo, Rae in the back since she was the only one of them who'd fit there. Bob called up the mapping app on his phone and two minutes later they were out on the boulevard and around the block heading west.

Not much traffic. Wide streets, flat desert-colored houses with tile roofs. They arrived at the Jacaranda Estates Mobile Home Community fifteen minutes after they ran out of the Forum Shops, and a few minutes more than that since the phone call was made.

The community was a perfect square, a quarter mile on each side, wrapped by a six-foot-tall concrete wall with flaking white paint. The guardhouse at the entrance was empty.

A small red arrow-shaped sign on the street opposite the guardhouse said "Manager, 300 Dodgers." The streets, it turned out, were named after baseball teams. "Dodgers" was the street leading away from the entrance and they followed it to number 300, which turned out to be an aging and thoroughly immobile mobile home surrounded by sunburnt zinnias and marigolds.

They parked and Lucas led the way to the door; they knocked and a woman in pink hair curlers opened it, looked at them, frowned, and asked, "Who are you?"

"U.S. Marshals," Lucas said, showing her his badge.

"You better come in. It's so goddamn hot out there, you could boil water on the sidewalk."

They crowded into the trailer, which smelled like cream of mushroom soup and Gerber's baby food—pureed peas, Lucas thought, an odor he wouldn't easily forget, either going in or coming out of a kid—and the woman said, "Gotta be quiet. I just put the baby down."

Lucas showed her mug shots of Deese, Beauchamps, and Cole. After a moment, she tapped the picture of Beauchamps and said, "He used to be here. Over on . . . Astros. 712. Haven't seen him in a couple of months."

"Who's living there now?"

"College student. Kelly something. Has a black-and-white dog; you see her walking the dog at night. I tell her, 'Listen, if you're at school and the air-conditioning goes out here, the power goes off, that pooch will die in there.' So then a couple days later she told me she made arrangements with the woman who lives across the way to make sure the dog is okay if there's a power problem. Nice girl."

"Is she related to this guy?" Lucas held up the Beauchamps picture. "A girlfriend, anything like that?"

"Don't know, don't keep track of that kind of thing. But I don't think so. I believe she rented it from them. This guy"—she nodded at the photo in Lucas's hand—"told me he was going to Alaska and he didn't know when he'd be back, exactly. He left me fifteen hundred bucks for repairs and said if it was more than that, I should kick out the renter and lock it up until he did get back."

"How do you know she rented it?" Rae asked. "How do you know they're not related?"

The woman shrugged. "I **don't** know. That's just what I think."

Lucas said to Bob and Rae, "Let's go look."

# CHAPTER TEN

A multi-dented Subaru Outback with lefty bumper sticker—"That's Ms. Liberal, Pro-Choice, Tree-Hugging, Vegan Hippie Freak to You, Asshole"—was parked outside the target trailer, which showed lights in all the windows even though it wasn't dark yet. Over the hum of the air-conditioning they could hear Taylor Swift singing "Teardrops on My Guitar."

Lucas said, "College student. Not a problem."

Bob hooked his arm. "What happened the last time you stuck out your face in front of a house, Lucas? We'll do this—it's what we do. You can go around and watch the back. There'll be a door or fire exit there."

Rae had already popped the hatch on the Tahoe and was pulling on a "U.S. Marshal" shirt and a vest. Bob joined her. When they were armored up, Lucas walked to the back of the trailer, where he could see the door, while Rae peeked through the window of the front door, then thc window beside it, and then Bob took up a spot at an angle to the door and hid his Glock in his hand behind his hip, ready to go.

Rae knocked and a moment later the door popped open, and Lucas heard Rae say, "We're U.S. Marshals. Could you step outside, please?"

A dog started barking inside, and then Lucas heard a woman's voice: "Be quiet, Willa. Shhh."

NOTHING WAS MOVING at the back door, so Lucas walked back around to the front. A short, stocky brown-haired woman was standing on the stoop. Rae held up her ID and badge and asked her if there was anyone else in the trailer and the woman said, "No," and Rae asked her if it was okay if they took a look.

"I really have a problem with law people pushing into my house," the woman said.

"We're not pushing," Rae said. "We're asking permission. If you say no, we won't. But we will get a warrant, which means we'll all be standing here for two or three hours, in the heat, until we do. And then if there's nobody in there, it'll all have been an annoying waste of time."

Bob added, "We're looking for some very dangerous people—the people you are renting from. There's a murder warrant out for one of them and armed robbery warrants out for all of them."

The woman: "What!"

Rae: "You see why we can't take a chance that you're hiding someone. The last time we went after them, they shot two law enforcement officers."

"What!"

Bob said, "We don't want to look at any of your personal papers or other possessions, we want to make sure we don't get shot in the back. That's the truth. So . . ."

The woman let them in, said her name was Kerry Black, not Kelly, as the manager had said. Bob and Rae cleared the place. That done, all five of them, plus the black-and-white border collie, Willa, crowded into the kitchen.

Black said she'd rented the trailer from a blond woman after seeing an advertisement on the Las Vegas Craigslist. "She said she wanted somebody reliable who wouldn't wreck the place and said Willa was okay. They wanted only three hundred a month, which was great for me. I couldn't even believe it."

Lucas: "How do you get in touch with them?"

"I don't. I mail the rent on the first of the month. If there are problems, I'm supposed to talk to the manager."

"You don't have a phone number?"

"No. All I've got is an address," she said. "I'll tell you, though, I watch my checking account and they haven't cashed my July or August checks yet."

"Not picking the checks up?" Rae said to Lucas. "Maybe they don't care about money."

Lucas asked if the owners had left anything behind, and Black said "Well, the furniture. There's some junk in a closet and some barbecue stuff and a grill."

"The junk in the closet—could we see it?"

The closet contained a cardboard box of Blu-ray movie disks and some country music CDs, old venetian blinds, an ancient vacuum cleaner with a frayed electric cord, a bowling ball in a bag that looked like it hadn't been opened in years, two cases of empty beer bottles, and a litter of dead flies. Black said she'd looked in there when she first rented the place, but then closed the door and hadn't really looked in since except when she'd played some of the movies.

"Did you put them back in the box?"

"No, they're sitting on top of the DVD player."

Lucas told her that they would talk to the FBI about sending a crime scene team around to check all the left behind stuff for fingerprints and asked her not to touch any of it.

"Do you think I'll get kicked out of here?" she asked. "I'm going to college, but I don't have any money and I'm waitressing my way through and this place is a super deal for me and Willa . . ."

"I don't know why you'd get kicked out. But if

the owners come back, you gotta call us. Be really, really careful if they do," Lucas said. He wrote down the address where she sent the rent in his notebook.

OUTSIDE, Bob said, "We've gotta have the crime scene guys check that grill."

Rae: "Ah, jeez, I don't want to think about that."

LUCAS SAID, "Somebody's lying to us, and I don't think it was that kid. I think it's the manager. Though I can think of some complicated ways that it might not be."

"Tell me," Bob said.

"Well, we set off an alarm back at the Forum. Somebody spotted one of us—probably me—and made a call here, where the phone was answered. That means there's a connection here. And I don't think it was the kid."

"She's got the cheap rent," Rae said.

"Yeah, but I don't think it's her. I don't think she's that good a liar. And I doubt they'd consider her reliable. I think it's probably the manager. I think she takes messages and relays them. Somebody spotted me in the Forum and called her. Then, she waited to see if we'd show up. That would tell them that we're watching the phone and we know about this place. So she's probably got anothcr burncr phonc that we don't know about that goes directly to Beauchamps or one of the others. And Beauchamps probably dumped that phone immediately after she called."

"If you're right, we've gone backwards."

"Unless Earl, the phone guy, can pull up the call she made. She probably called right after she took the call from the Forum and right after we showed up. If he can find it, we could still be hanging in."

"We could try for a warrant to search her trailer," Rae said.

Lucas shook his head. "We wouldn't get it. We don't have anything like what we'd need for a warrant. For one thing, it could be the kid. But it could be somebody like the manager's neighbor. She's home all day with the baby, nothing going on, then three marshals show up at her front door. She's gonna talk about it."

"I asked her not to," Rae said.

Bob: "Right. That was a half hour ago. I bet she's told only eight of her closest friends, after having them double-swear to keep it secret."

Lucas said, "I'll call Tremanty and have him call Earl. I don't think he can do what we want him to without any phone numbers, but we can try."

"Maybe get some dessert over at the Cheesecake Factory?" Bob said. "You know, while we wait for Earl to call back."

"I think we need to go talk to this Toni and Calvin Wright, see if they have anything interesting to say about the home invasion," Lucas said.

Bob groaned. "We're not going to get to the Cheesecake Factory, are we? Ever?"

"It's open late," Rae said. "And I want to talk to the Wrights, too. If I gotta be there, so do you."

LUCAS CALLED the Wrights using the number he'd gotten from Mallow, the Las Vegas cop. Toni Wright answered, said that Mallow had told them that Lucas would be calling. Lucas said, "I know it's getting late . . ."

"Not in Vegas. Come on over," Wright said.

The Wrights lived in a walled residential community called Kensington Gardens, in what would be the shadow—in the daytime—of two bland condominium towers northwest of the Strip. On the way there, Rae said, "Oh my God," and pointed. "Another Cheesecake Factory."

"I'm being taunted by God," Bob said, as they drove past.

"I don't think you're important enough for that," Lucas said.

TONI AND CALVIN WRIGHT resembled each other: dark-eyed with short dark hair, gym-conditioned, sleek as otters. "These men were all over us," Calvin said. "They knocked down the door one minute after we came in, we never had a chance. Toni and I study tae kwon do, so we can take care of ourselves in a straight-up fight, but they had guns. They knew what they were doing. Never had a chance."

"They said if we didn't open the safe, they'd rape me until I did or I couldn't," Toni said, and she started to cloud up. "There was nothing Cal could have done, either. They'd have killed him."

The men wore ski masks, but the physical descriptions fit Beauchamps, Deese, and Cole: Beauchamps, large and blocky; the other two, mid-height and thin. "Somebody else drove their car, but we didn't see him," Calvin said. "We know because when they went out the door, the car started up before they could have gotten to it."

"Could be the woman," Rae said to Lucas.

Toni Wright said her loss in jewelry would be over a half million dollars. "I had a collection of vintage Indian jewelry made by Charles Loloma, the most famous Indian artist ever. The thing is, the stones themselves aren't worth much—coral and lapis lazuli and turquoise, and so on. Some of the settings were gold, but really, in terms of dollars, not more than a few thousand if you melted it down. If they're looking for real money, they'd have to sell it intact, and there wouldn't be many buyers. Indian art dealers, that's about it. I've been trolling through some local places, seeing if I can spot any of it."

"If they sold it to Indian art dealers, how much would they get?" Lucas asked.

She said, "It's worth a quarter million, retail. So . . . you'd know better than me how much they'd get from a fence. I had twenty-two pieces, some of Loloma's best things. If they broke them down for the gold and the stones, it'd be a tragedy and be worth only a few thousand, if that."

"What about the rest of the half million?" Bob asked.

"I had a hundred and fifty thousand in a pair of earrings that Cal gave me when we got married. Great stones—three carats each, E color, flawless, brilliant cut."

Calvin Wright said, "Great stones, but they're nothing, like, unique. They're not like the Loloma stuff. Pull them out of the settings and they're totally anonymous."

Toni said, "The rest of it was gold and platinum bracelets, three watches, plus a ring by Belperron and a pearl necklace. Not really a collection, but the Belperron was worth a ton. I'd kill to get it back."

Lucas began, "This person, Belle Perron . . ."

"One name. Belperron is her last name, Suzanne Belperron, she was French. Long gone now," Toni said.

"So the ring would be, what, worth more intact or in pieces?"

"Oh. Far, far more intact. It's like the Loloma,

each one is unique," she said. "I gave the police copies of the insurance photos; we haven't settled with the insurer yet, there might be a lawsuit."

There had also been currency in the safe, mostly in dollars, but also an uncertain amount in euros and Chinese renminbi—the Wrights thought the total would be the equivalent of five or six thousand dollars. Toni Wright had managed to save her diamond-encrusted wedding ring by turning it around on her finger so that it displayed only its thin platinum band.

When they'd cleaned the safe out, the robbers had locked chains around the Wrights' ankles, with the chains looped around a couch. They'd put the Wrights' cell phones on the kitchen counter. "We had to carry the couch into the kitchen before we could get to our phones and call the police," Calvin said. "That took a while, fifteen or twenty minutes, you know, because we had to go up the steps to the kitchen and then down the hallway. It was a tight squeeze. And that goddamn couch was heavy."

Rae looked at Lucas and said, "It's them. No doubt about it. They did the couch thing in LA."

"One thing that you should know that I didn't think of until tonight," Calvin said. "It might not be important, but it was dark and we never saw their car, really. There's not much traffic here, and I **think** I saw their taillights going out the exit. They turned left, went west, but there's not a lot to the west of us—we're right on the edge of town. They could have been going to the parkway and then east, but it'd be a weird way to do it. Or they could have been going out to the Beltway, but that's right on the edge of civilization."

Lucas: "So, you think wherever they're hiding might be on the west side of town rather than downtown or the Strip or . . ."

"Or anywhere east, yeah. Don't know if that helps."

"The small stuff helps," Lucas said. "We add it all up and it helps."

"One other small thing, but I'm not sure I'm right about this because Cal says he didn't see it," Toni Wright said. "One of them, not the big man but one of the others, was wearing jeans, and there was something about one of his legs. It . . . It was fat around the knee, like he might have had a bandage on it. The other leg looked like, you know, nothing, but this one looked too fat. To me anyway. I wondered if he might have had to go to a doctor for something."

Rae: "You've got a good eye."

"There's a major medical center out here," Calvin Wright said. "If he's out here on the west side and he got bit by a dog, or something, he might have gone to their emergency room."

Bob said to Lucas, "He probably would have paid cash."

Lucas: "Especially if he got a prescription."

---

THEY LEFT the Wrights and ended the evening at the Forum's Cheesecake Factory. The air had cooled dramatically by midnight and had become light and pleasant. They'd walked over from the Bellagio. And since the casinos never closed, there were still people on the streets. Bob, who'd led the way, ordered a Very Cherry Ghirardelli Chocolate Cheesecake, Rae went with the Lemoncello Cream Torte, while Lucas chose the Hot Fudge Sundae. Lucas had asked the waitress if the sundae was decent and she said, "It's fabulous. I gotta tell you, if it was me, I'd be sticking my feet in that ice cream. I've been standing up for fourteen hours straight."

"Not in this one job, for God's sakes?" Bob said.

"Two jobs," the waitress said. "This one pays the rent, the other feeds the slots."

WHEN THE DESSERTS came, Lucas summed up: "We know they're here. The bad thing is, they probably know that we're here. They could go on the run again. We only found them because we got lucky with the phone. If they figure that out, and they probably will, they'll stop using Haar and throw the phone away. If we're going to find them, we've got to do it quick or we'll have to start over."

"Then what's next?" Bob asked.

"You guys check the hospitals tomorrow

morning, see if you can find the guy with the hole in his leg. I'll get back with Mallow and see who's fencing what around town and what places handle high-end Indian jewelry."

"Sounds like legwork," Bob said.

"Yes. In 105-degree heat."

"We should feel honored," Rae said to Bob. "We'll be doing actual detective-like things."

Bob sang, "I wanna be an airborne Ranger, fight and fuck and live in danger . . ."

"Think your partner is suffering from heatstroke already," Lucas said to Rae. And, "I'm going to bed."

# CHAPTER ELEVEN

The police raid on the Altadena house had spooked Beauchamps and Cole. Everything had been going so smoothly and had ended so cataclysmically, with both Nast and Vincent shot to death by the cops.

Cox wasn't an idiot but seemed oddly unaffected by the raid. She thought Nast was a jerk and had gotten what he deserved and didn't seem to register the fact that they'd been outrageously lucky to ride away untouched—that what had happened to Nast and Vincent could as easily have happened to her.

Her answer: "Well, it didn't, so why sweat it?" The three men looked at her, simultaneously shook their heads, and Cox went back to brushing her shoes.

---

IN VEGAS, they'd stayed five nights at the trailer park, all four of them. Cox slept in the bedroom with Beauchamps, but during the day Deese and Beauchamps went out, both men with beards now, wearing sunglasses and hats. When they were gone, Cox and Cole would test their new relationship, watching porn on the trailer's television and then trying out what they'd learned. Beauchamps seemed oblivious to their budding relationship; Deese watched them suspiciously.

Cox had gotten in touch with the Airbnb agent the first full day they were in town and by the sixth day the woman got them into two separate houses, cheap but fully furnished.

And they started talking about a house invasion: they needed cash and they needed it soon.

They'd lost the van in the raid and decided to go to two vehicles. They'd leave Deese's truck a few hundred yards from the target house and go in in Beauchamps's Cadillac. On the way out, after the robbery, Beauchamps and Deese would be dropped at the truck. There were a lot of surveillance cameras in Las Vegas, and cops looking for three men in a vehicle, in the area of the home invasion, would see only two in the truck and a man and a woman in the Cadillac.

That was all right with Cox—she was willing to be a getaway driver as long as she could pretend that she believed nobody would get hurt. The truth was, other people's pain didn't bother her much.

Not being as dumb a bunny as the men thought she was, she also knew that if people got hurt, the criminal penalties increased and the cops got more interested.

So Beauchamps and Cole did the basic research, scanning local magazines that took pictures at charity events, the women all in jewelry and their hottest dresses. When they had a list, they went to the cheapest all-cash motel they could find that had WiFi and used Cole's laptop to research the people.

When they'd whittled the list down to four candidates, they checked the houses on Google Earth, spotting getaway routes and possible security problems. They eliminated a condo right away and finally settled on the Wrights.

Deese picked up some current-looking license plates from a junkyard—five hundred bucks, no questions asked. They bought a railroad tie at a nursery, the kind used for landscaping, and two door handles at a Home Depot to affix to the tie, to make a battering ram.

When they went into Wrights' house, it had all gone smoothly, like old times. The robbery went well, Deese taking Nast's place as the frightener, but much of the take was in jewelry that would be hard to sell. They'd talked to their new fence about it and he suggested they not move more than a single piece of the Loloma, or two, each year.

"That Loloma stuff—it's all unique, it's all

documented with photographs, quite a bit of it is in books that all the Indian traders will have," the fence told them. "That's gonna be tough." He said that if he bought it, he might eventually make two hundred thousand dollars, but that could take ten years and with serious risk involved. He'd offer them twenty thousand—take it or leave it. After some grumbling, they took it.

They got ninety thousand for the rest of the jewelry: the diamonds and the pieces made by Belperron. The diamonds were no problem at all—they were excellent, and anonymous, stones. The Belperron would be resold to a fence in France, who'd move it in Europe, but that meant the take was further reduced because there'd be two fences involved.

The bottom line: the raid was a success but the take, including the cash, amounted to less than forty thousand dollars for each of the men.

Cole, on his own, lying low in Omaha, might stretch forty thousand dollars out over five or six months, but Deese and Beauchamps, with heavy casino and cocaine expenses, could cover a couple of months at best. Each of them gave Cox, as the driver, two thousand, which she thought was ridiculously stingy. She talked Cole out of another five thousand when they were alone, which meant that he wasn't covered for more than three or four months. And Cox knew that with her cocaine and casino expenditures the same as Deese's and

Beauchamps's, she'd be lucky if her money lasted a month.

THEY NEEDED more money but were hesitant to hit another house too soon. Would the marshals and the LA cops hear about the Wright raid and figure out where they were? They waited for any sign that the cops were looking for them but saw nothing.

They began to relax and to talk about a second raid, one that would get them out of Vegas. There was also the tempting prospect of a huge score—five million—but the information was funky. It involved a gambler named Harrelson.

And Deese, behind the backs of the others, had spoken to Ricardo Santos and Roger Smith about a payment that would allow him to truly get lost. Smith was at three hundred thousand, Deese wanted a million. Then came the call from Beauchamps's friend at the trailer park: the marshals had tracked them to Vegas.

"There's only one way they could get to the park and that's by tracking the phones. Either Haar sold us out or the feds are doing something we don't know about, some high-tech shit. We've got to get rid of the phones, like, tonight. We all have to change numbers," Cole said. "We have to think about going somewhere else."

Beauchamps: "Like where?"

"Miami, Seattle, Boston . . . Well, not Boston, too fuckin' cold . . . Maybe Houston. Someplace not in California or Nevada," Cole said. "We should split up. Do one last job, like the Harrelson thing, and retire for a few years. If it's what Larry thinks it is—five million, all cash—we should be able to do that. I could go to Omaha or Sioux City with my cut, a million and a half, and live there for eight to ten years in style."

"I'll believe the five million figure when I see it. But I sure as hell ain't going to Sioux City," Deese said. "I agree that we should split up. I need to get somewhere out of the way and lay low for a long time, like maybe forever. If I get picked up by anybody and they pull my prints, I'm dead."

"You gonna need money to do that," Beauchamps said. "Cole and I can go talk to Larry right now, tonight, and see if Harrelson and his old lady have gotten home."

"Gonna be dangerous, Harrelson is. The guy will be tough, he's gonna have guns, probably a heavy-duty security system," Deese said. He decided he'd call Santos again that night, maybe come down to eight hundred thousand. That'd have to be his minimum.

DEESE WAS SITTING on a couch in a T-shirt and a pair of Jockey boxer shorts, wrapping a new bandage around his calf. Ten months earlier, he'd been hurt by a man named Howell Paine, but inefficiently, he admitted: there'd been a fight, and Paine had bitten a chunk of meat out of his calf. That had led to his arrest and the chain of events that had led to his secret graveyard and the cannibalized bodies.

Though the wound was almost a year old, Deese had self-treated it and it had never properly healed. Instead of a skin-covered scar, he had a gnarled reddish-and-bluish lump of flesh that had become infected two or three different times.

He'd continued to self-treat the wound. A few days after they moved into the house, he'd gone out to the hot tub, where he'd scraped the wound open again on a drain cover. A pocket of pus had drained down his leg, and Beauchamps had told him he needed to go to the emergency room. Deese had resisted, but the wound had smelled bad enough that he'd eventually given in.

The wound had been opened and cleaned by an on-call surgeon at the medical center and he'd put Deese on antibiotics and told him to change the bandage daily until the new surgical wound had healed.

"We can handle Harrelson," Beauchamps told him.

"That's what we do," Cole added. "But first things first. We gotta get rid of all our phones. Now. Tonight."

---

THEY GOT RID of the phones.

Deese wanted to break them up with a hammer, but Cole argued against it. Instead, he and Beauchamps took them to a tough neighborhood beneath the Stratosphere Tower and left them on a concrete-block wall, from where he'd expect them to disappear in a minute or so.

"Better to have them walk around than to suddenly go quiet. That could pull the feds off our asses, at least for a few days," he told the others.

They agreed. "But then what?" Cox asked.

"Then we go talk to Larry about Harrelson," Beauchamps said.

"And we get a whole bunch of new phones," Cole added

LARRY O'CONNER was a short man with dull-brown hair, a skimpy brown mustache, and a serious potbelly. He dressed in double knits from head to toe because they didn't need ironing. He and Beauchamps had met years before at an Alcoholics Anonymous meeting in New Orleans. They'd both been sent to AA after convictions on minor burglary charges as part of court deals to avoid serving time. They'd both realized that neither of them was likely to stop drinking or go straight.

O'Conner had migrated to Las Vegas, where he made a living betting on sports and horse racing but had barely been getting by. Beauchamps had used him to connect with Las Vegas fences and had given him a small cut of the money that came out of those deals. That had led to O'Conner spotting Jim Harrelson, a golf hustler and poker player.

HARRELSON WAS good at gambling, much better than O'Conner. So good, he wasn't really gambling. He had a golf partner who everybody called Dopey, who carried a 9 golf handicap and could play six strokes better than that when he had to. Dopey, like O'Conner, was a drinker, and one night in a bar had bragged to O'Conner that Harrelson kept five million in cash on hand for his high-stakes poker games with LA whales and for his golf.

"The buy-in for some of those poker games can be a quarter million just to sit at the table," Dopey said.

And he and Harrelson had once taken more than a million dollars off two Phoenix financial guys who thought they were scratch golfers, Dopey told O'Conner, but they'd failed to prove it over a dozen rounds. All the bets were in cash, and Harrelson had fronted the money for their side of the bets.

"He took a banker's box of hundred-dollar bills out of the trunk of his car like it was chump change," Dopey said. "You know how much he keeps around? Five million. **All the time.** Said he wouldn't want to be caught short."

O'Conner filed the information away for possible later use.

Later had arrived.

THE MORNING AFTER they'd ditched the phones, and with new burners in hand, Beauchamps and Cole found O'Conner in a motel downtown. He'd been drinking for several days but wasn't too drunk to drive, he said. The night before, he'd gone to Tina's Wayside and had seen Harrelson's custom-yellow Porsche Cayenne in the parking lot.

"They're back. When he's here, he usually goes over to Tina's at night to hang out and figure out who's in town, where the big game is. His wife doesn't go with him, it's business," O'Conner said. "He usually heads back home by ten o'clock or so, especially in the summer. If you're gonna play golf in the summer in Vegas, you've got to be out there by six or you'll die."

Harrelson lived in an upscale neighborhood south of the airport, O'Conner said. That was also different than the situation in LA. In Beverly Hills, the houses were gated but not the streets. In Vegas, the streets were gated but not the houses—and, in Harrelson's case, the gates had guards instead of electronic remotes. But there was a simple way around it if Harrelson went home after dark.

His house backed up to a street that was outside the walls. And the walls were only chest-high and easily climbable. They could follow Harrelson home, and when he went on to the nearest gate Cox could drop them behind his house. They'd cross the wall and wait for Harrelson to pull into his garage and take him there.

If whatever they took from the house was too large to carry, they could always use one of Harrelson's cars to get themselves back out of the complex. The gates on the outbound lane opened automatically as a car approached.

WHEN THEY left O'Conner, Beauchamps asked Cole, "Tell me the truth: what do you think?"

"What I think is, these marshals are all over us. It makes me nervous that I'm not already on my way out of town. **Way** out of town. But—"

"You need the money after losing your stash in LA. And my idiot brother, the cannibal, is already hinting that he might need a loan. Geenie . . . Geenie doesn't have anything and never has."

"Cocaine," Cole said. "Blow and hookers and casinos. They'll get you every time."

"Not hookers. Dancers. But a lot of them," Beauchamps admitted. "And the blow. But what are we going to do? None of us could work a straight job. Maybe Geenie could get a sales clerk job, but she wouldn't."

"If we're going to hit Harrelson, I say we go tonight," Cole said. "We know he keeps a bundle on hand. Even if we don't get the five mil, we could get enough that we could all run somewhere else. We need to fly."

"I wish we had more time for the research."

"This isn't LA, where we had to do the research, checking out his old lady and all that. We already know who we're targeting and where he lives," Cole said. "We don't need any gate codes. We cross the wall, put a gun in his face, and take the cash. End of story."

"Aw, God." Beauchamps rubbed his forehead, up and down, then started the Cadillac and said, "You're right. Let's talk to Deese. See if Geenie thinks she can handle the driving and the timing again. I hate to be in a hurry. I hate it. But with the marshals here . . . As far as we know, every cop in town has our pictures."

THE TWO Airbnb houses were a mile apart. They'd wanted two houses here for the same reason they'd had two in LA: if the cops found the one, the other could fast become a refuge. They'd hoped to get two closer together, but the ones they got were the ones the Airbnb lady could get in a hurry and they hadn't wanted to do any house hunting personally. Even at a mile apart, in a suburb without traffic lights, they could drive between the houses in two minutes or walk it in fifteen.

When Cole and Beauchamps got back, they found Deese watching a cable TV hunting channel while Cox was sitting on a couch, pouting, as she flipped through a copy of **Women's Health**. She was using a butcher knife as a bookmark. Beauchamps asked, "What's wrong with you?"

"Your fuckin' brother, is what's wrong with me. What an asshole," she said, standing up and pointing the knife at Deese.

"What'd he do?" Cole asked.

"The usual. Trying to fuck me behind Marion's back," Cox said. She'd started calling Beauchamps Marion because the TV news stories about the gang usually referred to him as Martin. "He said he'd give me fifty dollars, for Christ's sakes. Fifty dollars?"

"Shut up, you fuckin' whore," Deese said, not bothering to turn his head away from the TV.

Cox, with her fists on her hips: "See?"

Beauchamps said to Deese, "I told you: keep your hands off her, goddamnit." To Cole, he said, "You're right. I don't see this working long-term. We go tonight, we split the money, we get out of here."

"I'm not going with the asshole," Cox said. "If you're going with him, I'll ride with Cole."

"She's fuckin' Cole," Deese said, still not looking away from the TV.

"Oh, horseshit," Cole said at the same time Cox said, "I am **not**," and Cole said, to Deese, "We had a pretty goddamn solid thing going until you showed up. We all got along."

Now Deese turned to the others and said, "What's this about tonight? Going?"

"We're hitting Harrelson," Beauchamps said. "We need to tool up and cruise the place. And we need to have our shit together when we do it."

"My shit's always together," Deese said. "But this is sorta sudden, huh?"

"We got marshals all over us," Cole said. "We need to get out."

Deese nodded. "Okay."

THEY CRUISED Harrelson's place in separate cars. Cox would be the driver that night and she wouldn't go with Deese. Cole and Deese were snarling at each other because Deese insisted that Cox was sleeping with both Beauchamps and Cole. So Deese and Beauchamps went together, Cox and Cole went in the Cadillac.

On the way to Harrelson's, Deese said, "When we're done with this, we get rid of Geenie. You know goddamn well she's fuckin' Cole. And she's also the weak link. I'll do it. Take her up north of here, dump her in the desert."

"I don't want to think about it. And so what if she's the weak link? We could drop her off at a shoe store and not pick her up. Don't tell her where we're going. The cops know our names anyway, so what's she gonna tell them?"

"You're not pissed because she's fuckin' Cole?"

"I'm not sure that she is. I don't like the idea of killing her. I'm not a killer. And she's a nice girl."

"She's a whore, Marion."

"No she's not. If she was a whore, she'd be fuckin' you if you'd offered her a reasonable amount of money, which you didn't. And if she was a whore, she'd have given you a price, which she didn't. Now shut up and drive."

"WHAT I'M most worried about is," Cole told Cox, "that the brothers will decide they don't need us. That fuckin' Deese likes killing people, it's what he does. You read the stories."

"He stinks," Cox said. "You ever smell his breath? It's like it got bad from eating all those dead people. Smells like he's got a dead mouse in his mouth."

"I don't care about his breath," Cole said. "I care about what happens next . . . Say this Harrelson story turns out to be true. He's got five million dollars in his house and we get it. If we split it four ways, we'll each get a million two fifty. But they get rid of us, they'd both get twice as much, two and a half mil each."

"I'm pretty sure I'm not down for a share," Cox said. "Or, at best, not a full share."

"Okay. Say they give you nothin'—"

"That ain't fair!"

"You're right. But say they give you nothin'. We cut it three ways and we'd each get"—he had to do the numbers in his head—"something like a million six five. That's still a lot less for the brothers than if they only split it two ways."

"You think they're planning that? To get rid of us?" Cox asked.

"I don't know. Finding out that they are, when Deese is standing there with a gun in his hand, then it'd be too late."

They drove on for a while, Cox finally saying, "I really want this money. If I don't get some money, I got nothing."

"Well, I want the money, too," Cole said.

Another minute, then Cox said, "Joan . . . the woman who fixed us up with the houses . . ."

"Yeah?"

"She makes all these real estate calls. She goes out to these houses with strange men. Alone. She carries a gun. I saw it, it's small, but she said it's powerful. She went to a concealed carry school and she liked it. She told me she's got four guns now and she goes out to a shooting range. She's even got two color-coordinated ones, blue and red. I'm wondering . . . maybe I could borrow one?"

"You know how to shoot?" Cole asked.

"Sure. I've gone shooting with Marion. It's not rocket science."

"It's not how to work the gun that's the problem. It's killing somebody that's the problem. We had rifles and shotguns on the farms, but the only pistol was this old rusty revolver, a .22. I take a 9mm into the houses with me, but I never have a round in the chamber because I don't want to have an accident," Cole said. "Maybe . . . Maybe when you start talking about guns, it's time to leave. Without the guns. Get in the car and drive away. We could take this car, go together. We could figure out another way to get some money."

"Like what?"

He shook his head. "I don't know. This robbery thing, this house thing, is the best gig I've ever had."

COX THOUGHT about that for a moment, then said, "I want enough that I can go back to LA and live like a star for a few years. That's all."

"The cops got your prints."

She shrugged. "So, they pick me up, I tell them everything I know about the three of you, which isn't anything they don't already know, and I tell them I was fuckin' Marion for money. That I didn't know you guys were crooks. That we ran out of the house in Altadena and you dropped me off in Pasadena, and that was that."

Cole, who was biting his thumbnail, nodded. "Could work. I'd be a little pissed if you hung a lot of it on me. But if you hang it on Marion and Deese, I'll be okay with it."

"I can do that," Cox said. "Hey! Harrelson's place is coming up."

THEY ALL CRUISED Harrelson's place, which was tucked behind tan adobe walls and a gate. Cole had asked Larry O'Conner how he'd managed to get inside, to cruise the house, and O'Conner admitted that he hadn't. What he'd done was, he'd gotten Harrelson's address and then spotted the house on a Google satellite image.

O'Conner had called up a map on his laptop, then the satellite image, and they considered the neighborhood of upscale houses, almost all with pools, only one or two without. Almost all the houses had multiple pitched roofs covered with red tile. Though large, houses were still crowded together, only a few arm's lengths between them, separated by thin screens of foliage.

Harrelson's house backed up to the exterior wall of the subdivision. A pool was set just inside the wall, so they couldn't cross in the middle of the lot, they'd have to cross between his house and the next one to the right. There was scrubby brush growing along the outside of the wall, so they'd have some concealment after Cox dropped them off.

"We could be seen from either house, so in and out fast as we can," Beauchamps said. "I don't know if they have armed security in there, but they could have."

"We'll have guns," Deese said.

"Yeah, but we don't use them unless it's to save our lives. Damnit, we need more time. If those marshals weren't here . . ."

WHEN THEY got back to the house where Beauchamps and Cox were staying, they agreed that they'd have to make some changes in the usual routine. If they even suspected that they'd been seen crossing the wall or in the yard, Cox had to be hovering nearby to make an instant pickup. If they got caught inside the wall, running would be virtually impossible—if they ran, Cox wouldn't know where to get them, and the place would be crawling with security and cops within minutes.

"If we spot Harrelson's car at the bar, after dark, we gotta go straight back to his place. We cross the wall and we hide there. In the brush. Geenie goes back to the bar and calls us when he's leaving," Cole said. "That way, we don't have to follow him back, there's no chance he could spot us."

"You know, if we're hiding in the yard and

Harrelson's old lady should come outside to the pool, we could grab her then and start taking the house apart. Maybe we wouldn't even have to go up against Harrelson himself," Beauchamps said.

"Larry said Harrelson carried money in his car," Deese said. "We'd miss out on that."

"Well, if we have a chance to grab her, I'd say we do it," Cole said. "Then depending on what the take is, we either get out of there or we wait until Harrelson gets back. We don't make the decision until we see what's what."

Deese: "What the man said."

Beauchamps nodded. "Sounds logical to me. That bar's got a big parking lot, Geenie could pull in there and sit for as long as she needs to."

That, they decided, was what they'd do.

AND IT WORKED perfectly, up to a point. They started cruising Tina's Wayside at nine o'clock, and Harrelson's yellow Porsche Cayenne was already there. "Can't be two of those," Beauchamps said. The Porsche was painted the precise tint of a Yellow Cab.

They headed back to Harrelson's house. The perimeter road didn't have much traffic after dark. They waited until there was a gap, then Cox pulled behind Harrelson's house. The three men, all dressed in dark clothing and wearing driving gloves, scrambled out and squatted behind a screen of eucalyptus trees. They carried with them a black backpack with guns in it, duct tape, ski masks, Geenie's book-marking butcher knife, a fifteen-foot chain with four padlocks, and three flashlights. They wouldn't need the battering ram because they wouldn't be knocking down a door.

They waited in the trees for five minutes, and then, during another carless interval, they crossed the five-foot wall. They landed in more generic landscaped brush on the far side of the wall, waited there for an alarm, a motion light to go on, a dog's bark, a questioning voice, and, when there was nothing, made their way slowly between the houses, with Harrelson's to the left. There were lights on in the house, but Harrelson's wife was apparently deep inside and they never saw her or even a shadow behind a curtain. They stopped behind a clump of decorative grasses next to Harrelson's garage door. Beauchamps opened the pack and passed out the ski masks and the guns and zipped the case back up.

O'Conner had told them that Harrelson usually had an early golf game in the summer and wouldn't linger at Tina's. He was correct.

Beauchamps's phone buzzed at nine forty-five. Cox was on the other end, and she said, "He's on his way. He'll be there in five or six minutes, if he doesn't stop."

"Stay way back behind him, don't try to get close," Beauchamps told her.

"I know, I know," she said. "I'm not dumb."

---

FIVE MINUTES LATER, she called again. "He's turning in at the gate. He's only a minute away."

Cole said to Deese and Beauchamps, "Get ready, he's here."

Beauchamps: "I'll lead. Clayton, you follow. Cole, you know the routine: you watch behind us, me'n Clayton will take him."

"But easy," Cole said, for Deese's benefit.

"LIGHTS," Beauchamps muttered. "Here he comes."

They saw the Cayenne pass under a streetlight. The yellow finish was unmistakable. The car slowed, and Beauchamps said, "Ready?"

Then Cole asked, "What the fuck is this?"

They watched, dumbfounded, as the garage door of the house across the street went up. The Cayenne pulled in and the door started down again. No chance they could get there in time to confront Harrelson.

"That fuckin' O'Conner got the address wrong," Deese said. "I'm gonna cut his fuckin' nose off."

"Not fuckin' O'Conner, fuckin' Google," Cole whispered. "I saw the map and they marked this house. You gonna cut Google's nose off?"

"We gotta get out of here," Beauchamps said. "Jesus H. Christ. We gotta get out of here."

---

THEY GOT BACK to the house without incident, fuming but sometimes laughing about it. Deese had thought it over and finally told Beauchamps that he was dealing with Roger Smith on a possible payoff that would see him out of the country.

"I'm telling you but not them other ones. If I get the cash, I'll give you enough to get you anywhere you need to go and get set up again."

Beauchamps shook his head. "Cole is my friend. I'll take you up on the offer, but I'm going to tell him it might be coming."

"Well, shit . . ."

Beauchamps said, "Clayton, something you never learned—being a killer instead of a robber—that to be successful, you sometimes have to trust people. I trust Cole."

Beauchamps told Cole and Cox about the possibility of getting money from Smith and that they'd get a cut, if only a small one, and Cole bobbed his head, said, "Terrific," and Cox said to Deese, "That's nice of you," the insincerity clear in her voice.

Later that night, when they were all in their separate rooms, Deese got a call on his burner. Roger Smith. He spoke low, and pool balls clicking in the background told Deese exactly where Smith was. Deese rarely yearned for anything other than money, cocaine, and sex, but he was suddenly overcome with yearning to be back in his old haunts in Louisiana, the green-baize pool tables, the smell of chalk, the squeak when twisting it on the tip of a cue. He pushed the yearning away, and asked, "You get my message?"

"Yes. I'm gonna do this, but I want to make a point plain. It's a lot of money. If you take it and don't hold up your end of the bargain, to leave the country, I'll find the best talent I can and hire them to kill you. You understand?"

"Man . . ."

"You understand?"

"Yeah, yeah."

"Don't be bullshitting me, **bon ami**," Smith said. "New Orleans is now off-limits for you. If you get the idea in your head of coming back here to put me down, you won't get two feet inside the city before I know it. We won't set no dumbass Lugnuts on you. So take the money and run and have a happy life."

# CHAPTER TWELVE

As the Gang of Four was doing reconnaissance and making the aborted run at Harrelson, Lucas, Bob, and Rae were pulling together what they'd learned in Las Vegas.

They'd planned to start the day by checking local hospitals for anyone who'd paid cash for a leg injury before the robbery at the Wrights' place; Bob and Rae would do that. Lucas would get together with Las Vegas's Sergeant Mallow to interview local fences about the missing jewelry.

"Here in Las Vegas, they've probably got a Yellow Pages listing," Rae said. They were sitting in the hotel's café, eating pancakes.

"When was the last time you saw the Yellow Pages?" Bob asked.

"This place is so wired up. It's like methamphetamine lighting. Makes me jittery. Gotta be more neon here than anywhere in the world," Rae said. “At night, the whole street out there looks like a slot machine.”

“Not by accident,” Bob said.

“You know what I’ve noticed?” Lucas asked. “Everybody looks so normal. You expect these hard-faced women and burnt-out guys and sleazy gamblers. But when you look around, it’s like every state in the U.S. sent a couple thousand residents here, dressed like they dress back home. Not even like the airport, where people dress up a little bit. They’re all dressed exactly like they do in Podunk.”

“Except they walk down the main drag here drinking out of martini glasses,” Rae said. “You don’t see that in Podunk.”

AS THEY ATE, they were looking at Bob’s printed-out maps to local emergency rooms when their planning session was temporarily derailed by a call from Earl, the FBI phone guy. He said that the phone they’d been watching had popped up again, and repeatedly, at several locations off West Chicago Avenue.

“I checked it out on a map and it looks like they were walking up and down an alley, like they were going back and forth between a couple of different places,” Earl said.

“Did you check the numbers they were calling?”

“Yeah, but they’re all to other burners. Not a full-time phone among them.”

"Huh. Don't know what that means," Lucas said. "Watch those other phones, too. Something's going on here."

Bob to Lucas: "Me'n Rae could go over there while you hook up with Mallow."

Lucas shook his head. "I want to take a look. Let's all three run over. You can drop me back if we don't see anything promising."

CHICAGO AVENUE turned out to be part of a neighborhood beneath a thousand-foot-tall observation tower that hung overhead like an enormous chess queen. When they turned down the block, Lucas said, "Goddamnit," and Rae said, "Yeah," and Bob said, "Well, now we know for sure that they know we're here."

They all recognized the neighborhood as a place you'd unload your burners if you thought the cops were watching and you hoped to confuse them. "Probably tossed them out the window," Bob said. "Free phones for your local dealers."

And it was not a neighborhood where Deese and the gang would be hanging out.

"Back to the original plan," Lucas said.

Rae: "Groan."

BOB AND RAE would focus on emergency rooms west of I-15, the north-south interstate highway that split the city right up the middle. They did that only because the Wrights thought the getaway car had gone west.

"It's weak, but it's what we've got. Everything we know about them has come from west of I-15," Lucas said.

Lucas would meet Mallow, who had a short list of fences where the Wrights' jewelry might be held.

LUCAS FOUND MALLOW waiting outside a Dunkin' Donuts on the east side of town. Mallow had said he wanted to walk to the first place they'd visit and the donut shop was nearby. He had a bag in one hand and a cup of coffee in the other and was wearing a loose, bright yellow shirt with its tail over his slacks. Lucas got his iPad out of the Volvo, left the car in the parking lot, and walked around to the front of the shop.

"A flatfoot at a donut shop," Lucas said. "You got no self-respect . . . You get an extra?"

"Hey, Cargo shorts and drivin' a Volvo, let's not talk about self-respect," Mallow said, tipping his coffee cup at Lucas's knees. There was a trash can outside the door. As they left, Lucas took the last donut, a double chocolate, and Mallow threw the bag into the can.

"You got me on the Volvo," Lucas said. "Where're we going?"

They were going down the block to a low stucco

building with a red neon sign that said "Alvin's Gems & Jewelry" and a door with an electronic lock. As they walked up, Mallow said, "Ring the doorbell. There's a camera aimed at the door, they know my face. I'm gonna hang back."

Lucas rang the bell and a moment later was buzzed through the door. He held it for Mallow, then led the way down a short hallway to the main room, where a woman was sitting behind the jewelry counter, looking at a television set.

Mallow said, "Miz Alvin. Ray around?"

Mrs. Alvin resembled some of the weeds that overgrew Las Vegas's vacant lots—thin, dry-looking—with yellow-white hair atop a puckered-up face. "Nope. He's up to the ranch."

"Didn't know you had a ranch," Mallow said.

"Did since Ray's dad died. It's north of St. George. He'll be back tomorrow," she said. "What do you want him for?"

"The marshal here wants to show you some pictures," Mallow said.

Lucas called up the photos of Toni Wright's jewelry on the iPad and spun it around to show Alvin. She looked at them carefully, then said to Mallow, "That's way high-end. We wouldn't handle that. Of course if we did, we'd want a good provenance. There's so much fake Loloma out there that you can't sell it if you can't prove where it come from."

Mallow said, "Right," letting the skepticism ride on his voice.

"Don't believe me?" Alvin said. "Look at the stuff we handle." She rapped on the glass top of the jewelry counter. "Most expensive thing in here is five hundred and forty-nine dollars, and we could be talked down. We don't handle no twenty-thousand-dollar Loloma."

"How about that princess necklace?" Mallow asked.

"Shoot. We didn't handle no princess necklace."

"Well, I know you did, and you know I know. You sold it to that Fitch guy up in Denver and he sent it along to Baltimore. What'd you take out of that? Fifty K? Is that where the ranch came from?"

She sneered at him, a rim of ragged teeth showing beneath her thin top lip. "You must not have checked the real estate market lately. You don't buy no Colorado ranch for no fifty K."

It was starting to sound like a lover's quarrel, so Lucas jumped in. "Mrs. Alvin, I'm a U.S. Marshal and I'm trying to track down a killer. That cannibal from Louisiana, you probably heard about him on television?"

She said, "Maybe," which meant yes.

"He's with this bunch who stole the Loloma jewelry," Lucas said. "If it turns out you or your husband handled it, and if you lie about it and we find out we'll put you in prison. We're not talking about thirty days for handling a stolen bracelet. We're talking about being an accessory to murder, which is the same as murder, and that's life in prison."

She twitched, maybe showing a little fear. "I'm telling you, we never saw that stuff. I'd know and we didn't." To Mallow she said, "You know who'd handle it, if anybody did."

Mallow said, "We're going there. We're watching your phones and theirs. If you call them, we'll be back. Like the marshal said, we're talking murder here, Louise."

"I hear ya."

LUCAS FOLLOWED MALLOW to the next stop, five minutes after the first, at a dusty storefront called Loco's Consignment & Furs. "This isn't the place Louise was talking about, that's next," Mallow said. "Thought we might as well stop since we're going right past it. Loco does some light fencing."

Inside, a young woman with close-cropped black hair, black eyeshadow, black lipstick, and black nail polish, with lots of silver rings piercing her earlobes, cheeks, and lips, looked at them and said, "If you're not from New Jersey, you gotta be cops."

"We're cops," Mallow agreed. "Where's Loco?"

"Dead."

"What?"

"He's dead. Funeral was last Saturday. Obit was in the paper."

"Then who are you?" Mallow asked.

"His daughter."

"We're looking for some stolen jewelry . . ."

The woman waved a hand at the store, which was heavy on leather furniture, gilt picture frames, and old but nonetheless high-end women's clothing, and said, "No jewelry. Not that I found anyway. I been in the store only since Monday. I wanna sell this junk and cancel the lease and get back home."

"Where's that?" Mallow asked.

"Oakland. California."

"How did your father die?" Lucas asked.

"In a bar. St. Arnold's Craft Brewery. The bartender told the cops that he was sitting on a barstool, grabbed his chest, and fell off. When he didn't get up, they went around and looked at him, and he might have already been dead. He definitely was dead when they got to the hospital."

OUTSIDE, Lucas put his sunglasses back on and asked Mallow, "Who was Louise talking about?"

"The Eli brothers. I was going to ask her what she thought about them, but she brought them up herself. They're downtown."

Lucas followed, a ten-minute ride. When they'd parked, Mallow pointed down an alley to the back end of another low stucco building with an open garage door instead of a normal entrance. "That's the legal front end of the Eli business. Somewhat legal—most of it fell off a truck somewhere. Walk down there and go in. Be cool. Pick up an item or two. Hang out at the back of the store, in the electronics. There's a black steel door on the left side; it goes into the back room, where the real hot stuff is. The door's always locked. When somebody comes out, grab the handle and yell for me. I'll be right outside. I can't come in, they know me."

LUCAS AMBLED DOWN the alley, walked through the garage door, and found a store with piles of crap and the stink of truck exhaust and diesel. There didn't seem to be any rhyme or reason to the crap. Stacks of slightly crushed rolls of Bounty paper towels were piled next to heaps of car wax bottles, with boxes of peanut bars on top of it all; cartons of nails sat next to a hill of tattered books; bottles of Softsoap sat on top of a couple of battered-looking speakers. The store itself was the size of two double garages, and the merchandise went to the ceiling. The shoppers seemed to be more browsers than people looking for specific items.

Lucas checked through a basket of Levi's premium blue jeans, found that they were all bootcut, let them go. An elderly woman sat by an old-fashioned cash register, chewing on a strip of beef jerky. She asked him, "You finding what you want, hon?"

"I was wondering if you ever get any accordions in here," Lucas said.

"Aw, hell, we had two Hohners in here last week; they both went in an hour. You keep checkin' back, though. We do get them in from time to time. There might be a concertina in the back by those ukes, if you'd be interested in that."

"Let me take a look," Lucas said.

He wandered toward the back, toward the black steel door. A rack of cheap-looking musical instruments sat within a few feet of it. Lucas took down an electric guitar, peered at the brand name on the headstock—ZziZZiX—plucked a string, which flopped instead of vibrating.

He peered down the fretboard, as if gauging its flatness, and heard the lock grind on the steel door. He put the guitar down, stepped to the door, and when it opened an inch he shouted, "Mallow! Now!" and yanked the it open. The man on the other side—skinny, gray-faced, with dark bags under his eyes, and startled—followed the door out into the sales area.

Mallow was coming fast for a man with a build like a bowling ball, and he jammed past the gray-faced man and yelled over his shoulder, "Shut the door!"

Lucas stepped inside and pulled the door closed and hurried after Mallow into a brightly lit room lined with built-in metal filing cabinets and with a couple of tables, a half dozen chairs, and an oversized television looming down from a wall. Four bulky men were standing around one of the tables, looking at something Lucas couldn't see.

Mallow spread his arms, his pistol in one hand, and cried out, "Hi, guys! What do we got going here?"

One of the bulky men shouted, "Fuck!" grabbed a plastic Office Depot bag off the table, and ran at Mallow and stiff-armed him. Mallow went down, and two of the other men jumped over the supine cop, the three of them then heading for the alley door. Lucas swung at the lead man, who put the plastic bag up to take the blow, and what looked like candy exploded from it. The man hit Lucas with his shoulder and Lucas went down and smacked his head on the concrete floor. One of the men stepped on his arm and Lucas hooked him by the pant leg, but the man pulled free. And Lucas could hear Mallow shouting for them. And then . . .

And then they were gone.

Mallow was on his knees, a drip of blood running out of his nose, and he croaked, "You okay?"

"Whacked my head," Lucas said. He got to his knees and almost toppled over, and Mallow came over and helped him get to his feet.

"You don't look so hot," Mallow said. He turned to check the fourth man, the one who hadn't run but who was now edging toward the exit. "Hey now, Tommy, stay put," he said. He pointed at a chair. "Sit." The man sat.

Lucas knelt down again, and Mallow asked, "You want me to call the meat wagon?"

"Nah, I'm looking for . . ." Lucas was patting the floor and came up with one of the candies that had exploded from the bag. Except that it wasn't a candy; it was a pill.

He stood up and tipped the pill into Mallow's hand. "OxyContin. Pure Purdue Poison."

Mallow turned to the man in the chair. "Tommy, what is this shit? Dope? What the fuck are you doing?"

"I'd already told them to take off when you busted in," the man said. "We don't deal no dope."

Mallow looked at all the pills scattered on the floor. "You're gonna have to tell it to the narcs, my friend." To Lucas he said, "Keep an eye on him. I gotta make a couple of phone calls. Don't fight him. If he tries to run, go ahead and shoot the motherfucker."

The man on the chair said, "Bart, goddamnit, you know me."

"I thought I did," Mallow said. There was a compact bathroom with a toilet, and a sink off to one side. Mallow stepped in, pulled a handful of toilet paper off the roll, wetted it in the sink, and wiped the blood off his face. After checking himself in the mirror, he walked down the hall to the back door and started talking into his phone.

They waited some more, not talking much, watching Eli squirm.

Fifteen minutes later, two narcs walked through the black steel door. Mallow pointed out the pills. The narcs checked one, and then the older of the two said to the man in the chair, "We're gonna need a lot of information from you, Tommy. You know, to keep you outta Ely. We wouldn't want to send a couple of Elis to Ely."

Ely was the state prison.

While the narcs were talking to Tommy Eli, Mallow pulled Lucas back into the hallway. "I've got a search warrant coming. Should be here in a few minutes," he said quietly. He tipped his head toward the metal filing cabinets. "If they bought that Indian jewelry, it'll be in one of those drawers."

"Okay. I think I'll sit down for a while," Lucas said.

"You're still looking shaky," Mallow said.

Lucas shrugged. "I'm all right . . . Maybe not ready to take on a couple of linebackers."

"Knocked both of us right on our asses," Mallow said.

"Got blood on your shirt," Lucas said.

Mallow looked down at the front of his bright yellow guayabera shirt. "Ain't that the way?"

WHILE LUCAS AND MALLOW waited for the search warrant, Bob and Rae had fought through three separate hospital bureaucracies and had come up empty. One the fourth try, at a northside medical center's emergency room, they asked the duty nurse if she knew of a man who'd been treated for a leg injury and who'd paid for the treatment with a stack of bills.

Instead of shaking her head and referring them to somebody else, her eyes narrowed and she said, "I'm not supposed to talk about **that**. You'll have to talk to one of the people in the director's office."

She made a phone call and pointed them at the elevators.

Bob said to Rae, "She said **that** like it was in italics."

"I noticed."

A tall carefully coiffed woman in the director's office looked at their IDs and then said, "We're not allowed to give out specific patient information without a subpoena. I'm sure you know that. I can confirm that we did treat a man about six weeks ago with a serious leg infection who refused to give us identification and paid us in cash. He said he didn't have any insurance, and the bill was substantial. Substantial enough that the cash payment was . . . extremely unusual."

"Can you tell me what kind of injury it was?" Rae asked.

"Yes. He had a large defect in his calf. The actual injury happened some time back, probably months ago, and apparently had been self-treated. A cyst developed under the wound. Our surgeon had to open the healed wound to drain the cyst.

And that's about as much as I can tell you without the subpoena."

"Can you tell us if the patient was given any medication that required a prescription?" Bob asked.

"Yes. He was given prescriptions for pain pills and also for antibiotics."

She wouldn't answer any other questions until Rae asked, "Can you answer a question about non-patients?"

The woman frowned. "Like what?"

"Was he accompanied by anyone?"

"I believe he was accompanied by a woman, perhaps his wife or girlfriend. One of our security guards reported that she brought him to the emergency room in a Cadillac."

"Do you do video of the cars at the emergency room?" Bob asked.

"Yes, we do. We archive the tapes after thirty days unless there's an inquiry during that time."

"So you wouldn't have the video anymore?"

"We do not," the woman said.

Bob said, "We'll be back with the subpoena."

The woman nodded. "We're always happy to cooperate with the authorities, but according to law we have to do the correct paperwork. It can be a pain, but it's the law."

When Bob and Rae stood to leave, the woman asked, "Can you tell me who the man is? The injured man?"

Rae said, "You heard about the Louisiana cannibal?"

"Oh . . . no . . ."

WHEN THE SEARCH WARRANT arrived at the Eli brothers' shop, delivered by two robbery cops, Mallow handed it to Tommy Eli, who frowned and said, "I gotta talk to my attorney about this."

"Talk to him all you want," Mallow said. "In the meantime, we're gonna search the place."

The cabinets along the wall, which looked like the ordinary filing type, were essentially keyed safes. Mallow asked Eli for a key, but Eli shook his head. "Bobby must have it. I don't know when he'll be back."

"Are those cabinets expensive?" Lucas asked.

"The best," Eli said.

"Too bad," Lucas said. To one of the robbery cops: "You got a pickax or a sledgehammer?"

"Yup. We also got a guy with the Jaws of Life. All we need to do is beat in the front of the drawer to bend them so we can get the jaws in the crack and then we can rip them right open, like ripping a door off a car. I'll go call him."

As he headed for the door, Eli called out, "Wait. I remembered. There might be a spare key."

———

THERE WAS a lot of jewelry. Lucas was no expert, but most of it looked like junk. Much of it was older, like nineteenth-century, with semiprecious moonstones or onyx and probably eight-karat gold. There was one flat-out safe, in which they found fifty-one thousand dollars and several hundred euros. In the velvet-lined bottom drawer of the eighth cabinet, they found five pieces of Charles Loloma jewelry that matched the photos given to them by the Wrights.

Eli said that the jewelry had been brought in by two men. He'd seen one of them before, a big guy who said his name was Richard. The other guy didn't mention a name, but was, Eli said, "An evil-looking fuck."

They were pushing him on it when one of the cops said, "There's another drawer."

He'd pulled the drawer out, which was shallower than the others, and then reached back into its cavity, where he found another handle. He pulled it, and in a second compartment were nine pistols, ranging from a piece of crap .32 to a .50 caliber Desert Eagle.

Mallow went off on Eli again and was still hassling him about selling guns illegally when a cop brought Bobby Eli into the room. Eli asked, "What the fuck?"

"That's what the marshal and I were saying," Mallow said to him. "What the fuck? We look in one drawer and we find guns, and we look in another and we find a buttload of jewelry stolen by the Louisiana cannibal. I never would have believed you guys would have joined up with an animal like that. I thought you were the friendly neighborhood fences. And then we've got OxyContin all over the goddamn place . . ."

"Wait a minute," Tommy Eli said. "The fuckin' cannibal?"

THE ELIS HAD two things relevant to the Gang of Four. The first was a scrap of lined yellow paper, ripped from a legal pad, with a license number scrawled on the back. While Tommy was paying the two guys who'd brought in the Loloma, Bobby had run around the block to watch them leave. He followed them to a Dodge Challenger with Oregon license tags. Bobby had written down the number, should it ever be needed.

Mallow called the number in to his office and was told that they'd get back to him as soon as they could.

The second was that in the negotiations for the Loloma jewelry, "Richard" had mentioned he hadn't gotten much sleep the night before because of the fuckin' planes taking off.

The Elis had written down the date that the Loloma had come in, and Mallow called somebody at the Las Vegas sheriff's office and asked them to call somebody at the Federal Aviation Administration to find out which way the planes had been taking off the night before they'd brought in the jewelry.

The narcs eventually took the Elis off to jail, though the brothers protested that they were victims, not perpetrators. The burglary guys were working through the office space inch by inch. They'd already solved a couple of burglaries and were hoping to solve more.

"That OxyContin was the biggest break we ever had back here," Mallow told Lucas. "We never had a way to get inside before. I'm a happy guy. Thank you."

"I'll be happy if you can help me get to Deese," Lucas said. "The rest of them are all yours."

LUCAS WAS STILL at the Eli brothers' office when Bob and Rae called about what they'd found at the medical center. "We got a subpoena on the way. We ought to know about the prescriptions and where they were filled inside the hour."

And as they were talking about that, Mallow waved at him and then called, "Got the car. It's a Hertz and it's already been returned. Hertz has video, and they'll give it to us, but they want some paper to cover their asses."

Lucas asked to Rae, "Who'd you talk to about the subpoena?"

"An assistant in the U.S. Attorney's Office. You need one?"

"Yeah. We need to talk to Hertz."

MALLOW DIDN'T WANT to go talk to Hertz because the Eli search was producing too much good material. Lucas talked to the assistant at the U.S. Attorney's, stopped at the federal building and got the subpoena from a pretty young woman who said, "We know about you. You're world-famous in the Justice Department."

Lucas said, "Right," but he liked pretty women and stayed to chat with her for a minute before he went on his way.

Lucas followed his iPhone GPS map to the Hertz office, which was in a car rental center south of the airport. The manager looked at the subpoena and then led the way into a back room, where he called up the video of the car rental. The renters were two men, one big and the other smaller, both wearing ball caps that obscured their faces.

At the end of the rental transaction, as the two were walking out to the car, one of the men half turned, and Lucas could see the side of his face. The manager hit a button and froze the image. "Oh, yeah," Lucas said. "Marion Beauchamps. That'll look good on the nightly news."

He also looked at the paperwork on the rental.

He'd never heard of the renter's name, Harold Weeks, but it was Beauchamps for sure.

"The license is valid and so was the Visa card he used," the manager said. He'd printed out all the rental information and gave a copy of it to Lucas.

Outside again, Lucas called Russell Forte in Washington and asked him to chase down the driver's license number and the Visa card.

Mallow called, said somebody in his office had talked to the FBI and the FBI had called the traffic controllers at the airport tower. The night before the gang had sold the Loloma jewelry, the planes had been taking off to the west. "There's one main east-west runway. There's a mix of residential housing out there under the flight path—apartments, town houses, single family homes. They'll be in there somewhere."

"We're getting close," Lucas told him. "We may want to work something out with your SWAT squad. These guys are hard-core."

"I'll talk to the sheriff," Mallow said.

RAE CALLED. All prescriptions were computerized and those issued by the hospital had been filled at a Walmart pharmacy. "Does that help?"

Lucas spotted the Walmart on his iPad: it was located off a stretch of the Beltway due west of the airport's east-west runway. "Yes. Everything points to the same neighborhood," Lucas said. "We need to get back to the hotel and figure out what to do next. I was planning to go to the TV stations and put Beauchamps's face on the news, but, now that I think about it, that might not be a good idea. If they run, we'd just have to track them again, but for now we sort of know where they are."

"See you at the hotel," Rae said.

Lucas had worked his way out to Paradise Road, on his way back to the hotel, when Sandro Tremanty called from New Orleans. "Hey, Dad."

"What's up?"

"I heard you're in Las Vegas," the FBI agent said.

"Yeah. We've followed them this far, crossed their trail a couple of times. We're starting to pin them down. Can't promise anything."

"You remember Dick? Ricardo Santos, the guy you met at Rog Smith's house?"

"The guy with the degree in chemistry," Lucas said.

"That's the guy. We've put a light tag on both Smith and Santos. I found out a few minutes ago that Santos jumped on a cut-rate airline at eight o'clock this morning, going to Vegas. He ought to be arriving there in about an hour."

"Oh-oh. Text me the details. I'm in a car; I just left the Hertz place by the airport. I'll turn around and go back. I'll get Bob and Rae headed this way."

"Do that. I'm trying to find a flight, but everything has a stop somewhere, they're all six hours or more," Tremanty said. "I can't get there until tonight. But if you're close to Deese, I'd like to be there."

"Jump right in," Lucas said.

# CHAPTER THIRTEEN

They had to hurry. Lucas did an illegal U-turn and headed back south, called the Hertz manager, spoke for a moment, got Bob and Rae on the phone. They'd been driving east toward I-15, on the way to the hotel, and were only ten minutes behind him.

"Unless he's got his own car, he'll have to rent one or take a cab," Lucas said, fast. "I was talking to the manager at Hertz. We're like old friends now. I want you to drive right up there like you're returning a car. He's expecting you and he'll turn your car around. Take a shuttle back to the airport; the manager says it only takes a few minutes. I'll talk to the airport cops and keep my car outside. Santos knows me but not you. I'll spot him coming off the plane and then you guys follow him to wherever he's going. If he rents a car, you should be able to jump on a shuttle and follow him right out of the place. If he's got a limo or gets a cab, I'll follow him."

"On the way," Bob said. "We should talk to our SOG guys here in Vegas in case we need them."

"I'll let you and Rae do that, you know them," Lucas said. "But get your asses out to Hertz now."

Lucas drove up the departures ramp at the airport, saw a cop, identified himself, and was pointed to a place where he could park his car. As he was getting out, a supervising cop jogged up to talk to him.

"You think anything will be going down here?" the cop asked.

"No. We're following him out of the airport, trying to see where he goes. For God's sakes, don't put any cops out there," Lucas said. "This is a smart guy, he'll spot them in a second. I've got two people on him, nothing will happen here."

Lucas, escorted by the cop, badged his way through security, located the gate for the incoming plane, which was still a half hour out, and managed to fractionally relax. A blank gray door that said "No Entry" was across the concourse from the gate, and Lucas got the cop to open it. There was nothing behind it but a stairway landing, with stairs going up and down.

"Could you stay with me? I'd like to hide here when he comes through."

"Not a problem," the cop said.

Bob texted from Hertz, said they were set, that the Tahoe was "cocked and locked."

"We're in in Terminal 1, the D gates," Lucas said. "Get down here as soon as you can."

FIFTEEN MINUTES LATER, Lucas and the cop sat waiting at a bank of one-cent slot machines when Bob and Rae walked up. Rae looked at the slots, said, "They won't let you get out of here with a fuckin' penny," and Bob said, "Tell us about it."

Lucas introduced the cop—"This is Judd Harlan"—and pointed across the concourse to the gate. "Santos will be coming out of there. We'll be behind there"—he pointed to the gray door—"and then you follow him. If he meets somebody, or gets a cab or a limo, you gotta let me know. I'll be at my car, I'll track him, and you can get back to the Tahoe and follow me. If he goes to Hertz, you drop in behind him and call me and I'll follow you."

Rae said to Harlan, "We'll need another one of your guys. We'll need him to stay way, way behind us, but if somebody meets him and he doesn't go for a rental or a cab we'll need you to run us through the airport to the parking structure, which we don't know about. We don't want somebody shooting at us because we're running."

"You got it," Harlan said, and he went off with his handset to call for a backup cop.

While he did that, Bob said to Lucas, "We talked to the head guy on the local SOG and they can gear up in an hour. You gotta tell me when."

The SOG was the marshals service Special Operations Group, a heavy-duty SWAT squad.

"We'll wait until we see where Santos is going," Lucas said. "If he heads out west on I-15, we'll want to get them ready."

"You think this too easy?" Rae asked. "Bob always worries about that."

"Maybe, but we're not there yet," Lucas said. "We thought it was too easy in LA until I got my ass shot."

"Santos is a complication," Bob said. "We don't know exactly what he's doing here . . . if he's doing anything. Maybe he came to roll some bones."

Lucas nodded and said to Rae, "By the way, I've got some news for you. Your heartthrob is coming to town. Tremanty. He's on his way right now. Maybe, you know, you'll want to shave your legs."

"Maybe I'll do that," Rae said. "When does he get here?"

"Don't know yet. He's trying to get the fastest flight out, but there aren't any more directs today," Lucas said. "He's gotta go through somewhere else."

Bob had a wide smile. "My, my. Sandro Tremanty, Rae Givens, Las Vegas, Nevada. There's a three-way made in heaven. What happens in Vegas . . ."

"You're such little boys," Rae said. "Shave my legs. Three-way. I mean, Jesus."

THE SECOND COP arrived with Harlan. They all went into the bay with the penny slots to wait. Bob walked through the banks of fake-neon dinging machines, checking them out. Rae started talking to Harlan and, after a bit, took a ten-dollar bill out of her pocket and slipped it into one of the slots. Bob took a chair a few yards away, and Lucas settled in beside him, to watch her lose her money.

After a minute, Lucas said, in a low voice, "I always meant to ask, never did because it's none of my business. You seem amused by the idea of Rae getting involved with Tremanty. I never quite figured out you and Rae."

Bob smiled and shook his head. "There is no 'me and Rae' except as marshals. She's smart, she's pretty, we like each other a lot, but nothing ever happened and nothing will. If I had a sister, she'd be Rae."

"Huh. I mean, does that ever bum you out? Even slightly?"

"No. Man, I like her better than anybody I ever met. But no heat. Not that way. We gossip about our relationships like a couple of old hens, but nope. Sister and brother."

"Okay. Sorry I asked."

"Surprised you didn't ask sooner," Bob said. "Everybody else has. And . . . here she comes."

Rae came over and said, "I didn't even win a penny. They took the whole ten dollars. Didn't win once. Oh, by the way, Santos is on the ground. He'll be here in five minutes."

Lucas took a dollar out of his pocket and said to Rae, "Let me show you how this is done." He slid the dollar into a machine, pushed the button, and won five. He pushed the payout button, took the slip, tucked it in his wallet.

Bob said to Rae, "That's all there is to it."

Rae said, "It's because I'm black, isn't it? Who would have suspected: racist slot machines . . . Hey, there's his plane."

THEY WATCHED as the plane taxied up to the gate and then they followed Harlan onto the stairway landing behind the gray door. Two men and a woman, all in dark business wear, were the first off, followed by Santos, who wore blue slacks and a pale linen sport coat and open-necked French-blue dress shirt. As they watched, he put on a white straw hat and sunglasses. He carried a brown leather backpack and a brown leather overnight bag.

"Guy knows how to dress and accessorize," Lucas said, peeking through the crack between the door and the jamb.

"Watch the hat," Rae whispered to Bob. A minute later, the two of them launched from the stairway landing. Lucas held the arm of the second cop until they were almost down the concourse and out of sight, then pushed him and said, "Follow Bob and Rae, but don't get closer than you are now. Not unless they yell."

Lucas and Harlan went out through a security lane and down to Lucas's car. On the way, Bob called and said, "He's heading for the rentals. You want me to crank up the SOG guys?"

"Not yet, we don't want a false alarm. Stay with him. I'll try to get behind you so we can change up."

BOB CALLED AGAIN when Santos was rolling down the Avis ramp. "Stay on the phone, I'll keep you up on where we are. We rode all the way to the rental place on the same shuttle. We're in the wrong vehicle, though. We're too big and visible, and it sorta looks like a cop car."

"This Volvo doesn't, I'm embarrassed to say."

Bob said, "He's turned north. He's in a dark gray Chrysler 300."

If he were going to the apartment complexes off the airport runway, Lucas thought, he should have turned south. North would lead to the Vegas Strip and downtown.

Bob, a few minutes later: "We've turned west on Hidden Well Road," and, a couple of minutes later: "North again on Las Vegas Boulevard."

Lucas got on Las Vegas Boulevard, spotted Bob and Rae fifty yards ahead, accelerated past them, said into the phone, "I got him."

"I'm turning here in case he's watching his mirror," Bob said. "I'll be back behind you in a minute."

Lucas was two cars behind of Santos, stayed with him through several traffic lights, got on the phone to Bob. "I'm afraid to pass him, he knows me. Are you back behind me?"

"Yeah, we're catching up."

"If he rolls through one of these lights on a yellow, I've got a problem. I think you ought to blow on by him. There are lots of Tahoes out here. Get ahead of him in case I get caught at a light."

"Doing that," Bob said.

A minute later, Bob and Rae's Tahoe sped past Lucas, Rae at the wheel. She slowed a bit as they came up behind Santos, then went on by. Bob said, "I'm in the footwell, so all he could have seen is a woman driving a truck."

"All right," Lucas said. "Don't outrun him."

They all got stopped at Harmon Avenue, Santos a half dozen cars behind Bob and Rae, Lucas another half dozen cars behind Santos. They went through Flamingo together, then Bob said, "Shit, he pulled into the valet parking at Caesars. You're on your own, Lucas. We'll be back as soon as we can turn around."

LUCAS DROVE SLOWLY toward the valet stand, stalled a bit despite a valet waving to him, waited until Santos was on the steps going inside, then drove to the valet, grabbed the phone and his bag, hopped out of the car, shoved his ID in the valet's face, and said, "Keep the car close, right out here, I'm working, I'm running, give me the ticket."

The valet passed him the parking stub and Lucas grabbed it and hurried up the steps through the door where Santos had disappeared. He stepped inside and scanned the crowd: there were several straw hats in the lobby, but he didn't see Santos at first, until he glanced toward the concierge desk and saw him talking to the woman behind the desk. She pointed across the lobby, and Lucas turned away and stepped back outside, where he watched through the glass doors as Santos walked across. He wished he had a hat like Santos's, anything that would disguise his appearance since Santos had seen him in New Orleans.

Rae jogged up. "Where is he?"

"Walking across the lobby."

Bob came up. "I dumped the car with the valet, goddamn near killed an old lady doing a U-turn on the boulevard. Where is he?"

Rae had stepped inside, waved them in beside her. "Scc his hat?"

They moved up behind him, the three of them spreading out across the lobby, and then into the gambling area. He was easy to follow through the various craps and roulette tables, but he disappeared into slot machines on the far side of the tables. Some of the machines were seven or eight feet tall, and the pale straw hat vanished amid their crazy flashing lights.

SANTOS WAS WALKING fast through the slots, the three marshals a hundred feet behind him. Gamblers wandered back and forth between the machines while bad rock music pounding down from the ceiling contributed to the sensory overload.

When Santos disappeared, Rae ran after him, the fastest-moving person in the place, lots of eyes tracking her. She got through the first area of slots, then stopped, looked back at Lucas, shook her head.

Lucas hurried into the slots, which were arranged in what amounted to a maze—short aisles leading into blocking banks of more slots—like they didn't want you to get out.

He called to Bob. "See him?"

Bob said, "No, I lost him. Where is he?"

He took a call from Rae. "You got him? Where?"

Then Bob came up. "We lost him. He's gotta be

right here," and Lucas heard him say to Rae on the phone, "Did he go in there?"

"Don't think so . . ."

They'd lost him.

WHEN LUCAS was sure that Santos was gone, he told Bob, "Go back to the valet stand and make sure he doesn't get the car back. Rae, let's find the closest taxi stand. I saw one when we were here the other day."

They looked for half an hour but didn't see him again.

When they got back together, Bob said, "I think I know why they were making those calls from here—it's impossible to track somebody. Too many people moving in too many directions. Santos might never have seen us, but he scraped us off because he knew he could do it and not take a chance that **he** might be tracked."

Lucas said, "That hints he's up to something. That he's here to meet with Deese."

Rae: "We know where his car is. We could stick a GPS tracker on it in case he decided to use it—but we'd need a warrant."

"Why would anyone give us a warrant?" Bob asked. "As far as we know, Santos doesn't even have a criminal record."

Lucas said, "Ahh . . . shit."

---

THEY SPLIT UP AGAIN and wandered around the casino, and eventually into the Forum shopping center, in case Santos turned up again. The Forum was an absurd place, gigantic statues of big-breasted nude Roman women and Greek gods with fountains spraying water over them. Tourists wandered around, taking selfies and eating crap. After a while, it became apparent that they wouldn't find Santos by just wandering. They located the hotel manager, who checked for him in the reservations and failed to find his name.

"Maybe he's like us: he's in this hotel for a reason but checked in somewhere else," Bob said.

"If he's checked in at all," Lucas said. "He comes here, shoots Deese or gives him a bag of money—or whatever he's doing—goes out to the airport and gets on a plane. He might not even need a hotel."

"Doesn't have a gun unless he got one here," Rae said. "Probably doesn't have a bag of money, either. They would have seen that at security and would have asked questions."

"There are ways to handle all of that if you need to: you wire a million bucks to a casino and cash it in here," Bob said. "I mean, maybe not a million, but a lot. After that, a gun is a matter of knowing the right guy. Roger Smith would."

"You almost sound like you know what you're talking about," Rae said.

"I read about it in a book," Bob said. "Books are always accurate."

LUCAS GAVE UP on Santos. He could be anywhere in Las Vegas. "We need to work the streets, out on the end of the airport flight path," he said. "It's gonna be tiresome, but what else can we do?"

"It'll be more than tiresome, it'll be pointless," Rae said. "There's gotta be thousands of houses down there. Are we gonna knock on every door?"

Lucas shook his head. "There aren't thousands of houses. I looked at the satellite photo. Maybe a few hundred under the path, where the airplane noise was loud enough to keep him awake. We know they're probably driving a pickup and an Escalade. So, we go down there and look for people on the street and ask if they've seen newcomers, renters, in a pickup or an Escalade. We have a chance."

"I vote we get something to eat, take a nap, and go out in the evening," Bob said. "There won't be people walking around in the streets when it's 105 degrees outside. We'll see more of them when it cools off a bit."

He was impatient to get going, but it was too hot, so Lucas agreed: they'd eat, go up to their rooms, nap or see if the internet might turn up anything—real estate searches, house rental agencies, meaningful maps—and reconvene in the late afternoon, move out to the streets.

"I hate it that we lost Santos," Lucas said. "Goddamnit, I hate it. He's going to meet Deese. He would have led us right to him."

# CHAPTER FOURTEEN

As Roger Smith's familiar spirit, Santos assumed that he was being watched by the FBI, either through his known cell phone or physically. Or, he thought, there might be a tracker on his car. Trackers were now small enough that it was unlikely that he could find it, considering everything else that was under the hood of a modern car.

When he left for Vegas, he thought the feds could be looking for a rental. He made two reservations, one at Avis and one at the Hertz desk at Caesars, under different names, each with its own credit card number. He'd been to Vegas any number of times and had some ideas about how to scrape off a trail: a fast pass through Caesars slots would shake anyone. He'd wind up at the Hertz desk, which was down a barren hallway, and any tracker would have to show himself, if he'd managed to follow that far.

He wouldn't have to identify himself; Santos could smell a cop.

HE'D PULLED the battery out of his known cell phone on the plane so that couldn't be tracked. He hadn't seen anyone following on the drive in from the airport, but he hadn't expected to, because the feds were better than that.

Fifteen minutes after entering the hotel, he was in the new Hertz car and out on Las Vegas Boulevard. A mile south of Caesars, he pulled into a FedEx store, showed receipts for five boxes being held for him there, got the boxes with a minimum of fuss and carried them out to the car.

When the air conditioner had cooled the interior of the car again, he opened the heaviest of the boxes, which contained five metal foil envelopes that he'd devised himself from thin sheets of copper.

The copper was soft enough that he could unfold the envelopes with his fingers and take out the contents—a slide and barrel, a frame, a trigger assembly with its single pin, and finally the magazine, in the first four—for a 9mm Sig P365, all separately wrapped. He didn't know if FedEx used an X-ray on suspicious packages, checking for contraband, but, if they did, they'd see nothing that looked like a gun. The final envelope, long and thin, contained the screw-on suppressor.

He assembled the gun without the suppressor—that took a minute or so—and shoved it under the front seat. The suppressor, which didn't look like much, went into the back of the glove compartment, where it was barely visible. He didn't have ammo for the gun, but that wasn't a problem in Las Vegas. There was a gun shop three blocks away, and he picked up a box of Federal Premium Hydra-Shok.

The remaining four boxes each contained a hundred and fifty thousand dollars in used hundred-dollar bills, wrapped in crumpled sheets of newspaper so the stacks of currency wouldn't shift around. The bills made two stacks, each a little more than three inches high, which fit nicely, and with plenty of room, in a standard FedEx box. They'd wanted the boxes to be lightweight, because they'd seem less worth stealing; and they'd broken the money into four boxes so, in case of theft, they wouldn't lose it all at once. All four came through fine.

THE DAY BEFORE Santos left New Orleans, he and Smith had gone for a walk in Audubon Park, across the pond from the golf course. The day was humid, but they were used to it, and the bees were out on the flowers and interesting to watch as they went about their work.

As they walked, Smith told Santos he was writing off the money. "It's a lot," he said with a shrug.

"But we can always go out and get more. Anyway, what you do with it is up to you. Give the money to Deese and tell him to get lost and never come back to New Orleans. Or, if you can get away with it, shoot him and keep the money. I don't care one way or the other because, for me, when you walk out the door, the money is gone."

Santos: "Really?"

"Yeah, really," Smith said. He stopped to sniff a rose, frowned, said it didn't smell like anything. "What the fuck kind of rose is that?"

"I'm not a rose connoisseur," Santos said.

Smith nodded, and they moved on, picking up the conversation. "From my point of view, I'd rather you get rid of Deese permanently," Smith said. "He's never going to do me any good, not now, not with all the murders and the fuckin' cannibalism. The feds could use that to turn him. Against me. And you, too, maybe. So, it's either his money to get lost with or your money to make his disappearance permanent."

"I'll think about it," Santos said.

"Think about this, too. He's a killer. You don't want to falter, because if you do, he'll kill you. And even worse, he'll probably try to kill me, and I'd have to jump through my rectum to keep that from happening."

"I'll think about that, too," Santos said.

"Lot to think about," Smith said. They passed another rosebush and, after checking for park cops, Smith reached out and plucked a blossom and twiddled it in his fingers as he walked, every few steps sniffing it. "Now I've got a rose. And it smells like something," he said.

Santos said, "You know what you sound like, don't you?"

"Yeah, I know," Smith said, with a tight, toothless grin. "This business is full of macho assholes. They think you're a fag, they relax. They believe it right up to the time you pull the church key out of your pocket and carve out an eyeball."

They walked on.

"You have to think about Deese's brother," Smith said. "I never really understood that relationship because they are so very different. At the same time, in their own psychopathic way, they seem to care for each other. Maybe because their father repeatedly beat the shit out of them when they were children."

"Shared experience."

"Exactly. Shared trauma," Smith said. "So if you kill Deese, you might have to do something about Beauchamps. That is, if he knew you were responsible for Deese's death."

"Okay. How about the others?"

"Don't care. They don't know about me, so I don't care what happens to them. If they see you kill Deese, if they're witnesses, then **you** might care. But I don't."

"That's all very clear," Santos said.

"You see any problems?"

"Not really. Well, maybe one: Davenport."

"Don't touch him," Smith said. "I don't doubt that you could take him, but the bigger problem is, he's part of a bureaucracy. A bureaucracy never stops. It keeps coming. If it takes years to pull you down, doesn't matter to them, they'll take the time. To them, you're just an active file in a computer and the computer keeps looking. That's why I hate to be crosswise with that fuckin' Tremanty. So far, he's made it a personal mission. If we went after him, though, and knocked him down, the whole FBI would be on our case. And they'd get us, too. Stay away from Davenport. Stay away from Tremanty. Fix our problem however you can, but don't go blowing over any cops, federal or otherwise."

AFTER PICKING UP the box of ammo, Santos continued south on Las Vegas Boulevard, then turned west on Warm Springs Road. A jetliner roared overhead as he made the turn, climbing straight into the hot blue sky to the southwest, on its way to Los Angeles.

He followed the car's navigation system to a neighborhood of dun-colored concrete-block walls and gated housing developments, turned down a street that opened up a bit, with shabbier houses under palm trees that had never been pruned. The nav system brought him to the address that Smith had given him, another dirt-colored house with a tile roof, with a circular drive in front. He drove on past, stopped at the end of the block, took the Sig out from under the car seat, screwed on the suppressor, and shoved it under his belt at the small of his back. He did a U-turn and went back to the house.

The driveway was empty, but when he pulled in and killed the engine he saw the curtain twitch in the window next to the front door. He got carefully out of the car, the gun poking him in the back, and rang the doorbell; a moment later, the door cracked open and a blonde looked out at him.

"What?"

"I'm Santos."

"You're way early," she said. "We didn't think you'd get here until tonight."

"Yeah, well, I got the last seat on a direct flight. So here I am. I feel like a **boudin noir** out here. Are you going to let me in or should I come back later?"

The blonde turned away from the door, and a man's voice said, "Let him in."

Santos reached back under his sport coat, as though tucking in his shirt, and touched the butt of the diminutive pistol. The blonde pulled the door fully open and said, "Come on in," and turned away and let him push the door shut.

The house was compact and poorly furnished—it came with the place, Santos thought, and smelled like carpet cleaner. Beauchamps was standing behind a breakfast bar to his left; the blonde was wandering into the living room to his right. Santos asked, "Where's Clayton?"

"Up in town. He likes them slot machines," Beauchamps said.

"That's crazy," Santos said. "He knows there's three marshals up there looking for him and that probably every cop in Vegas has a picture of his face?"

"Got a beard now, and he stays in the cheap places, goes to dive bars," Beauchamps said. "And, yeah, he's crazy."

The blonde asked, "Did you bring the money?"

"Yes, it's in the trunk of my car," Santos said. "But, it's for Clayton."

She smiled at him. "Don't suppose if we promised to give it to him . . ."

Santos smiled back. "No. That wouldn't be good enough."

Beauchamps asked, "What's this **boudin noir** you were talking about? You don't look like no coonass."

"My parents were Cuban," Santos said. "I've been in New Orleans long enough to dig the food. We Cubans have **moranga**. It's all blood sausage, though I gotta say a real **boudin noir** is better than any **moranga** my old lady ever bought."

"You're making my mouth water," Beauchamps said, flashing a smile. "Listen, you wanna bring the money in, or what?"

"Maybe come back later," Santos said.

"Let me go in the bedroom, get my phone, call Clayton and see where he is, if he can come quick."

"Okay." Santos looked at the blonde and said, "You're a beautiful woman. What's your name?"

"Thank you," she said, with a real smile. "It's Geenie. You're a pretty man yourself."

BEAUCHAMPS TOOK his phone into a bedroom as Santos was laying a shine on Cox. He closed the door, dialed Deese's new burner. When Deese came up, Beauchamps said, "The money is here."

"You got it?"

"No, Santos says it's out in the car."

After a long silence, Deese said, "Listen, I had to think about it when Rog said he'd send the money with Santos. I mean, why Santos? I know how they move money. FedEx lets you call up and tell them to hold your delivery so you can pick it up there. They could have sent it direct to us and we could have picked it up just as easily as Santos."

Beauchamps: "What are you talking about?"

"When Santos went to work for Rog a few years back, I asked around. There are some people who think he does the same thing I do, but he's not so . . . out there," Deese said.

"Not so much of a fuckup," Beauchamps said, to clarify.

"Not so out there," Deese insisted. "Everybody kinda knew who I was. Rog used me to scare people. Nobody knows who Santos is. He's supposedly a smart guy. Went to college. A guy told me that Rog used Santos when he didn't want to scare anybody but somebody needed to be gone. To disappear. There was a guy named Appel, German, and he disappeared, and everybody—everybody—heard he'd gone on to New York. Nobody heard from him after that. He fuckin' vanished."

Beauchamps looked at the bedroom door. "What're you saying?"

"What I'm saying is, you could have a problem. I can be there in twenty minutes, but if I was you I might put a gun in my pocket before I talk to him anymore. In case Santos has decided he'd like to keep the money."

"Ah, shit, man. He doesn't look like a killer, he looks . . . smooth. He looks slick and smooth, like a billiard ball."

"Which is one reason that people don't worry about him. Then, **poof**," Deese said.

"All right."

Beauchamps had a big Beretta in the chest of drawers. Big because it was meant to frighten home invasion victims. He hung up, got the gun, carried it into the bathroom, jacked a 9mm shell into the chamber, made sure the safety was on, flushed the toilet, and went back through the bedroom to the living room.

"He's on his way," he said to Santos. "He won't be too long. I can get you a beer, if you want to wait. Or if you want to go out, find a hotel or something . . ." He went into the kitchen, crab-walking sideways so that Santos wouldn't see the gun, and sat on a stool at the breakfast bar.

Santos cocked his head, looked at Cox and then at Beauchamps, and said, "Guess I'll wait. I'll take that beer."

Santos was thinking that if Deese was actually on the way, with the other man who was with them, it would then be three to one, assuming the blonde wasn't carrying a gun. By acting before then, the odds would be cut; and he suspected that Beauchamps had gotten a gun from the bedroom, the way he'd backed up to the refrigerator to get the beer.

Beauchamps was thinking about what Deese had said and how he himself would behave if he were Santos and there were six hundred thousand dollars on the line. He opened the refrigerator with his left hand and took out a beer while his right hand crept around to his back and grasped the Beretta.

Santos saw it and put up his left hand and said, "Wait," but Beauchamps saw Santos's arm going for his back and he pulled the Beretta and thrust it at Santos and pulled the trigger but nothing happened, and, in a flash, thought: safety. He thumbed the safety off and pulled the trigger again, and his hand hopped with the hard recoil as Cox screamed and ran across a coffee table and went down in a crash of cheap glass. And Santos got his gun out and fired at Beauchamps's face.

Beauchamps and Santos, five yards apart, both realized that they'd missed with their first shots, though that seemed almost impossible, and they both kept cranking on their triggers until Santos ran out of ammo and Beauchamps went down, firing his last, dying shot into the floor.

Santos, stunned, freaked out, patted his chest, looking for bullet holes. He found none. Although nearly deafened, he heard a crash in the bedroom and trotted to the door, found it locked, hit it with his shoulder, then tried to kick it in, felt weighted resistance.

The blonde had blocked the door with something heavy, and Santos had to get out. He didn't know how many shots he and Beauchamps had fired at each other, but it was a lot—the house stank of burnt gunpowder—and Beauchamps had not been using a suppressor.

His own gun, even suppressed, had been loud, and they weren't more than a mile from the scene of the 2017 Las Vegas massacre, which made him think that the cops might already be on their way.

He gave the bedroom door one last kick, and the blonde, who'd gone quiet, began screaming again. Santos took a spare magazine out of his pocket, jammed it into the Sig, and sprayed the whole load through the door and the Sheetrock walls. He heard one last crash of breaking glass from the bedroom and then hurried to the front door, to the car, and sped away.

At the end of the block, he saw a man standing in front of his house, staring at Beauchamps's house. He turned the corner and was gone.

COX THOUGHT she might have broken a leg when she ran into the coffee table, but it seemed to work all right, and she lay huddled behind the heavy wooden bureau she'd toppled in front of the bedroom door, her feet pushed against it.

When the shooting stopped and she took her hands away from her ears, somebody—it had to be Santos because Beauchamps would have called to her—tried to kick his way into the bedroom, but she rolled against the bureau and pushed back. Then Santos sprayed the bedroom with bullets, blowing out the only window. She closed her eyes and covered her ears again until the shooting stopped.

The front door slammed. She crawled to the window and looked out but couldn't see anything in the street, and she couldn't hear much at all, her ears still ringing with the muzzle blasts of the two guns, and then she saw Santos's car speed away, him hunched over the steering whccl.

She pushed the chest of drawers away from the bedroom door and stepped out. Beauchamps was dead, no question of that. When she looked at his chest, the word that popped unwanted into her head was "colander."

She began talking. "Oh, God. Oh, jeez. Oh . . . shit. Oh my God . . ."

She'd never seen a dead body before and this was an unsightly one, lying on the floor, eyes still open, looking at her, mouth slack, blood still oozing out into his shirt like a paper napkin sopping up spilt cranberry juice. She poked him once to see if he'd react but he didn't. And there were all those bullet holes . . .

Dead.

She had to get out. Cox shopped at Whole Foods and had one of their tote bags. She grabbed it, stuffed her purse and several pairs of shoes in it. She rolled Beauchamps up on his side and pulled out his wallet and then slipped her hand into his side pocket for the money roll he kept there. Grimacing at the warmth of his blood-splattered hand, she unclasped the gold Rolex and pulled it off his wrist.

His burner phone was sitting on the breakfast bar, and she threw it in the bag.

All that done, she ran to the door to the garage,

paused, saw two more paper grocery bags on the floor by the kitchen counter, grabbed them, ran back to the bedroom closet, stuffed the bags with the rest of her shoes, plus a plastic Tupperware box of jewelry, swept some cosmetics into the bag from the bathroom counter, added a baggie of cocaine, got her birth control pills and her sunglasses, yanked open the drawers of the other bureau—the one used by Beauchamps—saw nothing useful or valuable except for a wooden jewelry box that she thought might contain another Rolex, and maybe two, so she threw it in the bag also. She saw a box of 9mm ammo, grabbed it, and on the way through the front room picked up Beauchamps's Beretta by the barrel and dropped it in the bag, too.

With the two paper shopping bags and the Whole Foods tote, she stepped into the garage and tossed them in the backseat of Beauchamps's Cadillac Escalade. Didn't hear any sirens, but it hadn't been but five minutes since the shooting. Still, she ran inside, got an armful of clothing from her closet, carried it out and dumped it in the SUV. Went back to the bedroom again, yanked all the drawers out of Beauchamps's dresser and dumped them. The bottom drawer produced a bag of currency; she took it but didn't stop to count it. Finally, she went back to the toppled dresser by the bedroom door, took out an armful of lingerie, including everything she had from La Perla, and a bunch of bras and underpants from Victoria's

Secret, carried it all to the car, threw it in the backscat.

She pushed the button to lift the garage door, ran around to the driver's side of the Cadillac, got in, and backed into the street, taking a second to drop the garage door again to give it back the simple anonymity of the rest of the street. A man was turning the corner, on foot, shaded by a red umbrella, walking an overheated, panting black-and-white dog. She twiddled her fingers at him and he waved back. And she was outta there.

DEESE WAS on his way back to the house when Cox called on the burner and he asked, "Now what?"

She screamed, "He killed Marion! He shot Marion! Marion's dead! Marion's dead!"

# CHAPTER FIFTEEN

Lucas, Bob, and Rae spent a couple hours chilling out at the hotel. They took restless twenty-minute naps, gathered again and spent an hour making calls to home rental and real estate agents, with no luck. Late in the afternoon, with Lucas in the Volvo and Bob and Rae in the Tahoe, they headed south to the neighborhoods that were beneath the airport flight path. The heat was still ferocious, at 103 degrees, the sun like a molten glass marble.

They were making the turn off Las Vegas Boulevard onto Warm Springs Road when a cop car, lights and siren, blew by, and then another, and Lucas called Rae and said, "Maybe it's nothing."

Another cop was coming up behind, not running quite as fast, no lights or siren, and Rae said, "Looks like a big-time nothing."

"Let's tag along and see where they go . . . Maybe this is a high-crime neighborhood," Lucas said. But it didn't look high-crime. It looked empty, with hot stretches of tan stucco houses with tile roofs, separated by steaming blacktop, nobody on the street.

The cop who'd been behind them went by, while the cop ahead of them turned a corner. From that corner, they spotted a jam of cop cars outside a single-story house with an open garage door, cops going in and out. Another cop waved them off the turn down to the house. Lucas dropped his window and held his badge out. The cop came over, and Lucas said, "We're U.S. Marshals tracking fugitives. We think they live around here. We need to take a look in case you guys found them."

The cop looked at the badge, then turned and pointed down the street and said, "You see that green car down there?"

"Yeah."

"That's Lieutenant Harvey. He's running the scene. Park there and check in with him."

"How many dead?" Rae called from the Tahoe.

"One, is what I've heard," the cop said. "I haven't been down there myself."

THEY DROVE a block down to the scene, to the green car, and parked. On the street, they looked through the driver's-side window of the green car. The window dropped two inches, and a plainclothes guy in the driver's seat put a sandwich aside and asked, "Yeah?" chicken salad on his breath.

Lucas showed him his badge and repeated what he'd told the cop at the corner. The guy said, "Tom's inside. Lieutenant Harvey. Don't step on anything."

Lucas nodded, and as he started away, the guy said through the crack in the window, "Nice shorts, Marshal," and the window went back up. Rae stuck her knuckles in her mouth to keep from laughing, and Lucas looked down at his knees and said, "Best legs in Vegas, outside a gentleman's club. So fuck him. And all his relatives."

Another cop stood inside the door, in the shade, and when Lucas badged him he held up a finger and called, "Lieutenant. The feds are here."

Harvey, a short, fat man with a drinker's red nose and ratty white hair, walked over a minute later, frowned at Lucas, and asked, "Why are the feds here? Who are you?"

Lucas explained a third time, and Harvey stepped back and crooked a finger. Lucas, Bob, and Rae followed him through the door to where Beauchamps lay faceup on the kitchen floor, his chest dimpled with bullet holes in the middle of a blood-soaked shirt.

"Goddamnit," Lucas said.

"You know him?" Harvey asked. "Who is he?"

"Marion Beauchamps. He's got a couple other

aliases. He used to run a home invasion gang down in LA. He's the brother of the Louisiana cannibal, and we think the cannibal—Clayton Deese—was with him," Lucas said. "There's a guy who arrived in town a a couple of hours ago, from New Orleans, named Richard, or Ricardo, Santos. You really want to talk to him: this is probably his work. He's got a car we don't know about. He could be checked into Caesars. You can get a full bio on Beauchamps from Luanne Rocha, who's a sergeant in the Robbery Special Section of the LA cops. I've got her number for you."

Harvey wrote down Rocha's information. Another plainclothes guy, this one in a baby blue golf shirt over lightweight chinos, had come up to listen in and now said, "Shit, Tom, you already cleared the case. There's nothing left to do. Go down to Caesars and grab the guy."

Rae: "Let me tell you something. If you start running this thing down and you stumble over Deese, you can't go in with a sissy baby blue golf shirt. Deese killed a lot of people and ate some of them. He's got nothing to lose by shooting a few cops in baby blue shirts."

"I'll pass the word," Harvey said. "When I first looked at this boy, I had the feeling it'd get ugly." He nodded at the body on the floor and the puddle of now purple blood that had seeped out from beneath it.

Bob said, "Lucas here"—he tipped his thumb at Lucas—"was shot by this bunch back in May. Pretty much in the heart. Luckily, he doesn't have a heart. The thing you need to ask him about is the second house."

Lucas told Harvey about the double house arrangement in LA and the gunfight that followed.

"You think they got another house around here? And they shot you?"

"A second house wouldn't surprise us, and it's probably close by," Rae said. "These guys are assholes, but not dumb assholes. And they did shoot Lucas. He used to be a lot taller and better-looking."

Harvey shook his head. "All right. You know anything about a blond woman?"

"They may have a woman with them. Three guys and a woman. Now two guys. We don't know her exact status," Lucas said. "Beauchamps liked to chase women, but he didn't want to have to chase them too hard. Some of the women were okay, but some might have been more than available. They've got the blonde's prints down in LA . . ."

Lucas told him the rest of it—about Deese, Smith, and Santos, about Deese's brother Beauchamps, and Cole and the home invasions.

"I gotta make some phone calls," Harvey said, heading for the door. "A lotta phone calls." To the cop in the baby blue shirt he said, over his shoulder, "You got it, don't fuck it up. And change that shirt. You look like a target."

THE GOLF-SHIRTED COP introduced himself as Chuck Armie, and he walked them through the scene, staying away from a couple of technicians who were working through the bedroom. Harvey and Armie, with the head crime scene tech, had worked out the probable sequence of the shooting and laid it out for the marshals.

"Any of the shooter's blood anywhere?" Lucas asked.

"Nope. But there are all kinds of bullet holes in the living room wall, behind where he was probably standing. It's like the dead guy missed him six or seven times."

"That can happen," Bob said. "The unknown shooter didn't pick up his brass?"

"No. It's still here."

"Prints?" Rae said.

The cop nodded. "Of course."

"You know how he got out of here?" Lucas asked. "Anyone see a car? How about the woman?"

Armie bobbed his head. "The shooting got some attention, even with all the neighbors' windows closed and the air-conditioning on. Two cars left after the shooting: a small sedan, maybe a Corolla or a Civic or a Passat, silver in color, and then an SUV.

In that order. We got no plates. Your friend Santos is probably in the sedan, the woman in the SUV."

HARVEY CAME BACK. "We've got a fleet of uniforms coming in. We'll walk through the neighborhood, talking to everybody we can about newcomers. We've got guys on the way to Caesars."

Lucas handed him a card and said, "Call us if anything happens. We're really scratching around here." He looked at Bob and Rae and tipped his head toward the door. "We gotta make some calls ourselves."

On the way back to the cars, Lucas told Rae to call Tremanty. "We need to register the phone calls going to Smith. I've gotta believe that Deese will call him. And Santos, probably, too. You gotta get Tremanty to set it up."

Rae nodded.

Bob: "What else?"

They talked about it. The Las Vegas cops would be all over Caesars, but they didn't know Santos's face as well as Lucas did. They needed to find out where he'd gotten a second car and where he might be staying, if he'd checked in anywhere.

But Santos wasn't the problem. Deese was.

"Deese might be on his way out of town. Gotta believe the blonde called him and told him about Beauchamps," Lucas said. "We might've missed him."

"Don't say that," Rae said. "We got this. We got it."

THEY WENT BACK to the Bellagio. Bob said he was going to stand in a cool shower for ten minutes, Rae was planning to lie down to think until they moved again. Lucas got online. The first thing he found was a Hertz agency at Caesars Palace.

He called Rae. "I need to get over there. I'll walk. When Bob gets out of the shower, self-park the Tahoe at Caesars and call me. We might need wheels in a hurry."

At Caesars, he showed his badge to the manager at the Hertz booth and learned that a man who met Santos's description had returned a silver Corolla but had paid for it with an American Express card carrying the name Thomas R. Hobbs. The manager said, "The card went right through. He walked back around the corner. There." He pointed to the end of the hall. "He was either going down to the Forum Shops or he has a room here. Or, I dunno, maybe he was going to gamble. But if marshals are looking for him, that seems kinda unlikely . . . that you'd find him sitting in front of a slot machine."

Lucas scratched his head, nodded, said, "I'll look anyway. If the guy tries to rent another car, call me. Right away."

He gave the manager his card, and as he turned

away, the manager said, "You know . . . if he's, like, a fugitive . . . I don't know, this guy was carrying a whole bunch of FedEx boxes, like he was delivering them. Does that sound right?"

LUCAS CHECKED with the front desk, and one of the security men came out and told him that he'd already been talking to the Vegas cops and that there were three people named Santos staying at the hotel. They'd checked in two days earlier and appeared, from the registry, to be a husband, a wife, and a child. There was no one in the hotel named Hobbs.

"So if he's here, he's under a different name," Lucas said.

The security man nodded. "I've got no idea how you'd find him. If you could give me a photograph, I could show it around to the cleaning staff, see if they remember him. Kind of a long shot, though."

"Why is it a long shot? If he's in the hotel—"

"We've got almost four thousand rooms here, in six towers. Ninety-nine percent of the rooms have closed doors. Twenty percent have "Do Not Disturb" cards on them. What can I tell you? It's like finding one guy in a small city."

"Goddamnit." Lucas looked around the crazy place; he could probably see five hundred people of all sizes and shapes, scurrying through the lobby and in and out of restaurants and the casino, and he wasn't even in the main part of the building.

He went out and talked to the head valet, who said, "Man, I got ten people a minute coming through here. I don't remember the guy. Sorry. We could go down and look for the car."

Lucas gave him a card with his number on it, and Santos's car's license number, and asked him to look for it and to call him when he found it.

RAE CALLED HIM. "We're here."

"Cheesecake Factory," Lucas said.

On the way, the valet called. "We got that car."

Lucas hurried back to the front of the casino, and the valet took him to the parking structure and pointed out the car, which he said hadn't been moved since it was first checked in. Lucas looked through the windows and saw absolutely nothing inside.

"If he shows up and asks for the car, take a while to get it and call me," Lucas told the valet. "This guy is dangerous, so don't mess with him. Be polite."

He headed back to the Cheesecake Factory, called Harvey as he walked there, told him about the car.

"We'll put more pressure on the casino to find him," Harvey said. "That small city thing is mostly bullshit: there may be that many people here, but in a small city not everybody has to get off one of six elevators. We'll see if we can get a security guy on the elevator banks."

BOB AND RAE were waiting, pacing, and when Lucas showed up Rae said, "I caught Sandro at DFW. He was already on the plane. He'll be here in a couple of hours. He said he'd get the phone thing going with Roger Smith. Could be too late. He's sure Smith's got a secure phone. Santos might even be calling somebody else, one of Smith's employees. There's no way to know."

"We were right on top of Deese until that asshole showed up," Lucas said.

Rae shrugged. "Sort of. We had the neighborhood right. Didn't exactly have a fix on the house."

"I've worked deals where we had even less and it doesn't take as long as you'd think to narrow it down," Lucas said. "You talk to two or three houses per block, you'd find them eventually. Would have taken maybe two days. And if the Vegas cops had given us a couple of guys, we'd have had them in a day. Now . . ."

"What?"

"We're sitting on his first car. If he goes to a valet, the head valet will call me. What are the chances?"

"Slim, but not none," Rae said.

Bob said, "Two things: we've got no way to find him, unless he screws up. Even if we do find him, we don't have anything on him, not really. There's a chance that he doesn't know where Deese is, even if he did originally."

Lucas nodded. "That's a point. If he shot Beauchamps, he'd be a fool to have kept the gun, and I didn't get that feeling about him, that he's a fool. And if he shot Beauchamps, he's probably in trouble with Deese. He could be as much in the dark as we are."

"Maybe Tremanty will have some ideas," Bob said.

"Fuckin' FBI," Lucas said. "But maybe he will."

They got a table, ordered chicken and shrimp and tacos, and coffee and shakes, and Lucas told them about the car and the four thousand rooms in six towers, and Rae said, "Listen, we're not totally and finally fucked. Something good could happen."

"Yeah. And I could crack one of those slot machines for a million bucks."

"Drink your shake," Bob said. "You'll feel better."

WHEN THEY finished eating, they poked around Caesars, hoping to stumble over Santos, because they had nothing better to do.

Tremanty got there, called from the airport, and they agreed to meet back at the Cheesecake Factory.

Tremanty and Rae sat close together.

Tremanty had nothing.

# CHAPTER SIXTEEN

The second house was a mile from the first, the closest they could get from the agent who managed the Airbnb rentals. Cox, freaking out, almost drove straight to the second house. But not quite straight: she made one ice-cold stop.

A half mile out of the shooting scene, she pulled into a Shell station, took the cash in the bag she'd taken from Beauchamps's chest of drawers, counted it—forty-two thousand dollars—and hid it in the spare tire well, along with the pistol and the box of ammo. She'd managed to save three Rolexes, two in the wooden box and the one that came off Beauchamps's wrist. They went in the tire well, too. Cole had done the same thing with his stash in LA and had lost it all, but she couldn't think of anything better.

She left the cash in Beauchamps's wallet, a few hundred dollars. He had five thousand in the roll in his pocket and she peeled off two and put them in her purse.

It took only a few minutes and then she was on her way again. Cole had stayed at the second house that afternoon when Deese went out and was waiting for her. The garage was empty, and they put the Cadillac inside to get it off the street.

Cole asked, "Sure he's dead?"

"He's dead, he's dead. I managed to save some stuff: his pocket money, his wallet, some of my clothes. We can't go back there; you couldn't believe all the noise it made, the shooting. The cops'll be there."

Deese got to the house five minutes after Cox, just as she was finishing telling the story to Cole. The cannibal dropped the garage door and stalked inside and asked, "What the fuck happened? Are you lying? Did you leave him hurt, bitch?"

Cox, wide-eyed: "Deese! He was dead! Santos shot him like six times in the chest, he was about this far away." She spread her arms to demonstrate. "I got right down with him when Santos left. I tried to bring him back, but he . . . Deese, he was a mess. I never saw a dead person before, I mean, all the blood . . . Jesus."

She suddenly sat down on the floor, really falling, her legs giving way.

"What did Marion do? Just stand there?"

"No. Marion . . . Deese, I think Marion started it. He brought a gun out of the bedroom and he pulled it out and he pointed it at Santos but it didn't go off at first. I think he forgot about the safety thing. Then Santos pulled a gun out, and they both started shooting."

She went through the whole scene, once, twice, watching as Deese worked himself into a rage, ripping off his shirt, throwing it in a corner, shouting at her as she sat there on the floor. Cole eventually cornered him, talking quietly. "Deese, it wasn't Geenie who did it, it was Santos. And probably Smith."

"That's what she says," Deese shouted at him.

"Why would she lie? She and Marion were friends."

"Because she's a whore and whores lie about everything."

"I'm not a fuckin' whore," Cox shouted. "Marion was my friend."

Cole eventually managed to get Deese focused on Santos and not Cox. "Do you know what's going on?" he asked.

"You sound like you know," Deese shouted. "So tell me,"

"Your pal back in New Orleans decided you're too big a liability. He sent Santos out to kill you."

Deese looked at Cox. "You said he had the money?"

"He said he did. In his car. I never saw it. When he and Marion started shooting, I think Santos tried to stop it. He yelled, 'Wait!" but Marion had already pulled his gun out. One second before that, they were talking like old friends. It was like a cowboy movie," Cox cried. "They stood there and shot their guns at each other. And Marion . . . He shot Marion, like, fifteen times, or something."

"Fucker," Deese said. "I'm gonna kill that motherfucker. But a real shooter wouldn't have done it like that. If he was a real shooter, Marion never would have seen it coming."

Cole: "Whatever. We gotta get out of here. The cops know who we are. The best thing we can do is get the hell out."

Deese asked, "How much cash you got?"

"What we got from the raid, plus maybe ten K. So less than fifty," Cole said. "How about you?"

"Two. I was borrowing from Marion. I had a bad run of luck."

They both looked at Cox, who shrugged and lied. "I got Marion's billfold and his pocket roll. I haven't counted it, but it's not a lot," she said.

"Let's see it," Deese said.

Beauchamps's roll added up to three thousand dollars, and he'd carried six hundred in his wallet.

"What we got would just about get us to Ohio," Deese said. He took a turn around the room, breathing hard again, the anger and frustration climbing all over him. "That won't work."

"Farther than Ohio. Between us, we got almost sixty thousand," Cole said to Deese. "Let's split it. You take twenty, twenty-five. Geenie and I get the rest, because there are two of us. And most of it was minc to begin with anyway. You got a late-model truck you can sell it down in Miami, or somewhere, probably get another fifteen and go hide out in Puerto Rico until things cool off. You can live a long time down there on forty K."

"Maybe you can, but I can't," Deese said. "We got something else going for us: we know where there's five million dollars in cash. Harrelson's."

"No. We know where there's a rumor of five million dollars cash," Cole said.

"There'll be something, with him being a big-time gambler, and we need it now," Deese said. "There are too many cops around for us to hide here and work out another plan. Even if we get out of Harrelson's with a few hundred thousand, we're way ahead of where we are now. I agree with you on one thing: we gotta get out of here. Get out of Vegas."

Cole looked at Cox. "What do you think?"

"You're the criminals, not me," she said. Then to Cole: "If you and me had thirty-five or forty thousand dollars, even back where you come from if we had to rent a house or an apartment, it'd only get us six months. We **do** need more money."

Cole looked at Deese. "All right. Lay low until it's time to go, hit Harrelson tonight, and run."

"What if Harrelson isn't there tonight?" Cox asked.

"If we stay cool, if we don't leave the house, then

I don't know how they'd find us. We've hardly seen any of the neighbors around here," Cole said. "We could hunker down for a day or two."

"What about that Joan chick?" Deese asked. Joan was the agent who rented them the houses.

"She's only seen me and Cole," Cox said. "Her husband's a poker dealer here in town. Even if she suspected something, they're the kind of people who know when they should be looking the other way."

Cole bobbed his head. "Okay. We take the risk." He looked at his watch. "We'll go at nine. I'm going to watch the news, see if we're on it."

"I'm going to call back to New Orleans, see if I can figure out what the fuck is going on," Deese said.

"Another risk, the cops are all over the phones now," Cole said.

"The phone's clean, a throwaway," Deese said. "And I need to know."

DEESE WENT into the back bedroom to make the call and Cole and Cox drifted down the hallway to stand outside the door and listen, which they could easily do because Deese spent most of his time shouting.

The call went to a burner phone owned by a man named Larry Buck, who handed the phone to Roger Smith, who was standing next to him, because Buck was always standing next to him when Smith was out on the town. They didn't use names on the phone.

"It's the goddamn truth and you know it! You must have talked to that motherfucker. He wouldn't walk around the block without checking with you."

"I don't know what you're talking about, man. I don't. I haven't heard a word. I sent him there with four boxes of money. Six hundred K. He must've decided to keep it, unless . . . Hey, ask that chick, whatever her name is, who pulled the gun first? I don't think our guy would, he was just a deliveryman, he only had a gun because he was carrying all that cash, he's not a shooter."

"Don't tell me that, you motherfucker, you sent that fuckin' island beaner after my ass and he killed my brother. When I get my hands on him, I'm gonna eat his fuckin' liver with fava beans and Ritz crackers. You got that? You tell him that. Then I'm gonna come after your liver, you pasty-white, lying piece of faggot shit."

"Listen, listen, I'll try to get in touch, find out what happened," Smith finally shouted back. "If he didn't leave the money behind, then he's still got it and you still need it, right? Him giving you the money would prove that I'm telling the truth, right? I wouldn't have sent the money at all, if he was coming there to shoot you, for Christ's sakes."

"You get me that money, I'll think about it,"

Deese said. "I'm still gonna eat his liver, but get me the money, I'll let you keep yours."

WHEN THEY WERE DONE, Deese walked out of the bedroom and found Cox and Cole, leaning against the wall, advertising the fact that they'd been listening.

"We're not going after any money with you," Cole said. "If you go after that money, they'll kill your ass. That's nothing but a setup."

"Those fuckers," Deeds said. He had the burner phone in his hand and threw it at a couch. It bounced once and fell on the floor. "If it ain't a setup, it'd sure be some easy cash. It'd be the way to go. Better than Harrelson."

"Would you give us some of it?" Cox asked.

"Depends how nice you are to me," Deese said to her, giving her his nicotine sneer.

"Oh, fuck that," Cox said.

Cole said, "Geenie and I have developed a relationship, so you're not getting . . ." He tried to think of an appropriate word and wound up with "any."

Deese shook his head. "I'm in Vegas and I'm not getting any. How does that happen? If I—"

"Shut up," Cole said, in not quite a shout. "Get back on track. If you go after that money . . . Like I said, it's a setup. You go out there alone, they're gonna kill you."

"What would you do about it?" Deese cocked

his eyebrows at Cole and Cox. And with his funny squashed nose and rim of sharp teeth, he looked exactly like a giant weasel, Cox thought.

"If nothing else, we could be lookouts," Cole said. "I'd go that far, if you'd kick us out . . . fifty."

"Let's talk about it," Deese said.

THEY SETTLED into the house to talk and finally agreed that Deese would give them fifteen thousand each to be lookouts. While Deese and Cox were arguing about money, Cole turned on the television to see if they could get any news about the shooting. They couldn't, and after a while they were watching **Let's Make a Deal**, and Deese said, "Look at that guy. If I had to dress up like a fuckin' cockroach to win a few bucks, I wouldn't do it."

"We could use the money," Cox said. "You'd be doing us all a favor."

"Not if I had to dress up like a fuckin' cockroach," Deese said. He pointed at the next contestant. "Look at this chick. What's she supposed to be, a shrimp? She'd look better as the cockroach. I wouldn't fuck her with your dick, Cole."

After another half hour, during a talk show about the legalization of marijuana and the bad effects it was having on Vegas culture, Deese said, "I can't stand this shit. I'm going down to the Circle K and get some beer and chips and salsa."

"You'll get us caught," Cole said. "We agreed to stay inside."

"I can't sit here doing nothing. I need some beer. I got sunglasses and a beard and a hat, nobody will recognize me. I'll be fifteen minutes."

"No goddamn casinos," Cole said. "They got facial recognition there. They can look right through your disguise. They look at the way you walk and the shape of your shoulders, and all that shit. I read about it."

WHEN HE WAS GONE, Cox cracked the curtains at the front window and watched him rolling away. He'd taken the burner phone, but she had her own cold phone, and Cole agreed that nobody would have it.

"Let me see your arm," she said.

"What are you going to do?"

"Listen and learn," she said. She took her own phone out of her pocket and picked up Deese's. Deese's phone had no password protection and she brought up the last call made, and poked the number into her own phone.

LARRY BUCK answered, and Cox asked, "Is this the guy in New Orleans that the other guy called from Las Vegas?"

"Who is this?"

"This is the blonde who is with the other guy in Vegas."

"One minute."

Larry Buck covered his phone's microphone, and Cox couldn't hear what was being said. Then another voice: "This is the person the man in Las Vegas called."

Cox asked, "Did you really send money?"

"Yes."

"How bad do you want it back?" she asked.

"Depends on where else it might go," Smith said.

"What if the man in Las Vegas fell down the stairs and broke his neck?"

"I could see that happening," Smith said. "He's a careless walker. Where is he now?"

"He's out getting beer."

"Well, if something happened to him . . . I wouldn't get the money back anyway. So I wouldn't care who got it."

"If he somehow broke his neck . . . then this other guy who you sent here . . . why wouldn't he keep it?" Cox asked.

"Because I'd tell him to give it to you, no questions asked."

"Okay. We'll think about this. Tell your friend to stay here in Vegas. I'll need his phone number. If something happens to Dee—To, you know . . . We'll set up the payment. But I'm telling you, he has told us all about you. One person will make the pickup, probably me. If anything happens to me, that other guy will come to New Orleans and kill you. Since you don't know who we are, you'd never see it coming. We've done a lot of work in LA, and you probably know about that. We're not afraid of hurting people."

"Neither am I."

"We totally believe that," Cox said. "We're scared of you. But you should be scared of us. The money smooths it all out. If the other guy—the guy you're worried about—goes away, you should be happy with that."

"Let me get you the phone number for the delivery."

Cox wrote the number on the inside of her arm.

"Call me and tell me what happened," Smith said. "It's sort of like a soap opera, and I like soaps."

"Yeah? We were just watching **The Bold and the Beautiful**," Cox said.

"I caught that myself. We were probably watching at the same time," Smith said. And, "Good-bye."

When Cox hung up, Cole looked at her, chewing his lower lip, and when she asked, "What?" he said, "You know you're talking about murder."

"Not necessarily."

"That's what the New Orleans guy thought you meant," Cole said.

"That's his problem," Cox said.

"What are you thinking?"

"This lawyer I was friends with once told me

that when a guy gets shot, it's not necessarily murder. If a cop shoots him while he's doing a crime, that's not murder. If the guy shoots himself in the head, that's not murder. Murder's, like, a legal thing. Whether or not it's murder depends on who's doing the shooting."

"So . . . who'd do the shooting?"

"Not us. Remember how Deese keeps saying the cops won't take him alive? I believe him."

DEESE GOT BACK an hour later, carrying two twelve-packs of Coors and a couple of sacks of blue corn chips.

Cox asked, "Where in the heck were you? We were getting worried, we almost took off. And two twelve-packs?"

"No sweat," Deese said. "Rog called me. He wanted me to meet Santos at Circus Circus to give me the money. I said, 'Fuck that, I'm not meeting that asshole anywhere **he** wants to meet me.' So I went to find a place, and I did. And the two twelve-packs are so we don't have to stop if we need to get out of town."

"Where's the meeting?" Cole asked.

Deese squinted at him, and Cole said, "Come on, Deese, we already agreed. Santos might be set up to shoot you in the back. We'll watch out for you."

Deese popped a can of beer out of a twelve-pack, put the rest in the refrigerator, looking from Cox to Cole, then said, "All right. The Show Boat mall. Hundreds of people wandering around. He won't take a chance of shooting me in there. We'll tell him what time, we'll meet in a Chipotle's, won't wait any more than five minutes, he can come in any entrance he wants, so he'll know we won't ambush him."

Cole nodded. "Sounds like a plan."

"I gotta call Rog and tell him," Deese said. He went back to the bedroom to make the call. As they had before, Cox and Cole slipped down the hall and listened outside the bedroom door.

They heard Deese say, ". . . called Show Boat, it's a big mall. Seven o'clock, I'll be at a table inside a Chipotle's. It's on the ground floor . . . Nobody's gonna want to shoot nobody else in that place, they'd never get out with all the people around, the security guards with guns. Okay, well, you tell him . . . And tell him I got a gun, too."

COX AND COLE slipped back down the hall when they heard the conversation winding up, with threats from Deese's end, and probably from Smith's as well.

Deese came out of the bedroom a minute later and said, "We're all set. Seven o'clock. We'll all go in early and scout the place."

Cox had dropped onto a couch before Deese got

out of the bedroom and now she bounced to her feet and mimed punching Deese. "Now we're doing something. Now we're getting there. Nobody gets hurt. And we're out of Vegas, and fuck all those marshals."

Cole said, "Sounds like Smith knew all about what happened."

"Yeah, he did," Deese said. "I gotta think on that. That motherfucker. Maybe get the money and eat his liver anyway."

# CHAPTER SEVENTEEN

Tremanty was frustrated. Not angry, exactly, but unhappy, and as he sat next to Rae he was drumming his fingers on the tabletop. He had an overnight bag next to his shoe. His suit was rumpled and he hadn't shaved. "You're telling me that they know you're here."

Lucas nodded. "Probably. There are a couple of ways they could know, so we have to believe they do. Even if they don't, Santos could have scared them off."

"They could be most of the way to Idaho by now. Hell, they could already be there."

"The Vegas cops might get Santo's prints off the brass he left at the shooting. If they do, his ass is in a crack," Bob said.

"Yeah, yeah, but I'm not holding my breath," Tremanty said.

---

THEY WERE still talking, arguing, when a call came in for Lucas. He checked his phone and saw that it was from the Marshal Service's district office. Lucas, Bob, and Rae had checked in with the Vegas marshal on the way into town. He answered, "Yeah? Davenport."

"Davenport. This is Carl Young. Listen, we got a call, a woman trying to get ahold of you, and she asked for you by name. She said it's a matter of life and death. She said I should tell you the name Deese. I understand that's your cannibal guy. She wants your phone number and will call me back in two minutes. Should I give it to her?"

"Yes . . . Hell, yes! Tell her to call."

Lucas hung up, turned to the others, and said, "A woman called, mentioned 'Deese.' She's gonna call me."

Tremanty yanked his phone out of his pocket and pushed a number on speed dial. A moment later he said, "I need to trace a call incoming to Las Vegas. I can give you the receiving phone, it's on now. We need to know the location of the caller."

Lucas showed him the screen on his phone, the number, and Tremanty recited it into his phone, then repeated it. When he hung up, his frustration disappearing like cigarette smoke, he said, "Been here less than an hour and got us a tipster. Am I good or am I good?"

"We don't really know that yet, do we?" Rae said. Her tone was enigmatic, and they all looked at her for a moment before deciding not to press her.

TWO OR THREE minutes later, Lucas's phone rang, an unknown number. "Davenport," he said again.

"Is this Marshal Davenport?" A woman's voice, soprano, but with some whisky in it.

"Yes. What can I do for you?"

"Clayton Deese will be in the Chipotle restaurant at the Show Boat mall at exactly seven o'clock. He'll only be there for five minutes. He has a beard, and he's wearing a gray shirt, blue jeans, cowboy boots, and a red-and-blue LA Dodgers baseball cap. You can't call me back because I'm throwing this phone in the toilet."

**Click.**

Tremanty's phone buzzed. "Yeah?" He listened, then said, "Well, shit. But, thank you."

"Where is it?" Rae asked.

"On Las Vegas Boulevard north of here. Then it died."

"She said she threw it in the toilet," Lucas said. "And she said Deese is going to be at the Show Boat mall, at a Chipotle restaurant, at seven o'clock." He glanced at his phone. "We've got nineteen minutes to get there, wherever there is."

"I know where it is," Bob said. "You can check a map on your phone, but I saw it right up the boulevard. North of here—where that phone was. Maybe three minutes away." They were all hustling along behind Bob. "Not counting how long it takes to get to the self-parking."

They ran, weaving through the slot machines on Caesars main floor, setting off whirlpools of unhappy gamblers.

IN THE CAR, Tremanty asked, "Call the Vegas cops?"

Lucas: "What do you think? If we have a bunch of cops flooding the place, we'll never see him. He'll see them first and be outta there."

Bob said, "We'll really stink up the place if we don't tell them at all. We gotta tell somebody or we'll have major diplomatic problems."

"You're right," Lucas said. And Tremanty nodded.

Lucas, in the passenger seat while Bob drove, took out his wallet and found a card for Tom Harvey, the homicide cop they'd met over Beauchamps's dead body. Harvey had scribbled his personal cell number on the back. Lucas punched it into his phone as Bob ran a red light turning north onto Las Vegas Boulevard.

Rae was looking at her iPad, with a map of the mall's interior on it; she spotted the Chipotle's.

Harvey answered, and Lucas identified himself and told him what was happening. Harvey said, "Jesus, Davenport, we gotta have somebody on the scene. Let me round up all the plainclothes guys I got—"

"If the tip's right, he'll be there for only five minutes, starting at seven o'clock," Lucas said. "We're on our way, with an FBI agent, and will be there in three or four minutes, but we've got to park and then find the Chipotle's. So it's now fourteen minutes, no, thirteen minutes to seven, so do what you gotta do, but we can't have a bunch of uniforms running through the place, waving their guns around."

"I'm on the way," Harvey said, and he hung up.

Lucas said, "I'm dialing up the conference call," and all their phones started ringing. They checked to make sure they were all talking to one another, then tucked the phones away still turned on.

A MINUTE LATER, Bob made a wild left turn, and Rae directed him to the parking structure. Parked, looking at Rae's iPad map of the mall, Lucas and Tremanty worked through how they'd make the approach as Bob and Rae pulled on compact bulletproof vests.

They locked the truck and, outside the mall's entrance, stopped to catch their breaths, and Lucas said, "She said he'll be in the Chipotle's for five minutes. It must be a meet. I bet he's meeting with Santos, or maybe even Roger Smith. Deese, Smith, and Santos know me and Sandro. We gotta hang back. Rae and Bob, you lead. When you see him, move, and we'll come running."

Rae: "Time's up. We gotta go."

Everybody nodded, and Lucas said, "Inside and to your right," and they went through the doors into the mall. A few seconds later, Lucas grabbed Rae's arm, as she led the way in, and said, "Wait, wait. Jesus, the place is jammed." He turned to Bob and Rae. "You gotta get right on top of him. We can't have a firefight in here, everybody will panic, we'll kill ten people."

"Got it," Bob said. To Rae: "We keep people between us and him until we go through the door and then we've gotta be fast. Real fast."

Rae, tense, focused: "Yes. Watch his hands, Bob. Watch his hands."

LUCAS AND TREMANTY held back as Bob and Rae led the way.

Tremanty: "My God, there are a lot of people. Must be a special event."

There were forty or fifty people within a few dozen feet of them, strolling through the mall, drinking soda from plastic cups, some of them dragging kids along, dressed in T-shirts and shorts and athletic shoes and baseball caps.

"This is bad," Lucas said. He could feel the anxiety crawling up the back of his neck. People in the mall were looking at Bob and Rae and their bulletproof vests. He saw Rae talking to a blond woman in a cowboy suit, who, shaking her head, turned and hurried off into the crowd. And then Bob lifted his phone to his face and said, "I can see inside the Chipotle's and he's not in there."

"Then back off," Lucas said. "Get all the way across to the other side of the mall, like you're going somewhere else. That crowd doesn't like the looks of you."

"We're backing off," Bob said.

Lucas looked at the time. "Three minutes of seven. He's got to be inside if he plans to be there right at seven. Watch for his face, you have the description. But try to stay out of sight, and don't make another approach until after seven."

"Hope it's not some bullshit scam," Rae said, her voice sounding scratchy through the phone's speaker.

"It'd be weird, if it was. That woman knew me, knew Deese, knew we were here, and how to get ahold of me," Lucas said. "It's gotta be something."

BOB AND RAE went to a side hall that led down to a Nordstrom's. There were several circles of easy chairs in the hall, and they could slump down in a couple of chairs and still see into the Chipotle's. A woman sitting in the same circle asked Bob, "What's going on?"

"Waiting for somebody," Rae said.

The woman looked at Bob, then back to Rae, got her shopping bag and walked away.

Lucas and Tremanty joined them a minute later, sliding down into the seats of two other chairs, so low that nothing was sticking up but their eyes beneath the bills of their caps. Lucas said, "Six fifty-nine."

Thirty seconds passed, and then Bob muttered, "Hold it, hold it. On the left, the wall in front of the Apple Store, walking toward us, a guy with a beard."

"That's him," Rae said.

"Let him get inside and then wait for a minute," Lucas said, quietly. "Let's see who else shows up."

Deese went inside the Chipotle's and instead of getting in the food line stepped behind the front window and sat on a toadstool-like chair. A few seconds later, Tremanty said, "Holy shit, here we go . . ."

They all looked the other way, toward the opposite end of the mall, and Lucas said, "Santos. See him?"

"I see his hat," Rae said. "Never actually seen his face."

And Bob said, "Oh no. No!"

Lucas looked back to where Bob was looking and saw Harvey and two other men jogging down the center of the mall. They looked exactly like cops and not like anybody else in the mall. Lucas said to Bob, "Go! Go!"

Bob and Rae started across the mall, weaving fast through the crowd, toward the Chipotle's. They were halfway there when a man shouted down from the second level, "Deese! Deese! Cops! Cops! Cops!"

DEESE HAD TAKEN a window seat in the restaurant, next to a crowded table of jocko-looking guys eating plates of black beans and rice and doing high fives every ten seconds and calling each other bro.

When Cole screamed his warning, Deese exploded off the seat. A gun appeared in his right hand, and Bob shouted, "Deese! Stop!" and the jocks all went to the floor. A heartbeat later, Deese shot a woman out in the mall's center corridor, who went down, and then shot a man, and Rae screamed, "Stop!" and Lucas and Tremanty ran toward them, Lucas glancing sideways as he did and saw Santos, frozen, in the corridor.

Rae and Bob both had their guns out, but there was a virtual wall of humanity on the far side of Deese, as he, running, turned to his left. He would be running past Tremanty and Lucas and they both drew their weapons and moved to block him, but Deese saw Tremanty and snapped off a shot and Tremanty and Lucas both juked, and Deese deliberately shot the woman right in front of Tremanty, her blood spraying from the side of her head onto Tremanty's face.

Lucas still couldn't take a shot without a crowd in the background, and the mall had erupted into chaos by then, with shoppers and children running in all directions, screaming. The Vegas cops were thirty yards away in the wrong direction, so they couldn't stop Deese. A short man ran directly into Lucas's chest, sending Lucas staggering backwards, trying to keep his balance, as Deese went by fifteen feet away, past a Johnny Rockets. Then Deese saw Santos and he shot at him, missing. Santos reeled away, and Deese closed in on him, shot him in the back, then kept going.

Lucas ran after Deese after he shot Santos, but a woman toppled in front of Lucas and he tripped and went down. He scrambled back to his feet and saw Tremanty, with his hand pressed to the shot woman's face, looking wildly at him. Lucas ran after Deese again. He collided with another man, bounced off.

He could still see Deese, who turned and fired a shot at Lucas. There was another man closer to Deese who pulled a gun from his pocket and shot at Deese, who stumbled but continued on, and, looking over his shoulder, saw Lucas coming after him. The shooter looked at Lucas, who shouted, "No!" but the man shot at him, and somebody screamed behind Lucas, and he shouted, "Police! Police!"

The man held his gun upright, and then Bob was there, in his vest that said "U.S. Marshal," and he slapped the man in the face with his own weapon and the man went down. Rae sprinted past Lucas to where they'd last seen Deese, disappearing down a hallway to the left, and when they got there . . . Deese was gone.

"Where? Where'd he go?" Rae shouted.

They looked down the empty hallway, which ended with an exit door leading to the parking structure. They ran that way, past a short utility hallway to the left, and outside to the structure.

Where nothing was moving.

"Hiding between cars?" Rae said.

"I don't think so," Lucas said. "He scouted the place, he had lookouts. He'd know he couldn't get a car out of there."

They both looked back inside at the utility hallway and jogged to it. There were several doors down the hall, all of them metal, all of them locked. Lucas turned and saw a security guard in the main hall, where the shooting had taken place.

"U.S. Marshal," Lucas shouted. "Key! Need a key!"

The security guard ran toward them. One of the doors opened into an equipment closet, the second led to a storage area, the third to a loading dock with a dumpster. Lucas and Rae checked behind the dumpster and then inside it.

"He's gone," Lucas said to Rae. He looked back out into the main corridor. "But we've got shot people and we've gotta help if we can."

Lucas asked the security guards to watch the doors in the utility and the exit from the parking structure, and then he and Rae ran back to the corridor. Lucas checked Santos: two FedEx boxes were lying next to the green shopping bag he'd been carrying, and Lucas could see two more inside. Santos, on his stomach, his head turned, looked glassy-eyed up at Lucas and said, "Shot."

"Got help on the way," Lucas said. "Let me roll you over."

Santos had been shot on the left side of his spine, from the back, and the front exit wound was pumping blood. Lucas couldn't see an artery, but he'd seen an arterial wound once before and thought this might be one.

Lucas said, "This is gonna hurt," and he pulled Santos's shirt loose and pressed it into the wound as far as he could, packing the cotton in to nearly the full depth of his index finger. Santos groaned, again said, "Shot."

Lucas shouted, "Get me some help. Get me some help over here."

A moment later, a woman hurried up, said, "Nurse," and looked at the wound, then said, in what seemed to be an unnaturally calm voice, "You did what you could. I don't think there's anything else to do here until we have paramedics."

"Stay with him, would you?" Lucas asked, and the nurse nodded.

SANTOS SEEMED TO have passed out. Lucas picked up the green shopping bag, put the two FedEx boxes in with the other two, looked around, turned away from the nurse, pulled his own shirt loose, wrapped a finger in the fabric so he wouldn't leave prints, and ripped one of the boxes open.

Money. Lots of it.

The nurse was holding Santos's hand, and Lucas stepped over to Bob, who'd cuffed the man who'd shot at Deese and then Lucas. The man was bubbling blood from his nose. Bob had propped him up against the wall, and the man kept saying, "Active shooter . . . active shooter . . ." Bob said, "Yeah, but you shot the wrong guy."

To Lucas Bob said, "This guy shot that guy when he tried to shoot you." Bob pointed across hall. "I thought he might have been backing up Santos, so I swatted him."

Lucas turned to see a man leaning against the wall with two women working on him in a professional way, maybe doctors or nurses. Down the length of the mall, most of the people had cleared out, but small groups had gathered around the three other people lying on the floor in puddles of blood. One of the cops who'd come with Harvey was crouched over the first woman Deese had shot, Tremanty was still applying pressure to the facial wound of the woman who'd been standing next to him, his face, hands, and shirt splattered with purple blood.

Lucas asked Bob, "Did you fire your weapon?"

"No, no. I never could. Too many people behind him."

Rae had come up next to Lucas. "Neither did I. I never had a clean shot. I'm going to jog around the mall, see what I can see. Check that parking structure, even if he isn't there. Maybe I'll kick him out." She ran off toward the hallway to the structure.

Lucas called, "Careful, Rae. Careful," and she waved without looking back at him. Lucas looked around, didn't see anybody who looked like a paramedic, and said, "Somebody must've called for help by now."

Bob said, "Oh, yeah. I called 911 and they told me everybody was already on the way. They're coming . . . And I . . . My God! My God!" He walked away, one hand on the top of his head.

HARVEY SAW LUCAS and ran over and shouted, "Jesus Christ, what did you do?"

"None of us ever fired a shot," Lucas said. He

looked up to the mall's second level. "Deese had a lookout up there. He saw you guys coming, he yelled, and Deese started shooting. At anybody he saw. He must've planned that escape route."

"Ambulances on the way," Harvey said. He ran a hand through his thinning white hair as he scanned the chaotic scene. People were coming back again, peering at the wounded. "What a mess. What a fuckin' mess."

Lucas started stepping between bodies: a man shot in the chest, almost the same place that Lucas had been hit; a woman was shot in the upper leg, the bullet apparently breaking the bone. She was the first one Deese shot, Lucas thought. Nobody dead yet. The woman Tremanty was hovering over had been shot in the cheek, the bullet exiting behind the bone and passing through her ear.

Bob came over and said, "The man who shot at you, I left him with a security guard. He's some concealed carry guy, thought this was his big chance." He looked around. "How many dead?"

"None yet." Lucas looked at his phone. Seven minutes after seven o'clock. "It's been seven minutes from when the shooting started."

"Seems like a week," Bob said. "This is fucked up. Where are the ambulances?"

"We gotta go up, see if anybody saw the guy who yelled," Lucas said.

"Gotta ask about cameras is what we need to do," Bob said.

"You do that. I'm going up."

LUCAS TOOK an escalator to the second level, where people were peering over a railing at the floor below. He called, as loud as he could, "U.S. Marshal! Did anyone see a man shouting about cops? A man shouting about cops? Anyone see . . ."

He had no faith in the possibility of finding a witness, but he unexpectedly did. A woman in a red dress, pushing a baby carriage, which turned out to be full of magazines, raised a hand and called out, "I saw him."

Lucas went to her. "Tell me."

She pointed at the atrium's railing. "He was leaning over it, like he was waiting for somebody. I was sitting right over there." She pointed to some seating. "I noticed him because, you know, he was nice-looking. Brown hair. Thin. Like an athlete. Anyway, he was standing there for several minutes. Like he was watching. A blond woman walked up to him and said something and walked away again. Then—I wasn't exactly looking at him—someone yelled, really loudly, 'Please! Please! Cops!' I looked up and saw it was him. And then I heard the shots and stood up and started to run. I saw him in front of me, hurrying down the hallway, and the blond woman came up behind him and grabbed his hand and went with him . . . out of sight. I hid in that store over there. And when the shooting was done, I ran here to look over the railing with some other people."

Lucas got on his phone, called Harvey, said, "I'm right at the top of the escalator, I've got a witness who saw the guy who yelled at Deese. You need to send one of your people up here to take a statement."

"On the way," Harvey said. Lucas peered over the railing to the first floor and now saw paramedics beginning to move the wounded.

He asked the woman to wait, then called Bob. "Have you found a camera?"

"Yeah. We can see the Chipotle's, the area above the shooting . . ."

Lucas told him what to look for on the second floor, and Bob went away from the phone for a minute and then came back and said, "Yeah, we see him. We'll run it back and see if we can spot the blonde. We might be able to follow them down to the parking structure."

WHEN HARVEY'S COP arrived, Lucas turned the witness over to him, then went back down the escalator. Mall security guards had roped off the area of the shooting, and Rae, who'd come back after looking for Deese, said, "I didn't find him. People are streaming out of the place, it's a traffic jam out there. They're closing the mall."

"No hope?" Lucas asked.

"Nope. He's not hiding, he's gone."

He told her about the man and woman upstairs, and she said, "It's Cole and the woman who was in Altadena, the same one who was with Beauchamps."

Lucas nodded. "Probably."

"But then they must be the ones who tipped us off. If they are, why did they warn Deese?"

"You want the snaky reason?" Lucas asked. "Because they wanted us to kill him. They were working with Roger Smith and they wanted us to kill him."

"Then why was Santos—"

"Because he didn't know," Lucas said. "Smith didn't tell him. If the cops kill Deese, Smith is in the clear. If Santos pays Deese, Smith is in the clear. Either way works."

"You're making Smith sound like an asswipe," Rae said.

"There you go."

ACROSS THE MALL, Tremanty, covered in blood, was facing Harvey. They were arguing. Lucas headed that way, trailed by Rae.

Lucas heard Harvey saying, ". . . taking the blame for this mess. If you'd waited, we could have gotten a SWAT team here."

"That's bullshit. We were told he was staying for five minutes, and we had reason to believe the tip came from someone who knew what she was talking about. He's a serial killer, and a cannibal, and we couldn't wait," Tremanty said heatedly. He jabbed an index finger at Harvey without actually poking him. "It wasn't us who set this off, it was you guys. You came running down the mall, and I never saw anybody looking more like cops than you did. Deese's lookout saw you and yelled to him. If you'd walked down here separately, if you let us do it, it'd all be over with and we'd have Deese in custody. Lucas told you to stay away, told you we didn't need a bunch of cops—"

Lucas's phone rang just then and he turned away from the argument, and Bob said, "We tracked them to the parking structure, we got a silvery-golden Cadillac Escalade. And, guess what? There was mud splattered on the plates. Everything else was clean except the plates. Don't have a number, though."

"Goddamnit."

"It's not all bad," Bob said. "There's a Vegas cop here, says they have traffic cameras at the major intersections and we might be able to track the Caddy that way. To wherever they're going."

Lucas told him about the hallway and the loading dock, asked if there were cameras covering that. Bob went away for minute, came back and said, "Yes, there are. We'll look now."

"About that traffic camera video," Lucas said. "Get going on that, too. And keep me up on what you find out."

"Gotcha," Bob said.

RAE HAD WALKED away when Lucas was on the phone and came back with a handful of paper towels from a restroom, half of them soaked with water, and began toweling off Tremanty's face. He let her do it, holding on to one of her elbows to steady himself, and took a towel from her to wipe his hands. Then she dried his face, and said, "You saved that woman's life. She was bleeding out."

"But Deese is gone," Tremanty said. "We might not ever find him again."

Lucas said, "He might not have gone that far." He took the green bag off his shoulder, pulled it open, peeled back the flaps of all four FedEx boxes, showing off the money. "Smith was paying him, but we got the money. I don't know how much, but it could be a million."

Tremanty showed a flicker of a smile. "Santos is hurt, he's got a pile of money with him, and he's meeting up with the fuckin' Louisiana cannibal. That gives me something to work with. Deese won't be getting any more money from Smith, I can promise you that."

Harvey came over. "The sheriff is here, along with every reporter in Vegas. We've contained the press outside, we think, at least for now. We need to meet to talk about the story."

Lucas, Bob, and Rae all looked at Tremanty. After a moment, he nodded. "All right, I'll take it. We want to avoid a political clusterfuck, if we can. We need Bob's video of the guy who yelled at Deese. And his girlfriend. And the car. We need all the photos we have of Deese, including any video from the first floor. We talk to the sheriff and then—"

"The fuckin' press," Harvey said.

"Nothing wrong with the press," Lucas said. "It's the killing that's the problem."

They looked down the hall. The place had emptied out, leaving cops, crime scene techs, security guards and shredded bandage packaging scattered around the slowly congealing pools of crimson blood.

# CHAPTER EIGHTEEN

Deese had thought hard about how he'd pick up the money.

He'd sat in the bathroom, thinking; lay on the bed, picturing it. On the way across town, from the house to the Show Boat mall, he'd nearly hit a Rolls-Royce, distracted by the images playing through his mind.

What would happen if the marshals or the Vegas cops showed up, if Santos and Smith had betrayed him? If the feds got their hands on him, he was dead. So that wasn't going to happen. If he got jumped, he'd start shooting. He had his Glock, he had a full magazine, and chaos would be his friend. He could feel the cool pressure of the pistol against his spine.

The mall was right on Las Vegas Boulevard. He didn't get there fifteen minutes before the meeting, like a moron, to do some hurried, half-assed scouting. No, he got there two hours ahead of time and wandered through the crowd of shoppers, looked down hallways, tried doors, counted security guards. After half an hour of looking around, he found a possible escape route fifty yards from the Chipotle's.

HE PACED IT OUT.

If he could get a jump on any pursuers, he could make it to the short utility hallway that led to the loading dock with the dumpster sticking out of it. There were three doors in the hallway, but when he walked through another exit he found that he could get onto the loading dock and unlock one of the doors from there. If he could get through the hallway, close the door behind himself, lock it, and get around behind the dumpster, he could run along the mall's wall. Anyone chasing him would think that he was headed for the parking structure and be looking the wrong way.

All he needed was a five-second head start.

He walked out to his truck, drove around to the loading dock, and parked as close as he could—thirty yards away—in an employee parking area. He'd smeared some mud on the plates before he left the house and had suggested that Cox and Cole do the same with the Cadillac.

He called them now.

"I've been thinking—"

"Somebody should," Cox said.

"Shut up. I've been thinking it's possible that Santos is a shooter and he'll try to kill me. If he's going to do that, he won't show up at the Chipotle's. He'll try to spot me when I'm walking up to the place and take me out with a quick shot and get away in the crowd. That's one possibility. But if they're really going to try to pull something, I think it'll be a contract job, maybe with a guy right here in Vegas. You gotta watch for Santos and see if he's with somebody else, talking to somebody. If he comes alone, then they're probably going to pay. But if it looks like somebody's scouting me . . ."

BEFORE DEESE had left for the mall, Cox had confessed that she'd grabbed a bag of cocaine from Beauchamps's dresser drawer just before bolting from the house. She and Deese had done a couple of lines—Cole didn't use drugs—and Deese had taken the remainder after they'd snorted up those first cuts.

Now, outside the mall, in the parking lot, he did another line in the truck, then sat back, letting it light up his brain as he watched the cars come and go. A security car turned around the corner of the building a hundred yards away, and he sank down slowly in the seat until he was below the window. The car continued by without slowing.

And he waited.

The coke worked on him like a tape recorder stuck on repeat, playing the same scene again and again. Santos and he would meet at the restaurant, he'd take the money. He'd tell Santos to go right and he'd go left, down the hallway and out to the car. Again: he'd meet Santos, he'd take the money, he'd tell Santos to go right and he'd go left . . .

He ran it over and over.

And then the darker stuff: the looming cop, and he'd pull his gun and shoot his way free, shoot anything moving, causing a riot, his only way out if the cops showed.

He checked his watch: 6:45.

He unrolled the baggie, used a long thumbnail to cut some lines on the face of his cell phone. Had the iPhone designers been coke freaks? Hell of a coincidence, if they hadn't, because it was the absolutely perfect cocaine slab.

He snorted up two lines, waited for them to hit, snorted up two more, rolled up the small bit of powder that remained, pushed it into his back pocket, got out of the truck, checked his weapon, pulled his shirt over it, and walked into the mall.

Into what would become a shooting gallery.

COX CALLED. "We're right up above the Chipotle's. We don't see anybody who looks like anything. Bunch of fat tourists in shorts."

Deese looked at his phone as he walked up to

the Apple Store: one minute to seven. He could see the Chipotle sign ahead. Nobody in the crowd to worry him, not so far. No sign of Santos.

He took a seat at the front of the restaurant, next to a group of college assholes. Customers were walking by with fine-smelling black beans and rice. His mouth started to water and he looked toward the kitchen, but there wasn't enough time. No time, in fact.

He crossed his hands and his feet. And then, suddenly there was Cole.

"Deese! Deese! Cops!"

Deese uncrossed his feet and was standing up and pulling out his gun, which got hung it up on his shirttail for an instant, but no more than that, when he saw a big guy coming toward him, his eyes locked on Deese's, with tabs on his shoulders, the kind of tabs you see on a bulletproof vest, and he saw a woman starting to cross in front of them. Deese shot at the cop but hit the woman instead and she went down. Then he was running and shooting, and panic erupted in the crowd, and just as he was breaking away from the crowd he saw Santos, with his green bag, and shot at him, the motherfucker, but missed, and Santos lurched away, maybe looking for a place to hide, and Deese shot him in the back. And then Deese thought, Wait, is that the money in the bag?

He turned to look behind and saw there was a guy coming at him with a gun. Deese ran, and somebody shot at him, and his foot twisted violently sideways, but the injury wasn't crippling, and he was now at the hallway, then down it and through the door. He locked the door, ran behind the dumpster, then down the outside wall of the mall. Ten seconds later, he was in his truck and firing that mother up.

His foot . . . His foot didn't feel like anything. As he drove toward an exit to the street, he reached down between his legs and ran his hand up his wounded ankle: no blood.

He turned onto the street, kicked off his left shoe, ran his hand over his ankle. Nothing. He picked up his shoe and looked at it and found a wide groove in the heel. He laughed. Some motherfucker had shot the heel of his shoe but not him.

He was halfway home before his ankle began to throb and suddenly the fear climbed on him. He turned down a side street, then another smaller one, into a residential area, pulled to the curb, got out of his truck, and puked his guts out. He'd killed a lot of people, he guessed, and he didn't mind that so much, but he might have been killed himself.

He got back in the house, the taste of vomit in his mouth, the sweat streaming down his face. He could smell his own fear in the sweat, a corrupt odor, like a rat rotting after it died under the stove.

If he didn't vanish, he was a dead man.

And he was haunted by one question. That bag

that Santos had . . . A red bag? A green bag? . . . Was there money in it? Could he have slowed down enough to grab it? Where did the cops come from? Had one of the security guards spotted him? And that guy with the gun—that was that marshal, Davenport, who'd been shot in Altadena.

Where had their tip come from?

That fuckin' Smith; that was the only answer he had. Santos told Smith about the meeting location and Smith called the cops, hoping he'd be killed. Maybe hoping both of them would be killed.

COX AND COLE were immediately swept up in a panicked crowd, running down the mall. Maybe one or two of the shoppers had seen Cole screaming at Deese, but they were left behind in seconds. Down the main hall of the mall, down escalators, into the parking structure to the Cadillac, the screaming fading behind them.

They didn't know what had happened to Deese. Cole had lingered a second or two after he'd screamed the warning and he'd seen Deese come out of the Chipotle's and fire his gun. He hadn't seen if anyone had been hit.

They were afraid to call him in case the cops had his phone.

"Do you think he's dead? That one marshal was pushing right through the crowd. He wasn't but fifteen feet away from Deese," Cox said. She'd been watching from the end of the atrium railing, thirty feet from Cole.

"I don't know what happened, everything went crazy and I ran," Cole said. "There was a lot of shooting."

"Maybe it's on the radio."

They found a couple of local stations, but there was nothing but soft rock. Cox kept twiddling the dials. "It'll be on TV," Cole said.

"Sure. But should we go back to the house? If Deese isn't dead, if he got out somehow, they might be following."

Cox stumbled over a talk show in which the right-wing host was saying, "God help us, we've gotten word of a mass shooting, an active shooter, at the Show Boat mall. We don't have details yet, but apparently there are several dead and wounded, and the shooter is still at large. Police and ambulances are there, and more are on the way. If you are listening to this in your car, don't go to the Show Boat mall."

"Ah, Christ, now we **are** fucked," Cole said. "We're in it for murder now. Both of us."

"Maybe not, maybe not. Maybe if we get far enough away . . ."

"We gotta pack up and go," Cole said. "We'll clean the house out and head for the highway. We can be in Nebraska by noon tomorrow. People won't be able to see the car so well after dark . . . How much gas we got now?"

Cox thought running was the best idea, right up until they pulled back into the rented house's driveway, activated the door to the garage, and found Deese's truck inside.

"Holy shit," Cole said. "He got out."

DEESE WASN'T HURT. And nobody had been killed at the mall. Five people had been wounded, but nobody had yet died. Deese was standing in front of the television, which was tuned to a channel showing a helicopter hovering to the west of the mall, cameras aiming down at the squadrons of cop cars.

"They got pictures of all three of us," Deese said.

"What?"

"Watch for a minute, they'll show them again. They'll go from the helicopter, to the anchor lady, to the video cameras. Then they'll talk about who's to blame. I mean, which cops are to blame for this whole fuckup."

One minute later, the station cut from the helicopter feed to the anchorwoman, who introduced the video from the mall. Cox, Deese, and Cole had worn hats and sunglasses, so the videos weren't great. The most recognizable shot was of Cox, who'd looked up at a camera as they'd run down the hall. "I didn't mean to look up. I wasn't looking for a camera."

Cole said, "We need to cut your hair and get

you in a dress. Everybody will be taking a look at a blonde with long hair. We need to punk you out. After we cut it, we'll go red. We can buy some hair stuff on the way out of town, dye your hair at a motel."

"We got Harrelson," Deese said. "He's still got that money."

Cox: "What? We're not doing that. Are you crazy?"

"Why not? The cops don't know where we're at. We hit him tonight, an hour from now, get the money, and take off," Deese said. "The time between that and taking off is only about an hour, in the middle of the night. We could pack up and not need to even come back here."

They thought about it for a minute, then Cole said to Cox, "We need the cash. That hasn't changed. We're still in the game."

# CHAPTER NINETEEN

Bob called Lucas from the mall's video monitoring station. "Get the guys out to the car. The lookouts and Deese came in separate cars and we've spotted both of them. Vegas has stoplight cameras. We ought to be able to track them for a while. We might not get right on top of them, but the Vegas operations guys could get us close."

"I'll get them down there," Lucas said. "See you at the car."

Rae was still working with Tremanty, who now seemed dazed.

Lucas had once been tracking an assassin named Clara Rinker and, with the cooperation of the FBI, had managed to con her into making a call to an organized crime figure who had betrayed her.

Or so they thought.

In actuality, Rinker knew exactly what was

happening. She'd sent a burner phone to the target, saying that she didn't want to give him her real number in advance because she was afraid he could track it. She would call him on the burner.

A friend of hers, an Army ordnance sergeant, had put a pea-sized wad of C4 inside the phone, triggered by pressing a cell phone button. Lucas and the feds, eager to listen to the call, had gathered around the mafioso as the call came in, with FBI technical people waiting to trace it. Instead, Rinker had triggered the tiny bomb. The mafioso's head had been mostly blown off and his brains hit Lucas square in the face.

Lucas had freaked. "Get it off me, get it off me . . ."

HE REMEMBERED that moment as he looked at Tremanty, still covered in the woman's blood, from a bullet meant for the FBI man.

Lucas said to Rae, "We might be able to track them. Get Sandro back to his hotel. We can talk to you on a phone and you can catch us with a cab or a cop car. I think our boy needs to chill for a while."

"I'm okay," Tremanty said, but the glazed look never left his eyes.

"No, you're not," Lucas said. "I've been where you're at and it'll take time to get straight. So go get straight. Run in place, do some pushups, take a shower."

To Rae he said, "Take him. Get a cop car back to the hotel. Bob and I are going. Catch us when you can."

She nodded, and to Tremanty said, "Come on, Ess-Tee. Let's get you cleaned up."

Tremanty yawned—the result of shock—then said, "My clothes . . . my bag . . . still in the car."

"Damnit," Lucas said. He looked at his watch. "C'mon, we're three minutes from the hotel. We'll take you."

BOB WAS WAITING at the truck, and as they left the parking structure he hit the lights and siren. "They've tracked them both south on Las Vegas Boulevard, down to the end of the Strip, now they're looking for them farther south," he said, talking a mile a minute. "The problem is, the cameras are mostly along the busier intersections. If they turn off into a residential area, we'll lose them."

"So we work the street, like we planned," Lucas said. "With all those people shot at the mall, we'll get all the help we need."

Bob's phone dinged and he answered, listened for a moment, said, "Keep me up," hung up, and said to Lucas, "Still on the boulevard, but farther south. Down toward the house where Beauchamps got killed."

"Of course," Lucas said. "The backup safe house. It was bound to be close."

Tremanty asked, "This isn't live, is it? You're not actually seeing live video?"

"No, it's all recorded," Bob said. "We're a half hour late."

THEY DROPPED Tremanty and Rae at the Bellagio, and as Rae led Tremanty away Bob said, "He looks pretty shaky."

"I could tell you about that," Lucas said.

Bob's phone dinged. He answered, listened, and hung up.

"Gotta get more south. They were headed right for the Beauchamps site. Maybe we'll get lucky."

"Sun's below the horizon," Lucas said. "Gonna start getting dark. Damn, I wish we had another hour of light."

"It is what it is," Bob said.

They were rolling fast down the boulevard, siren squawking at the red lights, trying to catch up with a couple of Vegas cop cars that were leading that way. Bob's phone dinged again. He listened, hung up, and said, "They got them at Sunset, still heading south. But there's no camera at Warm Springs, so if they turned there—"

"Bet they did," Lucas said. "We're gonnna need a map, and maybe twenty or thirty cops knocking on doors."

The phone yet again. Bob listened, hung up, said, "You would have lost your bet. They went on south past Warm Springs, because they picked them up at Blue Diamond, where there is a camera. They turned east there. We won't see them again, we're outta cameras, unless there are some in store-fronts. We need a map of the residential areas east of Blue Diamond."

Lucas got Rae's iPad from the back, called up a map, studied it for a moment. "Maybe . . . two square miles of houses. That's where they'll be, if they didn't see the cameras and are trying to dodge them. Let's find out how many cops we can get in there. If we can get enough cops, we'll spot them tonight."

"Assuming they hang around," Bob said.

"Yeah. That," Lucas said.

BOB TOOK another call and was told Las Vegas Metro cops were moving into the area, rendezvous-ing at a CVS pharmacy on what turned out to be Windmill Lane, if you were going east, Blue Diamond if you went west. When they got there, nine Metro cop cars were already in the parking lot, with more coming in behind. They parked and found an improvised command post run out of a van by an assistant sheriff named Deborah Case.

Lucas introduced himself and Bob to Case, told her they'd been at the mall, and she asked, "You have anything for us?"

Lucas shook his head. "Nope. Looks like you're

doing what we'd be doing. Give us a few blocks to cover, we both have experience doing that."

"You have a vest?"

"Yes."

"All right." She pointed at another cop. "That's Lenny. Lenny'll tell you where to go."

Lenny had a large-scale map that he'd broken down into quadrants and then smaller squares. He assigned Lucas and Bob to a square on the edge of a densely packed subdivision.

"We're looking for a white Ford F-150 SuperCab—that's the model with the smaller doors in back, the back-hinged kind. And we're looking for a silver or maybe champagne Cadillac Escalade," Lenny said. "Both have mud on the plates, and there aren't a hell of a lot of mud puddles around here at this time of year so if you see muddy plates, that's them. Both plates are white, we think California and Louisiana. Nevada plates are light blue with a yellow or orangish scene at the top or bottom."

"We're thinking a couple doors per block," Lucas said.

"We're saying two doors per side of each block. There are a lot of houses per block out here, and you get some of those curved streets and you can't see very far along them. Use your best judgment," Lenny said. "We're telling people to look for houses with vehicles parked outside that have Nevada plates and aren't the target vehicles. You wouldn't want to knock on the door and have the fuckin' cannibal open it on you."

"We'd probably try to avoid that," Bob agreed.

"I don't have any extra radio chest packs for you guys. I do have a handset you can use," Lenny said.

Bob took eight seconds to figure out the handset, and he and Lucas headed for their square. Rae called a few minutes later and said, "Where are you? I want to get in on this."

"How's Sandro?" Lucas asked.

"He wants to come, too. He's shaking it off, I think, now that he's got the blood out of his eyes and mouth."

Lucas told her about the rendezvous site at the CVS. "You guys might as well get your own assignment. But stay in touch."

Lucas and Bob had drawn a roughly rectangular area. On Rae's iPad, Lucas counted a hundred and twenty-four houses arranged in fourteen adjoining blocks of differing sizes. He and Bob conferred over the iPad, agreed that they should probably try to hit about forty houses to be sure of covering the area.

They parked the Tahoe and locked it and started walking through the warm, lingering twilight. Lucas had never been in a subdivision quite like it: the houses were large but only a few feet apart. Some had no lawn at all, nothing but a concrete slab right up to the front doors. Others had postage-stamp lawns, gravel, and a few desert shrubs. One startling lawn, hard green under the streetlight, turned out to have plastic grass. All the houses had three-car garages, usually a double-door and a single-. Most were white, though the neighborhood was sprinkled with pastels, green, beige, tan. The streets were empty.

Bob worked one side, Lucas the other, looking at the houses with their lights on. Only a few had both the lights on and vehicles outside, and they chose those. The people inside were cautious. One man shouted at Lucas, after Lucas rang the doorbell, "I'm calling the police!" Another yelled, "We don't want any!"

They'd been knocking on doors for an hour, into darkness, when Bob got a call on the handset. "This is Lenny. Marshal?"

"Yeah, this is Bob Matees."

"We got them. We're sure. We're setting up the SWAT to go in. There are lights on in the house but no visible vehicles. But, then, there wouldn't be, huh? Anyway, we're informing you. If you want to come back to the CVS, we'll lead you down to the house and you can watch it go down . . . If you want . . . I understand you got shot the last time you did this."

"That was the other guy," Bob said. "See you in five minutes." He whistled for Lucas, then shouted: "They got 'em!"

They ran back to the truck and took off.

---

AT THE CVS, Rae jogged over, trailed by Tremanty. He was wearing a fresh short-sleeved shirt, no bloodstains. "It's them," Rae said. "A neighbor said they were driving a silver Escalade and a white pickup, that they'd only been there a couple of months—two guys, no blonde—but picked Deese out of a photo display as the driver of the truck."

"How far from here?" Lucas asked.

"Not a mile. East down Windmill, then over a block. The neighbor said the house was an Airbnb, renters coming and going every week before these two guys showed up. It's them."

"When's the SWAT going in?"

"They were ready, they're closing in right now. We're welcome to go down that way, but they want us a few hundred yards out . . . They'll be doing it in fifteen minutes or so. Not a lot to think about."

"I thought we'd be doing this," Lucas said.

Tremanty nodded. "So did I. But I don't care as long as I get Deese."

CASE, the assistant sheriff, had set up two rings of pursuit cars around the target house. One ring one block out, the other ring three. If by some weird chance Deese and the others broke past the SWAT squad, the net would collapse on them.

Lucas, Bob, Rae, and Tremanty, all in the Tahoe, moved up to the first ring and parked. Bob asked Tremanty, "How's the head?"

"Okay. I stood in a shower for ten minutes with cold water in my face. I won't forget it, but I'm not stumbling around like a clown anymore," Tremanty said. To Lucas: "What'd you mean when you told me you'd been there?"

Lucas told him about the murder of the mafioso, about clawing at his face and coming away with a handful of brains.

"Aw, Jesus," Tremanty said. "That's, uh . . ."

"Yeah."

BOB'S HANDSET BURPED. "They're going in," a voice said. "Everybody locked and loaded?"

"Like John Wayne said," Bob said.

Lucas rolled a window down. If there was shooting, they'd be close enough to hear it. There was nothing, and a minute later the radio burped again. "The house is empty. Stand down."

"Goddamnit," Tremanty said.

Rae said, "We need to look."

THEY HAD TO WALK the last block to the house, where they found Case and the SWAT commander running the scene. The house was typical of the neighborhood, with both garage doors up. A white Ford F-150, with mud-smeared license plates, was parked on the single-bay side.

Case, the assistant sheriff, was standing at the

front door. Lucas, Tremanty, Bob, and Rae walked across the concrete lawn and looked past her into the house. Lucas could see clothing on the couch and sacks of junk food on a kitchen counter. "They may be coming back. For the truck," Lucas said to Case. "You should shut down the scene."

She said, "We're already there. We'll leave the outer ring in place—the Cadillac won't get in here—but it's probably too late."

She pointed, and Lucas turned to look. Three blocks away, a group of vans were parked at the side of the street, with a dozen people standing in the street iself, looking down at them. "TV," Case said. "If they're paying any attention to the media, they'll see us."

"How many guys are you leaving here?" Tremanty asked.

"Eight unmarked cars, parked on side streets, a block out from the house. If they come in, we'll see them. And we'll have the manpower to take them down. You can go on in, if you want."

She went to do something else, and Lucas, Bob, Rae, and Tremanty stepped inside the house, cruised the living room and the two bedrooms. There was high-end clothing in the closets and on the floor, in boxes and bags. "After the mall, they must've known there'd be a massive manhunt," Tremanty said. "They're on their way out of town."

"That Lenny guy said the Highway Patrol is all over the roads going out of town," Bob said.

"I . . . don't know," Lucas said. "If they were planning to run straight from the mall, they would have packed a lot of this stuff up. What would it take, five minutes? And why leave the truck? It's a hell of a lot more anonymous than the Cadillac."

"Even in the LA shoot-out, they took stuff," Bob said.

"It's weird that they'd be out, wandering around town, with everybody and his brother looking for them, and with those videos on television," Tremanty said.

"They're up to something," Bob said.

Rae: "Yes."

After a moment, Lucas said, "It's a snake hunt now. There's nothing for us. Unless something changes."

"What're you saying?" Tremanty asked.

"I'm saying we go back to the hotel and bag out," Lucas said. "Play some blackjack. Bob could pick up a little weed at one of the stores on the Strip, get mellow. Rae . . . I don't know what Rae might do. Read an art book. We can take the handset to stay in touch with what's going on here."

Rae: "Really?"

"Ah, fuck it," Tremanty said. He looked around the parking lot, the cop cars stacked up around them. "You're right. We're out of it."

# CHAPTER TWENTY

Cox, Cole, and Deese left the house a few minutes before eight. Cox wasn't talking much, after an argument with Deese. Deese, she'd said to his face, was dragging all of them down. "All of my life, I haven't done nothing really bad, and you're dragging me down. The cops are looking for me. And maybe for murder. Why'd you have to go and shoot all those people?"

Deese had smiled at her, his yellow teeth dull under the overhead LED lights. He was eating Cheetos, his lips orange with the cheese. "You're in it now, bitch," he said. "You're a genuine outlaw. They gonna put you on a table and stick a needle into your arm, unless you disappear."

Cox had started to cry, and Cole said, "Stop that. We'll figure this out. Who's gonna do what tonight?"

Deese: "What's there to figure out? We almost did it already."

Cole said, "Man, I'm doing my best to get you out of this mess. Marion and I ran our LA ring for three years and never had a speck of trouble until you showed up. But we're doing a raid tonight, and that's what I do best. We got to get organized—the chains and padlocks. Gotta look at some maps and satellite pictures. There's lots of shit to do."

THEY GOT the backpacks ready, and the guns and chains and padlocks and masks, and looked at satellite pictures. Cox turned on the TV and found a news station. All the talk was about the shootings at the mall, with some memories of the Las Vegas music festival massacre in 2017, which killed fifty-eight people and left more than eight hundred injured.

"Shit, we're small-timers," Deese said.

They ate mac-and-cheese microwave dinners, hauled their gear out to the Cadillac, and took off. Cox found another news station. They were halfway to Tina's Wayside when the woman newscaster said, "We're getting word of a SWAT team raid believed connected to the shootings at the Show Boat mall. Our reporter, Jennette English, is with Metro police on Windmill Lane."

Cox flinched. "Oh my God, they got the house."

Deese: "What?"

"That's where we were," she said. "We were on the first street off Windmill Lane. We can't go back. They've got all our clothes, everything. My shoes."

Cole: "Jesus, we got lucky. They couldn't have come in more than a few minutes after we left."

"Fuckin' cameras, I bet," Deese growled. "When I was in London, they could track people all over town, step by step, with their cameras. Bet they've got them here, too."

"What do we do?" Cox asked.

"If they were tracking us, they know the cars," Cole said. "This car. And the truck. They'll be checking everything that looks like us. We need to get out of sight right quick."

Cox started to cry again. "I want to go home."

"We really need to get out of sight," Cole said.

"It's a Cadillac," Cox wailed. "You can't park a Cadillac in the woods without somebody looking at it."

"No, but you can hide it . . . Turn left at the next light."

COLE TOOK THEM to a Cadillac dealership five minutes way. The place was closed, but there were rows of parked Cadillacs facing the street, with a few empty slots. "What if there's a guard?"

Cox asked, as she backed into one of the vacant spaces.

"I'll handle it," Deese said.

"Aw, jeez, you're gonna kill a security guard?"

Deese didn't say no. Instead, he looked around the crowded lot, then asked Cole, "How'd you know about this place? This is pretty fuckin' smart."

"Saw it when we were out driving around," Cole said. "We still gotta get down to Tina's without being spotted to see if Harrelson's there. That's not for an hour yet. We need to wipe the dirt off the license plates—at this point, it's a giveaway."

They did that, then settled in to wait.

A foil sack rustled in the backseat. "Anyone want some Cheetos?" Deese asked.

THEY ARRIVED at Tina's Wayside at ten minutes after nine o'clock, in full darkness, and immediately spotted Harrelson's Yellow Cab–colored Porsche Cayenne sitting under a light in the parking lot. "Aw, man," Cole said. "He's here."

"I hate sitting around in this Cadillac," Deese said. "Find a place we can wedge it in, where you can't see it."

They drove once around the parking lot, decided on a spot in the street that ran parallel to the backside of the lot, between two other SUVs, from where they could still see Harrelson's truck. More waiting. The last time, Harrelson had left at ten o'clock. And he did on this night, as well.

One difference: there was a short, round-headed man with him. They both got into the Cayenne and Deese said to Cox, who was driving, "Gotta go! Gotta go fast! Fast! Go! Go!"

She threw the Cadillac into gear, yanked the SUV out of the parking space, and hit the gas. "Not too fast," Cole said, "We don't want some cop stopping us."

"Gotta take the chance," Deese said. "Fast! Fast! Go! Go!"

Cox knew the route from the first attempt. They didn't see any cops—"I bet they got every spare car covering the house," Cole said—and they made it to the wall across the street from Harrelson's with three or four minutes to spare.

Cole and Deese had pulled the ski masks over their heads, checked their guns. Before they left the house, Cole had unscrewed two wooden legs from a coffee table. These made satisfactory clubs, each two feet long, with sharp, ninety-degree corners at the top end. Cole handed one to Deese and said, "Your leg. Don't kill anybody."

Deese hefted it and said, "Maybe I shoulda worked with you guys instead of working for fuckin' Smith, that miserable piece of shit. I used to have this walking stick . . ."

"Right," Cole said.

Cox would find a place to ditch the Cadillac not too far away. If something went wrong, they'd call and she'd come in a hurry. If all went well, they'd take one of Harrelson's cars and leave town in that. As they came up to the wall, she slowed, and Deese said to her, "Don't you run off. Don't you run off to the cops. If you run off and leave us here, after I get out of prison, I'll find you and cut you open and eat your liver right in front of your eyes."

"Jesus, Deese," Cole said. And to Cox: "You'll be okay. Stay in the game."

They were at the wall, and Deese and Cole, now in complete darkness, were quickly out of the SUV and over it.

AS WAS THE CASE with their first attempt, the subdivision seemed dead: no cars on the streets, nobody outside, no voices or music or people in swimming pools. The flicker of television screens danced behind a few curtains, but as part of Las Vegas, with its all-night reputation to live up to, the place was a failure.

Deese and Cole squatted behind a shrub across the street from Harrelson's house, which was dark except for one yellow-bulbed lantern by the front door. When Deese tried to brush the shrub a bit to the side, he got a handful of thorns and spent the next two minutes pulling them out of his palm and cursing in a stage whisper.

Those two minutes were well used, it turns out, as they scanned the street for trouble. Cox called, "Harrelson just went past, two people in the car . . . He's turning into the gate right now . . . He's inside the gate."

"Go," Cole said. "Walk, don't run."

They walked across the street, up to Harrelson's garage, then around the corner and behind another shrub that matched exactly the one they'd left the moment before.

Cole asked, "Ready? Got your table leg?"

"Yeah, yeah, if you got your gun. This mask keeps sticking to my tongue."

"Quiet. This is them."

LIGHTS ON the street now, a car moving slowly. Then the garage door's lifting mechanism engaging, the overhead light coming on, the door starting up. Cole said, "Not until you hear the garage door starting to come down or a car door slam. We don't want him inside the truck with his keys. Step high when you cross into the garage, you don't want to trigger the safety laser beam and reverse the door, getting it going back up again."

"I got it, I got it, you told me a million times."

The Yellow Cab Porsche was at the curb, then in the driveway, pausing to let the garage door go all the way up and disappear. A second later, the door started down again, and Cole said, "Go!"

They scrambled around the prickly shrub and the corner of the garage, high-stepped over the beam, and stooped behind a black Lexus sedan. The Porsche was on the other side of the sedan, and, beyond that, behind the single-bay garage door, was a tan Jeep Sahara. A door slammed on the Porsche, then another, and as Cole and Deese peered through the back window of the Lexus, and out the other side, they saw the short, pumpkin-headed man walk between the Lexus and the Porsche and turn away from them, toward the door to the interior of the house.

Cole said, "Now," and stood and stepped around the end of the Lexus behind Pumpkin Head, who didn't see him, and then Harrelson emerged from behind the Porsche, and he did see him and tried to reverse his course but Cole pointed his gun at Harrelson's head and screamed, "Freeze! Freeze or I'll kill you, motherfucker."

Pumpkin Head lurched, surprised and in shock, and turned. Deese, coming up behind and to the side of Cole, hit him on the forehead with the table leg with a resounding crack that sounded like a dead branch being broken.

Cole said, "Jesus," as Pumpkin Head went down flat but somehow kept the muzzle of his weapon on Harrelson. "On the wall, on the wall, motherfucker. Put your hands up on the wall. Put them up."

Pumpkin Head struggled to his hands and knees, groaning—"Ow! Ow! Ow!"—and Deese kicked him in the ribs. And when Pumpkin Head went down again, Deese stepped over his body and said to Harrelson, "Don't make me beat you to death. Open the fuckin' trunk on the Porsche."

Harrelson, red-faced and angry, but not obviously frightened, said, "I gotta get my keys outta my pocket. We're not gonna fight you. And don't hurt Dopey no more."

"I'll fuckin' kill him if I fuckin' feel like it, fuckin' Dopey," Deese said.

Harrelson took a key fob out of his pocket, pushed a button, and the back hatch of the Porsche opened up to reveal a set of golf clubs and a gym bag. The bag was full of golf shirts, two pair of golf shoes, and a plastic bag full of dirty shirts. Deese pulled up the floor mat: nothing there but a spare tire and tools.

"I'm gonna ask you only once," Deese said. "Where's the money?"

Dopey/Pumpkin Head was still on the floor, still groaning, but now it was "Ahhh! Ahhh! Ahhh!" Deese kicked him again and he yelped, and Harrelson said, "I've got a roll in my pocket, and Dopey has a thousand, probably."

Deese lashed out with the table leg and hit

Harrelson on the side of the face, opening a gash across his cheekbone and knocking him against the garage wall and then down on his butt. A rake hanging on the wall fell on top of him.

Deese said, "Get the fuck up or I'll break your fuckin' kneecaps."

Cole said, "Easy, we don't want to kill him. We won't get the money if we kill him."

"I'm not gonna kill him, but if he doesn't tell me about the money I'm gonna cripple everything but his mouth." Harrelson was struggling to get up, and Deese kicked him in the thigh and he went down again, and Deese asked, "You wanna play golf in a wheelchair?"

"There's more money in the house . . . Maybe a few thousand."

Harrelson had dropped the fob when Deese hit him, and now Cole scooped it up and said, "Get him in the house. When we go through the door, you might hear an alarm pad start to beep. We'll give him ten seconds to disarm it. If he doesn't, we gotta run. Stand back, because I'll put a bullet in his brain for our trouble and then one in Dopey's. You don't want to get the blood on you because of that DNA shit." Cole doing his fright bit.

"Got it," Deese said.

"Alarm's turned off," Harrelson muttered. "Don't hurt us and I'll get the cash. The cash we've got."

---

THE DOOR to the house opened, and a blond woman with big Texas hair stuck her head in the garage and said, in her Texan drawl, "What the f—" before Deese hit her in the face and knocked her on her ass and back into the house. Harrelson shouted, "Hey!" and Cole stuck the gun in his face.

Harrelson asked, "What? You're gonna murder me in cold blood?"

Deese said, "Fuck, yeah, and enjoy the shit out of it," and pointed the gun at his head.

Harrelson didn't flinch, and Cole said to Deese, "Remember the money," and Deese said, "Okay," and shot Dopey in the hip, the discharge sounding like a cannon in the enclosed space. Cole jumped, Dopey screamed, and Harrelson shouted, "Stop it, for Christ's sakes. We'll give you the money."

GLORIA HARRELSON was crawling across the kitchen floor, dripping blood from her nose and coughing. Deese wagged his gun at Harrelson and said, "Get in the house," and Harrelson walked past Cole and into the house and said, "We gotta get an ambulance for Dopey."

Deese: "Fuck him, let him die."

Dopey's hair was scraped back into a ponytail, and Deese said to Cole, "Put your gun on this asshole," meaning Harrelson, and when Cole did Deese backed up to Dopey and grabbed his hair and dragged him, screaming, into the house and dumped him on the floor. Gloria Harrelson was still crawling toward the kitchen, and Deese asked, "Where do you think you're going?" and kicked her in the ass and she went flat on the floor and began weeping.

Harrelson said, "One more thing and I'll be on you like white on rice."

"And you'll be a fuckin' dead hero," Deese said.

"And you won't get one penny, you piece of shit!" Harrelson shouted.

Cole said, "We're gonna need that money. Where is it?"

"I got my roll, and there's more money in the safe," Harrelson said. "Don't mess with Gloria anymore."

"Gimme the roll," Cole said.

Harrelson dug in his pocket and pulled out his roll of bills, mostly hundreds, and Cole thumbed them and said, "Maybe three grand."

"Not enough, nowhere fuckin' near enough. I'll tell you what, we don't get enough money, I'll take it out in pussy," Deese said to Harrelson.

"Don't do that," Gloria wailed from the floor.

Cole said to Deese, "We've been here too long. Cut the bullshit. We want the safe open. And if we don't have it in a minute and thirty seconds, I'm gonna kill them and we're getting out."

"Don't do that," Gloria cried. "Safe's in the family room."

Deese kicked Dopey and said, "Gimme your cell phone," and Dopey groaned and said, "I'm bleeding real bad," and Deese said, "Give me the fuckin' phone or I'll kick you to death."

Dopey fumbled the phone out of a blood-soaked pocket and Deese stomped on it. The he waggled his gun at Harrelson and said, "The safe."

As Harrelson and Gloria led the way to the family room, Deese leaned close to Cole and said, "I'm pretty fuckin' good at this."

"Man . . ." Cole just shook his head.

The safe was concealed in the side of a cabinet in the bar. Harrelson pulled open the cupboard-style door to reveal a four-foot-high steel box with a combination dial. He spun the dial a couple of times, then leaned closer and stopped sequentially at four different numbers. He popped the safe open and stepped back. Cole said to Deese, "If he tries to fuck with me, shoot him."

Deese pointed his gun at Harrelson, and Cole got down on his knees and began pulling drawers out of the safe. He dumped a lot of jewelry on the floor—gold chains, a couple of diamond necklaces and rings, some emeralds, a sparkly gold Panther brooch by Cartier. Cole slipped the brooch in his pocket. The bottom drawer turned up a stack of cash. Cole fanned the cash out and said to Deese, "Maybe six or eight."

Deese pointed the gun at Gloria's head and said

to Harrelson, "Where's the money, asshole? Where's the money? We know you got it."

"In a safe-deposit box, dummy," Harrelson said, "Downtown. In the bank."

"We know you used to keep it in your car."

"Everybody in town **knows** that and it's bullshit, and always has been. I was never stupid enough to do that. How much did you hear? Three million? Five million? I bet it was five million, right? Well, think about it. You gonna drive around a town full of assholes with five million in cash? You get rear-ended and there's a fire? A junkie breaks in? You're out three million. Or five. Whatever you heard, it's bullshit."

Cole: "Let's go." And to Harrelson: "We need the keys to that Lexus."

Deese: "Ain't got enough money." He shoved Gloria Harrelson in the chest, hard enough to knock her back on a couch. "Listen to me, bitch. Where's the money?"

She began crying again, then choked out, "In the bank, in the box. Honest to God, that's the truth. It's in the box."

"Fuck it, you're coming with us."

Cole: "What?"

"She's coming with us," Deese said. He turned to Harrelson. "We want two million in cash tomorrow morning when the bank opens. You don't get it to us, I'll kill her. You call the cops, I'll kill her. If we gotta run with her, I'll kill her. But first we'll bang her so hard they'll probably find her pussy lyin' in the street."

Harrelson: "You fuckin' punks don't know what you're—"

Deese struck with his pistol, raking Harrelson across the face, ripping another jagged cut down across his cheek and nose. Harrelson staggered backwards, fell on the floor. Deese pulled the stocking off his face. "Look at me. You know this face? It's been on TV . . . All over the TV."

Gloria groaned, "Oh my God, it's the cannibal."

Deese turned. "That's right. The cannibal. I'm gonna roast your tits over a slow fire, we don't get that money."

Gloria: "Oh my God . . ."

Cole said, "Deese, I don't—"

"Shut the fuck up," Deese said. He waggled the gun at Gloria Harrelson. "Out to the car. And we need those keys."

Harrelson said, "Don't mess with her. I swear to God, I know people here, we'll track you down. And I'll pour a gallon of gas on your head and set you on fire."

"You do anything but get that money to us, you won't be doing that because you'll be dead, along with your raped-ass old lady."

Cole: "Jesus Christ."

Harrelson to Cole: "Don't let that motherfucker touch her."

Cole opened one of the backpacks and told

Deese, "Put your gun on him," and to Harrelson: "I'm gonna put a chain around your waist. You fight me, the cannibal is going to kill you."

Cole threw the chain around Harrelson's waist, fastening it with a padlock. When the padlock was secure, he led Harrelson to a living room couch and looped the other end of the chain around the couch and locked it.

He showed the two padlock keys to Harrelson and said, "These'll be on the kitchen table with your cell phone. You call the cops, the cannibal will kill your wife. Think about it. There won't be any point in calling anyway because by the time you get the couch into the kitchen, we'll be long gone."

Cole got the other chain out of the pack, and Deese asked, "What're you doing?"

"Got to chain up Dopey."

"If Dopey's alive, the asshole will call an ambulance, the cops'll come in."

"Goddamnit, Deese."

Deese kicked Dopey's wounded hip and said, "Fuck you," and shot him in the head. To Harrelson: "There. Now you don't got to call nobody."

COLE, shocked deep in his heart, drove, Deese sat in the back with Gloria Harrelson. Nobody spoke until Cole backed the Lexus out of the garage and into the street. When they were rolling, Cole punched up his speed dial and called Cox and asked, "Where are you?"

"Hiding behind a pile of dirt."

"How do I get there?"

"Take a left out of the gate, go about three blocks to a construction site. You'll see a pile of dirt on the left side of the road as high as a house. I'm behind it . . . Did you get the money?"

"It's complicated," Cole said. "It's fucking awful, is what it is."

"Oh no."

AT THE PILE of dirt, Cole told Cox what had happened, and she whispered, "He killed him? And we . . . We can't kidnap her. This is terrible, this is awful. Oh, God, Cole, we gotta get away from this maniac."

"I'm thinking about that," Cole said.

"You got your gun?"

"Yeah. But I never shot anybody."

COLE USED A DIME to unscrew the California plates on the Cadillac and transferred them to the Lexus. When Deese asked why, he said, "Because I don't think the cops know the California plates, but they'll know the plates on the Lexus if Harrelson calls them. Now we're driving a Lexus with California plates, which is different from anything they know. Here in Vegas, driving a Lexus is like driving a Ford."

Cox asked, "Should I erase my fingerprints? From the Caddy?"

"Too late for that, honey," Cole said.

She tried anyway, using a sock to rub the steering wheel and the center console and door handles. As she did, she kept muttering, "Oh, God, Oh, Jesus," and looking over at the Lexus, where Deese waited in the backseat with Gloria Harrelson.

When Cole was finished with the license plates, he pointed to the passenger side and then walked around to the driver's-side door and got in. Cox got a sack out of the back of the Cadillac and said, "At least I saved some shoes." In the car, she turned to look at Gloria in the back and asked, "You okay?"

Harrelson just sobbed.

"She's bummed out because I've been feeling her up," Deese said with a grin. "There's some nice stuff under all them clothes."

"Don't do that," Cox said. "Please don't do that, I can't stand it." To Cole: "Where are we going? We can't go back to the house."

"Don't know," Cole said. "We got to figure that out."

"I know where we're going," Deese said. "We need to head north on Highway 95. About two hours . . . We got gas?"

"We got gas. But if we're gonna try to do this, we need to make another stop at a Walmart."

Deese: "What for?"

"We need to buy a couple of metal file boxes."

Deese: "Why?"

Cole told him. Deese said, "I didn't think of that."

"You don't think a lot," Cox said. "Period."

# CHAPTER TWENTY-ONE

Lucas estimated that he'd been asleep for all of fourteen seconds when his phone rang. He groped at its lighted face on the bedside table, looked at the time and caller: one o'clock in the morning, Tremanty.

When Lucas answered, Tremanty said, "The local office got a call from a guy named Harrelson and they eventually called me. Harrelson's a gambler who's believed to have a lot of cash on hand. Deese and some other guy, probably Cole, crashed his house tonight, thinking that Harrelson had five million bucks there or in his car. He didn't. So Deese and the others took Harrelson's wife and they're holding her for ransom."

"That's nuts," Lucas said.

"Exactly. Deese shot a friend of Harrelson's. Killed him. To make his point. And he pistol-whipped Harrelson. Deese says he'll rape Harrelson's wife and then kill her if Harrelson does anything but pay the money. If they see cops, if they don't get the money, then they'll rape and kill her. Harrelson believes them."

"How do they know it's Deese?"

"He was wearing a mask when he came in, but he took it off. To further make his point."

"Harrelson called you anyway?"

"The guy's not stupid," Tremanty said. "He figures if he pays, they'll kill his old lady anyway to eliminate a witness."

"How's Deese gonna . . . Harrelson wouldn't go with him after the payoff . . . There'd still be witnesses . . ."

"We're not dealing with a genius here. While Deese isn't so bright, he's perfectly willing to kill at the drop of a hat. In New Orleans, that's almost the same as being bright. He's telling the truth, though: he'll rape and kill the woman if he doesn't get the money. Probably rape the woman and kill her even if he does. He's gone over the edge. They'll call Harrelson in the morning and tell him where to deliver the money."

"What do you want from me?" Lucas asked. "I'll do anything you say."

"Actually, I'm calling you to update you and to see if you might have any idea on how to handle this. I'm heading over to the office. We're keeping the Vegas cops out of it, for the time being."

"I'll get with Bob and Rae," Lucas said. "We'll be in touch."

BOB AND RAE were early-to-bed types and looked stunned when they stumbled into Lucas's room. Lucas, a night owl, felt fine. But after fifteen minutes, they concluded that they didn't have much to offer. Lucas called Tremanty and told him such.

Tremanty told him to hold on for a few seconds, apparently walking somewhere, and Lucas could hear voices in the background. When Tremanty came back, the voices were silenced.

"Listen, Lucas . . . Man, the thing is, Harrelson looks like you. Like us, actually, but I'm skinnier, I don't have the shoulders, and I've got to run the team. And he's clean-shaven, and all. What I'm saying is, we need somebody to put on a golf hat and a golf shirt and be Harrelson tomorrow for the money drop. If there **is** a money drop."

"I can do that," Lucas said. "What's the plan?"

"Harrelson has to go to the bank to get the money. They may be watching him—in fact, I'm betting on it—so we're flooding the zone. Our idea is, Harrelson goes to the bank at nine o'clock, when it opens, in a pink golf shirt and khaki slacks and a baseball cap. He takes the cap off out on the steps and looks around so that if they are out there, watching, they'll see him. You're already in the bank, in your pink shirt and khakis, and he gives you the cap, you put it on, and you come out fifteen minutes later with the bag."

"That should work if they're watching the bank," Lucas said.

"It's what we've got right now. At least we'll have somebody in play if they call."

"What do you want me to do right now?" Lucas asked.

"Go back to bed. Try to get some sleep. We've spoken to the bank manager and we'll get you inside at seven o'clock. So, set your alarm for six. Or I can call you then. We'll brief you when you're at the bank, what we know at that point."

"What do you want from Bob and Rae?"

"If we need to go in heavy somewhere."

"I'll tell them," Lucas said.

The situation felt weird to Lucas: he was usually the guy in charge, running the team, and was not used to being one of the pawns. He told Bob and Rae what they'd be doing. And then they all went back to bed.

HE WAS UP a few minutes before six, and Tremanty called right at six o'clock and said the plan hadn't changed, except that the agent in charge had talked to the sheriff. The FBI would handle it, but the Vegas cops now knew what was happening.

"It's a political thing, you know, after the mall," Tremanty said.

---

LUCAS CLEANED UP, found the bank on Google Maps, called Bob and Rae to make sure they were awake—they were, but they'd be going to the FBI office with their gear, and Bob would be going out to a shooting range—and took the Volvo to a parking structure near the bank and walked over right at seven. Tremanty was waiting inside the door with two other FBI people, including the Las Vegas agent in charge. Lucas could smell the stress.

"We'll have seven more agents around you, running a box," the AIC said, poking a finger as Lucas's chest. "Don't try to beat any yellow lights."

"We want you to talk to Harrelson on the phone," Tremanty said. "He's already up, but he won't be here until nine. We want you to hear the way he speaks. You'll have his cell phone in the car. We'll be tracking the cell and any incoming calls. And we'll have both a Cessna and a chopper in the sky, tracking cars. And there'll be a GPS tracker inside the money bag."

"What if he asks for identifiers? What if he asks, what tattoo does your wife have on her ass?" Lucas asked.

The AIC said, "Ah. We got that. When you answer the phone, you'll make sure it's on speaker. You'll be carrying a handset that'll come back to us, and Harrelson, and you'll have an earbud in your ear. If Deese asks about the tattoo on his old lady's ass, Harrelson will say, 'Property of the Hells Angels,' or whatever, and you answer the question."

"Cool," Lucas said. And he laughed. "'Property of Hells Angels'?"

"The problem is, of course, that they'll think about aerial surveillance, and all that, and they'll try something tricky," Tremanty said. "They'll have two or three vehicles, maybe a stolen one in addition to the Cadillac and the Lexus, and they'll dump one or two of them. Something tricky anyway. Like driving into a parking structure and running out on foot. Or whatever."

Lucas asked Tremanty, "How's Santos? Is he going to make it?"

"Yes, but he's messed up. Lost a kidney, a chunk of his stomach. A slug barely missed his spine, but he might have some nerve damage that'll affect his legs. Won't know about that for a while."

"I'm asking because he lost us in Caesars and we were right on his tail," Lucas said. "He dumped his car with the valet and disappeared into the crowd. I'm thinking Deese and his crew could do the same thing, and we could wind up with guns in a crowd again."

"Don't want that," the AIC said, with a touch of sweat in his voice. "I mean, Jesus, we really don't want that. You wouldn't believe the PR hassle we've got after that thing at the mall. We're smoothing it over, but it looks like ten years of good relations with the local cops just went down the drain."

Tremanty: "If those fuckin' cops hadn't come running down the mall—"

"Don't start," the AIC snapped. "I already got a headache. So does the sheriff. We don't need to hear any more about it."

Tremanty nodded.

Lucas asked, "Real money?"

"We've got that going," Tremanty said. "Not two million, but enough to look like a lot. One-dollar bills, wrapped up in bundles, with hundreds on the outside. Two hundred bundles, so you'll be carrying a little less than forty thousand. The money bundles will be supplied by the bank but will come from Harrelson. If you lose it, it's Harrelson's loss."

"All you have to do," the AIC said, "is be Harrelson. That's it."

"Sounds easy," Lucas said. "It never is, though."

"Not only that, you have to wear silly clothes," Tremanty said, handing him a sack. Lucas looked inside and found a new pair of khaki slacks and a pink golf shirt.

"Where'd you get these in the middle of the night?"

"This is Vegas," Tremanty said.

LUCAS GOT on the phone with Harrelson, who had a touch of a dry, Southwestern accent. His vocal range and Lucas's—mild baritones—were a near match, which helped.

"I'm sitting here on my bed all freaked out," Harrelson said. "I do love that girl, and that goddamn cannibal has her. I might have taken him on, but there were two guns and it only would have gotten all of us shot."

"You did okay," Lucas said. "Tell me the whole story, beginning with when they caught you in the garage."

"I already told the FBI agents . . ."

"I want to hear you talk, see if I can fake the way you sound."

"Oh. All right . . . Well, I pulled into my garage . . ."

As Harrelson spoke, Lucas turned the phone upside down so he could still hear him but could simultaneously practice the same accent. When Harrelson finished, Lucas said, "I hope I got it."

"So do I. You gotta save Gloria, man. Those people are animals."

"See you here at the bank," Lucas said. "Nine o'clock."

OFF THE PHONE, Lucas asked Tremanty, "How do I sound?"

"Like a Minnesotan trying to imitate George Bush."

"Thank you."

———

DEESE AND HIS CREW would know the bank didn't open until nine, so the feds expected that Harrelson wouldn't get a call until a bit before or after.

The bank's employees began showing up a few minutes before eight and were taken aside, one at a time or in small groups, and briefed on what was about to happen. They were asked to turn off their cell phones until the agents told them it was all right to turn them on again. That caused some complaints, especially from parents who said they needed to check on school arrivals, and Tremanty agreed to allow necessary calls but only with an agent monitoring what was said. That generated some complaints about privacy, but Tremanty used quiet, friendly persuasion to tell them to go fuck themselves and their privacy issue.

Lucas: "I like the way you did that."

"It's how you would have done it . . . Go change clothes."

He did, and when he came back the AIC whistled and said, "You're so pretty, I might date you myself if I didn't already have a wife."

"I understand the attraction, but I'd never date a feeb," Lucas said.

"Hate that word 'feeb,'" Tremanty said.

"That's why real cops call you that," Lucas said.

HARRELSON WAS outside the doors at five minutes to nine, carrying a cloth shoulder bag.

They let him stand there in the sun until exactly nine o'clock, when a security guard opened the doors and Harrelson walked in.

Lucas didn't think they much resembled each other, except in size and coloring; Harrelson also had a bit of a gut, but that wouldn't be hard to fake. He also had white gauze bandages on his forehead and cheek, which the feebs hadn't thought about, but they rounded up the bank's first aid kit and stuck some gauze on Lucas.

Lucas doubted that the Deese or his crew would risk getting close enough to see the differences. Harrelson had parked in the bank's parking lot in the Yellow Cab Porsche and asked Lucas if he'd ever driven one.

"I've had 911s for twenty years, but I've never driven a Cayenne."

"I've had both, it's the same thing, you'll be fine," Harrelson said, as he handed over the car's keys. "You can fake using the fob to unlock it, but I left it unlocked."

He gave Lucas the golf hat and his cell phone and took a pile of clothes out of the shoulder bag—Harrelson would change into black slacks and a black shirt, with a straw hat, when he eventually left the bank.

Tremanty came up with a box full of bricks of cash and a black box the size of a cell phone—the GPS tracker. He loaded them into the bag, with the tracker at the bottom. The money looked good at a glance, but if anyone riffled them they'd imme diately see the one-dollar bills under the hundreds. "Forty grand," he said. "From Mr. Harrelson."

"Don't worry about taking care of it," Harrelson told Lucas. "I wouldn't mind getting it back. But if it gets away, I got more. Do what you have to do."

Lucas nodded. "I've met a couple of relatives of kidnap victims. I've never seen anyone as cool as you are."

"I make a lot of money as a gambler," Harrelson replied. "You make money that way by dealing with the reality you actually get, not what you wish you'd get. I'm freaking out, though, I'm just not showing it. I'm trying to deal with the reality."

"We'll get her back," Tremanty offered.

"Yeah, maybe," Harrelson said. His face revealed nothing.

Tremanty looked at his watch. "You've been in here for fifteen minutes." To Lucas: "Time to go. Get lucky."

"Take it from me: luck won't have anything to do with this," Harrelson said.

Lucas pulled down the golf hat low and headed for the door.

# CHAPTER TWENTY-TWO

The last two miles of the trip north had been over dirt roads, out into the desert, the Lexus occasionally dragging bottom. The last leg took them up a steep rocky track until the headlights caught a silvery reflection below a south-facing bluff.

Cox: "This is it?"

From the backseat, Deese said, "Yeah, this is it. You think anybody's gonna find us out here?"

"I don't even know where I am myself," Cole said.

They were looking at an old Airstream trailer, sitting up on concrete blocks. It looked like it'd been rolled and somebody had tried to fix it with a bumping hammer. There were lights at both ends of the trailer, but nothing moved until they popped the doors on the Lexus, and a corroded man's voice said, "Hold it right there, motherfuckers, or you gonna die."

Deese yelled, "Ralph! It's me! Clay! . . . Deese!"

A man wobbled around the end of the Airstream, carrying a pump shotgun. He might have been anything between forty and sixty, heavily bearded, and wore denim overalls over a T-shirt. A hole was ripped through one knee, like Cox had seen everywhere in West Hollywood, but this hole had nothing to do with fashion. "What do you want?"

"Place to bag out," Deese said. "One night." To the others he said, "Ralph's a miner."

"Whyn't you go to a motel?" Ralph asked.

"Had trouble with the cops."

"I hope to hell you didn't go leadin' 'em up here," Ralph said.

"No, no, we're clean," Deese said.

"Well, shit. You might as well come in and tell me about it."

DEESE HAD a heavy hold on one of Gloria Harrelson's arms and he dragged her toward the Airstream and she started weeping again, and Ralph asked, "What's wrong with her?"

"We had some trouble with a guy who owes us money. Lots of money. This is his wife. We took her as security."

"How much money?"

"Two million," Deese said.

"Holy shit," Ralph said. "You're gonna throw me a piece of that? Rent?"

"Yeah, yeah, we'll take care of you," Deese said.

They trailed behind him to the Airstream. The trailer seemed solid enough, when they climbed the steps. Cox could hear a chugging sound from outside, and when she asked Ralph told her that it was the diesel generator on the other side of the hill.

The inside of the Airstream was like the inside of a pill capsule—much of the original finishes had been ripped out, except a café-type table with couch-like seats on either side. A bed was visible in a room at the far end of the capsule, with an added real-house-type door for privacy. "I don't got much to eat except frozen pizzas and some canned Boy-are-dee," Ralph said.

"We're okay," Cole said.

"Exactly what kind of trouble you in?" Ralph asked Deese.

"Hard to explain," Deese said.

"Deese ate some people back in Louisiana," Cox said. "And tonight he killed a man."

She was obviously serious, and Ralph laughed. "If somebody asked me, that's what I would've guessed. How'd them people taste?"

"Okay," Deese mumbled.

"You barbecue them?"

"Man . . ." Deese said.

"Love me some barbecue, like your daddy used to make," Ralph said. "How'd you ever come to do that anyway?"

Deese, now exasperated, said, "Look. Remember

when we'd all go deer hunting and haul them carcasses out of the woods? All that meat? I'd hauled some of these deadasses back to my place to bury them and carry them back there, behind the house, but it was just . . . meat. I got to thinking about it. And so one day . . ."

Cox: "Yuck! That's disgusting. That's probably why you smell."

"What?"

"Let it go," Cole said. "What are we doing?"

Deese shook his head and turned back to Ralph. "I want a place to sleep for a while and then we'll get out of here. You still got that old green motorcycle?"

Cox said, "He shot a whole bunch of people in a mall down in Las Vegas. Then he kidnapped Gloria here."

"Jesus Christ, Clay, you leave anything out?" Ralph asked.

"Hey . . ."

Ralph glanced at Cox with a teasing grin on his face. "Is there a reward for him?"

"Not as far as I know," she said, still serious. "He was being chased by the FBI and the U.S. Marshals, and then the Los Angeles cops, and now the Vegas cops." She glanced at Cole. "Did I miss anybody?"

"The Louisiana cops," Cole said.

"Oh, yeah, them too," Cox said.

"Well, shit happens," Ralph said. "We gotta figure out where we're all gonna sleep. I could spoon up with this one here." He nodded at Cox.

Cox said, "Fuck that, you old monster."

"WE GOTTA lot of talking to do before morning," Deese said to Ralph. "You still cook up some meth?"

"From time to time," Ralph said. "Getting tougher, though."

"Probably gonna need a few hits to stay awake tomorrow," Deese said. "How about that old motorcycle? You still got it? Still work?"

"Works fine. It's the only way I can get up to the mine."

"We're gonna need to take it with us. And your truck," Deese said. "Anyway, we'll talk later, tell you about it. Right now I'm gonna take Gloria in the back room for a few minutes."

Gloria had been snuffling all the time they were in the trailer and now Deese pushed her toward the bedroom.

"Don't let him do this, don't let him do this," she pleaded with them, looking mostly at Cox. "Don't let him . . . You know what he's going to do."

Then the two were in the bedroom and the door slammed.

Ralph asked Cole, "How much do you want for this one?" and nodded at Cox.

"What's wrong with you people?" Cox asked. To Ralph: "Fuck you." And to Cole: "We gotta get out of here. You got the car keys."

Ralph took a couple of steps back and lifted his shotgun. "Can't let you do that. I'm gonna need some of that money Clayton's after. Sit down and take it easy and we'll talk to Clayton when he gets done."

Gloria Harrelson cried out from the bedroom, and Cox said, "You know what he's doing back there."

Ralph took another couple of steps back and sank into a rickety wooden chair, the gun still up, and said, "Well, hell. That's what women're for. Always has been, always will be. Might rip off a piece myself, if Clay says okay. Been a while since I been down to Vegas."

"If you do that, you'll have to kill her so she doesn't come back on you," Cole said. "That'd be cold-blooded murder."

Ralph pulled at the top of one ear, then said, "Well . . . yeah, I guess. That seems to be baked in the cake anyway."

They could hear sex sounds from the bedroom, and Cole asked, "You got any music here?"

"I got a radio," he said. "It's behind you. The right knob turns it on. It's old rock and roll."

Cole turned, saw the old brown Bakelite box, turned the right knob, and Led Zeppelin came up with "Whole Lotta Love."

"I hate that old shit," Cox said. They heard another cry from Gloria Harrelson. "Turn it up louder."

DEESE SPENT forty-five minutes in the bedroom, then came out, pulling up his pants, and said to Ralph, "I used some of that baling wire to tie up her leg to the bed. You can't get them windows open, can you?"

"Not without a crowbar," Ralph said.

Deese glanced at Cox. "What?"

"That was awful," Cox said.

"Really, it was pretty good," Deese said with his yellow grin. "I had to whack her a time or two to get her started, but after that it was okay."

"Aw, Jesus," Cox said, looking away from him. They could hear Harrelson sobbing again from the bedroom.

Deese said, "About tomorrow. Here's what we're gonna do."

"Whatever it is, it won't work," Cole said. "It's about ten to one that Harrelson's called the cops. You can't never do the money exchange and get away with it. What we really need to do is get out of here, get north. We could go up to Seattle or Portland, I'd school you in the home invasion business, we could pick up a couple million in a few months."

"You know why people don't get away with the

money?" Deese asked. "Because they don't do the exchange in Vegas."

He turned to Ralph. "Remember that time I came out here and called you and you said you'd busted out at the MGM and were temporarily homeless? You were living down below?"

Ralph smiled. "Really? That's how you're gonna do it?" And a second later: "The motorcycle and the truck! You're smarter than you look."

DEESE LAID OUT his plan and, when he finished, said, "That's why we had to come up to see old Ralph here. The truck and the bike. Cole drives the truck up and back, no reason for anybody to look at him. I take all the risk on the bike. I don't make it, you're no worse off. If I make it, we got two million dollars. I believe we'll make it."

Cole bobbed his head. "That's not a bad plan. It all depends on the truck and the bike, though. I'm looking around this place"—he waved a hand around the interior of the Airstream—"and I'm not impressed with the maintenance. If the bike blows up, everything blows up."

"The bike's fine," Ralph said. "I ride it every day, and I keep it up. But even if you had to get off and run, it's only a few blocks."

They talked for a while longer, and Deese said, finally, "We leave here by six, we get down to Vegas by eight. I make the call to Harrelson at nine. It'll be all over, one way or the other, in fifteen minutes."

"What about Gloria?" Cox asked.

"We'll figure her out tomorrow," Deese said.

"They might want to talk to her, to know that she's still alive," Cole said.

"Well, tough shit. That's what I'll tell them. I'll tell them I got her stashed in a house, that I know all about tracking cell phones and so they're not going to talk to her. And if they don't pay up, I'll cut her throat, dump her in the desert." He hesitated, thinking about it, then said, "And they'll believe me. Because it's true."

WHEN THEY were done talking, Deese went back to the bedroom, and the crying and beating and sex sounds started again, and Ralph said, "I got a hard-on like a telephone pole. Almost like being there."

"Shut up, old man," Cox said.

Cole said, "I'm not going to listen to this. Let's go sit in the Lexus. Maybe we can lay the seats down and sleep there."

Ralph twitched the shotgun at them. "You can do that, but why don't you use that key thing to open it up from the doorway here and then leave it with me. You act like you might want to leave us and we can't have that."

Cole looked at Cox, then at Ralph and the

shotgun, and nodded. "Come with us. We'll need the key for the seats."

OUTSIDE, in the Lexus, they got in the back, with the seats reclined, and when they'd made themselves as comfortable as they could for sleeping Ralph said, "Sleep tight," and went back inside. Cox asked, "What do we do?"

"I think . . . we try for the money," Cole said. "Deese's plan will work. If we pull it off, we go up north, somewhere in the Midwest, get jobs, rent an apartment, and lie low."

"I don't wanna—"

"I know what you wanna. You want Southern California or Miami, or something like that. But we need to put some time between us and this mess. The more, the better. They got our fingerprints and DNA, and all that, and if they ever pick us up we're done. We need to be careful little kids until we can work out better IDs and get out of the country. If we get a half million dollars from this deal, we can make it down to Panama and live for ten to fifteen years on it. By then, nobody will care about all this."

"I don't believe that. People got shot. People are dead. Gloria's been raped and she's a witness. And both of us are part of what she saw."

"Gloria's good as dead."

"No."

"Oh yes. There's a logic to this. Like Ralph said: it's baked in the cake," Cole said. "Doing what Deese's done, there can't be any witnesses. They'll kill her and haul her out to some old mine, or something, and bury her and nobody'll ever find her. That's the way it is. We gotta take care of ourselves. So Gloria's dead."

"Still . . ."

"Listen. They'll catch Deese or kill him, the FBI will. After that, nobody'll really care about the rest of us. And ten to fifteen years from now, they'll care even less. I've been to Panama. It's a real decent place. A girl like you, even if you don't want to be with me . . . There are all kinds of American expats down there, guys looking for women to hang with. You'll hook up with some guy . . ."

"I'll hang with you, at least for now," Cox said.

"Well, that's fine. I do like you. We got to be careful, though, when Deese and I get back tomorrow," Cole said. "We need a piece of that money and he might want to keep all of it. I've got my pistol, but he knows that. So we'll have to be really careful."

He reached into his back pocket, pulled out the Panther pin he'd palmed when they raided the Harrelsons' safe. "Didn't tell Deese about this—I saved it for you. I looked at it, it's a Cartier. That's a jeweler, top-end. It's got some diamonds, and shit. I thought you'd like it."

Cox took the pin, turned it in her hand. "Oooh. It's so beautiful, John. That's the best gift I ever got. So . . . It sparkles, doesn't it?"

"Yeah. That's why I grabbed it."

Cox pulled herself forward, pulled a bag out from under the front passenger seat, groped inside it, and produced Beauchamps's 9mm. "Deese doesn't know about this, either."

"You know how to use it?"

"Oh, yeah, I shot guns like this a few times." She pulled back the slide, let it snap forward. "All cocked and ready to shoot. All I have to do is push this safety thingy forward. Marion told me that if I ever have to shoot somebody to get as close as I can and then keep pulling the trigger until the gun stops shooting."

"You can do that?" Cole asked.

"With Deese? Yeah."

"This time tomorrow, we could be in Denver."

"Or dead," Cox said. She didn't mention the money in the bag.

# CHAPTER TWENTY-THREE

Lucas shouldered the bag of money, pulled open the bank door, trotted around to the Porsche, pushing his gut out as he went, waved the key fob at the car, and climbed inside. Everything looked just like the inside of his 911. The earbud was in his right ear, the passenger side, already wired into the handset. Tremanty said in his ear, "Okay, you looked right. I would have bought it, if I were Deese."

"Now I sit and wait," Lucas said. "I don't see anyone on the street coming my way."

"They'll make you drive," Tremanty said.

He sat there for three minutes and then the phone rang. He put it on speaker, held it next to the handset, and Deese asked, "When was the last time you and Gloria got it on?"

"Saturday . . . No, Sunday night," Harrelson said in his ear.

Lucas said, "Ah, let me see, Saturday . . . No, wait, Sunday night. Sunday night."

"All right. Go on out to Howard Hughes and turn right. We're watching you. Better not be anybody following you."

"There's nobody. I got your money. Gimme Gloria. Where do I get Gloria?"

"You get Gloria after we get the money."

"That's fucked up," Lucas said. "This is a lot of money for nothing. Don't hurt her. Remember, I'm a witness, I can identify you as well as she can, so don't hurt her. There's no need to hurt her."

Deese: "Keep driving."

Tremanty, in the earbud: "That was good, Lucas. That was great."

LUCAS DROVE out to Howard Hughes Parkway and turned right. Tremanty said, in his ear, "Okay, the box is rolling, you're in the box. The Cessna's up on top of you, thank God for that yellow car. And, yeah, we got you on the GPS."

Deese: "Drive on up to Sands. Don't drive too fast. Don't go gettin' stopped by no cop."

Lucas: "I want to talk to Gloria."

"When we got the money, Gloria will call you from a gas station," Deese said. "We'll turn her loose three blocks from the station."

"That doesn't sound real to me," Tremanty said in his ear. Lucas couldn't reply without Deese hearing it. And Tremanty, talking to somebody else, said, "Let's stretch the box a bit, stretch it out a vertical block on both ends. They'll do that tricky thing now."

Lucas was looking in his rearview mirror. He couldn't see anybody obviously tracking him.

Deese: "I don't know exactly where you're at now, but you gotta be close to Paradise. Take a right on Paradise."

"I'm still on Sands," Lucas said. "I'll take a right on Paradise."

"Got that," Tremanty said. Lucas could hear him talking to the FBI agents driving the box.

He came back to Lucas. "They're starting to worry me. Nothing tricky yet. But if they take us way out in the desert, we'll lose the box."

Another voice, in the background, maybe the AIC. "Yeah, but they'd never be able to lose the Cessna or the chopper out there. I don't think that's it. I think they'll do the trick here in town."

Lucas could see the intersection of Paradise Road coming up. "I'm at Paradise," he said into the cell.

Deese said, "Take a right and keep going."

"I'm going," Lucas said. "Where am I going?"

"You're going until I tell you to stop."

Tremanty: "That road runs down to the airport and stops. Something's got to happen in the next minute or so."

Deese said, "You should be coming up to

Harmon Avenue. Take another right. Tell me as soon as you do. The second you make the turn."

Lucas came up to Harmon and said, "Taking the right on Harmon."

"That's the Hard Rock Hotel on your right. Go past it, you'll see some grass and trees, and shit, and you'll see a bridge with a red balloon tied to one end of the railing. Turn there onto the bridge and stop. Tell me when you have."

Tremanty: "Tighten the box. Get tight. This is the tricky part. Cessna says there are some people in a drainage channel, farther down. He can't see what's going on."

Lucas turned at the red balloon. "I'm on the bridge. I've stopped."

Deese: "Get out, walk to the bridge railing on the driver's side, throw the money off the bridge into the ditch. Get back in the car and drive away."

"We're tight on you, around the corner, ten seconds," Tremanty said in Lucas's ear.

Deese: "Throw the money, throw the money, motherfucker. Get out of the car and throw the money in the ditch."

Lucas got out, carrying the bag. He looked down to the drainage channel, could see people a hundred yards away to his left. It looked like there was a homeless camp under the bridge—piles of trash, wrecked shopping carts, plastic sheets rigged as tents.

"Throw the money, motherfucker, then get back in the truck. We're watching, Gloria's got the gun in her mouth right now."

Lucas threw the bag down into the channel and stepped back to the car but didn't get in. A second later, he heard a harsh buzzing coming from under the bridge, and then an Army-green dirt bike rolled out from under it and buzzed up to the bag. The rider was wearing a helmet with a blacked-out faceplate. He glanced up at Lucas, snagged the bag with one hand, and roared off down the channel toward the homeless camp.

And then the bike and rider disappeared under the bridge.

Tremanty was in his ear. "Where'd it go? Where'd it go?"

"I'm going down to the bridge," Lucas shouted into the phone.

He left the Porsche on the bridge, ran around the end of it and down a slanting retaining wall into the channel and toward the second bridge as another car came in from the left and two FBI agents jumped out and looked down at him. Lucas shouted, "He went under the bridge."

Tremanty, in his ear: "That's not a bridge, there's no bridge there. Where'd he go?"

Lucas ran toward the camp and around a tent there made of a blue plastic tarp . . . and found himself looking into a tunnel.

An emaciated bearded man said, "Hey, man . . ."

"Where'd he go?" Lucas shouted. "Where'd the bike go?"

"What'd he do, man?" the thin man asked.

"Where'd the fuck he go?" Lucas shouted again, grabbing the man by his shirt and pulling him up on his tiptoes.

The man pointed a finger and said, "You can see those tracks? Almost ran over my ass."

LUCAS LET HIM GO and ran in the direction he'd pointed, found the motorcycle tracks where they disappeared into the tunnel. There were sparks of light in the darkness, and Lucas turned to one of the FBI agents who was coming up behind and shouted, "Get on the radio and tell them where he went and which tunnel it is. See if they can figure where it comes out. You don't have a flashlight, do you?"

"In the car."

"Get it and throw it down to me. I'm heading into the tunnel."

The agent broke away, and Lucas stepped into the darkness, which wasn't quite absolute. As his eyes adjusted, he could see there were more people inside, spots of illumination from flashlights and from kerosene lanterns—old-timey glass-and-metal vessels that put out a golden glow stronger than many of the other sources.

Behind him, the agent ran down the sloping embankment and shouted, "I'm coming with you."

He handed Lucas the flashlight from his car and had one of his own. The two of them ran into the tunnel, following the track of the motorbike.

The tunnel was dotted with lights and each one signified another camp. The floor of the tunnel was covered with sand, ankle-deep in spots, with the freestanding tents/tarps fastened to the walls. There was crap all over the place: food wrappers, McDonald's cartons, old discarded blankets clogged with damp sand. The series of lights ended with a single kerosene lantern a hundred yards in and the heavyset woman who sat next to it with two shopping carts draped with a blue plastic tarp as a tent.

"You cops?"

Lucas grunted as he went by.

And she called out after him, "I think he shot somebody. I heard a shot. I think."

LUCAS AND THE AGENT continued running down the tunnel; it had smelled bad from the beginning, but the stink got heavier as they ran. The agent pulled the tail of his jacket up over his mouth and nose, and called, "I think this is their toilet," and Lucas nodded and pulled his shirt up over his nose. He took it down once, to see if he could talk to Tremanty on the handset, but the handset was dead.

Lucas had lost track of time, but thought they

must have been running for five or six minutes, when they saw a light ahead. They ran on for another minute, to the end of the tunnel, where seven-foot-tall grates blocked it top to bottom. One side of the grate had been pried open far enough for a man to squeeze through.

A body lay by the grate, a man's, with a bullet hole in the head. And beside the body, the green motorcycle and the money bag, empty except for the GPS tracker. The bike had no license plate.

The agent, who looked like a teenager, said, "Murdered somebody," and then he gagged from the smell of the tunnel. And maybe the sight of the body.

Lucas said, "Nothing we can do now. We gotta go up."

They went up and found themselves standing under an enormous ultra-modern Ferris wheel. To the left, they saw a parking garage for the LINQ, a casino.

The agent said, "Jesus, we're right on the Strip."

Lucas lifted the handset and called Tremanty. "You there?"

"Lucas? Where the hell are you?"

"We're at the exit of the drainage tunnel, right behind the LINQ, under that Ferris wheel—that white Ferris wheel. We've got a body, a motorcycle without a license plate, an empty money bag, and a GPS tracker."

"Be there in two or three."

---

TREMANTY ARRIVED in two, or three, with a squadron of other FBI cars. He walked up to Lucas and said, "We're screwed."

"Gloria Harrelson's screwed, when they take a close look at that money," Lucas said. "The guy in the airplane didn't see anything?"

"No. He wasn't looking here. We were a half mile away. Any ID on the dead guy?"

"Didn't have a chance to look."

Lucas turned to the agent who'd run the tunnel with him. "Go down there and see if there's a VIN on that motorcycle. I don't know where you'd find it. But . . . Here, I'll come with you."

One of the other agents, a slender man who looked like anything but a biker, said, "The VIN's usually on the steering column. Let me go down. Gimme a flashlight."

Tremanty walked a few steps away and got on his phone. "We're gonna need the name and address that goes with a VIN we're about to get and we need it right now. **Right now.** We'll have it in a minute."

And a minute later the agent in the tunnel shouted, "Yamaha," then called out the vehicle identification number. Lucas wrote it down, and Tremanty relayed it to whoever he was speaking with on the phone. He listened and a moment later said to Lucas, "Jesus, it's a '96."

And after another moment said, "It goes to a Ralph Deese . . . in Beatty, Nevada."

"Where's that?" Lucas asked.

Tremanty shrugged and spoke into the phone: "Find out where Beatty is. See if they have a police force."

He listened for a while longer, as Lucas paced around him, and then said, "Get me that number."

He hung up and said, "No police force, but they've got a sheriff's substation. I hope somebody's home."

Somebody was.

Tremanty put his phone on speaker, and Lucas and the other agents gathered around him as he spoke to a sheriff's deputy. The deputy said, "Yeah, I've heard of Ralph. I think he lives up in the hills somewhere, but I don't know where exactly. That's what I heard anyway. I can't guarantee that it's right. The people here pretty much ran him out of town. Must've been four or five years back, before I got here."

"Why was that?" Lucas asked. "Why'd they run him out?"

"Everybody said he was a bad man. People think he raped a girl up here, but she couldn't ID him. And he must've been wearing a condom, or something, because the guy before me ran her down to the hospital and got a rape kit done that came up negative on DNA. There's rumors around that he might have killed a guy out in the desert, an ex-partner of his. He's supposedly a prospector, but he never came up with any gold, far as I know."

The bottom line was that Ralph Deese no longer lived where the motorcycle put him and nobody knew where he currently was, though the deputy said he'd ask around.

Tremanty hung up and said to Lucas, "Asking around is going to be too late."

Lucas said, "Listen. When I was talking to Roger Smith back in New Orleans, he said that the Deese brothers had an uncle out here. That's got to be who this is. He said the uncle was a miner, that he looked for turquoise. I remember because that seemed like a weird thing, to mine. You think there'd be some kind of claim, or whatever they do out here. Something with a location and a name."

"I dunno, but I can find out," Tremanty said. "Give me one more minute."

# CHAPTER TWENTY-FOUR

The gang's day began at five in the morning with an argument: Ralph wouldn't be going to Las Vegas because they were taking his truck and they only had room for two. Cox argued that they should take both vehicles, the truck and the Lexus, and abandon the Lexus when they released Gloria.

"That ain't gonna work. Gloria will know about the truck, and we couldn't outrun a fuckin' Prius in that thing," Deese said. "Me'n Cole are going down, that's all we need. Right now, Gloria doesn't know where she's at, and we'll keep it that way. You and Ralph wait here, watching her."

"I gotta stay with Ralph?"

"Yeah, you gotta stay with Ralph."

Cox looked at Cole, who looked at Ralph and said, "You touch her, I'll beat you to death with a fuckin' shovel. I ain't joking."

Ralph held up both hands. "She's safe with me."

"That's the way it's gonna be," Deese said.

Cox and Cole went outside, and Cox said, "Gloria knows who we are. We're really . . . I don't know. Ralph is crazy as a bedbug."

"Then keep your gun close."

They went to the Lexus and retrieved the gun, keeping an eye on the trailer. "Like Marion said, start pulling the trigger, that's all you gotta do, if Ralph comes after you. Easy as pie."

"Easy as pie, but you said you never shot anybody."

"Never had to," Cole said. "But now we're in a bad spot, Geenie."

"Ah, jeez . . ." She took the gun and tucked it into her back waistband, under her blouse. "You gotta be careful, Cole. We're going to somewhere warm."

"Like hell?" He grinned.

"Panama, like you said."

"I'll be careful. When we get back up here, you slip me that gun," Cole said. "If Deese is gonna pull something, that's when it'll be, when he feels safe."

The door of the trailer popped open and Deese stepped out. Cole kissed Cox and said, "We oughta be back by noon. If we're not back by, say, two o'clock, you get in the Lexus and head north, up to Reno. Dump the car and take a Greyhound back to LA. Like you never heard of us."

"Ah, that's not going to happen," Deese said.

He walked over to Ralph's motorcycle and said, "Help me get it in the truck."

"You're sure it works?"

Deese paused, said, "One way to find out."

He straddled the bike, fired it up, rode a hundred yards down the track and back, then killed the engine. "Good as the day it was made."

He and Cole lifted it into the truck, put the tailgate up, and locked it. "Let's go."

Cole kissed Cox again and she gave him a squeeze and said, "See you," and a minute later Deese and Cole were rattling down the track toward the highway.

THEY WERE in Las Vegas at seven-thirty, and Deese sent Cole into a McDonald's for Cokes and a sack of Triple Breakfast Stacks Biscuits; they both ate two—in the truck, in the parking lot—and then Cole drove them to the drainage channel and the entrances to the tunnels, with Deese pointing the way.

"I'll be hiding under that bridge when he throws the money in and then I'll ride like a motherfucker right into those tunnels."

"Where do they come out?"

"That's the important part. If you're not there, they'll catch my ass and nobody gets no money. You gotta be there. That's why you're driving."

Deese pointed the way again, the turns, until they got to a spot under the Ferris wheel that had a couple of parking places for security personnel and was directly above the exit from the tunnels. "Ralph says their cars are hardly ever here. As soon as Harrelson throws the money, I'll yell into the phone and be here one minute later. One minute. You jump out of the truck with the money box, meet me down there."

"There's bars across the tunnels looks like a jail cell," Cole said, peering into the drainage channel.

"They can be pushed open."

"Yeah, but if it turns out they can't be, if somebody locked them since Ralph was here, you're fucked."

Deese nodded. "Okay, you're right . . . Pull in there."

Cole pulled into one of the empty spots, Deese climbed out of the car, crossed a low fence, and ran down into the channel. There was some garbage and paper trash at the tunnel entrance. As Cole watched, Deese grabbed one of the gate bars and yanked it a foot or so outward, almost enough to squeeze through. He yanked again and it moved another foot. Then he pushed it back in place and ran back up to the car.

"No sweat," he said. "Soon as I call, you run down there with the money and yank it open."

Cole said, "It's after eight. We need to find a

place for me to sit. And we need to get the bike off the truck and get you down in that ditch at the Hard Rock."

Deese grinned at him. "You nervous?"

"Fuck, yeah. I always get nervous. But I'm always there."

THEY FOUND A SPOT in a parking lot across a street from the bank's lot. The bank's was ringed by fifty-foot-tall pine trees, but it was easy enough to see between them. And there'd be cars coming and going from the lot where Cole would be. "I can watch him only until he gets in the truck," Cole said. "Then I gotta go, if I'm gonna get back to the Ferris wheel."

"Yeah, but you'll see him when he gets there and gets out of the truck and make sure it's him and not some cop. When you call me after you see him come back out of the bank, I'll wait three or four minutes before I call him. That'll get you on your way to the Ferris wheel. It'll take him another five minutes to get to me. You'll have plenty of time."

"Yeah, yeah."

"You getting spooked?"

"A lot of timing's gotta be right. When we were hitting those houses, we knew exactly what we were doing," Cole said. "We knew who was inside the house, what we'd get, where the cops were. This is a crapshoot."

"Just take it easy when you drive out of here. A goddamn fender bender and I'm dead and you won't get a nickel," Deese said.

THEY DROVE BACK to the drainage channel, unloaded the bike, lifted it over a fence, and Deese rolled it down the slope to the sandy bottom and pushed it under the narrow bridge. A few street people were sitting outside the tunnel entrance, watching them, but made no move to come over to the bridge. "What are you going to do if one of the bums grabs the bag?" Cole asked.

Deese said, "Won't happen. If it does, I'll handle it. You better go."

"We could still walk away," Cole said.

"Go! Go!"

Cole went.

HE WAS IN his surveillance spot early, ten minutes before nine. Five minutes later, he saw the Yellow Cab Porsche turn into the bank's parking lot. He saw Harrelson get out of the car—pink shirt, khakis, sunglasses, bandages on his face. He reached back into the car, got a floppy-brimmed golf hat, pulled it on. No question that it was him. Reached back into the car again and pulled out what looked like an empty green shopping bag. He walked toward the bank. Cole punched his burner, calling Deese, and said, "We're on. He's waiting outside the bank."

Deese clicked off without a reply.

Cole waited for what seemed like a long time. He supposed Harrelson would have to get back into the bank vault, count out the money. Cole once had a safe-deposit box and whenever he took out the box, bank people escorted him to a private room to load or unload it. That would suck up some time.

People came and went from the bank. Fifteen minutes later, Harrelson came back out, climbed into the Porsche . . . and waited. Cole thumbed the power button on the burner, and when Deese came up he said, "He's in the car. I'm outta here."

THEY'D DECIDED Deese would make the call, so that Cole wouldn't have to do it while he was driving. Cole rolled out of the parking lot, up to Sands, took a left, and headed for the Strip. By the time he got there, Harrelson should be getting close to the Hard Rock. He worked his way to the back of the LINQ parking garage; a security car was parked in one of the spaces he was planning to use, but there was nobody in it.

His phone rang, and Deese shouted, "On the way." Cole hopped out of the car, got the two metal cash boxes from the backseat, crossed the fence, and ran down into the drainage channel to the metal grates blocking the tunnel entrance.

He yanked the grate bar to one side, stepped through, ran twenty or thirty yards down the tunnel, far enough that a GPS wouldn't work, and opened the metal boxes; the boxes would act as a Faraday cage if there was a GPS tracker in with the cash. The concept for such a cage had come out of the research he'd done with Beauchamps and the gang in L.A. They'd worked hard on that, he thought now. Beauchamps had been a smart guy, and he, Cole, was also a smart guy. How they'd ever gotten a dumbass like Deese hung around their necks . . .

Fifteen seconds later, he heard the distant motor grind of the dirt bike and saw a tiny dot of light, its headlight, getting closer.

Thirty seconds later, Deese was rolling to a stop. He tossed the money bag at Cole and said, "Dump the money, dump the money."

Cole began transferring the money from the bag to one of the metal boxes, all they'd need. As he was transferring the last few bricks of cash, he found the GPS transmitter.

"Transmitter," he shouted at Deese, who'd killed the bike and dumped it on its side. He turned and threw the transmitter farther down the tunnel, then looked up at Deese, who was pointing a pistol at his head.

He barely had time to flinch.

---

COLE THREW the transmitter down the tunnel and turned back, and Deese pulled his gun out of his belt and shot Cole in the forehead. Cole sagged over the empty metal box. The muzzle blast had been deafening in the tunnel, but Deese took a second to shoot Cole again in the head, then picked up the money. He patted Cole's jeans pockets, found the truck keys, jogged to the end of the tunnel, squeezed through the gate, pushed the bar back in place.

He was back in the truck in thirty seconds.

He had one more stop to make; he'd be back at Ralph's in two hours for the cleanup. Too bad about Ralph. The old fucker had to go, along with Cox and Gloria Harrelson. At that point, he'd be well into the wind, running free, with two million bucks and a high-powered Lexus.

# CHAPTER TWENTY-FIVE

The FBI SWAT team was sent home, on standby, and Bob and Rae showed up at Lucas's hotel room, where Tremanty was working the phones, with various federal agencies, trying to find out who serviced mining claims.

Another agent was trying to work through Nevada state agencies to see if any of them tracked turquoise mining, while Lucas called a variety of raw stone dealers asking about a prospector named Deese. In the meantime, the Ney County Sheriff's Department was interviewing people around Beatty, Nevada, in an attempt to find someone who knew where Ralph Deese had gone after being run out of town.

They got a break: the Bureau of Land Management showed Deese had a current claim southwest of Beatty, apparently within a few hundred yards of the California border. The BLM provided a GPS location, and a federal satellite image showed them a silver oval—a trailer—parked on the site, which was in a mountainous area well off a lonely dirt road.

The image's resolution was high enough that they could make out a pickup truck and what might have been a motorcycle parked next to the trailer. The image wasn't current: it had been taken four months earlier.

"Four months ago, but it was still active then," Lucas said. "If this Ralph Deese guy would be willing to take them, it'd be a perfect hideout." He tapped that screen. "And there's that motorcycle."

"There's some possibility that they're still in Las Vegas. Or they've headed north," Tremanty told the agent in charge. "You need to keep people here in case there's a break. I'm going to take my team, including the three marshals, north to the Deese claim. We'll need the chopper quick as you can get it for us."

The AIC agreed: the chopper would be waiting at a commercial heliport south on Las Vegas Boulevard, near the airport.

"Get us some handsets. I don't think cell phones will work out there," Tremanty said.

The AIC said he'd send four handsets, all of which could be used to talk to the helicopter, and the chopper was equipped with a satellite phone for longer-distanced calls.

"We'll take the Tahoe—we're all gunned up and it's right downstairs," Bob said to Tremanty.

"It's gonna be hot out there. We're talking Death Valley a few miles away. We're gonna need lots of water, and you and Lucas have to change clothes. You need boots or sneaks and long-sleeved shirts and hats. Rae and I already have our gear. We'll get the water and meet you at the car."

THEY MADE IT back to the hotel to change. Lucas and Tremanty both had cross-training shoes and jeans; they both wore long-sleeved dress shirts, because they had nothing better and no time to go shopping. Lucas still had Harrelson's golf hat, and Tremanty bought a hat at a casino convenience store on the way to the car. At the car, they found Bob and Rae loading two-liter bottles of water into two lightweight Osprey Talon backpacks. They were both dressed in light combat camo shirts and pants, with camo boonie hats.

"We're gonna need the gear bag," Bob said. "We've got two rifles, one semiauto and one fully auto, and a sniper rifle. We should be able to handle anything they throw at us."

Fifteen minutes later, they were crossing the tarmac to the waiting FBI helicopter, a commercial version of the military Black Hawk. The pilots had already filed a flight plan. They lifted off, circled over a golf course, and were gone.

---

THE PILOTS had given Tremanty a headset so they could talk. On the way to Deese's mining claim, Lucas, Tremanty, Bob, and Rae pored over the satellite images of the site that Rae had downloaded to her iPad. Bob had experience looking down at deserts from Black Hawk helicopters and tapped the road that came closest to the mining claim and the dimly visible track going into it.

"If we try to go in with a sheriff's convoy, they'll see us coming before we even get to the approach road. Let's see . . ." He checked the scale at the corner of the image. "They're up on a ridge, the car would have to come around this mountain. That's fifteen miles away. If they're watching, it's perfectly possible that they'd see us at fifteen. And it looks like there are parts of those roads where we wouldn't be able to drive more than fifteen miles an hour, even in a Jeep, and maybe less in spots. On the approach road, depending on whether he cleared it with a bulldozer or just wore it down by driving over it, we could be down to three or four miles an hour."

Lucas: "And?"

Bob tapped the screen again. "If the pilots are willing to do it, we could land over here, behind this mountain—that's, what, two miles, or a little more? They wouldn't hear us. This isn't sand dunes out there, it'll be hard soil with sparse vegetation and some sand at the surface, so the walking will be fairly easy. Walking—hurrying—we could do it in a half hour, and they wouldn't see us coming."

Rae, who'd been quiet for most of the trip, said, "One problem: will the pilots put us in there? I know from experience that they don't like—uh, what do they call it?—informal landings. Especially in a desert. They don't know what they're going to kick up. Dust and dirt, and all that."

Tremanty: "If that's the way to go in, I'll talk to them. Give me the iPad."

The helicopter was fitted with nine decent but not luxurious passenger seats, the front three facing the back of the pilots' seats. Tremanty more or less duckwalked out of the back, around to one of the front-facing seats, put on the headset, and tapped the copilot on the shoulder. The rest of them couldn't hear the conversation, but it went on for a while. And then Tremanty duckwalked back.

"They're willing to take a look. We'll swing around and come in from the southwest, fairly low, from fifteen miles out, so the trailer will be in the sound shadow of the mountain. If the image is correct, there's a hard-packed spot where they think we can put down, but they'll have to eyeball it first," Tremanty said.

The flight out took forty minutes—the pilots told Tremanty that they were pushing 200 miles an hour. At one point, well outside of Las Vegas, they crossed an enormous suburban subdivision.

Rae: “What are those people doing out here?”

“Cooking their brains out if they don’t have AC,” Bob said. “You really, really wouldn’t want to have a power outage here.”

THE LAST PART of the flight hugged the gray-and-tan desert terrain; at one point, they flew over a dozen huge, perfect green circles created by center-pivoting irrigation systems over some kind of crops, but what the crops were, none of them knew.

The pilots said something to Tremanty and he pulled the headset back on and asked for a repeat, then said to the others, “We just crossed the California line. We’ll be coming around for the approach.”

Bob had a heavily padded plastic case in his arms containing a bolt-action .300 Winchester Magnum sniper rifle. He’d taken it to a Las Vegas shooting range that morning, prior to joining the FBI SWAT team, to make sure it was still sighted in. He’d been satisfied then, but even with the padding he was worried about what the helicopter’s vibration might do to the heavy telescopic sight. He’d carried it cradled in his arms for the entire flight to give it further protection.

“Don’t want to shoot from more than two hundred yards out, if I have to shoot,” he said. “I hate this fuckin’ vibration.”

---

THEY WERE SLOWING, then slowing dramatically, then dropping. There was lots of dust thrown up that blocked the view, and the chopper eased back up and sideways for several hundred feet. Tremanty was wearing the headset again and said, "They see a rock. It's flat and wide enough to land on. We're going that way. Still well behind the hill."

Rae was unzipping the equipment bag and pulling out a scoped M15 and then an unscoped M4. She handed the M15 to Lucas along with a thirty-round mag, slapped another mag into her own weapon, and asked Tremanty, "Do they see any snakes?"

Lucas took the rifle and said, "Not that funny."

"Just askin'."

They hovered over the reddish brown flat rock, a space some fifty yards across with a few desert plants pushing up out of the cracks. They settled, tipped a bit, settled some more, and were down.

Lucas got on his knees and unlatched and pulled back the side door and was hit by a wave of heat. He climbed out, followed by Tremanty, Bob, and Rae, all looking like an **Outside** magazine combat team in fashion-approved desert wear.

TREMANTY was carrying a backpack with the iPad, two bottles of water, and a pair of binoculars;

he had a Sig P226 in .40-caliber on his hip. Lucas had the other pack with four bottles of water, plus his pistol and the M15. Both Bob and Rae had sidearms, and Bob broke the sniper rifle out of its heavy carrying case and slung it over his shoulder. Rae carried the M4 and a ton of ammo.

The copilot spotted their exact location on the satellite image and oriented them, pointing them toward the Deese mining claim, which was on the far side of a low mountain ridge.

"We're all gonna feel like jackasses if they left there ten years ago," Bob said.

Rae: "They didn't. I got ten bucks says we'll find them all right there. Deese and Uncle Deese and Cole, this blond chick, and Gloria."

"Nobody take the bet," Bob said. "It'd be bad luck."

Lucas was pulling the chest straps tight on his pack. "Let's stop bullshittin' and start walkin'."

Tremanty pointed, "That way," and asked, "How come everybody's got a machine gun except me?"

"Only one machine gun, and I got it," Rae said. "Because I look hot with it. I might get a job modeling them."

Tremanty said, "Hmm."

Lucas nodded and said, "You could do that. Make the big bucks, too. Camo bikini, machine gun, hip-hop hair . . ."

Tremanty, again: "Hmm."

Rae said to Tremanty, "That's tension talk, the

way Davenport goes on, being a wiseass. He always does that when we get close to the shit hittin' the fan. Ignore him."

LUCAS LED OFF, followed by Bob and Rae, with Tremanty trailing. The first mile had both uphill and downhill pitches, nothing severe, but not quite as easy as Bob had suggested. There were scattered rocks, like in the pictures taken by the Mars rover, and plants that bit. The heat was ferocious, the kind that burned the sweat off your face before you even got damp; it felt like a bad fever. They crossed two vehicle tracks, invisible on the satellite photos, apparently sworn in by three-wheelers. Rae saw a fist-sized spider, which she claimed was a tarantula and "can kill you as fast as a rattler."

From the back, Tremanty said, "Untrue. In fact, they're barely poisonous. They **can** bite, but the bite's not venomous."

Rae: "Killjoy."

Lucas: "I think I'll fuck with one to find out for sure." He looked at the mountain, licked his lips, and said, "Sooner or later, we'll have to start climbing. That's when it'll get hot."

A half hour out of the chopper, they passed a low red rock bluff that threw a shadow out onto the desert. Bob pointed at the shadow and said, "Water stop. Two minutes."

Lucas checked his watch. "If Deese left Las

Vegas the minute he got the money and made no stops, and didn't drive more than five miles an hour over the speed limit, he'll be getting here about now."

"Except for the bad road coming in," Tremanty said. "That'll slow him down. But we oughta trot this next part."

THE NEXT PITCH was a slight uphill that continued on for most of a half mile. The footing was good, a layer of sand over a harder crust. They crossed an arroyo, with a deeper sandy floor, saw a motor track closer to the mountain they were skirting and moved onto it. "Looks like it's going toward the trailer. We're getting close," Rae said.

They crossed a rocky hump, still on the track, down into another arroyo, and up a higher hump and around the heel of a bluff, and the trailer was there, four hundred yards away. They backed off, behind a clump of brush, where they could see the trailer without being seen.

"Old Airstream," Tremanty said, looking at the trailer with his binoculars. "Pretty beat up, like a salvage job."

A dark sedan was parked outside the side door. Tremanty put the binoculars on the car and said, "Yes! That's Gloria Harrelson's Lexus."

"Told'ja," Rae said.

Bob said, "If they're watching, they'll see us if we try to get closer on the track."

Lucas: "Why don't we backtrack, get a drink, and come up behind that ridge."

He pointed downhill to a ridge that would cover an approach from the south side of the trailer. They wouldn't be able to get all the way in, but they'd get closer.

THEY ALL TOOK long drinks after fishing the bottles out of Lucas's backpack, and Lucas took a final look through the binoculars. Not much to see: everything around the trailer was deathly still, although, after a moment, he became aware of a vibration. He slid the glasses sideways, saw the silver oval of a propane tank. There was a surface pipe leading to the trailer. And there was another snaking away from the tank and up the hill and out of sight.

"Okay. There's a propane tank, probably for heat in the winter, but you feel that vibration? I think he's got a generator back there, behind the tank. He'd want it away from the trailer so he wouldn't be breathing the fumes."

"Does that help us?" Rae asked.

Bob was looking at the trailer through his scope and said, "It could. It's gotta be running the AC. If we could slide around the trailer, we could kill the generator, and somebody would either have to come out and see what the problem was or die of heatstroke."

They passed the binoculars around and speculated about the Lexus. Had the gang driven the car to Las Vegas? Were they already back? They'd seen a pickup on the satellite image and it was nowhere to be seen. Neither was the motorbike.

"He had to have taken the truck," Lucas said. "That's how he got the bike to Vegas."

"Then he's not back yet," Tremanty said.

BOB SAID, "If we get down below that ridge and keep going right, you see that hump? We could low-crawl across there and get behind those bushes or trees, or whatever they are, and get back to the generator without being seen."

"One of us could," Lucas said. He looked at Rae. "You."

"Why me?"

"Because if we drive somebody out of the trailer, we'll need the sniper out front. I'll call the shot, Sandro will talk to me about it. And if we get spotted, we'd want the machine gun up high and behind the trailer to pick off runners coming out the back."

She nodded. "Okay."

THEY BACKED OFF their vantage point, screwed the caps on their bottles of water, talked about the plan, and headed downhill and around behind the ridge that would block the view from the Airstream.

Five minutes later, they were walking back up the ridge, only four hundred yards to the right. Rae took Tremanty's backpack with a handset and a bottle of water and slid even farther to the right, crouching as she approached the track to the Airstream, eventually going to her knees. She waved once and was out of sight, crossing the track, before heading up the hill to the generator.

Lucas, Tremanty, and Bob crept up the ridge and lay in the skimpy shade provided by a circle of shadscale bushes. They could no longer see Rae, and nothing was moving around the trailer.

Then Rae called: "You were right, Lucas. There's a generator back here and it's running. It's got a lockdown cover on the switch, but I can get at it with a stick. Want me to throw it?"

Lucas looked at Tremanty and Bob. They both nodded. "Throw it," Lucas said.

A moment later, the vibration stopped, and Rae said, "Done."

NOTHING HAPPENED for a minute or two, then a door opened and a blond woman looked out and then stepped outside. She looked around for a moment, shaded her eyes, looked down the approach track, went back inside the trailer, came out a moment later and went to the Lexus, got inside and started it, got back out, leaving it running, went back to the trailer, came back a minute later with what looked like a six-pack of beer or soda, and got back in the car.

"I can take out the tires if we need to," Bob said.

"She is not going anywhere," Lucas said. "She's waiting for Deese and the others. They're all down in Vegas. She's in the car for the air-conditioning."

Tremanty: "What do you suggest?"

Lucas said, "I suggest we wait."

"There's probably nobody else inside—we could take the trailer," Tremanty said.

"Too late," Bob said. They turned toward him and he pointed. A cloud of dust was rising from the track far away, but not too far away, a few miles at most. "If she has a way to call them . . ."

"Okay," Tremanty said. "We wait. Need to get tight under the bushes."

Rae called: "You see them?"

"We do. Sit tight."

# CHAPTER TWENTY-SIX

Deese didn't feel even mildly bad about Cole, but he felt something. He couldn't put his finger on it, exactly, but loneliness might have come closest. There was no longer a single person in the world he could talk to. His half brother was dead. He'd shot a man with whom he'd shared a kidnapping and a home invasion. His uncle was a crazy old coot who lived in a shithole shack in a shithole place to whom he could talk to for, like, maybe ten seconds before wanting to shoot his ass, which he planned to do just as soon as he got back. And, finally, his former boss wanted to shoot him.

Then there was Cox. Deese had plans for Cox when she got back to the shithole, plans she wouldn't survive any more than Gloria Harrelson would. The Nevada desert was the final resting place for hundreds of murdered men, women, and children at least, the unmarked graves stretching out from Las Vegas in both directions along I-15, and they'd simply be filling two more. No problem.

He didn't dwell on all this, being too busy driving and planning, and he didn't have a soul for such concerns to cloud over, but the clouds were out there somewhere. Time and cocaine should clear things up.

AFTER KILLING COLE, he'd driven the pickup, following a zigzag route, out to Las Vegas Boulevard, then to the Wynn Las Vegas, where he'd stayed a couple of dozen times and where he was familiar with the self-parking option. He drove into the garage, cruised along for a few minute looking for a specific car. He found it and parked in the first empty space closest to it, which was three down.

There was nobody around and he just sat there for a couple of minutes more, then got the screwdriver he'd brought with him, crawled from his car to the next one over and unscrewed its front license plate, which was from California, then crawled along to the next car with California plates and unscrewed its front plate. He then crawled to the car he'd spotted when he drove in, which also had California plates, replaced first the front plate and then, nervously, because he was more visible, the back.

He'd heard on the burglar/car theft hotline that

nobody really knew what their license plate number was; people hardly ever looked unless there was something radically different, like a Kansas plate replacing one from Nevada. Stealing the plates from a Lexus and replacing them with other California plates, the owner probably wouldn't notice.

And stealing the front plates from cars that were parked nose in, the owners likely wouldn't know they were gone until they'd parked elsewhere, maybe not until they'd driven several other places. They wouldn't know when or where the plates were taken and not be looking for them at the Wynn.

He'd put the stolen plates on the Harrelsons' Lexus. A routine check by the Highway Patrol would show that the plates on the dark gray Lexus were current. Ralph's crappy old pickup wasn't going to get him to Miami, but the Harrelsons' Lexus would—in comfort.

HE CRAWLED BACK to the pickup with the plates, put them in the cab, pulled his hat down, walked to the lobby, paid his parking fee, and drove out of the garage to the boulevard and headed north. When he'd left Las Vegas behind, he reached into the backseat and pulled the money bag up to the passenger seat. He reached inside the bag, pulled out a banded stack of bills.

It was a half inch thick, all hundreds. He riffled the stack with his thumb, put it back in the bag, and attempted to tally the number of stacks in his head while driving. He knew the number he came up with wasn't entirely accurate, but when he realized he was well past a hundred he was happy. He had the money, he was loose.

He would have whistled a happy tune if he'd known one.

EARLIER THAT MORNING, after Deese and Cole had left for Vegas, Cox sat on the couch, watching Ralph Deese slopping his way through an oversized bowl of Raisin Bran.

"Supposed to be good for my heart. That's what the lady at the store said," Deese told her, a white rim of milk on his mustache. His nose was virtually in the bowl. "Problem is, it makes me fart. Which I guess you're gonna have to live with. Unless you go outside, which I don't recommend. Even the lizards don't go out in this heat."

Cox looked out the window, over which Deese had put some self-stick reflective film to cut the glare. Still, it looked like a scene from hell out there. Yellow, like the world was on fire. Cox was a beach girl and had spent much of her life looking at the Pacific Ocean, the biggest body of water on the planet. If she went out the door and spit, she thought, that'd be the wettest place within fifteen miles.

She and Ralph mostly communicated in grunts.

When he'd finished with his Raisin Bran, they exchanged a few grunts, from which she understood that he was going up the hill to "take a dump," as he put it.

"The toilet doesn't work?"

"This ain't no hotel," Ralph said. "You wanna take a shit, you'll find a trench up the hill in the shade of the bluff. There's a shovel there, you throw dirt on the turds. Wanna pee? Do that anywhere out there. I usually pee off the porch."

Now she grunted. "Whatever . . ." And he went out, carrying his shotgun. She'd already peed once, behind a bush, because there'd been no door on the toilet, no privacy. That wouldn't have bothered Ralph.

A moment later, Gloria Harrelson called from the bedroom: "Help me!"

Cox sat there for a moment, undecided, then finally got up and walked in and took a look. Harrelson had initially been bound with wire to the bed, but the wires had cut into her leg, so wire had been replaced with chain they hadn't used at the Harrelsons' house. It had been looped around an ankle and a wrist and padlocked, holding the woman on her back. Deese had the keys.

Both the ankle and wrist were chafed and red with still-drying blood. Purplish dried blood from a bloodied lip covered her chin, and a cut on her cheekbone had trickled blood down into her ear. She had a black eye, the eyebrow crusty with yet more blood. And the room was infused with the smell of urine. Harrelson was naked, her clothes strewn on the floor. She'd managed to partly cover herself with a tattered cotton blanket.

She looked up at Cox and pleaded again, weakly, "Help me . . . Please help me . . ."

"I can't," Cox said. "They'd kill me."

Harrelson bit at her lip and started to weep, and then said, "Give me some water? Please give me some water . . ."

"That I can do," Cox said.

She went back to the refrigerator and got out a bottle of Dasani, carried it back to the bedroom, and handed it to Harrelson, who grabbed it with her free hand and drank the entire thing in a half dozen long gulps.

Cox waited until she was done, but when Harrelson said, "You've gotta . . ." Cox shook her head and walked away.

Harrelson continued calling out from the bedroom, but Cox dropped back on the couch and put her fingers in her ears until the calls stopped.

COX THEN SPENT a few moments contemplating her future. Not a promising one, she concluded. Cole and Deese both could place her at home invasions they had orchestrated, and those two, plus Gloria Harrelson and Ralph Deese, could testify that she was involved in a brutal kidnapping that had involved an even more brutal rape.

Cole, she thought, would take care of her as far as he could, but what would happen if they were all caught and the police offered to cut a deal with Cole for implicating her? There was a major difference between ten to fifteen years in prison and life, especially when you were Cole's age, in your early thirties. After ten to fifteen behind bars, he'd still have a shot at a life when he got out.

Would they get caught? She closed her eyes and thought about it. Probably, she concluded. There were too many people chasing them and those people were smart and there were a lot of them. Deese, the cannibal, was a big deal for the cops. They might get away with it for a while, but sooner or later they'd be cornered. Especially if they stayed on the run with Deese.

Her mother had told her that she'd have to take care of herself, that nobody else would. And nobody had taken care of her mother, that was for sure. The woman was drinking herself to death while dating men who invariably beat her, an ugly race between liver failure and homicide.

She could go out and get in the car and take off, Cox thought. She had Beauchamps's money, plus a few thousand dollars of her own, a little sack of gems, three Rolexes—a grand total of sixty or seventy thousand. Tempting.

But then there was Ralph with his shotgun. He was not likely to let her walk. She could probably work her way around that.

Eventually, she decided that running alone wasn't the ticket. She needed Cole and his connections. With Cole, she could find a fence for the jewelry. And Cole knew how to disappear. She'd have to wait for them to get back.

When they came back, would Deese really share the money? Or would he try to kill them? That seemed as likely as not. The logic of the situation seemed to point only in one direction if she was going to get out alive.

RALPH DEESE came back, looked at her, said, "They oughta be in Vegas by now."

She grunted, he nodded, then his eyes drifted back toward the bedroom. "Well," he said. "Time for a little morning pussy. If you'll excuse me . . ."

Deese headed for the back. He didn't bother closing the door, and Cox heard him say, "How you doin', cutie-pie?"

Through the open door she saw him take off his clothes, his erection bobbling around like a fishing pole below his flabby gut.

Clayton Deese, Cox thought, as the screams began again from the bedroom, was going to kill her, and then Cole, and then Gloria Harrelson, and probably Ralph as well. Harrelson was driving her crazy. The goddamn woman shouldn't fight it, she should go with it. Screaming didn't help. Not with the Deeses.

Fuck it, she thought. The Deeses didn't give a shit about anybody—not Cole, not her, probably not each other.

She reached beneath the couch cushion where she'd been sitting and pulled out Marion Beauchamps's 9mm. The gun was loaded and cocked, and all she had to do was click the safety off and pull the trigger.

She clicked the safety off, tiptoed down the length of the Airsteam to just outside the bedroom door, where she could hear Harrelson's sobs as Ralph's flab slapped against Harrelson's flat stomach. Then Ralph grunted, which, in Cox's experience, meant that he was done. He'd lie on her a minute, resting. Then, if Cox knew men, he'd get up and look for his pants, unless he decided to bring his stupid cock out to show Cox.

Which is what he did.

COX WAS STANDING outside the bedroom door when Ralph stood up, turned from the bed, and saw Cox standing there. He grinned at her, the Deese family's yellow teeth on full display, and said, "Hey there, you want some of this?"

Cox said, "I thought I'd give you some of this instead."

She brought the gun around and shot Deese in the chest. The gun bucked hard against her hand and she almost dropped it. The muzzle blast was deafening, and she put her free hand up to an ear, which was ringing like an old-fashioned telephone. Deese took a wide-eyed step backwards, then toppled onto the bed, pinning Gloria Harrelson's body beneath his suddenly dead bulk.

Harrelson cried, "Oh, thank God, thank God."

Not quite, Cox thought, grimly.

She stepped over to the door, where Ralph had propped up his shotgun in the corner. When she pushed the safety, a little knob to one side of the trigger, it popped out on the other with a red ring around it. That meant it was ready to fire, she figured.

She stepped back to the bed and said, "I'm sorry," and moved the muzzle of the gun to within an inch of Harrelson's heart and pulled the trigger. It clicked, but nothing happened.

"What are you doing?" Harrelson shrieked. She shrank away, as far as she could with the chains. "What are you doing? What are you . . ."

Cox thought, Shit, and pulled hard on the shotgun's forestock, popped an empty shell out of the chamber and new one in. She again aimed the gun at Harrelson's heart, as the woman tried to push away from her, and this time when Cox pulled the trigger the shotgun bucked, the blast deafened her, and Harrelson died, a bloody red hole in her chest.

Cox rubbed her face and thought, Done.

Now, in this entire world, there were only two men left who knew what had happened on this long, horrid trip: Deese and Cole.

SHE REMEMBERED from somewhere—a movie, she thought—that the cops did tests on people's hands and arms to see if they'd fired a gun. That could be a problem. She managed to prop open the small bedroom window, get the shotgun muzzle an inch or two outside, with Ralph Deese's dead hand wrapped around the stock of the weapon, his face near it. She pulled the trigger with his dead finger and left the gun on the floor next to his body.

Now what? Her mind felt cold—or cool anyway. If she had been kidnapped and mistreated, if the gang hadn't allowed her to leave . . .

Harrelson had been chained to the bed, but there were several feet left over. Cox crossed the bedroom, not worrying too much about the blood spattering the floor and walls, and got a length of the chain and wrapped it around her waist, then yanked it back and forth to bruise herself. She didn't want fresh blood, just bruises, and a lot of them, from below her breasts to her hips.

The process hurt, but she kept it up, until the

whole area between her breasts and hips were crossed with bruises and vividly reddened flesh. When she was satisfied, she put the chain down, went to the kitchen area, found a plastic bag, filled it with ice from the refrigerator, and wrapped that around her waist.

Done right and given time, she thought, the bruises would look old.

AND WHAT ELSE?

WELL, there was the jewelry and cash. She went out to the car and got it, took it inside, found a garbage bag, put the jewelry and all the cash, except for a couple of thousand dollars, in the bag, cinched it tight. She carried the bag outside, into the sun. When the men had taken the pickup, they'd thrown some tools out of the back, including a shovel.

She carried the shovel to a lonely, stunted tree on the edge of an arroyo, a hundred yards from the trailer, paced off six feet from the tree, dug a hole through the sand down into the crusty subsoil, put the bag in the hole, covered it with a couple shovelfuls of sand, smoothed the sand with her foot, erasing all signs of the hole. She walked a short distance up the slope, found a bluish rock the size of a dinner plate, brought it back, placed it on the cache site, and brushed some sand over it.

Nothing more to do now . . . Except kill Clayton Deese.

She could do that, if he didn't see it coming.

Cole, she'd have to think about. She really did like him. But a girl had to take care of herself.

She went back in the trailer and washed her hands and arms again, then took off her blouse and washed her entire upper body. Put her blouse on again. Washed her hands and arms again . . .

DEESE WAS an hour north of Vegas when he realized that the gas gauge hadn't moved off full. When he and Cole got in the truck, he'd checked and assumed they had a whole tankful. But now he had no idea how much gas he had left. He really didn't need to run out, not with two million in cash in the truck and his face all over television screens.

He was trying to decide whether to go back for gas or risk going ahead when he saw a sign for a gas station and convenience store. Two miles later, he slid up next to a row of gas pumps. He pulled his hat down, went inside, paid twenty dollars for gas, and a few dollars for two cold Pepsis and a candy bar, went back out, and pumped the whole twenty into the tank.

He was well out in the desert, not a lot around. One other car was parked at a second row of pumps when he pulled in, but the woman driver finished filling her tank before he was done and drove off.

When he put the nozzle back on the pump, he checked again to make sure he was alone, then opened the back door on the truck, looked in the money bag, giving himself a minute to reassure himself of its being there and to enjoy it for a minute. He took a stack of bills in his hand and riffled through them and . . . what?

He pulled a bill out. A dollar bill. Near panic, he pulled out another stack: same thing, a hundred-dollar bill top and bottom, nothing but dollar bills between. That fuckin' Harrelson had ripped him off. He was gonna . . . What was he gonna do? One thing, he was gonna cut Gloria Harrelson's head off and leave it on the highway where somebody would find it and return it to Harrelson.

Consumed with the fury of the moment, he got in the truck and drove off, the pedal to the floor, until the old vehicle began to scream and a speed limit sign that read 80 flashed by and he realized he could blow it all right there. He backed off, from 97 to 70, his head almost down to the steering wheel, fantasizing about catching up with Harrelson and skinning him alive.

"Honest to God, I'm gonna do it. I'm gonna catch that motherfucker and skin him alive," he shouted into the steering wheel.

An hour later, still fuming, and defeated by his attempts to figure out how much money he actually had—he thought maybe thirty thousand, mostly in ones, so how the hell do you spend thirty thousand dollars' worth of one-dollar bills?—he turned off the highway and onto the dirt road that would take him to Ralph's place.

COX saw him coming. Gun was ready, safety off.

She had to get close.

# CHAPTER TWENTY-SEVEN

When the dust from the oncoming truck appeared below them, still a couple of miles away, Tremanty said, "We want to take Deese alive, if we can. Any way we can. If we can get him alive, I can bring down Roger Smith's whole gang. The rest of them . . . You know, whatever's necessary."

"Is that the same thing as not givin' a shit?" Bob asked.

"In that direction," Tremanty said.

"That could be a problem," Bob said. He'd propped his scope on Lucas's backpack and was watching the approaching truck. "The woman's been in the car ever since Rae cut the power. Nothing else is moving, and the trailer door is wide open. It's gotta be a furnace inside. I don't think there's anybody in there. Nobody alive anyway."

"Then where are they?" Tremanty asked.

"I can't answer that question," Bob said. "But I don't think they're in the trailer."

"He and Cole could have taken Mrs. Harrelson down to Las Vegas," Tremanty said.

"If they did, nobody knows where she is or we would have heard," Lucas said. "My personal feeling is, she's probably in a hole up here. Deese had no reason to turn her loose. Not after what you guys found in Louisiana."

"Yeah, well, I still want him alive," Tremanty said, "if we can get him that way."

"You know, it's my call," Lucas said. He wiped sweat out of his eyes, blinked against the glare. "All due respect to the FBI, I'm the one in charge of chasing him down. If we can get him alive, we'll do it. If we have to seriously risk somebody else's neck, I won't do it. I'll green-light Bob."

"I won't have any trouble pulling the trigger," Bob said. "Not after looking at all those people in the holes, including some that he ate."

"Goddamnit, Lucas . . ."

"Lucas is right, Sandro," Bob said, lifting his face away from the scope. "But there's more than one way to skin a cat. From here, I could punch a bullet through one of those rivets in the trailer. Or a kneecap. I might possibly be able to knock him down without killing him. I can't think of why we'd do that, what the circumstances might be, but we can keep it in mind."

Lucas said, "Give me a handset."

The truck was still a mile out—they couldn't see all the twists and turns in the approach track—and maybe as much as five minutes, given the rough approach road. Lucas called Rae and told her what they'd been talking about.

She agreed. Take him alive, if possible. Shoot him if he looked like he might kill somebody else. Tremanty was on the handsest to the helicopter, who relayed his questions to the FBI office in Las Vegas, and, after a moment, he looked at Lucas and shook his head. He listened for another minute, then said into the handset, "We think Deese is coming in now. I gotta go."

He clicked off, and said to Lucas and Bob, "No sign of Gloria Harrelson. And the body in the hole? They printed the guy and put a rush on it. It's Cole."

"Holy shit," Bob said. "The guy's a—"

"He's a cannibal. And now he's eating his own," Lucas said. "Whoever that woman is, I think she's in trouble. She's got the keys to the car. She should have taken off."

"Unless she's working with Deese," Tremanty said. "Maybe we should have run down and grabbed her."

"He's thirty seconds out," Bob said.

The truck came over a low rise, and the woman got out of the car. They were looking at her right side and back, and Tremanty, with the binoculars, said, "She's got a pistol in her back pocket."

"I see it," Bob said. "What the heck is going on? Is she gonna shoot Deese?"

DEESE, in the truck, first saw the door open on the Lexus, then Cox climbing out, carefully facing him. Probably wondering where Cole was. And he noticed the trailer's open door, and that wasn't right. Every time somebody left the door open for even a second, Ralph would yell at him. And it was just hanging there, wide open, a dark rectangle against the blast of reflected sunlight that was the aluminum capsule. He came up to Cox and the Lexus, but he didn't stop. Instead he circled her, drove back to the trailer, stopped outside the door.

BELOW THEM, ninety or a hundred yards away, Deese got out of the truck, turned toward the open door, paused—a perfect target—and Bob asked, "Lucas?"

Tremanty, hissing: "No."

Lucas: "Not yet."

Deese went into the trailer.

DEESE BLINKED, in reaction to the heat and the darkness. No lights on, few windows, it took a minute for his eyes to adjust, and he first made out

Ralph's body as being something like a lumpy pile of clothes outside the bedroom door. Then, when he realized it was a body, the thought popped into his mind that Ralph had killed Gloria Harrelson. But no . . .

"Ralph?"

Nothing. He glanced back at the door, to make sure Cox wasn't about to shoot him in the back, then walked up to the body. "Ralph?"

It was Ralph all right, lying in a stinking puddle of blood with a hole in his chest. Flies buzzing around, more crawling around the edge of the puddle. What the hell had happened? Must have been Cox, there wasn't anyone else.

He looked past Ralph's body to the bedroom and saw a naked leg with a few links of chain wrapped around it. He stepped over Ralph and saw Harrelson, sprawled naked on the bed, with a plum-sized hole in her chest. Not much visible blood; it probably soaked into the mattress beneath her. A shotgun lay on the floor, its butt overlapping the bloody puddle from Ralph. He picked it up, wiped it off on the sheet tangled under Gloria Harrelson's legs.

Looked back at Ralph, back at Harrelson. From the look of both of them—Harrelson's pussy and Ralph's cock—Ralph had taken advantage of the situation.

Deese said to Ralph, as he swung his foot over him, "At least you came before you went, you old asshole." Ralph, he thought, would have liked that.

He cackled at the line, lost track of what he was doing, and when his foot hit the blood on the far side of Ralph's body it slipped and he lost his balance, fell on Ralph's bare chest, one hand went down in the puddle.

"Ah, shit. Shit." He got up, went to the sink, but only a thin trickle of water came out; the pump wasn't working, the power was out. How'd that happened? Another mystery. He popped open the refrigerator, took out a bottle of water, opened it, washed his hand, dried it on his jeans.

He picked up the shotgun again, a cheap Mossberg that had seen better days, the barrel hot enough to iron with. He shucked a couple of shells into the sink, his hands now slippery with sweat, fished them out. Two shots. He looked around, saw a green-and-yellow box sitting on a windowsill, took out four more shells, shoved in five, pumped once to get a shell into the chamber, and shoved another into the magazine.

Buckshot. Bless you, Ralph, you dead motherfucker.

Planning to kill both them bitches anyway.

THEN COX was at the door of the trailer, or just outside it. She shouted, "What'd you do to Cole, you big fat cocksucker?"

Deese thought, Fat? and looked down at his gut. He was six feet tall and weighed a hundred and seventy pounds.

"Cole went away," Deese shouted back. "You and me got some things to do, sugarpuss."

He heard her running away and hurried to the door, but when he got there she was behind the truck bed, looking at him. He stepped outside, the gun hanging from one hand. He grinned at her and said, "No place to run."

She asked, "Do I look like I'm running?"

Her hand came up, and Deese realized that she had a pistol in it and he opened his mouth to shout, or something, and she pulled the trigger and the slug smacked into the door behind him. He dove back through the doorway and rolled away from it as two more shots poked holes through the trailer, both slugs blowing past a couple of inches above his body. He shouted, "Hey, hey, hey!"

He heard the truck door open, and when he peeked through a window he saw she was inside the truck, not looking at the door—she was looking at the money.

He eased back over to the door and shouted, "We can work something out."

"What'd you do to Cole? Did you kill him?"

"He was a witness against both of us," Deese shouted back.

In the truck, Cox frowned, and thought, Well, that's true.

---

ON THE RIDGE, Bob asked, "What're we doing? Somebody tell me. I can't think, I've got to focus on what I'm doing here."

Lucas said, "If it looks like he's going to kill her, take him."

"Wound him. Wound him, for Christ's sakes," Tremanty said. "Or let it play out."

LUCAS ASKED, "What about the chopper? We could try calling the chopper, tell them what the situation is, see if they'd be willing to hover a few hundred feet up. She couldn't reach it with that pistol, even if she tried, and he couldn't with the shotgun."

"Something's going to happen, I don't think there's time," Bob said. "I'm getting really fuckin' sweaty here. Somebody wipe my forehead, I'm gonna mist up the lens."

Tremanty handed a radio to Lucas and said, "Call the chopper." He produced a handkerchief, and as Lucas thumbed the call button, Tremanty wiped Bob's forehead. Lucas called the chopper, told them what they needed.

"Two minutes," the pilot said.

COX SHOUTED, "It's mostly one-dollar bills, you big fat chump."

Deese: "Take a bunch, run over to the Lexus, and take off. There are license plates there in the truck. Put them on the car, drive up to Reno or back to LA."

"You'll shoot me."

"No I won't. I promise," Deese shouted.

"You liar."

The truck was only ten feet from the door of the trailer, and Deese was dying in there. He had to get out, one way or another, and the damned Airstream only had one door. One of the windows had to be an escape hatch, he thought, but he didn't know which one. And the trailer was so beat up, it might not even open.

He shook his head, made sure the safety was off on the Mossberg, then rolled into the open door and fired three rounds directly into the driver's-side door of the truck and then rolled back behind the wall. One second later, a single shot blew past his face. He scrabbled back six feet.

He'd missed, somehow, and the bitch almost killed him. And even if she hadn't, he thought, the heat soon would. Had she gotten out of the truck? He risked a peek at the window and, sure enough, saw her looking toward the trailer door, over the top of the truck bed.

Then she panicked. As he was peeking through the window, he saw her aiming the gun that way and he dove behind the refrigerator as she peppered the trailer with bullets.

Then they stopped, and he thought, Out of ammo.

He crawled back toward the door, peeked, saw her running toward the Lexus. He pushed himself up, stepped into the door, and swung the shotgun toward her.

LUCAS SAID, "Take him, take him."

Tremanty: "Wound him."

Bob said, "Fuck!" and pulled the trigger.

As he pulled the trigger, Deese took a step down to the ground.

Deese didn't know what had happened; he didn't feel any immediate pain, but his leg blew up beneath him.

AS DEESE FELL, the woman got to the Lexus, which was still running, jammed it into gear, and hit the gas. Lucas said, "Tires."

Bob took his time, fired once, and the front tire went expensively flat. Not explosively flat, but with a genteel release of air pressure. Cox kept going, throwing a ton of dust in the air.

"Run-flats," Bob said in disgust.

"Take another one," Tremanty said.

**Bang!** And the rear tire was gone, but the car rolled on. **Bang!** And an off-side tire went. They were so preoccupied that they never heard the helicopter until it passed overhead, got in front of

Cox, and slowly lowered itself until it was hovering fifteen feet above the road and directly in front of her, a menacing dragonfly to her bug. The Lexus stopped and a moment later the driver's-side window dropped and a hand poked out and waved. She'd quit.

"What happened to Deese?" Bob asked.

They all looked back to the trailer. Deese had vanished.

"I hit him hard. Maybe too hard," Bob said. "He was stepping down, I was aiming at his knee but hit him in the groin area instead. He's gonna lose the leg, I think. And if I took out his femoral artery, he's dead. Shit. He fell right into the slug."

"Crawled back inside?" Tremanty suggested.

"I think he crawled underneath," Lucas said. He got on the radio to Rae, told her what had happened.

"He didn't crawl out here. I can see the whole back of the trailer," she said. "I could lay a few rounds in there, in the dirt, see if it chases him out."

"Hold off," Lucas said. "We should get this woman out of the way. We know Deese's hurt, he's not going anywhere."

"Not to say that he couldn't kill you with that shotgun," Bob said. He was watching the trailer through the scope, his finger hovering a quarter inch off the trigger.

---

DEESE WAS under the trailer, which was, in a way, a relief, cooler than inside. On the other hand, somebody—he had no idea who but probably a cop—had shot him, and the pain was blinding him. He knew he was bleeding bad.

Pretty much a done deal, he thought. He still had a last wish. If only he could get a peek at a cop . . . He still had three shells, he thought, three or four. If he could get a peek at a cop, he'd kill him, a good-bye kiss.

He pushed himself flat, glanced down at his leg, surprised by the amount of blood beneath it. The pain was bad but seemed to be diminishing. The heat must be getting to him, he thought, because he was getting light-headed. If he was going to get a cop, it had to be soon.

BOB STAYED behind the ridge with the rifle still propped on Lucas's backpack, waiting for some sign of motion inside or underneath the trailer. Tremanty and Lucas slid sideways along the slope until they were beside and slightly below the Lexus, then Lucas raised his rifle, and Tremanty his handgun, and Lucas shouted, "U.S. Marshal! Come out of there. Come out on this side."

The passenger-side window rolled down, and she shouted, "They raped me. They made me fuck all of them. They chained me up . . . That old man raped and killed Mrs. Harrelson. And he was going to kill me."

Lucas shouted, "Come out of there."

Tremanty half stood, loping toward the back of the Lexus, and when Lucas saw him moving he shouted, "Sandro! Get down. Don't do that. Get—"

**Boom!**

The shotgun. Tremanty flew away from the car and halfway down the slope. Lucas looked at him in horror. And then Tremanty rolled over, got to his knees, turned to Lucas, and said, "Missed."

"Jesus. Don't do that shit. I already did it enough for both of us." Lucas looked back at the Lexus. "Come out of there."

Up on the hill, Rae had seen the shot and had seen Tremanty go flying, and she sprayed the ground behind the Airstream with a burst from her M4.

Cox slipped out of the Lexus and down to Lucas and Tremanty. Rae was shouting into her handset, "How's Sandro? Is he hit?"

Tremanty said into his handset, "No, but my back is full of cactus stickers."

Rae said, "What were you doing? My God, I'm gonna kick your ass when I get back down there."

Lucas asked Cox, "How many people in there? In the trailer?"

"None. Well, two, but they're both dead. This guy Cole was sorta taking care of me toward the end, he left me a gun to keep Ralph off me. But

Ralph went back into the bedroom—" She broke off and began to cry.

"Where's Mrs. Harrelson?"

"Ralph . . . Ralph raped her. And then . . . he had this shotgun—**that** shotgun, the one Deese has—and after he finished with her, he shot her. Right in the chest. I had that gun, but I was so scared. But I knew he was going to kill me next. So when he came out of the bedroom, I shot him first."

She began weeping again, gasping for breath. "I was so scared . . ."

Lucas wasn't entirely buying it, but he still had a Deese problem. He left Tremanty to take care of Cox and scuttled across the ridge back to Bob.

"He's under there, all right, I saw him. But I didn't have a shot," Bob said. "I'll tell you, he'll bleed to death if we don't get him out of there soon."

ALL DEESE WANTED was one more shot, one more shot. He was sure he'd missed with the first one; he'd pulled around too quickly. The machine gun had scared him. He hadn't been hurt, but he knew he couldn't move backwards. He inched sideways, very light-headed now. There was a bunch of crap under the trailer, a pile of four-by-four timbers, each about five or six feet long, that smelled of creosote, an old pot with the bottom rusted out, some baling wire, a pile of narrow boards that might have been a wooden floor.

He slid one of the boards out of the pile to prop up the gun barrel.

One more shot, he thought. Was that too much to ask?

He moved another board to get it out of his line of sight and looked straight into the cold black eyes of a **Crotalus scutulatus**, the Mojave green rattlesnake, North America's most poisonous rattler. It struck him in the face and he panicked, jerked away, slapped at it, missed, and it struck him again, in the nose, and again in the cheek, and he screamed and rolled away, crawling blindly out into the sun, his fear of the snake greater than the fear of a bullet.

Bob and Lucas saw him crawl out, and Lucas said, "Wait! No gun. I don't see the shotgun."

Lucas yelled at Tremanty, who was still talking to Cox. When Tremanty looked up, Lucas pointed, and Tremanty looked that way, and Lucas said to Bob, "Let's go. But let's be careful."

"He screamed," Bob said. "What was that?"

"Dunno," Lucas said. He shouted, "Rae. Rae. Come down, be careful. He's out in front." To their right, Tremanty and Cox were walking carefully toward the body in the dirt but were still fifty yards way. As Bob and Lucas got close, Rae turned the corner of the trailer and put her machine gun on Deese.

Bob called, "Is he dead?"

Lucas moved up, Bob now pointing his handgun at Deese's body, Rae her rifle. Lucas knelt and said, "Still breathing. A little anyway."

Deese twitched, or shuddered. He tried to push up, failed, got his face turned out of the dirt, looked at Lucas with sightless eyes and said, "Sssnna . . . Sssnna . . ."

"What?"

Bob backed a couple of feet away. "I think he was trying to say 'snake.' Jesus, look at his face."

Lucas looked, six holes pocking Deese's face, around his nose, already turning blue. "Oh, shit!" Lucas lurched away from the trailer, stood well back to try to look under it. Saw nothing but a pile of dusty lumber and an old rusted pot.

Rae waved Tremanty and Cox up. The helicopter had landed on a piece of desert hardpan and sat there, waiting for customers.

"Is he dead?" Cox asked.

"No, he . . ." Bob began. He looked again. "Well. Maybe now."

Cox said, "Good," and spit on the body.

# CHAPTER TWENTY-EIGHT

They left all the bodies where they lay and called in an FBI crime scene team. The team arrived, by helicopter, with generators and lights, at three o'clock. Backup ground crews arrived two hours later, along with a couple of cars from the local sheriff's office.

Cox at first seemed willing to talk. Rae went up the hill and turned the generator back on, and when the air-conditioning came up they sat in the trailer in one end, trying to ignore the bodies at the other end, and she gave a partial statement.

She had originally gone with Beauchamps, not knowing exactly what he did for a living, she said, knowing only that he liked to dance and spend money.

When she found out what he did, she said she wanted to leave but they wouldn't let her. When Beauchamps and the others left on a job, they chained her to a bed but left her with a TV remote and a pile of magazines.

She pulled up her blouse to show off her bruises. “See? You can see the chain links, like, right here.”

The gang wasn’t cruel, but she couldn’t leave. Later, she said, Beauchamps told her that Cole also wanted sexual privileges and she’d begun sleeping with both of them. She’d refused to sleep with Nast, but wouldn’t say why. When Rae asked if it was because Nast was black, she said, “Well, yeah, I guess . . . No offense.”

She also said that Vincent hadn’t wanted to sleep with her because he was “different.”

“Not gay. He just, I dunno . . . Sex didn’t do anything for him.”

She refused to sleep with Deese because he smelled bad and ate people and was evil and called her a whore, which she insisted she most certainly wasn’t. When Tremanty and Lucas began picking apart her story, she began to cry, said, “You’re being mean.” And then she said, “I didn’t do anything. I didn’t do anything except I wanted to party. They picked me up and kept me.”

Crying her bright blue eyes out, she asked for an attorney.

LUCAS, Bob, Rae, and Tremanty made recorded statements at the scene for an assistant U.S. attorney; the entire scene was comprehensively photographed. Just before dark, they rode the helicopter back to Las Vegas; Cox was transferred by ground to a federal holding facility.

The next day was spent with paperwork, and the Vegas AIC held a press conference with Tremanty and Lucas, in which they gave credit to the hard work of the Metro cops, the Ney County Sheriff's Department, and, of course, without saying so—they had behind-the-scenes spokespeople to do that—themselves.

The cannibal was dead. Good riddance.

When it was all signed, sealed, and delivered, Lucas, Bob, Rae, and Tremanty agreed to rendezvous at the Cheesecake Factory at seven o'clock to eat and talk about the case, before flying out the next day. Bob and Lucas arrived right at seven, Rae and Tremanty were late.

"I think they're, uh-mmm, you know . . ." Bob said.

"Good for them," Lucas said. "Everybody oughta uh-mmm. Not enough of that going on, in my opinion."

"Tremanty's gonna wind up in Washington, sooner or later," Bob said, over a cherry shake and cheeseburger. "I hope she doesn't go with him. I mean, I wish them the best."

"But you don't want to break up the team."

"She's my best friend," Bob said.

"Are you uh-mmming anybody at the moment?" Lucas asked.

"As a matter of fact, I am. There's a high school gym coach . . . Anyway, she's divorced, friendly, and likes to work out. Don't know what will happen there . . . Maybe something."

RAE WANDERED IN a few minutes later. Her hair was damp, but neither Lucas nor Bob mentioned it, until she said, "That's right. Don't say a fuckin' thing."

"We're trying not to," Lucas said.

Tremanty ambled up a moment later. His hair was damp as well, but they didn't say a fuckin' thing.

Cheeseburgers, fries, shakes.

"You got Santos anyway," Lucas said. "That's gotta be some kind of wedge you can use to get at Smith."

Tremanty shrugged. "Don't know. Cox is a witness to the Beauchamps shooting, but she somehow wound up with the most expensive defense attorney in Las Vegas, where defense attorneys don't come cheap. She says he's doing it pro bono for an indigent client, but that would be like the first time forever."

Bob: "You think Smith . . . ?"

Tremanty nodded. "Of course. If she testifies that Beauchamps shot first—that Santos was acting in self-defense—we can still get Santos, maybe, on the attempted money transfer, aiding a federal fugitive. But you know, Deese was never convicted of anything. Now he can't be because he's dead."

"Sorry," Bob said.

"Not your fault," Tremanty said. "You were trying **not** to kill him and he stepped right into the slug. So . . . it all gets complicated. Whatever happens, it'll cost Smith a lot of money. A bundle."

"And the cannibal is dead," Rae said. They raised their milk shake glasses and clinked them together. "The cannibal is dead."

THEY ALL FLEW the next day, Bob, Rae, and Tremanty to New Orleans, Bob and Rae in business class, Tremanty in the back. Rae suggested that Bob give up his seat so Tremanty could sit next to her.

Bob laughed. That wasn't going to happen.

Then Rae suggested that she give up her seat so the two men could have the leg and hip room, but Tremanty said, "Rae, you're taller than me."

Bob and Rae flew business into New Orleans, as did Lucas into Minneapolis, on the Marshals Service tab.

HARRELSON didn't flinch when told of his wife's death. He nodded and walked away, turned at the door of the FBI office and said, "Thanks for tryin'." When he got home, he sat on the bed and looked at his wife's clothes in the closet and sat there and cried and couldn't stop. That went on for a while.

COX'S excellent defense attorney proved valuable: in the end, she wasn't charged with anything because all the government could prove was that she'd stayed with the gang. In her favor, there were those chain bruises, carefully photographed by the defense attorney's excellent photographer, and the fact that she'd called Lucas to tip him off about the meeting between Deese and Santos.

She was required to testify against Santos as part of her no-prosecution deal.

Santos was in the hospital for three weeks, then transferred to the federal holding facility in Las Vegas. He'd lost a kidney and suffered nerve damage near his spine that affected control of his left foot. He could walk with the help a small brace that kept his foot pointed forward, but not run well.

He also had an excellent defense attorney. And when it was all over with—it took nearly a year—he pled guilty to handgun violations and attempting to aid a federal fugitive. He told the court that the money he was delivering actually was Deese's own money, not Roger Smith's. "A hidden stash," he said.

He was unaware of any illegal activity by Smith; he worked in Smith's law office as a consultant on drug violations by Smith clients, of which there were many. With no prior convictions, he was given three years in prison.

His three years—he'd actually serve thirty months—cost Roger Smith three million dollars in cash; money well spent, in Smith's view.

Thinking about it drove Tremanty into an occasional frenzy.

KERRY BLACK, the college girl who'd rented Beauchamps's trailer in Vegas, kept sending off rent checks that were never cashed, and because Beauchamps owned the trailer under a false name, nobody ever picked up on it. She got two whole years out of the place, before graduating and moving on. The checks went to a mail drop store. When the rent on the mailbox ran out, the store bundled up the envelopes and returned them to the post office, who forwarded them on to Black's new address. She really wasn't sure that she should spend the uncollected money, but life is life and she eventually did.

TREMANTY AND RAE remained an item. Their relationship caused a two-day breach in Rae's relationship with Bob. They had desks facing each other, and Rae came in one morning, humming to herself, and Bob stared at her until she asked, "What?"

Bob blurted, "You look like the most thoroughly fucked woman in the continental United States."

That was on a Monday. She forgave him on Wednesday afternoon.

THERE WAS one lonely body at the cannibal's place that was never found and molders there still beneath the tangled brush and among the slithering snakes.

COX and her excellent attorney remained tangled in the court proceedings until Santos pled out. Then she walked. But not far. She rented a Jeep, drove to the site of Ralph Deese's Airstream, which had been hauled away as evidence and eventually junked. She dug up the money and jewelry she'd hidden there. Altogether, a bit over sixty thousand dollars, enough to be a star—at least for a while.

At a dance club in Santa Monica called Lancer's, she met a smart guy who didn't want to talk about himself because, it turned out, when he eventually did talk, in her bed, he revealed he was on parole for an armed robbery conviction. When she pressed him about what he was planning to do in his post-prison life, he confessed that it'd probably be more armed robbery. It was his only real skill set.

"There's a better way," she said. "Would you

know any guys who are, like, really big and frightening?"

Of course he did. He'd just gotten out of High Desert State Prison.

Cox still had the Panther pin given to her by Cole and she wore it as a talisman for good luck, though, truth be told, his face was beginning to fade in her memory. A year after the shootings in Vegas and at Ralph Deese's trailer, she and her new home invasion gang were driving Rocha, the LA robbery cop, insane.

ON A WARM EVENING in early September, Virgil Flowers had taken off his cowboy boots and had his feet up on Lucas's backyard dining table, waiting for the barbecue ribs to get done. His very pregnant girlfriend, Frankie, shuffled around the yard after her son Sam, and Lucas's son Sam, both nine, who were playing a species of football that involved a lot of wrestling, the occasional head-butt, and, every once in a while, a muffled curse.

Frankie demanded, "Who said 'asshole'? Which one of you little f . . . who said 'asshole'? You should be ashamed."

Her son said, "You said 'asshole,' Mom."

Frankie: "I was quoting, that doesn't count."

Lucas's grass-stained kid shouted, "Dad! Frankie said 'asshole'!"

---

VIRGIL, normally stationed in Mankato, in southern Minnesota, had been working in Minneapolis on a murder at the University of Minnesota. Frankie had driven up to the Cities to renew their acquaintance.

Virgil pointed a beer bottle at Frankie and asked Lucas, "Isn't it true that if we don't get married, the kids'll be little bastards?"

Lucas said, "Yup. They will. Had that same problem myself, with my first daughter. Her mom wouldn't marry me and she went on and married this rich guy who adopted my kid—I had to sign the papers, but he's a good guy, so I did. Technically, I think that means she isn't a little bastard anymore. But she was for a while."

"I hate the idea that some kid's a bastard. I even hate the word 'bastard,'" Virgil said. "You ever look the word up on Google? The synonyms are, like, 'scoundrel,' 'villain,' 'rogue,' 'weasel,' 'good-for-nothing.' I'm gonna get her to marry me, one way or another."

"Between the two of you that'd be, what, six marriages?"

"Yee . . . aah, I guess," Virgil said, pausing to add them up. "One of mine didn't count, though. That was more, like, an overnight camping trip."

"If you had to get a divorce, then you were

married," Lucas said. "And if you're gonna marry this one, you're gonna need a plan."

Virgil took his feet down, and said, "Like what?"

"Let me think for a minute," Lucas said.

Weather came out of the house. "You got a call," she told Lucas. "From Elmer. I told him you'd call him right back."

"Quiet," Virgil said, "He's thinking about how to get Frankie to marry me."

"That's a heck of a lot more important than anything Elmer might have to say," Weather said.

"Exactly."

Lucas: "How about this? Tell her that you want to get a marriage license, in case she changes her mind. It's good for six months here in Minnesota. Then you wait until she goes into labor and you show up with your old man . . ."

Virgil's old man was an Episcopalian minister.

"That'll work," Weather said. "About halfway through labor, you'll do anything to get your mind off of it. Even get married."

"Seems treacherous," Virgil said. "I like it. A lot."

Weather handed Lucas his cell phone. "You gotta talk to Elmer. He seemed . . . disturbed."

Virgil: "Oh-oh."

Elmer Henderson was a former governor of Minnesota, now a U.S. senator. He'd been appointed to the job by the current governor after the previous senator had been shot to death in Washington. According to the local political pundits, the appointment had come only after considerable arm-twisting. The current governor was not numbered among the brightest half of Minnesotans and initially had wanted to appoint his sister to the job.

Lucas took the phone, pressed recall and then speaker, and Henderson instantly picked up. "Lucas?"

"Senator . . . or Governor . . . Elmer?" Lucas said.

"Lucas. We've got a nasty problem," Henderson said. "Nasty. When can you get here?"

"Washington?"

"Yes, of course. Can you make it tomorrow? I'll send a plane."

Virgil shouted, "Senator . . . Virgil Flowers: could he get shot again?"

Henderson asked, "Is that that fuckin' Flowers? Ah, jeez . . ."

Lucas: "Well? Could I get shot again?"

Henderson: "Look, guys. I can't promise anything . . ."

# LIKE WHAT YOU'VE READ?

Try these titles by John Sandford,
also available in large print:

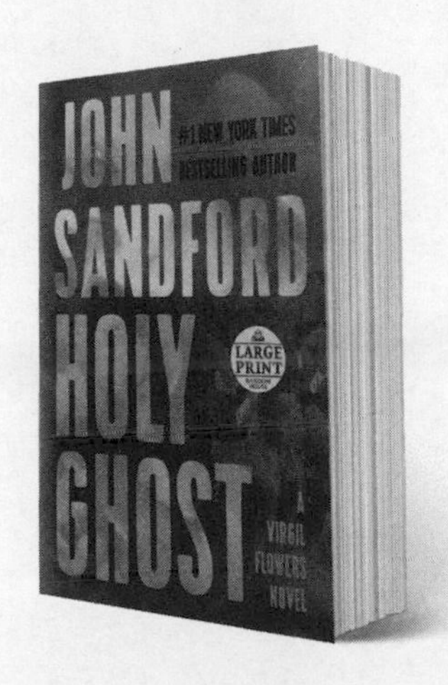


**Holy Ghost**
ISBN 978-1-9848-2752-4

**Twisted Prey**
ISBN 978-0-525-59378-2

**Deep Freeze**
ISBN 978-0-525-52312-3

For more information on large print titles, visit
**www.penguinrandomhouse.com/large-print-format-books**